CHARLIE THORNHILL
DUNCE OF THE FAMILY
BY
CHARLES CARLOS CLARKE

FIRST PUBLISHED IN 1864

This book has been edited and abridged by
Veronica Bellers and Susan Duke

We are grateful to Rev John Fellows for kindly allowing us to use extracts from his biographical details of Charles Carlos Clarke.

We would also like to thank George MacMillan for his generous and learned help translating the Latin and Greek quotations.

INTRODUCTION

Charles Carlos Clarke was born in 1814 and was educated at Trinity College, Oxford which he described as a "stronghold of happy prejudice". He took holy orders and became a curate, marrying and having twelve children. His stipend was never enough as one can well imagine, particularly as he was a keen follower of hounds and horse racing. He took to writing as a sporting journalist - *"Crumbs from a Sportsman's Table"* was published in 1865 and was a collection of his articles. *"Charlie Thornhill"* was his first novel and published in 1864. As well as adding to his income with his pen he set up a crammer in the Old House, Esher, Surrey. Describing this move into teaching he wrote "I was once a curate, contented but not rich on £100 per annum and house rent ….I found neither my house nor my income large enough for my wants….The Government came to my aid. It was decided that, while Greek iambics were required to make a gentleman, spelling was indispensable for an officer of Her Majesty's service…. I at once turned my attention to tutorial responsibilities".

Charles Carlos Clarke was a keen and knowledgeable horseman and hunted with the Pytchley regularly. He was known as 'The Gentleman in Black', and it is thought that these lines of Whyte

Melville, the bard of the Pytchley Hunt in Northamptonshire, could well have described Carlos Clarke.

Next comes the parson,
The parson, the parson,
Next comes the parson,
The shortest way to seek.
And like a phantom lost to view,
From point to point the parson flew,
The parish at a pinch can do
Without him for a week.

Carlos Clarke has a charming and intimate style of writing, it is as if he is sitting at a fireside with his audience around him, recounting his story. The reader is included in his opinions and even in his dilemmas as his tale unfolds. We can feel ourselves to be members of his circle of friends, comfortably taken back to Victorian England where this interesting and amusing novel is set.

The editors and abridgers of *"Charlie Thornhill"* are descendants of Charles Carlos Clarke through one of his daughters, Eveleen. In today's world we are all overwhelmed by the wealth of printed material that we wish to read, and this may be why modern novels have become shorter and brisker. We, Charles Carlos Clarke's great-great-granddaughters, would like a wider and younger readership to enjoy the fun of *"Charlie Thornhill"*. Instead of plodding through that Victorian landscape carefully noting every detail as they did at that time, the speed of the novel has been stepped up to more of a trot. We have shortened the book and inspected each sentence to be sure of clarity while making every effort to retain the charm and entertainment of Charles Carlos Clarke's original book.

Susan Duke & Veronica Bellers

NOTE: The biographical details here have been taken from the Introduction in the unabridged book which was republished by the R.S. Surtees Society in 2004. That fascinating introduction was written by the Rev. John Fellows.

CHAPTER 1

"Hearken to me, gentlemen,
Come and you shall heare,
I'll tell you of two of the boldest bretheren,
That ever borne y-were"
– Ballad Poetry

Circa 1848

It was a beautiful evening about the middle of spring. As the sun was approaching the horizon, a small pleasure-boat containing two people pulled into a creek on the river Lee, a mile or two from Cork. Half a dozen rude steps led through a rustic gate to a very small, neatly kept lawn. The neatness of the place was remarkable and the cottage itself was utterly without pretension. It consisted of about four small rooms, with a verandah looking to the east and south which gave an ornamental appearance to the building. A few creepers, already putting forth their earliest leaves, added a certain amount of character to the house. In the semi-obscurity of a setting sun it was almost *triste* and the deep shadows upon the little lawn seemed melancholy, not always displeasing, nor very un-Irish.

A man and a woman disembarked from the boat. The woman had moved a few steps on to the lawn and now stopped, watching her companion as he fastened the boat. They were both eminently handsome, and still young. The woman was about seven-and-twenty, of very delicate and lady-like proportions. Her face was sufficiently beautiful, but its charms were enhanced by fidelity in suffering, of truthfulness, of dependence. It told, too, of anxiety, but not for self – of care for others deeper than for any suffering of her own. The man was also a very handsome person. He was considerably older, though still an active, up-right and well-made man. He had the appearance, essentially, of a gentleman; but he had a restless, unsettled gaze, and a face in which there was written in a strong hand – impulse, sensuality, self-will. There was no command either of self or others in those handsome large dark eyes, or in that full lip and ruddy complexion. He was dressed in a sombrero and a pilot coat, which he had just put on, and which he buttoned as he leisurely approached his companion.

"Oh! Arthur, Arthur, how happy we might be here but for these wretched separations; and if not here, elsewhere; all places are the same to me, if you could only be as you once were with me and the children."

"Better perhaps as it is, Norah".

"No! Impossible. Whatever the sorrow, whatever the mystery, surely it may be better borne when shared with your wife?"

"You would only be teased by the daily annoyance of my difficulties, and could never relieve them."

"Try me, Arthur. For what did I marry you? Was it because you were rich; because you promised me a great house and many luxuries? Did ye come courting like a fine gentleman, when ye cantered over on your ragged-looking pony?" said Norah, with a touch of humour, in spite of her anxieties;

"And in that old shooting-jacket that old Mike begged to frighten away the birds? It wasn't till the day we were married I knew you'd a decent coat to your back."

"You married me because you loved me; and it would have been better that you had been buried first," said the man, bitterly. "It's no use, Norah; don't ask me. I can tell you nothing, except this, that I must leave you again for England. Be a good girl and take care of yourself and Kathleen and the boy. Some day we'll try and leave this place and every sorrow behind us; but it can't be yet. What do the children do with themselves all day?"

"Hubert goes to school in the morning, and seems to be getting on well; but I hardly know much of his school fellows. Kathleen is my dear companion. Hubert is usually fishing all the afternoon; and is always teasing to know when he's to have the pony you have so long talked about."

"Let him fish, Norah; it's an innocent amusement, as long as he does not fall into the river: but keep him away from horseflesh; the less he ever knows of it the better; it's been very little good to me. But now I must go to meet Burke. I have a word of business to say to him to-night."

"Well! Don't be long. But don't bring Burke here; I've seen him once, and I don't like him. Arthur, dear Arthur, these men frighten me; they are at the bottom of all our sorrow and mystery; trust me, and confide in me. If I can do nothing else for you, I can pray for you, or die for you, but I cannot leave you."

Arthur Kildonald was the son of a man of small but independent property in the west of Ireland, who without influence or position was too much of a gentleman to work for his bread. Arthur had had, as a boy, a very moderate education, but he had had the advantage, or could it be disadvantage, of a close proximity to a garrison town and his father's idle habits and congenial disposition had brought him into continual intercourse with the officers. The young man grew up singularly handsome, and with all those tastes for riding and shooting and every sort of sport. At an early age he was an adept at all games of skill and of chance. His dexterity as a pigeon-shot found him no unwelcome supplies of pocket-money and his horsemanship procured him many a good mount in amateur steeple-chases. A naturally good disposition soon gave way to the contaminating influences of self-indulgence and gambling. Very little remained to him at the age of five-and-twenty, but a questionable recklessness in money matters, which was occasionally mistaken for generosity, and a certain softness of character which rendered him the prey of designing women and men. With the former he was supposed to have had some successes – an idea which his vanity encouraged. With the latter he was always either a tool or a hero. He had much physical courage which served him in moments of danger or difficulty.

His father's death opened the realities of life to him. Up to that period he had been entirely ignorant of his social position. He woke to find himself an orphan which gave him little trouble, and a beggar, which was a crushing evil. Hitherto he had not felt the want of money; now, and henceforth, his life would be a struggle with the world. It so happened that the small property from which his father may have received the rents, came under the hammer, and was bought by Mr. Thornhill of Thornhills, an English gentleman of large fortune, at a price which just served to pay off the mortgages, a few personal debts, and to provide funds for the funeral. Arthur Kildonald believed that a great wrong had been done him by the Thornhill family and though at the time they were quite unknown to him, he cherished a most foolish, almost frantic, antipathy to them all. The name of Thornhill stank in his nostrils; and a savage longing even then possessed him of some day wiping out an imaginary stain upon his position in society. From that time he led a life of dissipation, supported by the association which he formed with gamblers of every degree and more especially upon the turf. His connection with these men led him frequently to England. Indeed, for several years he had lived at least eight months out of the twelve in that country. A charming manner and congenial pursuits gave him an *entrée* into, at least, the fringes of society.

Such had been, and still was, the man who now moored his skiff on the left bank of the Lee, a short way lower down the stream from his own house and on the opposite side of the river. He stepped lightly on shore, lit a cigar and walked leisurely inland towards a small inn which he quickly recognised by a horn lantern swinging inside the door and shedding its dim lustre over a circuit of a few hundred yards.

"Is Mr. Burke here, Patrick?" he asked the publican.

"Is it Lawyer Burke, him as rides the bay cob, yer honour?"

"The same, and a very handsome cob it is," said Kildonald; "A little light below the knee, but a fine mover. How long has he been here?"

"He's taken his first tumbler, and maybe he'll be wanting a second by this time. Will I hold a light to yer honour?" said Patrick, as he preceded Kildonald to a small but tolerably comfortable little room, where there was a small turf fire, and Mr. Burke was enjoying a good hot glass of whiskey punch which had been brought to him upon his arrival some ten minutes before.

Patrick busied himself for a minute or two about the fire and then looked at the tumbler and then at the little kettle whilst the two gentlemen saluted each other in the customary manner of men who meet pretty frequently but without great love for one another. As soon, however, as the door closed, Burke, drawing his chair closer to Kildonald, asked somewhat abruptly –

"You got my letter, I suppose about the Corinthian Handicap?"
"I did."
"Can nothing be done to stop Sir Frederick Marston's horse Benevenuto?"
"Nothing in this case; the horse must win if all goes right; he's a stone better than the mare and there's nothing else worth mentioning in the race."
"By God, he must not win! It'll ruin me;" and Burke moved uneasily on his chair. "Listen, Kildonald; I know he belongs to Sir Frederick Marston; but can money do nothing with his trainer? Is he to be got at?"
"Simply absurd. Where we can give hundreds he can give thousands. Besides, I know the trainer, and nothing of that kind can save you."
"I tell you every man has his price." said Burke.
"And I tell you that Turner cannot be bought; if he were to be, it's beyond your purse and mine; he's the straightest trainer in England."
"Who will ride the horse?" asked Burke.
"It is not known; it's a gentleman's race, and will be run on its merits."
"A gentlemen's race! Come, Kildonald, there's hope yet. They're worse than jockeys, and a great deal poorer."
"I go to England to-morrow," said Kildonald. "Lord Castleton might have the mount, but can't ride the weight."
"Can you? You've ridden Sir Frederick's horses before this: if you can manage this you may stand two thousand to nothing on it. If not – the game's over, and once over with me, you know what follows."
"Enough, enough, sir; I have submitted to these threats too frequently not to know what is coming." At the conclusion of Burke's speech Kildonald had risen quickly from his seat, his breath came rapidly, his voice quivered with passion, and his face wore a paleness terrible to contemplate. It had in it a shade of fear, which in

a constitutionally brave man bespeaks an inability of action. A lion before the braying of an ass is said to stand cowed, or to crouch trembling at the unearthly sound; and a man of physical power in the meshes of his own vices is an object equally pitiful.

"I have said it is impossible. I am in your power, but I will not be reminded of it every time your accursed avarice makes me an unwilling tool in hands that I despise. You – you – you forget who I am."

Burke, too, had risen, and the fancied advantages of birth and the real advantages of manner and appearance were very obvious. Burke was a broad-shouldered and singularly vulgar-looking man in his middle thirties; his head was large, his features coarse, and a profusion of red hair and whisker gave him a fierce appearance. Low cunning was the predominant expression of his face, but it was mixed with the roistering air of a middle-class horse-dealer. He was really a sporting lawyer.

"Faith, Mr Kildonald, I'll not forget *what* ye are." And here Burke paused, for he was not sure how far he could drive his confederate. "However, it's impossible, is it? I'd like to see the thing on the cards that's impossible with you and me. If Sir Frederick's horse wins this that'll be seven thousand to Thornhill alone, and ..."

"Hold," said Kildonald; "did you say Thornhill? Has he much money on it? Quick man! Has he backed Sir Frederick's horse for a stake? Tell me at once." And such was his vehemence that Burke could not help seeing that his point was gained and the name of Thornhill would prove his safeguard; so he replied without much hesitation, and with quite as little truth, that Thornhill had backed the horse heavily. In fact, he put a finishing touch to his last *coup* by asserting that the Irish property must be on the market before long if Thornhill lost.

Kildonald's thoughts were most opportunely directed into a new

channel. He had two objects in view, both of which seemed once more within his grasp; an opportunity to gain a safe retreat to the Continent to escape Burke's blackmail over an injudicious and youthful marriage with a gipsy beauty. The other was an opportunity of revenging himself upon the family whom he unjustly regarded as his oppressors and the usurpers of his birthright.
"Will Sir Frederick give ye the mount?"
"He will," answered Kildonald laconically.
"And can he win as he likes?"
"Or lose, I suppose you mean."
"Perhaps I do."
"Then why not say so? There's no necessity for any delicacy about the matter, unless ye think Patrick's maybe, at the keyhole."
"If he is he'll catch nothing but a cold in the eye."
"And what's to prevent me winning and landing a stake worth double of your paltry offer?"
"Because winning is never a certainty, and it wouldn't suit us to do so."
"It's dangerous but I can do it," said Kildonald, thoughtfully. "I can make it a certainty at say three thousand to nothing."
"It's a certainty." And without another word Kildonald quitted the room.

CHAPTER 2

THE BATTLE

"And like the impatient steed of war,
He snuff'd the battle from afar." – *Marmion*

England – Dr. Gresham's Tutorial – circa. 1848
"Go it, Charlie, keep your head up: by Jove, that's a finisher!" said Bob Wilkinson, the cock of the school, as the baker's boy dropped to a well-delivered left hander of his opponent. "Beautifully done! You must win now; about two more rounds will settle it," added he, as he pulled back Charlie to his second's corner. "Here, give us the sponge, and carry the pail over to the baker; fair play's a jewel, you know;" saying which he threw the damp sponge at the baker's backers.

"I hope old Gresham won't turn up before the finish; what a row there'll be if he finds it out," said a dark-eyed young Pickle, who seemed quite as much alive to the fun as to the danger of the Master's arrival. "Another five minutes and we shall win, and we'll give Thornhill a jolly feed at old Mother Tucker's, after second school tomorrow."

"Don't let him close, Charlie – keep well away; well stopped!" said his second, as the baker made a vigorous but ineffectual attempt to rally: "now go in;" and Charlie Thornhill – for it was he – finding the baker a little short of wind after his last effort, followed him up and terminated the round by a "one, two, three" of so scientific a character, that Muffins, as he was politely called, failed to come to time: and the Dunce of the Family was hailed the victor, amidst the cheers of his school fellows, and the sad disappointment of the "cads".

"Don't you think he had better go to Payne's, and have a coat of paint on that left eye?" said Reginald Glanville, who considered personal appearance before all other things.

"Never mind his beauty, Dolly, he'll be handsome as paint itself when he's had a raw beefsteak on his left eye." said a young ruffian with a flat nose and a shock of red hair.

Dr. Gresham would with pleasure have pounced upon the actors in the late scene; but as he was engaged at the moment in a private lecture, in which the question at issue was the probable consequences to the world of the conquest of Syracuse by the Athenians instead of the Romans, there was no prospect of his securing an offender for himself.

His junior master, Willis, was of a different opinion. Whilst our young friends had been exulting in the successful termination of an hour's charming sport, Mr. Willis had been watching the proceeding in secret and now presented himself unexpectedly among them to inquire more minutely into particulars, and to be sure that his eyesight had not deceived him in the persons engaged. Having satisfied himself upon these points, taken another view of the cheerful chief actors in the drama, added a note or two to his memoranda, and buttoned his coat across the chest with a sort of conscious rectitude of purpose, he departed.

Charlie Thornhill

* * * * * *

"Wer lügt, um einem Andern zu schaden, der ist ein böser Bube: wer aber lügt, um sich selbst aus der noth zu helfen, der is ein schuldige memme." – German proverb

"He who lies in order to frighten someone else, he is a wicked rascal: but he who lies in order to help himself when in jeopardy is guilty of low cowardice."

"I say, Russell, we shall get into a horrid row about this fight of Charlie Thornhill's. I knew that brute Willis would be sneaking somewhere. Thornhill is certain to be flogged and so will any fourth-form boys that were caught."

"I don't believe he put my name down at all" said Russell throwing himself into a chair; "If he did it's only learning a book of Homer and we can swear the cads began it. I told Thornhill to come up here after dinner and Wilkinson and O'Brien, and the rest of the fellows who were in it. I can't think why Willis makes such a horrid row about it."

This conversation was going on in one of the studies between Russell and Glanville, who had come up from their house to the study to get up their afternoon's lesson, and to agree measures for mitigating the Head's anger, which was said to be great.

"Oh! Here come the other fellows." said Glanville "I wonder whether Willis has said anything about it to Thornhill." The door opened, and in walked half a dozen of the principal abettors of the late affair of honour, the victor among them.

"Did Willis say anything at dinner about it, Thornhill?" said Wilkinson, who came in at that moment with two or three books under his arm and a short but formidable stick laden with lead at the top, which added materially to his appearance as a conspirator.

"Yes; he said a great deal about his duty. You know he always does. And he said it would be a very serious matter for the fifth and sixth form boys that were there." said Charlie.

"Say the cads began it," said a bold, confident voice, which proceeded from a handsome but unabashed junior, who was in the study more by sufferance that right.

"That's all very fine," said Charlie; "But they didn't. Cadwallader owned to me that he was entirely to blame."

"Then if I were you I should lick Cadwallader for getting me into a row. It's entirely his conceit. I suppose he would have the wall side. It's his fault!"

The fight had taken place on a green sward close by the side of the river and within no great distance of the school. It was a public thoroughfare, used alike by the Doctor's boys for the purpose of walking or boating, and by the townspeople as a short cut to a more distant part of the parish. It is not surprising that it gave rise to an occasional squabble between the two, which ended not infrequently in a fight, as in the present case, when two young gentlemen met, whose vanity or obstinacy lay in that direction. There can be no particular pleasure in walking in close proximity to a very dirty wall, abutting some still more filthy buildings, in preference to about fifty yards of green grass which ran between it and the river. Yet this was the particular fancy of these young gentlemen and on that account an honour coveted particularly by the boys of the town. It was certainly mortifying enough that the blood of a Howard or bone of a less aristocratic scion of a banking or brewing interest, should have to yield to the superior weight of young Muffins, Slaughter or Codfish, as the case might be, backed by a turbulent crowd of young cordwainers, leathersellers and publicans, all bent upon "smashing the swells," as they were pleased to call the little aristocrats of one of the most celebrated schools of its day.

"I don't think it's worth telling a lie about," said Thornhill, "at all events." And as he spoke he blushed and hung his head, having evidently made a remark which was not likely to meet with general approbation.

"Well, that's all very fine," said Russell. "You're certain to be flogged, anyhow, and we may be sent away; the least is a book of Homer, or an imposition of a hundred lines every day for a fortnight. It's just enough to prevent one's going up to the Castle on Saturday. By Jingo, how black your eye's getting."

"I think it's as well to tell the truth about it, if Thornhill don't care," said Bob Wilkinson. "As to that confounded Willis" – and here he brought down his leaded stick, which, we regret to say, was used for knocking rabbits on the head and other poaching purposes, upon one of the two study tables with dangerous violence – "he ought to have his neck broken. There's not another master in the school would have sneaked in that way."

"The long and short of it is, we did start it," said Charlie. "There's no denying it; and I should not like to look the old Doctor in the face and tell him a crammer. He always behaves like a gentleman to us, and we shall get off pretty easy if we do the same by him."

It will be observed that the speaker was singularly deficient in the learning which gave a boy power in those days: he wrote neither longs nor shorts, nor Greek iambics; he was miserably dull at all scholarship, but he had a great reputation as a runner and jumper, a cricketer, a horseman, and an oar. He had a handsome, cheerful face, indicative of determination rather than passion; a good manner, but thoroughly boyish in all its ways; and an utter freedom from anything like affectation; he might be said scarcely to know what fear was. He had no great flow of high spirits, but was rather thoughtful, and his humour took the turn for droll images and illustration rather than for wit or repartee. Books he hated; but he never gave his masters reason to doubt him, as he honestly confessed to all the help he got from the upper boys when accused of it; and whilst his place was amongst his juniors in school, he was always to be seen arm-in-arm with his seniors out of school. The truthfulness of Charlie Thornhill was, unwittingly, the secret of his popularity.

"There goes the bell, and I haven't looked at my Horace. I'm sure to be called up; give us a construe, Cleverly, that's a good fellow". said Charlie.

After afternoon school and before the locking up for the night, it was the custom of Dr. Gresham, or one of his masters, to read prayers. On the evening in question the prayers were finished and the monitor had called over the roll but the Doctor did not leave his seat and his arched and strongly-marked eyebrows contracted with an unwonted frown.

"Wilkinson, Russell, Glanville, Cleverley," said the Doctor; and then there was a pause, whilest he prepared his pencil with a knife; then he continued in a voice more awfully sonorous than before striking dismay into the palpitating bosoms before him, "O'Brien, Jenkinson major, Walker, Thornhill, and Cadwallader stand out;" and out they stood. "The monitor has brought me your names as being concerned in another disgraceful scene with the town's boys. Follow me into my study. The monitor will attend."

Here was a pretty state of things. The chapel was the recognised place for the settlement of all such public wrongs. Nothing but the most heinous offences ever found their way to the Doctor's sanctum, which consisted of all the mystery which oaken book-cases, Elizabethan windows, crimson curtains, coats of arms, and the oldest folio volumes could impart. If the Doctor was heavily learned in school, grandly solemn in chapel, playfully erudite in society, he was simply awful and sublime in his study. Here complaints of private wrongs were heard, and grievances redressed: the Doctor's study was a temple cut off from vulgar tread and approachable only by sixth-form high-lows. Their case was evidently a heavy one; and they followed the monitor in melancholy silence into the precincts of the unwritten law.

The great man – and he was a great man, of great and varied learning - was already seated. Ponderous tomes of reference ornamented the chairs and tables, even the very floor. Manuscript sheets lay before him and rolls of uncorrected letter-press in Greek, Latin and Sanscrit. The room, handsomely furnished as it was, smelt of the mighty ancients and the Doctor was the high priest of the whole. Here and there a sixth-form exercise of Sapphics or Alcaics, or a translation from Shakespeare into Greek iambics, with the Doctor's nervous corrections and erasures, alone connected him with the little world below.

"And so…so….so you've been fighting again, I hear; ay, ay. What is the meaning of this?" said Dr. Gresham with a curious, absent hesitation, as if he were looking for a Sanscrit root in the middle of it all. "You've been fighting," said he, with a grim smile.

"Yes sir."

"And with whom, with whom was it?"

"With the cads, sir," said O'Brien, the descendant from the Kings of Ulster.

"With whom, sir?" said the Doctor, not unmindful of his dignity.

"Oh! I beg your pardon, sir. With the snobs - the towns' boys, I mean sir."

"And which was the aggressor, young gentlemen?"

A silence of some seconds. "I was, sir" said Thornhill.

"And who is I, pray?" The Doctor loved to forget names.

"Thornhill, sir."

"Thornhill, Thornhill. And whose house is he in? And in which form? Have you got your remove, boy?"

"No, sir. I shall have it next half."

"Not if you don't do better than last time," said the Doctor who became suddenly alive to the claims of Charlie to distinction. "Not if you don't do better. Did you know my orders about fighting with the town's boys? Did you know that I intended to flog the first boy that was caught, or send him away? You're very likely to get your remove, some of you – some of you." And here the Doctor gave another short laugh, which boded better for the delinquents. "And – come nearer, Thornhill; nearer still, boy. Why, you have got a black eye!" And here the venerable sage looked as if that was a most unreasonable result of a three-quarters of an hour's fight.

"If you please, sir, we found Muffins – I beg your pardon, sir, I mean the baker's boy, quarrelling with one of the little fellows, and ---"

"And you went to help him. Well – well, I shall see all about it to-morrow; but don't go out from the school fields until you hear from me again. Thornhill – Thornhill – ay! I must flog Thornhill; he's been sent down twice in the last week, and now he's got a black eye in a fight with a baker. Stay. Monitor, bring Thornhill into the upper school tomorrow morning at ten o'clock, and the names of the rest who were with him. Take care, take care, young gentlemen. Wilkinson and O'Brien, you're old enough to know better; but I've got my eye on some of you. Go along, go along;" and the Doctor was already deep in his new work, an edition of Aristophanes.

The immense advantages of flogging would fill a volume. What a horrible thing is the promiscuous laceration of the back, arms, and shoulders, by a cane! Always at the mercy of momentary impulse. But there is a dignity in flogging. It comes after a night's reflection, and leaves an opening for extenuating circumstances to appear. Besides, where there is life there is hope, and no one knows what may happen to divert the execution of a sentence, however just.

Strange to say, on the following day, after morning chapel, the Doctor's own servant, Mr. Bandy, appeared in Willis's house, with a desire for Mr. Thornhill "to step this way."

Many were the conjectures as to what had taken place, when half an hour after, a fly was at the door. Charlie Thornhill was on his way to meet his brother, with undefined fears and a heavy heart, but without his flogging. It was not known until some days after that a mysterious fate had robbed the boys of a kind and generous father. Squire Thornhill had been shot on his road back from Bidborough races. But we must retrace our steps, to explain the position of our hero, and the circumstances which left him fatherless at so early an age.

CHAPTER 3

"MY FRIEND GEOFFREY"

"Celui qui remplissait alors cette place était un gentilhomme"
The place that is most fulfilling is surely the home of a gentleman.

One of the most beautiful places in the midland counties of England isThornhills. One extremity of the park is remarkable for its natural variations of soil, luxuriance of heather and fern, its gnarled and twisted oaks and masses of woods and water. At the other end it has rich cultivation within which stands the house, a noble specimen of the early Tudor style. The magnificent hall opens on every side, but one, to rooms of grand and lofty proportions, lighted, or rather obscured, by deeply mullioned windows, not infrequently enriched by the emblazonment of heraldry and still retaining the shields of the new nobility to whom it had been granted at the close of the Wars of the Roses when the Lancastrian Henry rewarded some of his most active followers with the spoils of the extinct Yorkists. On the walls still hang the well-preserved memorials of the hunt or of war. A fine black oak staircase leads to the upper storeys of the house, the brightness and smoothness of which must have put to the test the hilarious guests of the first Mr. Thornhill, an eminent banker and goldsmith of Charles II's reign. Amidst the tattered banners and the rusted spears and swords of more exciting periods were scattered tusks, foxes' masks and brushes, hunting whips of every age since the days of the Merry Monarch, and fishing apparatus from the time of Izaak Walton [1] to the most approved methods of modern invention, all these adorned the walls with rich profusion. Amongst the hunting pictures on the walls was a fine full-length painting of the grandfather of the present proprietor of the place in hunting costume who had set the example of keeping the county hounds without a subscription, an example which had been duly followed by both his successors. It was, indeed, pretty clear that claret had beggared the descendants of the knightly family who had benefited from Lancastrian Henry's gift. I can say nothing about the respectable money-lender who took the place for a bad debt and called the lands after his own name: he probably had but little knowledge of country pursuits, and was more at home in Lombard Street than on his estate of Thornhills; but there can be no doubt that a taste had come down through the days of hawking and harriers, until the name of Thornhill of Thornhills included the very quintessence of a country life.

In a mixed aristocracy, like that of England, such a family as the Thornhills was certain to hold its own. High connections, an unencumbered estate of about twelve thousand a year, and a character for a certain amount of talent, derived chiefly from diplomacy in minor courts and the representation of the county on high Conservative principles, made them respected by the highest rank and looked up to by men of almost every position. It must, however, be admitted that they shone amongst the provincial aristocracy rather than in that heterogeneous mass of beings called London society. The father of Geoffrey Thornhill, though he had

---

[1] Izaak Walton wrote "The Compleat Angler" published in 1653

refused a baronetcy and married a peer's daughter, Lady Charlotte, had lived almost entirely amongst his tenantry, until at the end of the London season he invariably filled his house with overworked politicians, overfed loungers, sportsmen and idlers of every degree. Then Thornhills became the house of the county. No duke rivalled the profusion of its hospitality

But Lady Charlotte grew old and her husband grew old: and as will happen in the nature of things, the property and the hounds descended to Geoffrey Thornhill. Everybody worshipped him, as in duty bound. The men ate with him, drank with him, shot with him and hunted with him; and the women set their caps at him. He was the delight of all hearts, as who should not have been, who was the handsomest and one of the richest men in the county? He had his faults: a little hastiness of temper, and a turn for dissipation and gambling but he was full of generous impulses, and never could say "No" to himself or to other people. When Emily Carisbrooke, the eldest daughter of Sir George Carisbrooke, and one of the prettiest girls in the country, married him, she was looked upon by her acquaintances as the most fortunate of women.

In truth Geoffrey Thornhill was tall and handsome: his features were especially good, perhaps better than the expression of his face, which announced sensuality and weakness of purpose. He was graceful, and well made, as quite a young man; indulgence gave a fullness to his figure in after years which was only kept in check by violent exercise on horseback and on foot. He had a peculiarly pleasant smile, which played about his mouth, and as he passed a life almost entirely free from anxieties and amidst the gratification of almost every wish, it is scarcely to be wondered at that it was ever present. He was by far pleasanter in company than out of it; not an uncommon thing. He was a selfish man and rather thoughtless of little kindnesses which cost some sacrifice, but lavish in all things that cost him none.

Having never felt the want of money, he was liberal and open handed, without being truly generous or charitable. To his wife he was never unkind but he frequently pained her by open admiration of other women, and by attentions which had not escaped the observation of the world in which they lived. He was an excellent friend. As far as a mount, a day's shooting, or a hundred pounds could be of service to an acquaintance, Geoffrey Thornhill was not wanting; but he would have foregone no pleasure for the sake of anyone; and regarded a death in his circle only as pain insofar as it deprived him of an anticipated enjoyment. He was affectionate in disposition; fond of his boys, Tom and Charlie, and proud of them; but careless of their real good. His greatest favourite was his only brother, Henry, a London banker, and of tastes, habits and disposition the complete reverse of himself. This attachment was mutual. Each saw in the character of the other some want of his own; the hard-working, thick-crusted man of business, who had a mind intent upon nothing but money, who spent from 10 a.m. until 4.00 pm every day of his life in the counting-house, admired the unembarrassed *nonchalance* and careless generosity of his brother; whilst Geoffrey could not but admire in his brother Henry that perseverance, steadiness, and strict principle in which he felt himself to be deficient. Be that as it may, the most amiable trait in the character of either brother was fraternal love.

But little remains to be told of Geoffrey Thornhill. He was an adept at all sports and athletic exercises. From his cradle he had been brought up amongst horses and guns; and education completed what nature seemed to have begun, by making him the most finished sportsman of his day. His feats and skill live in the recollection of his acquaintances, and are still quoted as unrivalled even in our own times. He could hunt his own hounds, if need be, after a night of hazard or whist. He knew as much of his covers and his fields as the keepers themselves, and was equally conversant with the favourite haunts of the birds. He was as willing to encounter danger against the poachers by whom his neighbourhood was infested. Constant excitement seemed necessary to his very existence. His almost universal mode of travelling was by relays of hacks, and he performed the most astonishing distances in the shortest possible time. Need I say that such things as these made him the most popular of men? Where could he have found an enemy?

CHAPTER 4

AN ENGLISH GENTLEMAN'S CASTLE

"Haec res et jungit, junctos et servat amicos"
One sees it as a business matter, the other as a service to a friend.

"How do you go to Bidborough, Thornhill?" said an *habitué* of Brookes's, as Geoffrey Thornhill lounged in the bay window about 11 am on a lovely morning in May, with "The Times" in one hand and a straight riding whip in the other, having left his hack at the door in charge of a red-waistcoated man. "I ride to Marston's for dinner today" replied Geoffrey Thornhill, "It is only twenty-seven miles to Woodlands Abbey, and I have sent on a hack half way; Marston rides on with me to the course to-morrow morning. How are they backing the grey?"
"What, Benevenuto, for the Corinthian Stakes? Oh! They back him at evens; there are only four to start; and he is quite safe to win, unless he dies in the night. Do you know anything about him?"
"Yes" said Thornhill "they had a trial yesterday, and he is said to be seven pounds better than the Maid of the Mill; so that there can be no mistake. I've just backed him for another thousand."

"Who rides him?"

"Kildonald. Between ourselves that's the most awkward part of the business; but Marston thinks himself under some sort of obligation to the man, and he makes a great point of having the mount. As it was offered to him long ago, I can hardly see how he can help himself now. I don't like Kildonald."

"Perhaps you are prejudiced and dislike his countrymen in general."

"On the contrary, I have a particular fancy for Irishmen; that is, of the lowest and highest classes; the former are not understood, and the latter have not always had a fair reputation." said Thornhill.

"Kildonald scarcely comes up to that standard; and how the deuce he manages to live as he does I have no idea. He has the most elastic conscience about women and horseflesh I ever knew." observed the club member. Thornhill, nodded an adieu to his friend, and mounted his hack to ride his first stage towards Bidborough.

Now I must say a word about Bidborough. It had a singular pre-eminence. It was and is the very stupidest country town in England. During eleven months and eight-and-twenty days of every year it enjoyed a tranquillity perfectly marvellous. Yet it was not without inhabitants. Of course it had a parson. It was a fine large living, some £1,500 a year and usually reserved for the second son of the "great family", as the Earl of Bidborough was called. There was a lawyer; but I apprehend that the greater part of his business consisted of the agency to the "great family", and a few others, who trusted him with the collection of rents and the drawing of leases. Like all other robberies, those can be most effectively perpetrated in the dark. There was also an apothecary; he would have done well, but for the adoption of hydropathy; which has a tenuous hold on reality but had penetrated to these remote and mysterious regions. The place itself consists of a long ill-paved street, ignorant of *trottoir*, in the midst of a down county. It had a mouldy smell and grass-grown appearance. It was itself purely agricultural in its population, though situated in the middle of one of our cloth manufacturing districts. But for the conversation at Brookes, the reader would be puzzled to know what attraction could have taken Geoffrey Thornhill to such a spot.

The fact is, that though Bidborough itself was unknown, its racecourse had a universal reputation. It was more or less a private meeting; the tumult and turmoil of a great race-course were wanting; and a considerable number of the races were devoted to gentlemen riders. This in itself, independently of other circumstances, made it more select, and, consequently, a more agreeable rendezvous than usual.

The present season was expected to be remarkably good. The great house was full, and the neighbouring gentry had determined upon a revival of the former days of splendour. Of late years it had been upon the wane; but there was a general feeling, a tacit understanding amongst racing men, that Bidborough was to be the fashion.

The gentlemen of England had determined that Bidborough races should be more attractive than ever; and the great point of attraction was to be "The Corinthian Stakes," a handicap race for gentlemen riders alone. Of starters there would be but four; but the money which was on the favourite, a fine three-year-old, the property of Sir Frederick Marston, called Benevenuto, gave some idea of the opinion in which he was held by the great patrons of the turf.

The ride from London to Sir Frederick Marston's was sufficiently interesting. At St. Albans Geoffrey Thornhill mounted his second hack, and was not long in reaching the seat of Sir Frederick where he was welcomed with as much cordiality as is consistent with true good breeding. Geoffrey was a favourite everywhere; and Lady Marston was no exception to so general a rule.

Sit Frederick and Lady Marston were still young; that is comparatively with Thornhill. Marston had been one of the young men whom Thornhill loved to have about him; a good shot, a horseman, a *bon vivant* and a congenial spirit in many ways. Ten years in point of age, when a man first appears, make a vast difference and establish an influence which not infrequently lasts through life. For his part Frederick Marston had more to thank Thornhill for than he ever understood. A long minority and a taste for dissipation made him the object of attack to every well-born sharper; and it was as well for him that he found a home where he might indulge his tastes to a certain extent, without falling into the hands of those who would have been merciless in the face of such temptation. He was reserved for better things. At thirty he married a woman every way suited to him, whose charms of conversation and manner made his home cheerful, and whose beauty of person accorded well with the hospitalities dispensed by one of the richest country gentlemen in England. He had a pack of fox-hounds in a country only second to Leicestershire and Northamptonshire; a gallery of pictures on which care, knowledge, and money had been lavished; a deer forest in Scotland; a villa at Como; and yet he was dissatisfied with his lot. Fortune had denied him two things. He had been married five years without a child, and he had kept a string of horses for seven, but had never won a great race. For the former disappointment there was no accounting, and at present there seemed to be no remedy: for a winner no expense or trouble would be spared.

What were the awful mysteries of a former and less civilized age, which drove a woman from the table of her lord as soon as she had satisfied the cravings of nature, whilst he and his comrades were left to indulge in a prolonged repast? Be that as it may the custom has obtained in this country, and at the time I write of was remarkably popular. In France society was differently constituted. Women did not relinquish the right to preside over the after-dinner conversation of their husbands, and the mistresses of kings and councillors became mistresses of the world. Still with no less certainty did Lady Marston and her guests rise at the usual time, and amidst a rustling of silks and satins, and the profound salutations of one devoted slave of the door, retired to the drawing room. Sir Frederick and Thornhill drew their chairs closer together; the butler appeared with one fresh and cool bottle of choice Lafitte, and they proceeded to discuss questions in which, as the reader may feel an interest, he shall be allowed to participate.

"And how are the boys, Thornhill?"

"Well; and at school. Tom is at Eton, and Charlie is to join him. I hope it may be for his good."

"Ah! My friend Charlie must be getting a big fellow now. I like that boy, Geoffrey, there's something very original about him."

"Originality has its drawbacks, Marston: and if your young favourite was less original and more fond of work it might be better for him. However, Eton will do that for him, perhaps."

"It must be singularly changed since my day if it does," said Sir Frederick. "If I were bent upon giving a naturally indolent boy full opportunity for indulging his favourite weakness, I should certainly select a public school for him."

"Why so?"

"Because a cub or an ass may be licked into shape; a stupid fellow may be brightened; an impudent fellow may be taken down; but there's no cure for idleness in a public school: and it's almost the only fault that could not be cured there. How does Tom get on?"

"Admirably. He's a great favourite, comes home surrounded by chums, who all admire and copy him, and has never missed his remove. However, he has plenty of brains. Charlie's my *bête noire*, and seems proud of his nickname, The Dunce of the Family."

"I wish he were a poor man's son. I prognosticate great things for Charlie," said Marston good-naturedly. "Tom can take care of himself; but younger sons are not always so well taken care of. I suppose he must have a profession."

"It's early days to think of that. I believe he'll have his uncle's property; for, between ourselves, Fred, I've nothing to leave him. Every shilling of Thornhills is entailed, and the Irish property too; besides which the latter is saddled with my wife's settlement and is scarcely able to bear the burden."

"Your life is not insured?"

"Not for a halfpenny."

"What a thoughtless fellow you are, Thornhill! I ought to have been your mentor, not you mine."

"Times have improved with you. But you haven't told me what to do with Charlie; he's nearly fourteen so I must make my mind up soon."

"Send him to Henry Reynolds."

"What! The Rector? My dear fellow, he knows Charlie too well, and me too."

"You don't know him, if you imagine his love for you or Charlie would ever interfere with his duties."

"You think so, Marston? You ought to know; but I own it did not strike me."

"He's the truest-hearted gentleman in this county: and no man doubts his learning. His living is but small and his family large: so that you may benefit him and yourself too."

"I must have another chat with you about Reynolds. The boy is idle, fond of horses and dogs, with a strong will, good manners and appearance and would make his way at Eton."

"The worst thing that could happen to him. He would never learn a lesson, or write a piece of Latin, or do a copy of verses for himself. As to his horses and dogs, he's a Thornhill, I presume! Cramwell tells me that the Duke[2] finds the present system very defective and

---

[2] Could this be referring to the Duke of Wellington who was Commander in

determines on instituting an army examination. This is only the thin end of the wedge; that examination must soon become competitive; and the result will be open government appointments, civil and military. Old Cramwell is delighted at the prospect. At first he shook his head, but soon gave way; for he discovered some consolation in the very pretty pickings to be got for his party by an increased staff of principalships, inspectorships, commissionerships, and a number of other ships, which the old duke good-humouredly, with an eye to his own profession, called 'ships of the line.'"

"Then," said Thornhill, "They may get more learning into the army, but they will lose caste. If the modern system is to be forced upon us, what is to become of Eton and Harrow, and half the good schools in England?"

"They'll soften down, Thornhill, to meet the times. I learnt nothing at Eton, and I don't suppose Charlie would learn much more. You can teach him to be a gentleman, and that's about the use of Harrow or Eton to two thirds that go there. It happens to be just the knowledge that your boy doesn't need. And now let's go to the drawing room, as you will take no more. Emily will be expecting us by this time. Thompson, have a fire lighted in the smoking-room in half an hour's time."

* * * * * *

"A wife well-humour'd, dutiful, and chaste."

The hospitalities of Woodlands Abbey were charming. The master could be agreeable; nay, more, he could be, and was with his intimates, a very fascinating person: but Lady Marston far outshone her husband in her character of hostess. To say she was one of the most beautiful women of her day was to say the least in her praise.

Chief of the British Army until his death in September 1852?

Her mind was cultivated to an extent scarcely conceivable in days when ornament takes the place of substantial merit. Her manners had a charm which pertains only to such as have embellished English sincerity with the elegances of the best foreign society. She was kind, but graceful; even warm, but courteous; a woman of the world in the midst of home duties; thoughtful and tender, but not the less witty and conversational. She received Geoffrey Thornhill kindly, inquired enthusiastically after his wife and his boys, of whom she knew him to be prouder than of anything. She regretted the absence of other company, but congratulated herself and Marston upon their accidental presence in the country at this time, when they could be of service to so old a friend.

After half an hour's pleasant conversation in the drawing room, she said "But we shall see you back after the races, and then perhaps you will give us a day or two more, as we do not leave till the end of the week." She took her leave and her candle together, and the men were left to their devices.

A smoking-room is an essential in a gentleman's house; and Marston's was not behind others in its comforts. The barbarism that invites a man into the open air of an evening, to the chill and fog of an English climate in the month of May, to enjoy his post-prandial tobacco, is deserving of severe reprobation or silent contempt; and both Sir Frederick and his guest did not deny themselves the luxury of arm-chairs and a fire, in a room embellished by the coaches of Henderson, and favourite horses and hounds by all the best sporting artists of the day.

It scarcely required these to remind our two friends of the importance of tomorrow. It had been the subject uppermost in their minds for some part of the day; and though Marston was too well accustomed to winning or losing a race, and Geoffrey Thornhill too careless of a few hundreds, more or less, to let his present bet tinge his general tone with one shade of anxiety, still they had both quite enough at stake to be glad to talk over the probable chances of success.

Thornhill puffed a few clouds of smoke before him, and from behind them inquired after the grey.

"All right," said Marston, "he never looked better; shall we call in Turner?"

"No! never mind about Turner, Fred. I believe Turner to be as honest as the day, but those fellows have temptations which we know nothing about."

"I took every precaution; it is my opinion that the horse can't lose – and that he will win the Leger if he keeps his form. He is better than he ever was before, certainly a stone better than when he won at Northampton."

"I'm glad to hear it. If I'd seen you yesterday I should have backed him for the double event. We'll go in good time tomorrow, and see what Musgrave will do about the Leger. Burke, that Irish fellow, was at Tattersall's and wanted to lay against him for the Corinthian; though I hear he laid out all he had at Doncaster some time ago."

Here they both relapsed into silence: but after a couple of minutes, Geoffrey asked who was to ride Marston's grey.

"The very best gentleman rider in England!" said Sir Frederick, with enthusiasm, as if his friend Thornhill must be satisfied now. "The very best in England, bar none."

"You mean Kildonald; I quite agree with you. There is no one like him: and as to the young ones, they are no use with him whatever. He has the finest hands, and he combines monstrous power with great elegance. He can do anything with his horse; in fact, he knows too much."

"You don't like him, Geoffrey?"

"I don't like his friends. He's a pleasant, gentlemanly fellow enough;

but that fellow Burke is in every robbery, and I think Kildonald is in with him."

"They are compatriots; but there can't be much in common between such men as Burke and Kildonald," said Marston the least suspicious of men, he scarcely believed in the existence of premeditated rascality. At this moment came a knock at the door, and a servant entered, slowly and noiselessly, as is the wont of gentlemen's servants. "What horse is to go on to-morrow to Sittingdean for Mr. Thornhill, sir? Turner is gone with Benevenuto, and left no orders."

"Send the roan mare and my black hack. We shall start from here at ten, and tell George to be ready at Sittingdean at half-past eleven. What sort of a night is it?"

"Rains fast, Sir Frederick," and the man left the room

"So much the better for the grey; it can't be too heavy for him; every drop that falls will be ounces in his favour: it's a certainty so long as he lives till the morning." And the sanguine baronet indulged in a prolonged yawn, which reminded both that they might retire for the night.

"Good night, Marston; breakfast at nine. And you think it is a certainty?" said Thornhill for the last time.

"As certain as a thing can be. Good night!" And they both took their candles and made their separate ways to bed.

CHAPTER 5

TO THE COURSE

**"The rugged mountain's scanty cloak
Was dwarfish shrubs of birch and oak."**

The rain was over, and by nine o'clock it was as fine a May morning as ever shone upon the earth. The sun was high in heaven, and the still wet blades of grass and early hedgerow leaves were glistening like diamonds. There was a genial warmth about the day already, early as it was, which made it rather the harbinger of the coming summer than the expiring effort of departing spring. All nature rejoiced; the birds carolled blithely as they flirted merrily in the tender shadows of the opening leaves. The feeling was irresistible and Thornhill had but little difficulty in shaking off the blue devils of the night before when he threw up his window and welcomed the morning air. Lady Marston was already at the breakfast table with one or two inmates of her house, whom we have not before noticed, her brother Lindsay, and a young Belgravian, scarcely of presentable age. Marston himself, too, was on the steps of his house, giving some orders about the horses, and returned to the breakfast room just as Geoffrey

Thornhill entered by an opposite door.

Breakfast is a cheerful meal in a country gentleman's house; perhaps the most so of any. It is to the day what youth is to life: somewhat too short, but a season of promise – alas not always to be fulfilled!

"Shall we say half an hour later for dinner, Mr. Thornhill?" said Lady Marston. "Perhaps eight o'clock will suit you and Frederick better than our usual hour?"

"Thank ye, Kate. Eight o'clock will do capitally for us," said the baronet kissing his hand to his pretty wife.

"Adieu, I wish you luck," came the rejoinder. And the gentlemen were gone.

Time is no laggard when a cheerful day's sport is before such men as Sir Frederick Marston and Geoffrey Thornhill. In half an hour they were ready for their proposed journey; the roan mare and the black hack having been gone some hours earlier, they prepared for an exhilarating ride through beautiful country to Sittingdean, a village within a short distance of the course, and where their second horses awaited their arrival.

About the same time, but on the opposite side of the country, a party of a very different kind was verging towards the course. Over a long strip of common land, decked here and there with dells, and clumps of stunted box, and straggling gorse, rumbled one of those half-houses, half-waggons, drawn by a dull, badly-fed cart horse and a thriving donkey, the common attendant on a gipsy encampment. It was accompanied by some half dozen swarthy looking Bohemians, two of whom were women, whose scarlet neckchiefs and fantastic head dresses proclaimed their profession. A short distance behind these came three more people, consisting of a man, whose sharp features, high cheekbones, and twinkling gray eyes had no characteristic of gipsy life: his face was indicative of low cunning; and his dress consisted of corduroy breeches, unbuttoned at the knee, and blue dress-coat with metal buttons and large pockets protected by heavy lapels on the outside. His companions were a woman of about forty years of age, bearing the remains of much beauty, disfigured by intemperance of every kind and now haggard and worn by sickness and premature decay; and her son of about twenty, singularly athletic, finely made, and with a face which, in the midst of all its grandeur, exhibited a ferocity more like that of uncivilized life than the ordinary daring of depraved nature. There was a recklessness about him as of one smarting under wrong.

"And where are we now?" said the younger man, in an impatient tone, "Near the course?" and he halted to survey the scene.

"That's Sittingdean to your left, and that's the racecourse to the right, where ye see the tents in the hollow; this bridle-path is the way to Stapleford over the common: but ye know the way?" And here Mike Daly (for so he was called) turned with a malicious half-look towards the woman, Mary Connor.

"Ay, ay! I know every stone and every tree of the road: it's burnt into my very soul with a scar that twenty years have never healed. What do you ask such a question for?" and her face turned almost livid as she placed her hand on her side, and her eyes flashed with unwonted light.

"I've had my wrongs too," said Mike, "And it's not in this country. Faith, a home's a home, if it is but a pigstye, and –"

"Your wrongs indeed!" said Mary with a look of withering contempt at the speaker. "What do you call wrongs? Have you seen your home, as you call it, destroyed; your only parent dying with a curse on his lips for your unborn child; your daughter stolen and your hopes of happiness withered; your love trampled on; your very supplications for bread derided by one for whom you had sacrificed everything in this world, and in the world to come?" and such was the vehemence with which the words were uttered, that Daly, accustomed as he was to such outbreaks, dropped behind, abashed at the insignificance of his own misfortunes.

"Silence mother!" said George; "Think of this world, and leave the other to take care of itself. What has it ever done for us, that we should concern ourselves about it?" And with a daring fierceness he strode onward at a pace that bid fair to out distance his companions.

"Ah! Like father, like son," continued the Irishman, in a sort of soliloquy. "He drove us from our homes, to get the rent; and now ---. But wait awhile, wait awhile; it's lawyer Burke that'll see the poor folk righted." And at this moment a turn in the narrow path they had been following brought them round the corner of a small covert, whence the race course came full upon their view.

The younger man had outstripped the other two, and was now mingling with the gipsies, who regarded him with looks of distrust. He was poorly clad, and nothing but his manner expressing himself, and a certain air of hauteur, served to separate him from the lowest grade of ruffianism. He was no sooner joined by his mother and Mike Daly than the three plunged at once into the crowd, now beginning to collect from every side. They had almost reached the course, when in crossing one of the rides, cut in every direction through the heath, a horseman, on a small active horse, brushed rudely past almost trampling upon the young man whose left hand seized the bridle, and he raised his stick with the other. A harsh cry from his mother arrested his arm, and permitted the horseman to pursue his course unmolested.

"George! George! For God's sake hold; leave him, leave him to – to – to Heaven. Yes, yes, there is, there is a God. He only deserted me when I deserted myself. His punishment will come soon enough;" and the broken sobs of the woman were for some moments too violent for suppression.

"Look at him; look, George. Shall you forget him?"

"Do I ever forget an enemy?"

"Is he an enemy?"

"He would have trodden us under foot, like the rest of his accursed race; damn him. Who or what is he, that I am not as good?"

"He is Arthur Kildonald: my enemy, but your father."

A sullen scowl crossed his face: and his mother rose at the same moment from a hillock on which she had sunk, he took her by the hand, and led her towards the railing which separated the stand from the course. "My father? Arthur Kildonald? No; I'll not forget him. Let us be going."

CHAPTER 6

THE RACE

"Puncto mobilis horæ
Nunc prece, nunc pretio, nunc vi, nunc morte supremâ,
Permutet dominos et cedat in altera jura." Hor., *Ep*.ii.

The sting of fickle time.
Pray now, now be rewarded, now be strong, now the highest point is death, we exchange masters and submit to another law.

The bell had already twice rung for saddling: and the first two races had been run rather to the disappointment of the gentlemen and the success of the professional bookmakers. In the first race an outsider had won by the jockeyship, as was asserted, of Kildonald; in the second the favourite had been defeated on the post by a beaten horse, and the race pulled out of the fire. In the interval before the Corinthian Handicap, the race of the day, the conversation turned partly on the merits of the horses, partly on that of the riders. Sir Frederick Marston turned away from the course and ambled back to the where the horses were being unsaddled

"Captain Kildonald made a fine race of that, Sir Frederick," said a neat-looking, well-whiskered individual, with a small betting-book in his hand, and a tooth-pick in his mouth. "He never took a liberty with his 'oss, and they all come back to him at last. He's a nasty beggar to ride, for he wants you to get all you can out of him, and you mustn't get it out too fast."

"He rode the horse very well, very well indeed, Smithson," replied the baronet: "few men can ride better. There's many a jockey might give *him* 5 lbs; but he scarcely looks himself today, somehow or other."

"He leads such a life."

"Does he? What is it – gambling?"

"Bless you, yes!" said the man, who was called Smithson, who was a good sort of fellow, and found living by his wits easier and pleasanter than being behind a counter, the natural sphere of his operations; "Bless you, yes! Play! All night and all day. He must have some pretty good nerve left to live as he does."

"Do anything, Sir Frederick? Want to back your colt?" said a yellow-looking, stout, heavy-jowled man, in shiny black clothes, and a most respectable look, who had been a stocking-weaver in the midland counties, and was now the largest bookmaker on the Turf.

"Nothing more, thank you, Pearson. I've backed him for all I intend; and I hope he'll win."

"Well, Dorrington, what have you done about Benevenuto?" asked Sir Frederick to a well dressed gentleman who joined the group.

"Backed him like the devil," said Lord Dorrington to his inquirer. "It's a comfort to know that he's *meant*. He *does* belong to a gentleman, and he'll be well ridden."

"He's a very easy horse to ride," said the young Marquis of Droughtmore, himself no mean performer over a country, though a little too heavy for the flat. "He has a great turn of speed, and comes when he's called upon. Are you staying here, Dorrington?"

"Yes, at Henry Corry's. It's about three miles from here, across the heath."

"What a handsome gipsy!" said Wilbraham, who just joined them, pointing to the figure of an athletic-looking young fellow, with magnificent eyes, who was watching a bare-knuckle fight, but keeping the corner of his eye stealthily upon somebody unseen. "He'd do to put into training to lick anyone for £200. Come, Thornhill, you back the Bohemian, and we'll put him into form in no time. Why he must be six feet two, if he's an inch; and what a pair of shoulders! His face reminds me of somebody. You are not handsome enough, Dorrington, or I should say it was you."

At that very moment, mounted on the grey colt, led by Turner, Sir Frederic Marston's trainer, and looking the perfection of a gentleman jockey, came Arthur Kildonald. He was a tall, singularly good-looking man but very spare. His length of thigh gave him a great appearance of power, as well as ease upon his horse; and it was plain to see that what strength he had was above the saddle. He was beautifully dressed; and his colours, dark purple and buff, became him admirably. It was impossible not to notice him. At the best of times his face was not a good face: it wanted honesty or expression, with all its beauty. Now it was deadly pale, and wore a troubled look. Not far from the horse, amid the crowd that walked by his side admiring his condition, and entering a last bet upon the race, was our old acquaintance Mr. Burke. To a very close observer, one significant glance passed between the latter and Kildonald, before he was lost in the crowd. At the same instant Lord Dorrington turned suddenly from the gipsy to the rider. The likeness was sufficiently manifest: there was but the difference between the savage and the civilised man, for the rest the resemblance was complete.

I have already said that the Bidborough Meeting was select rather than large. It embraced country gentlemen in the Stand, their carriages and wives on the opposite side of the course. The great earl, Lord Bidborough, was there, talking to Thornhill, Sir Frederick Marston, and a few more of equal rank. The labourers, servants, and artisans of the neighbourhood appeared in more than a just proportion; their smiles and many-coloured ribbons were the pleasantest part of the scene. The greatest betting men were there, including the nobility and gentry of England, the real patrons of the Turf: the idlers who backed their fancy for a pony were there in great numbers. The fine, independent, top-booted farmers and yeomen appeared in great force; and in smaller numbers the *mimi, balatrones, et hoc genus omne*[3]. The small betting man was not to be found: there was no place for the minor bookmaker, for the lawyer's clerk, or the embryo City man.

I write of a day when the chief proprietors of racehorses were to be found amongst the nobles and gentlemen of England; horse racing had not yet become a simple trade. It was presumed that the object was to win. There were always rogues, as there have been before and since the days of Dan Dawson[4] but racing was not yet the business of a nation, and the pleasure of the few; what betting there was, was done *con amore.*[5]

The course was being rapidly cleared. Policemen were active, and the huntsmen and whips of the Bidborough Union Foxhounds were forming a serried rank of inquisitive yokels some distance below the Stand. The ladies were closing their glove books and eagerly expecting the race of the day. The last dog had already been cleared from the course by at least five minutes. Three horses had gone down besides Benevenuto: two were entirely out of it, and the third ridden by Lord Castleton, had nothing but an outside chance against

---

[3] Actors, buffoons and people of every kind.
[4] Daniel Dawson was indicted and convicted of poisoning horses in 1811.
[5] For the love of it.

Sir Frederick's horse. The preliminary canter confirmed preconceived notions, that the race was a foregone conclusion. One chance alone remained to the fielders: that Kildonald should make use of his horse all the way.

They're off! The multitude hold their breath: a murmur: they come: the grey winning. "By heavens! What's Kildonald about? He's at work already; Castleton wins. No, by Jove! The grey does it now. Castleton, Marston; d_____ it, he's stopped him!" shrieks Lord Dorrington and twenty more voices at the same moment, as the mare, quietly ridden by Lord Castleton, is landed a winner by a neck. "It's a cursed robbery!" "It's a swindle!" "He could scarcely help winning, as it was!" "An infernal piece of rascality from beginning to end!" And epithets not complimentary, and curses both loud and deep, were uttered against the rider of Benevenuto, as he rode to the weigh-in. It was all over; and the blank looks and empty pockets of the Grand Stand told it all quite plainly enough. Kildonald, amidst the yells of the populace and half protected from personal injury by the police, entered the Stand. His lips were quivering with suppressed passion and every muscle of his pale face was working. Turning sharply round, his eye lit upon Geoffrey Thornhill, who was replying in no measured terms to the condolences of the men by whom he was surrounded. The word "swindle" or "swindler" rose sharply over the hubbub. Kildonald glared like a tiger, and, forcing his way towards Thornhill, demanded in tones scarcely audible, but hissing from between his teeth, whether Thornhill applied that epithet to him.

"I echo, sir, the sentiment of every man on the course who ever saw a race in his life when I repeat that it is an infernal robbery;" and as he spoke, Thornhill's face, before rather expressive of disappointment, coloured with an effort to control his temper.

"Swindler?" rejoined Kildonald, now utterly beside himself; and as he spoke he raised his right hand, in which he held the whip with which he had been riding, and made a blow at his antagonist. His arm was instantly seized, but not before the whip had slightly grazed Thornhill's cheek. An insult so gross drove all power of restraint from Geoffrey Thornhill and with one blow he knocked Kildonald into the arms of a bystander. The quarrel was too unseemly to proceed; the friends of either party hurried them away; and whilst Geoffrey Thornhill rejoined his friends in the Stand, Kildonald mounted his hack and rode straight to the cottage of an acquaintance with whom he was staying, about half an hour's walk from the course.

"You were imprudent, Thornhill," said Marston, some two hours later, when every trace of passion had left his friend Geoffrey, and nothing remained but a consideration of his position in the quarrel.

"I was. But I was robbed of a very large stake." Thornhill blushed again at the recollection of the indignity.

"Admitted. But why did you strike that unfortunate blow? He must leave the country; and your expressions no man can gainsay, though some may blame."

"Good heavens! Marston, how you do talk. Is a man to lose several thousands by such rascality and stand by and profess to respect it? I had no idea that Kildonald would have heard me; but as it was a robbery, and I had said so, it would not have been dignified to have denied it."

"That was impossible, and now *que faire.*" At that moment a gentlemanly-looking man, well known on the turf and in society as a Major Doyle, a mutual acquaintance of Kildonald and Thornhill, of irreproachable character, approached and said in a grave measured tone.

"I beg your pardon for the unpleasant intrusion, but my instructions leave me no alternative. I am desired by Mr. Kildonald to state that he remains at my house, which is on the heath, and barely two miles from here, until he can have the necessary arrangements for a meeting with Mr. Thornhill. The exigencies of the case preclude all apology, and demand as much despatch as possible."

"Accept my excuses, Major Doyle, for not at once receiving you by appointing a friend to confer with you. The circumstances are such as to require consideration, and I will forward a note or send a friend this evening to your house." replied Geoffrey Thornhill. The Major raised his hat with an elegance characteristic of an Irish gentleman, and Thornhill replied with a bow as distant as courtesy permitted.

"Marston, I should ask you to do me the greatest favour that one man can do for another; but one friend older than yourself in length of friendship, and older than either of us in years, must be consulted."

"But you will not fight him?"

"Undoubtedly."

"Why he's a swindler – a common blackleg".

"We say so. But remember, he has a little world of his own, which will not believe it. Unfortunately it is not capable of direct proof, and we have only acted on our convictions. Yes; I must fight him."

"What, then, do you propose?"

"Go home to Lady Marston; keep your own counsel and mine. I shall ride round by Corry's: he is the best fellow alive in cases of this sort. He has had hundreds of them on his hands. He will give me some dinner, see Major Doyle this very evening, and I shall be with you two or three hours later than otherwise. Your hack will not take long going from Sittingdean, which I can reach from Henry Corry's by the lower side of the heath. Adieu, my dear Marston. Let's send your groom for the horses, and I'll be off. The last race will be over by the time they are at the back of the stand."

CHAPTER 7

THE CHALLENGE

"Captain, I thee beseech to do me favours." Shakespeare, *Henry V*

When Geoffrey Thornhill had mounted his hack, and desired Marston to tell them at Sittingdean that he should be there by ten or half past, he turned with a loose rein over one of the paths of the heath, which led amongst clumps of firs and broken patches of sand and gorse to the villas and country houses scattered over the face of the landscape. The sun was setting; and at another time Thornhill would have probably given a passing thought to the beauty of the scene, or to its adaptability for fox-hunting. He might have admired his clean shaped, active hack, as he picked his way over the stony and sandy road before him. At present his mind was engrossed with other matters. He had lost a sum of money he could ill spare at the moment; but "sufficient unto the day" was a favourite proverb of Thornhill's, as it is of many a man in pecuniary matters. No man understood that philosophy of money better than he – at least, if spending or losing it with a cheerful indifference constituted a philosophy. He was constitutionally courageous too; and though he was impulsive, and apt to say things which he sometimes regretted, he never shrank from their consequences. His was the regret of a noble mind sorry for having inflicted pain on others, rather than for its effects upon himself. He was not a man to abstain from injustice, or to shrink from acknowledging it.

If a man is ever justified in egotism, it is when he sees a probability or possibility of being shot through the body within the next four and twenty hours. Geoffrey Thornhill saw that possibility very plainly before him; and his constitutional courage did not serve to shut out the prospect. The consequence was a gloomy ride to Corry's, in which he peopled the world with his wife and his boys. He rang the bell and asked if Mr. Corry was at home. He was, and was about to dine: but Mr. Thornhill's card should be taken to him. In a minute the servant returned with a request that he would sit down for five minutes; Mr. Corry was dressing. The five minutes elapsed before he had sufficiently admired a Titian, a very fine copy (to Thornhill it made very little difference), when Harry Corry appeared.

"Delighted to see you, Thornhill, delighted; we dine directly," said he ringing the bell. "Mr. Thornhill will dine with us Thompson; and desire Gregory to see to his horse. We've only three or four men here whom you know. Like to wash your hands? Come with me."

"I beg you a thousand pardons, my dear Corry; but I must have five words with you at once."

"No, not a word; nothing before dinner on any consideration; we have just a soup, a fish, and a haunch; an early one from your old friend Lascelles[6]." With these words he hurried Geoffrey Thornhill into a dressing-room and left him to make his ablutions.

---

[6] We are almost sure that a family called Lascelles were old friends of the author's family. Letters from Charles Carlos Clarke's grand daughter, Margaret Collyer, to a member of the Lascelles family are in our possession. Editors

Henry Corry was a man better known almost than anyone in London. He was a bachelor of moderate fortune, good family, and heir to an earldom. He was a man of exquisite taste; his dinners and his pictures were few, but excellent. He associated generally with men younger than himself. His conversation amused them and his highly-bred quiet, restrained them. His reputation as a man of the world was at its height; and there was no one to whom men in difficulty, would apply with more certain prospect of a solution. In all matters connected with fighting or women, he was an arbiter from whose dictum there was no appeal.

The dinner was good, as well it might be, from the care bestowed upon it; the conversation as vapid as might have been expected from a certain restraint arising from Thornhill's presence. Rumours of events had reached most of Corry's guests. Every one was anxious to put him at his ease on the subject evidently uppermost in his thoughts; but the very desire to do so produced a constraint, unnatural to any of the party. Corry himself, not having been at the races, was sublimely ignorant of the whole transaction and set down the loss of spirit to the loss of money; though he admitted to himself that it was something new in the constitution of Geoffrey Thornhill or Lord Dorrington.

"They must have been confoundedly hit," thought he.

"That's a good picture on the mantelpiece," said Wilbraham, a traveller, and would be connoisseur.

"I think it is; it's the only Claude I have here. That and the Titian, with a couple of Watteaus in the small drawing-room, with half a dozen of less value, are all I have in this place."

"What a charming repose!" said Mr. Hammond, who seemed himself to have just awakened out of a sound nap. "That small Spanish picture in my room, I presume a Murillo, has one of the most beautiful faces I ever saw."

"Talking of faces, what a splendid face was that gipsy boy's whom we saw on the course today, just before the race. Dorrington found out a likeness, and a very remarkable one;" and here the speaker, quite a young man named Putney, blushed, on remembering to whom the resemblance related.

Thornhill hastened to relieve his embarrassment. "Yes, I noticed the likeness myself, talking to Lord Bidborough, as Kildonald rode down. That's an admirable haunch of yours, Henry Corry. You were not on the heath today?"

"No! but I took a walk about a couple of miles to the right of the course, and I rather think I saw Putney's handsome gipsy; he was not far from Doyle's cottage at the time, and seemed to be looking after something – the poultry, I suppose. But, Geoffrey, I beg your pardon, I know you told me you wanted to speak to me; and now that we can leave these men with such a good substitute as that bottle of Lafitte, I dare say they'll excuse us for five minutes, before we make up our rubber." With these words the host rose slowly, and Thornhill and he left the room.

"And now, my dear fellow, how can I oblige you? I see there is something wrong." And Thornhill related to him the occurrences of the day.

"This is unfortunate: three days hence you may be able to treat him with contempt, if the world looks upon it in the same light that you do. Today it is impossible!" and he rang the bell. "Order the brougham round, directly."

"Yes, sir;" and the man disappeared.

"Now, Geoffrey, go down to those men, and wait for me. I shall be gone half an hour."

No sooner were Corry and Thornhill gone to the drawing-room, than the tongues were unloosed, and they began to speak plainly.

"He must fight, I suppose," said Lord Dorrington, who, however, helped himself to a bumper of claret with as much *nonchalance* as if fighting was the ordinary occupation of the species.

"I should rather say not," said Putney, who had lately been gazetted to a troop in the 10th Hussars. "One don't fight with robbers; at least it's optional; and Kildonald is a robber to all intents and purposes, as much as if he stole my purse." And here, the junior captain yawned at his unwonted exertion. "Much more so if the extent of the plunder is taken into consideration; but Thornhill will fight; he has most chivalrous notions on such points."

"He is in good hands, at all events. The claret, please, Wilbraham. When Kildonald is shot, there'll be one scoundrel less in the world, at all events, and we can very well spare him." Here the door opened and Thornhill re-entered the room.

In the meantime the brougham had driven rapidly towards another part of the heath, and after an application to the bell, Corry descended at the door of Major Doyle's cottage.

"My compliments to Major Doyle, and I shall be glad to speak to him on business of importance;" and Corry tendered his card – whilst through the narrow passage of the house came an occasional ominous rattle of dice; and as the adjoining door opened, something like "Eleven's the nick," smote on his ear,

"Ah!" thought the sobered man of the world, "now that there is no one left to devour till tomorrow, they are preying upon each other. Good heavens! To think that a man like Thornhill must place himself upon a level with these men, whose hand is against every man, and whose reputation is not worth half an hour's purchase".

"Major Doyle, I presume" said he, seeing that a gentleman had entered the room almost suddenly enough to extinguish his cogitations.

"Major Doyle, at your service," replied that individual.

"My business is pressing, Major Doyle, and unpleasant. With its purport you are already acquainted, when I say I come from my friend, Mr. Thornhill of Thornhills." Here both gentlemen stopped and looked at one another with considerable uneasiness.

"I fear your mission can have but one result. I cannot affect to misunderstand the necessity. It will be needless for us to enter into the cause of this unhappy quarrel – but the sooner the meeting can take place the better."

"It gives me pleasure to meet with such promptness," said the major, whose Irish propensity was about to be indulged so unhesitatingly, and partly anxious about the loss of a day's racing.

"And me pain!" rejoined the other, who saw neither credit nor profit to his friend in being first swindled and then shot.

The two gentlemen, however, being so far *d'accord*, laid their heads together, and were not long in making such arrangements for the following morning, as to give the major plenty of time for the transaction of his favourite business, before the calls of his favourite diversion.

When Henry Corry returned to his house, he at once sought Geoffrey Thornhill. He was playing a rubber, and finished it as unconcernedly as he would have done, had his friend returned with an invitation to dinner. Thornhill's was a strong, perhaps an uncommon mind; it never utterly refused to see things in their true light, but carefully postponed the prospect to the latest moment. Perhaps I am wrong in saying that it was a strong mind; the action of it was in this respect almost involuntary. It is but due to him to add, that when he took the trouble to realise a hard position, he acted with a characteristic boldness, which was not the less genuine because he recognised the reality and extent of his danger.

"My dear Thornhill", said Corry, taking him into an adjoining room when the rubber was over, "Knowing your determination to return to Marston's tonight, instead of sleeping here, as I wish you to do, I have succeeded in arranging matters for tomorrow morning at eight o'clock. At the ninth milestone on the Sittingdean road, between this and Marston's, I will meet you tomorrow morning at half past seven; we can go in my carriage, and you can send Marston's back to the Royal Oak. To avoid exciting suspicion, Major Doyle will come at the back of Sittingdean, by another road; Kildonald sleeps at Sittingdean tonight, and he will pick him up on his way tomorrow. I know you too well, my dear fellow, to impress upon you punctuality in such a matter; and you know me well enough to tell me whether there's any thing else in this business in which I can be of service to you. In case of accident, the place is the back of the old ruin in Owlston Park, and the time eight o'clock."

"Thank you, thank you, Corry, a thousand times; and now let me ring for my horse."

CHAPTER 8

HOMEWARD

"L'homme propose et Dieu dispose."

When Geoffrey Thornhill started on his road to Sittingdean, the moon was not yet up. For the first mile or two from the cottage, the road was tolerably good and the night was not absolutely dark and he pushed on at a rapid pace, not from a feverish anxiety, but from a wish to reach his temporary home as early as possible. The atmosphere, however, was still and heavy and it was not long before he felt the heat somewhat oppressively. As the road advanced into the common it became more full of holes and ruts and mindful of the possibility of laming his horse at such a distance from Sittingdean where he expected his second hack, he pulled him into a walk and allowed him to pick his way at leisure. He lit a cigar and at that moment the moon rose over the tops of the low fir trees which skirted the road irregularly on either side. Thornhill knew the road pretty well; he remembered that for about a mile the deep sandy lane with heavy blocks of loose sandstone, a steep and dark bank on either side, were overgrown with gorse bushes, heather and stunted trees and terminated in a very sharp descent. From there the rest of the road, on so light a night, was capital galloping ground into Sittingdean, from which place an hour and a half's sharp riding on a fresh horse would bring him to his journey's end. He could afford a quarter of an hour's leisurely riding, whilst he smoked his cigar and considered his position and his course of action for the morrow.

His thoughts could not be cheerful: they turned naturally towards his home for though a thorough man of pleasure he was warm-hearted and impulsive. His love for his children was genuine and deep and his pride in his eldest boy, his accomplishments and his person, was unalloyed by any selfish feeling. Had Thornhill been less spoilt by the world he would have better appreciated the happiness of his home. He had married a woman amiable, good and elegant, with country tastes and habits, and an intense admiration for her husband, but not a strong character. She exercised little influence in her house or over her husband or her children. Mrs. Thornhill had sailed calmly down the stream of her life, an admirable example to her neighbours, a good village Lady Bountiful, a favourite with everybody; but she had had no power to moderate the selfish pleasures and indulgences of her husband.

In this fit of blue devils, rather than in serious meditation, Thornhill rode on. Having cleared the worst part of the road, he had reached the very steep descent between the scattered firs and box which threw a gloom over this part of the heath, and was just beginning the descent, when we leave him to turn to others whose interest in the story is greater.

* * * * * *

One hour before Thornhill had started from Henry Corry's villa, Mike Daly and the handsome gipsy George appeared having, apparently, walked from the neighbourhood of Sittingdean. They seemed, by the road they were taking, to be making their way across the heath towards the gipsy encampments in the close neighbourhood of the race course itself, ready for the morrow. By this route they would cross the road which Geoffrey Thornhill must follow on his way to Sittingdean, as that was the only horse road, the bridle paths being invisible and quite useless in the dark to any but walkers who knew them tolerably well.

"Hist, George, aisy; I hear a step."

"No such thing," said George in a hoarse whisper, which trembled with emotion; "Kildonald can't be here this two hours or more; he was not likely to start till eleven or later. What's the hour?"

"About half-past nine or ten."

"Then halt here; he must pass by this road; there's no wind, and we can hear every sound that stirs. These tall dark firs would hide Satan himself," and as he spoke he seated himself under a tree within ten paces of the narrow defile to which I have before alluded. Mike did the same.

"What rascally work did Lawyer Burke do at the races, Mike? He ought to pay ye well for this night's work."

"He cares about his good name back in Kerry; but to protect it, Kildonald must die; killing people does not come cheap though. He won't see me want."

"He's a scoundrel, Mike; a low, beggarly scoundrel, that gets the oyster and throws you the shells, but I must avenge the man who sired me and who left my mother ruined." Here George listened once more, but nothing was to be heard, and he resumed his listless attitude against the tree.

"How do ye know what time Kildonald is coming Master George? Maybe he's already gone, and I'll never have such a chance again for such a pot of money, and you neither for your vengeance."

"How do I know his time? I've been to the cottage, and where there are women you may know anything." George was a bit of a philosopher, and a close observer of human nature.

"Now I hear a horse," said he, as a slow even step, occasionally striking a stone, and breaking into a momentary jog, smote his ear. "It's close at hand, Mike, the time has come! Steady!" and they simultaneously rose and approached the edge of the road, under cover of the firs.

* * * * * *

About an hour or rather more after Thornhill had left Henry Corry's villa, the stable-gates of Major Doyle's unpretentious tenement, which was rented for the race week by himself and a betting man or two, opened and a smart clever-looking hack emerged, carrying no other than Arthur Kildonald. The moon was now up, and the way lay clearer than in the earlier part of the evening. The gambler's face was pale and the passion which tore him found ready vent in accelerated pace. His reflections were not pleasant; he held, it is true, Burke's note of hand for £3000, a means of escape from this country, but the deliberate robbery of which he had been guilty in the morning would anyway have necessitated that absence because he had been found out which carried with it some very painful inconveniences. He would have liked to retire like a graceful actor, regretted for a time and with a hope of an occasional return. All his hatred, too, for Geoffrey Thornhill, his absurd and mistaken prejudices against him as the purchaser of his Irish property and his fear of Thornhill's bold and resolute nature, lashed him into a fury, as he trotted sharply over the uneven ground that entered upon the road over the heath. One other circumstance had not escaped his notice; amongst his own set he had lost caste. It's a bad thing to be found out. Besides Major Doyle, perhaps scarcely anyone of the party he had left would have hesitated to do what he had done. They attached no discredit to the dishonesty that he had committed but they bore very hardly upon the discovery of it and regarded that as a serious blow. This was not a pleasant subject for contemplation; he was to be shunned by his own set; though Major Doyle's notions of honour forbade him to desert his late guest. The duel itself was one in which no credit could accrue to him. His opponent was too popular a man to be shot at with impunity and now the quarrel, though unavoidable, was of his own seeking.

"Fool, fool!" said he to himself, "why was not I deaf; or dumb? Why did my accursed ill luck throw me in the way of that villain Burke? And poor Norah and my children! Good God, if anything happens tomorrow, what's to become of them? I must trust Doyle." In this spirit he rapidly neared the dark and broken descent which the others had reached some time before and was forgetful of the badness of the road, which for a hundred yards was almost perpendicular. He was already urging his horse to continued speed, but with a fearful plunge and a violent snort which would have unseated a worse horseman, the hack refused to proceed.

* * * * * *

The whist party which we left at Henry Corry's was not one to be disturbed by ordinary circumstances. It consisted of pure men of the world, not without natural feelings, certainly not without refinement, but well exercised by constant friction against society which hardened while it polished. Corry himself was depressed more than might have been expected by the forthcoming duel, a rare occurrence and an unlawful one in the present day. The four or five men who surrounded the card-table divided their attention more than usually between unpleasant anticipations and their cards; but as the stakes were high, it can hardly be said that the former had so much of the attention as the latter.

"Five pounds on the rubber, Corry," said Wilbraham, who had been silent some time, in deference to his host, but who felt compelled to say something pleasant to break the silence. "Certainly. Which do you wish to back?"

"Dorrington, of course; he always holds cards."

"Be it so;" and Henry Corry again relapsed into silence. He was leaning against the mantelpiece, with his back to a small fire, which had been lighted during dinner. The room in which they were playing was furnished in a most elaborate manner. All that money could command, combined with taste, was to be met with there. The ornaments were of the most refined character. Sèvres china of the most beautiful description; statuettes from the choicest originals; marqueterie and ormolu, with handsome mirrors proportioned to the moderate dimensions of the room; few pictures, as has been said, but valuable, and handsomely bound works of the best authors; rich hangings and luxurious chairs of various shapes and kinds, combined comfort with elegance, seldom to be met with in a country villa so far removed from large cities.

"How's the game, Seymour?"

"Dorrington and I win the trick: we are four to three, and a single up. At present your fiver looks well."

"The room's hot," said Corry. "Would you like a window opened for five or ten minutes? Putney, are you afraid of the draught?"

"Not I," said the captain. Corry opened a window partially, which looked on to the lawn. At the same moment a horse came down the road from the heath at a fearful pace, and a ring at the door-bell announced an unexpected guest. Sharp, quick, and agitated tones of enquiry were heard in the hall, and as the servant threw open the door without the announcement of any name, an unwelcome figure stood before the astonished party.

It was Kildonald. Not withstanding the pace he had evidently ridden, his face was perfectly ghastly: large drops of perspiration stood upon his forehead, his hair was matted with damp and hung in dishevelled locks over his brows; terror seemed to have utterly taken away his speech, for he reeled and staggered into a chair, with scarcely ability to say,

"Quick, quick, for God's sake! Thornhill -----" Here the whist-players rose and Henry Corry came forward with a cold and resolute manner, saying,

"To what, sir, am I to attribute this honour? Pray explain." But he was cut short by Kildonald, who repeated in more collected, but no less earnest tones,

"Thornhill is murdered! Quick – quick, gentlemen. Villains have been beforehand: his blood be upon their heads, not mine. He lies on the road by the glen, four or five miles from here, before you come to the Sittingdean road. Pray send out at once. But I fear it's too late." The bell was rung.

"Gregory, saddle Lord Dorrington's mare and my hack instantly; and tell Jervis to bring round the brougham again. Mr. Kildonald's horse is at the door." Here Henry Corry followed his servant out of the room. "And let one of the men on whom you can depend go down to the nearest constable and bring him up here, to wait till our return."

In ten minutes' time they were on the road, the brougham following them, as best it could, over the rugged road to the scene of the terrible catastrophe.

And there on the road, at the top of the descent, beneath a dark mass of firs and box, lay the lifeless body of Geoffrey Thornhill.

CHAPTER 9

TIME FOR REFLECTION

"Pompa mortis magis terret quam mors ipsa."
It is the trappings of death that terrifies, rather than death itself.

So terrible and unprovoked a fate creates alarm under the most ordinary circumstances. The excitement is not lessened when the victim is wealthy, popular, and high-born. In the present case there was something doubly terrible. The next day he might have had on his own hands the blood of a fellow-creature. It is our happiness to live in a day when the true courage of a Christian gentleman may exhibit itself in declining to risk his life, or to risk taking the life of another[7]. This relic of barbarous chivalry has passed away from before us. Perhaps we are to thank a more plentiful admixture of middle-class blood, with its prejudices in favour of long life and respectability. If there still remains an argument or two for the admirers of the duel for meting out proper punishment for certain offences, we can always reply that there is a higher chivalry which

---

[7] Duelling became illegal in Britain in 1819 but continued, particularly in aristocratic and military circles, almost into the twentieth century.

enables us to bear those insults.

The coroner's inquest returned a verdict in accordance with the evidence – "Wilful murder by person or persons unknown." He could make nothing of it. That Kildonald was an object of much suspicion is not to be wondered at. The evidence at first was so strong that the magistrates were much censured for not having committed him to take his trial. After continued remands, and a very heavy bail, it was found necessary to discharge him. Two or three circumstances spoke strongly in his favour – or rather against the supposition of his having committed the murder.

First of all it was very clear that Arthur Kildonald had left Major Doyle's house long after the time that Geoffrey Thornhill had quitted Henry Corry and his guests. Indeed, it might have been presumed that when Kildonald left Doyles' cottage, Thornhill was already near to Sittingdean. There was also a strong presumption that Kildonald went out unarmed and it was clear that the murder was committed with a pistol, though the weapon remained undiscovered. The idea even that Thornhill had waited for him, and fell as the result of an equal combat, was negated by the fact that a blow of a very violent character had been given on the temple, though death was caused by the bullet, which had penetrated the brain. The two men had no means of ascertaining the movements of each other, and were not likely to have anticipated by a few hours the vengeance which the morning would have accorded them. The purse and watch of Thornhill had either escaped the vigilance of the assassin, or were purposely overlooked; his betting book, and a small pocket-book which he usually carried, were gone. In a word, an impenetrable mystery veiled the event, which grew no lighter as time rolled on. The gipsies were not forgotten; and a few desperate characters who frequented the heath about race time were taken before the Bidborough justices, but nothing could be made of them; and before the end of a month the town and neighbourhood had resumed their wonted stupidity and quiet.

It was not long before the recollection of Thornhill and his many accomplishments was confined to the police and his own immediate friends and family. Lord Dorrington and his set went their ways, some to their farms, none to their merchandise. The covers were quiet at Thornhills; they still held pheasants and foxes; and the new heir would probably take back the hounds when he came of age: and the widow in the meantime would issue the customary invitations, and Thornhills would be much the same.

"Terrible business, the death of poor Thornhill," said Captain Boldthrow, on the steps of Crockford's, a month or two after the catastrophe. "It must have quite spoilt Corry's Bidborough party. The widow's jointure is small, rather. She has the manor-house and £1200 a year."

"Charming woman!" rejoined his companion, Dicky Calthorpe of the Blues. "Twelve hundred a year is not to be got every day. By the way, do you know the lost betting book has come to light in a very mysterious manner? It came directed to Marston, from Dublin and it seems to have been given to the guard of the Cork mail by a fellow in a labourer's dress, as they changed horses at some place or other. I'm afraid it will break up our shooting party for next year. Does any one know anything about Thornhill's horses?"

"Most of them will be sold on Monday week. I met Geoffrey Thornhill's brother, the banker, just this minute in Pall Mall, and he told me all about it. He and Marston are the trustees."

By the time the horses were sold, and the season came round again, "the best fellow in the world" was as much forgotten, almost, as if he had never existed.

But there were others whose memories were not so short. Sir Frederick and Lady Marston had not ceased to sorrow for their old friend, and lavished their regrets in affection for his widow and children. The shock to Mrs. Thornhill had been great indeed. She mulled over their early days and wondered whether she had done all she might have done to make the home of Geoffrey Thornhill what it ought to have been. God bless her! She tried to discover a fault in herself where none existed and to hide some provocations which had been too apparent until now. And the boys often looked back to their last parting from their indulgent, good-humoured father. Tom had been on the bridge at Eton, and Charlie at the office of the southbound coach, as he started on his journey to Dr. Gresham: they little thought that it was for the last time. "Sublatum ex oculis quærimus invidi."[8] Amiable as Geoffrey Thornhill was, he had never appeared so amiable to his family as now.

But time, the great assuager of ills, wrought its usual effect. The boys returned to school. Tom plunged into every amusement, and, gifted with great capacity, was equally a favourite with the masters as with his schoolfellows. He exhibited a disposition singularly akin to that of his father. He was eminently handsome and had already begun to appreciate the advantages of his new social position. It was impossible, too, for a clever, intelligent boy like Tom Thornhill not to see that his father's death had made a sensible difference in the estimation in which he was held. As a youngster every one was ready to give him a construe, or to do his verses. As he grew older, he became the fashion: the sincerest flattery is imitation. They copied his dress, his manners, and his slang; his juniors admired him, his equals courted him, and his seniors delighted to honour him. His name was in every mouth. There was nothing too good for him, nothing he could not do and if a too confident parent ventured during the holidays to sound the praises of man, woman, or child, the answer was, invariably, "You should see Tom Thornhill." Is it to be

---

[8] "We search with yearning for what has been taken from our sight."

wondered at if his mother regarded him with intense admiration?

As for Charlie, at his father's death it had been ascertained that he was just beyond the age at which he could be received at Eton. It was wisely determined that instead he should return to Dr. Gresham. The school was at that time half the size of Eton but its scholarship and its flogging were equal, if not superior, to anything of its day. Dr. Gresham himself was a man of most brilliant talent, sound learning, and, rarer still, of varied accomplishments, which great scholarship, for some reason or other, was generally supposed to exclude. But he was more than this. He was a most admirable schoolmaster, combining a happy playfulness of disposition with a power of influencing young minds to an almost incredible extent. Into these hands Mrs Thornhill, on the advice of her executors, once more entrusted her younger son.

The distinguishing feature in Charlie Thornhill, as at present exhibited, was a lively distaste for every species of learning. To say for what he had or had not talent, was equally difficult. He hated classics; but this cannot be said to have implied any love for mathematics: his contempt for the models of antiquity was quite unaccompanied by any regard for modern literature. The leading article of the "Times" and the "Arabian Nights' Entertainments" alike failed to excite any warmer feelings than sheer indifference. His principal reading was the sporting periodicals of the day but if he could indulge in cricket, boating, a run with the beagles, or even the more modest pleasures of a rat hunt out of school with his bullterrier, Rosie, he seldom denied himself those enjoyments for the sake of any literature.

As the son of Mr. Thornhill of Thornhills, Charlie had been a boy of some consideration among his fellows. He had a large house in which to ring the bells, handsome stabling to show his schoolfellows, a keeper at his service, as far as the rabbits were concerned, and a horse that went by the name of Master Charles's mare. In these distinguishing marks of Fortune's favour the world shut its eyes to his position, that of a second son. So he accepted this position for the present, but did not shut his eyes to the future.

"What a quiet fellow you are, Thornhill!" said Teddy Dacre one day as the two boys leaned over the parapet of the school gardens, and a large open court abutting on to the street in front of the school chapel and library. It was a fine old building of the reign of Edward VI, the founder of the school. It was a place in which most of the boys lounged about at odd times, and in which they were now waiting for the twelve o'clock calling over, having just come out of the second school. "What a quiet fellow you are, Thornhill, you never do anything now." Teddy Dacre who was a delicate, handsome boy about sixteen years of age, looked at his friend.

"That's because you do it all for me, Teddy."

"Oh, I don't mean school work: I mean licking the snobs and poaching at Birdington. What a lot of rabbits there are there! Do you know Swan and I were nearly caught by the keepers at Grassfield, setting night lines?"

"Were you? What do you think Gresham would have done if he'd caught you?"

"Oh! I don't know. He couldn't have flogged us, you know, because he never does flog fifth form fellows."

"No. And that's one reason why I don't poach at Grassfield and lick the snobs, Teddy. You see, when he could flog us it didn't matter much, because you took your chance; now it's a shame, because he wouldn't like to expel us for it; and so we put the old Doctor in rather a fix. I think it's a shame."

"What a jolly form that fourth form was!"

"So it was," said Charlie, with a sigh. "And I almost wish I was back in it. But tell us about the fishing."

"Well, Swan and I were coming back from the big perch hole close by the side of the water, when who should we meet" (Teddy was not so good at his English, you see) "but that big keeper with the black whiskers and the smooth white terrier. He came straight up to us, of course, and asked where we had been. So we told him we'd been to the warren for a walk."

"That was a lie, Teddy."

"So he said. And then he took hold of Swan's rod and as his pockets were full of night lines and hooks he was obliged to let it go. Then he told us to go with him to the Hall; and as we walked along by the side of the brook, when we came to the big hole we – we --- we ----"

"Bolted, I suppose?"

"Shoved him in, and then we bolted. We knew he could swim, because he told us so once before, when he found a hole in the bottom of his coracle."

"You'll be found out; for he's got Swan's rod, hasn't he?"

"Yes; but that doesn't signify. It's got no name on it."

"Teddy, 'pon my soul, you're incorrigible. I suppose your governor's a magistrate?"

"Of course he is. What of that?"

"Only the next time he commits a vagrant, or a poacher, or any of those fellows, you go and listen to the case. Now I'm going to calling over, and then if you like, we'll go swimming."

The walk to the bathing-place was beautiful. It was about a mile from the school, along the banks of the river, which were broken into ledges of sand and ironstone, and interspersed with low bushes, gorse, and firs. The stream flowed with a broad and powerful current; now shallow and rapid, now in a still and quiet corner eddying and turning back again upon itself. The greater number of the fellows who intended bathing had run on ahead in company with Nixon the bathing-man, an amphibious, otter-like sort of person, who was engaged to take care of the bathing-places, and to give what instruction and help might be wanted in swimming. He was a cunning old dog was Mr. Nixon, and under his ostensible profession of bathing-man he concealed that of dealer in contraband game, spirits, tobacco, and terriers. He always had a few ferrets, and not infrequently a gamecock or two. His wife was the cook, washerwoman, and general store dealer to a certain portion of the school and dispensed the most extravagant tea, sugar, twopenny loaves, pats of butter, and gooseberry and rhubarb tarts, that can well be imagined. Nixon had been a soldier; and the iniquitous old rascal added much discipline to leaven his own laxity of morals. Charlie Thornhill and Edward Dacre set out with the idea of catching up with this worthy and his companions. Before long they had left the precincts of the school behind them, and were following the beaten track by the side of the eddying river.

"Thornhill, what sort of a fellow is your brother Tom?" said Dacre, stopping to strike a light for a cigar.

"Are you going to smoke, Teddy?"

"Yes. I always do. So do you, Thornhill, sometimes, for I've seen you. I do it for my chest," added the boy, laughing as he spoke, and pulling away at a very horrible and highly adulterated cabbage leaf. "So they can't say much if I am caught. Come on Charlie!" said he laughing again and puffing away harder than ever to keep it alight.

"Here's the sixth form bathing place. What a jolly spot."

"Let's stay here, Thornhill. But you've not told me yet about your brother Tom. I've a cousin at Eton, and he says he's the best fellow in the school."

"So he is," said Charlie sitting down on the bank. He always grew enthusiastic on this topic at least. He had but two at present: one was fox hunting, and the other his brother Tom. "So he is; he's a splendid fellow, Teddy. He's such a good looking fellow. And can't he ride? My poor governor's horses were rather too big for him; but he kept two of them, and Sir Frederick Marston says he's to have two more this winter. He's going to Oxford next year. And he's such a good natured fellow, too. He gave me this watch last holidays and a new gun: it's as light as a feather, and such a killer."

"My cousin at Eton says he's the cleverest fellow in the school, only he never reads," said the other.

"Ah! Tom can do without reading. You should see him do his holiday task, he always does it all in the last three days. He'd astonish old Gresham with his Greek iambics. Lord, how I do hate verses! You haven't a brother?" This was said in a melancholy tone seeing not having a brother as a deprivation.

"No; but I have some sisters. They're stunners, too, I tell you."

"What do you call them?"

"Why, the eldest is Alice: she's dark, with such jolly hair," rejoined Dacre, who was almost as enthusiastic about them as Charlie was about his brother. "And the other's Edith: she's fifteen. You should just see her ride after my uncle's harriers. She jumped such a place the last time we were out!"

"Why, I didn't know you were a sportsman, Teddy."

"Well, I don't care much about it. It's such a bore. I like lying on the lawn and reading novels best. I think I shall bathe, it's so hot."

"Come on then."

"Oh, I shall bathe here; the sixth form fellows don't come until the afternoon. It's such a nuisance to have to walk any more."

"You'll get a licking if any fellow sees you."

"Nobody will see me; so here goes." And he commenced preparations by taking off his coat at once.

"That's just like you, Dacre." And thinking that a good thrashing might be useful to all boys of sixteen, Charlie Thornhill ceased to remonstrate, and sat himself down on the bank to smoke.

Where Charlie's mind had wandered did not seem quite clear; perhaps he was thinking of his mother, or Tom, or his best friend, Lady Marston. He might have wandered back to the days of the squire, or he might have been wondering what would become of himself when it came to be his turn to scud through the world, when he was roused by a sudden cry for help. Dacre could swim and he looked rapidly round, expecting some trick, when the boy's head rose to the surface, near an old oaken stump in the bed of the river. The face was just above the water, and as the limbs below struggled convulsively, the face sank again with a look of such agony and a stifled cry of such terror that Charlie was left no doubt as to the reality of the situation. Stripping off his coat and waistcoat, he plunged in and swam to the stump. Taking the precaution to seize this with his left arm, he stretched down with his right hand in the direction of Dacre. For a few seconds his efforts failed to raise his friend's head, but at length, by the exertion of all his strength, Charlie succeeded in dragging Dacre to the tree. Here he held it firmly, and ascertained the cause of the poor fellow's submersion by the weight of weeds which had attached themselves to his legs and feet. He was just calculating upon his capability to get the boy safely to the shore from the tree on which he was lying, when fortunately he heard the voices of Nixon and his companions. "Quick! Quick!" shouted Charlie Thornhill. "Quick, Nixon! Help! Help!" And as the sounds reached them they all came running down the bank in time to see Charlie, almost exhausted by the strength of the stream, the weight of his own clothes, and the apparently lifeless body of poor Teddy Dacre, which he still supported with difficulty. A small round boat made of tarpaulin lay on the river's bank, close at hand. In a moment Nixon was in it and steering with one paddle down stream to the tree; but he was scarcely in it before it began to fill, and Nixon, within three feet of the boys, abandoned his coracle and took to the water.

Once on the old stump, a favourite place from which the sixth form boys were accustomed to take headers, he was able to relieve Charlie of part of his burden, and in another minute they were safe on shore, with Teddy Dacre between them. Having got rid of the water, and restored animation by the best means in their power, with the assistance of a labourer who was fortunately at home, they got Dacre to a cottage; and after rest and cordials they returned on their way to school.

Of course Dacre and Charlie were absent at dinner and the cause of it was not long in transpiring.

"Nearly gone, Teddy," said Thornhill as they walked along.

"Oh! Charlie, Charlie, how can I ever – " and here Teddy burst into tears.

"There, Teddy, old fellow, never mind that; you'd have done the same yourself: it's all over now."

"Except the licking: perhaps they'll let me off, as I was so very nearly drowned."

"I shouldn't if I was a sixth form fellow, I can tell you: I'm all for justice: and though I don't think you ought to have been drowned, I am quite sure you ought to be thrashed."

The next day at twelve o'clock a lower form boy came into the school gardens, and said, "Thornhill, the fellows want you in the six-form private room."

"Do they – who told you so?"

"Scott told me to tell you."

"All right," and he went.

When he arrived there was no doubt about the business on hand. Teddy Dacre, looking very foolish stood at the foot of a long table, around which, in various attitudes, sitting or standing, were several sixth formers: "Thornhill," said the head boy, "tell us all about this, for the water has washed it all out of Dacre." Thornhill related the circumstances as succinctly as possible.

"Then he was bathing in our place?"

"Yes."

"Desecrating our Nereus, the protector of our streams and groves: no wonder the divinity seized him by the leg – I wonder he ever let him go."

"He was very nearly drowned," said Charlie, suggestive of a reprieve.

"Thanks to you that he wasn't quite: 'Fiat Justitia, ruat coelum.[9] He must be punished. Who is the prepositor for the day? Humphreys, prepare the block. As to you Thornhill, you're a good fellow, and the school ought to be as proud of you as if you were a senior medallist, or Ireland scholar. Is there anything that we can do for you?"

"Yes, let off Dacre. The only use of punishment is to deter himself and others from the same thing; and he didn't look as if he would ever forget what happened."

"You'll be an honour to the woolsack, if you take to that line. We will let him off, as justice has been avenged. Dacre, respect the rights of your superiors, and write a copy of twenty verses on 'The Advantages of Obedience'"

Dacre looked at Thornhill, he was both relieved and grateful. As they left the room there was a buzz of applause, and the hum of many voices amongst which rose one distinctly, which said "By Jove, that fellow Thornhill's not such a fool as they take him for."

---

[9] 'Let justice be done, though
   The heavens fall.'

CHAPTER 10

OUR HOLIDAY

"And this beauteous morn
(The prim'st of all the year) presents me with
A brace of horses."
Two Noble Kinsmen, Act III, Scene I.

As vacation after vacation came and went, seventeen year old Charlie Thornhill increased in stature and popularity and confirmed the good opinion that had been formed of him. His friendship with Dacre continued uninterrupted from the date of the circumstances detailed in the last chapter. The one seemed never to forget the obligation he was under; the other had forgotten everything connected with it.
"A note for Mr. Thornhill", said John the doctor's own man, as he threw open the door of the hall; "where's Mr. Thornhill?"
"Not here, John, but as you seem rather groggy about the pins, I'll take it for you," replied a very precocious-looking young gentleman as he scrutinised John's crooked legs. John did not think an encounter of wits worth his time, so retired, gravely placing the note upon the table to take its chance.

"I say, Forester, where's Thornhill?"

"How should I know?"

"Well, you had better find out pretty quickly, and take that note, or you may get a licking. I think I know where it comes from: it's to ask him out for holiday Sunday.

"How do you know that?" said Forester.

"Because I know that old Thoroughgood meant to ask Charlie Thornhill to the steeplechase on Saturday, and I saw his groom in the school lane. He wants Thornhill to ride one of the ponies: so just be off with the note at once, young fellow, or you'll get a licking. If he's not in Dawson's study, he's at old Mother Shipley's; she keeps his bullterrier, Rosie." And true enough at old Mother Shipley's was Charlie, helping himself and Rosie to stewed beefsteak, and anxiously inquiring after some rats, which he hoped were not intended for meat pies, to judge by the tone. They were really to decide the merits of a rough-coated terrier, and the smooth highly-bred bullterrier which Charlie was stroking and feeding alternately.

The note indeed proved to be from old Squire Thoroughgood to ask Thornhill, with some half-dozen schoolfellows, to spend what was called Holiday Sunday at the Cliff, a charming spot about ten miles from the school, and an especial favourite with all the boys. There lived Squire Thoroughgood – an honest, independent, country gentleman of the old school. He had a good estate, a good-looking family of five boys, a clear conscience, and an admirable digestion. He was a man of middle size, about sixty years of age, white haired and fresh complexioned, well built, and active for his age, still an adept at all sports, and encouraging their practice in every man, woman and child who he could convert to his theory. He believed that nothing in the world equalled fox hunting – and that in it was inherent every virtue; above all other, truth and courage. So far did he carry his principle, that when compelled to admit that the bishop of the diocese was an honest man and a gentleman, he always asserted that the bishop was a sportsman by disposition and taste, and only prevented by the peculiar circumstances of his case from subscribing largely to the county hounds. All Thoroughgood's sons were taught to regard hunting, shooting, and fishing as equivalent to the three R's. and beyond them in most respects. There was always a stable full of horses and ponies, down to the rough Exmoor of the youngest boy, who was now, however, about fifteen, and promoted to a clever, well-bred animal, fourteen hands and a half high, with considerable pretensions as a hunter. Once every year, on a particular holiday Sunday, it was this gentleman's practice to send to Dr. Gresham's for a detachment of schoolboys, whose known propensities had rendered them friends of the young Thoroughgoods, or favourites of the squire: and of course the proceeding was in accordance with the old gentleman's notions of what was right. The Holiday Sunday extended from Friday night until Monday morning at 10 a.m. at which time every boy was expected to be again in school. Excuses were unknown; distance was no apology; illness alone constituted anything like a valid reason for absence. Saturday therefore, the day *par excellence*, and Mr. Thoroughgood took care that it should be a pleasant one.

On the present occasion, as heretofore, the grand climax was a boys' steeplechase. Considering that Mr. Thoroughgood was a country gentleman, and neither a dealer nor a proprietor of a travelling circus, things looked pretty favourable for sport. There were three good hunters in the establishment, which without being in racing condition, were quite capable of galloping two or three miles over any country with a proper weight on them; and two more horses had been sent from a dealer's stable in the neighbourhood, not quite so fit to go, but not bad conveyances for a couple of schoolboys. There was always the chance of a tumble; and each confident in his own skill, as long as his pony was certain to jump, would have taken any sort of odds that came within the bounds of possibility. On Friday afternoon, accordingly, Mr. Thoroughgood's phaeton, licensed on great occasions to carry six small men, the groom, or five schoolboys, conveyed a tolerably noisy party from the school gates to the Cliff, where the hospitable Squire, with a son or two on either side, was waiting to welcome his juvenile guests.

"Now, boys, be off to your rooms: dinner, sharp, in half an hour;" and out came boys and carpetbags with an equal alacrity.

"Mind that bag," said Dacre, "There's a pot of patent blacking for my black boots."

"Now then, stupid," said Wilkinson to another, "don't sit upon that — you'll crush my tops:" whilst Charlie Thornhill, quite awake to the emergency, collared his own property, and was soon mounting towards his bedroom, leaving his comrades to follow, which they soon did. Everyone had a cutting whip, and two out of the five had to open their bags with a penknife, having left their keys behind.

Dinner passed off as such dinners must. There was plenty to eat and drink, and a bottle or two of champagne enlivened the conversation of the youngsters; but it was manifest that the serious business of the meeting was deferred, in every respect, till the morrow. One thing Charlie heard, and which somehow gave him a new interest in the proceedings: the Misses Dacre were staying in the neighbourhood, and his curiosity would be gratified, as they were to be in the squire's party for the day. The surprise did not seem to affect Teddy Dacre to an equal extent; he had some misgivings on the score of his horsemanship, and did not appreciate feminine badinage, of which he was pretty certain to get his share. A very jovial game at whist followed dinner in which each told his partner pretty plainly the state of his hand before playing, and in which there was none of the villainous retrospection of the game so common amongst amateurs.

Wilkinson retired early to look at his breeches, which had been fabricated from a pair of white moleskin trousers for the occasion, and Teddy Dacre to polish his boots with the very best patent French varnish, which could not be trusted to any hands but his own.

Morning always shines brightly upon schoolboys when there's no particular reason for the contrary. To-day nobody could have seen a cloud. It was early spring; and March was for the present enacting the lamb. Every one of the five had been out of bed before daybreak to see what sort of a day it was likely to be; and each had returned to bed fully persuaded that it was sure to rain, until the light gray morning eased their minds of that anxiety.

"Come in," said Thornhill, as a knock came to the door. "What in the world do you want, Teddy?" and the misty outline of Master Edward Dacre, in a white shirt with black sleeves, made its appearance in Thornhill's room. "It can't be time to get up yet."

"Well, I don't think it is, quite," said Teddy, as he nervously twitched up a pair of drawers, and sat down at the foot of the bed. "Do you know, these colours of mine are uncommonly cold? I don't think shirt sleeves are quite the thing for the middle of March."

"But you'll soon be warm enough if you should happen not to get into the brook, which George Thoroughgood says is quite full of water: the governor's delighted, because he says there's no danger of broken backs. If you are not warm enough, put a couple of jerseys underneath. But why didn't you borrow some colours? You could easily have got them. I had some sent to me from Turner, Sir Frederick Marston's trainer, as soon as I got scent of the thing."

"How does it look, Charlie; not very bad, does it?"

"Bad! Not at all. You're quite a swell compared to Russell. He's sewed two scarlet sleeves on to a black cloth waistcoat. Your shirt has a very sporting look in front, not quite up to the mark behind."

"I wish to goodness I could get off riding, Charlie." Here Charlie sat bolt upright in bed in thorough bewilderment. "My sister Edith does chaff so, you can't think. I wonder whether George Thoroughgood would let me off, and ride for me?"

"Bless your innocent heart, my dear boy, he can't ride the weight by two stone. Besides, what would the Squire say? It isn't honest, Teddy; 'pon my word it isn't".

"I don't see that."

"Why, you came here, and ate the squire's dinner, and brought your traps, and you've made your shirt into a sort of Prussian sentry-box, and you're going to breakfast and of course all that's the same thing as entering for the race. It's deceiving the Squire. You are such a shifty bird, Teddy; and all because you're afraid of a woman." And here the speaker curled himself up again, and gave a grunt indicative of fatigue.

"Yes; and so would you be afraid if you knew her."

"I don't know about that," said Charlie, with some few misgivings on the subject; "but I know this, she wouldn't put me off from such a jolly lark as we are going to have today. Why there are two and thirty fences, lots of timber, a double post and rails, and the brook, as I told you before, quite full of water. Only just fancy!" And it was a lovely picture certainly but Teddy Dacre did not seem to take so cheerful a view of it in his shirt and drawers, as Charlie Thornhill did from underneath the bed-clothes.

* * * * * *

**"Teach the youth tales of fight, and grace
His earliest feat of field or chase."**
Lady of the Lake, c. vi, II

"Here they come at last," said old Thoroughgood, pretty nearly tired of waiting for his breakfast, as the clock struck a quarter past nine, one full quarter of an hour beyond his usual time. The old gentleman might have been justifiably vexed at the delay and with any other person would have been so; but a schoolboy was to him what a tortoiseshell cat is to Aunt Tabitha – it breaks nothing, it steals nothing, it inconveniences no one, it can do no wrong.

"I beg a thousand pardons, sir," said Charlie, walking shyly into the breakfast room; "I really was so tired." And here we may remark that the pleasure of lying in bed constitutes one of the supreme blessings of a schoolboy's holiday. On the morning in question it is but fair to say they were all up and had performed their ablutions in good time; but encasing themselves in their new and heterogeneous costumes caused considerable anxiety and involved, in most cases, some ingenious contrivances. Large trousers had to be drawn into tight pantaloons. The long had to be made short and the short long. There were as many button-hooks at one time as there were buttons. The assistance of the valet was *selon les règles*[10] but we can scarcely recount the fact without blushing, that, from the old housekeeper down to the very youngest, the kitchen-maid, every one of them had a finger in the pie. Boot tops came up too high, equally obstinate breeches refused to meet. Each seemed to have stepped into another's shoes, whether they fitted or not; and this usually depended upon the size of the elder brother. Before long, however, they had all followed Charlie Thornhill and were passed in review before Squire Thoroughgood and his sons, whose curiosity had been roused to see whether the devices for steeple-chasing costume were more or less as ingenious as those of previous years. They proved to be nearly upon a par with those of their predecessors.   Charlie, indeed, by the addition of an extra pair of woollen stockings, made an appearance not unworthy of his sporting reputation; and the harlequin jacket he had borrowed, with its black cap, though a little tight across the

---

[10] **According to the rules**

shoulders, pre-eminently qualified him for taking the lead. Wilkinson came next in order and in weight, and, as far as his purple-and-orange jacket was concerned, presented a very tolerable figure; but having hired his top boots from the post boy at "The Dragon of Wantley," at a moment's notice, his legs had a melodramatic appearance between Charles II, and a French Jacobin. Dacre's shirt was declared to be an admirable substitute for the white and black family colours, which it was intended to represent: and with his Wellington boots, which had been varnished to a turn from bottom to top and coaxed to meet a rather shrunken pair of leathers, the only ones in the party, gave him a not unflattering resemblance to a magpie. Billy Russell, or "The Honourable William" as he was called, made the most of a rather limited wardrobe. He had the black cloth waistcoat and scarlet sleeves already noticed and had deliberately thrust into a pair of top boots of antiquated form his white-cord trousers, on to which a pretty housemaid, bribed by half a crown and a kiss, had been employed for half an hour in sewing mother-of-pearl buttons, to give an appearance of realism at long distance. The light-weight of the party little Tommy Bosville, in the most correct of breeches and boots, with his black jacket and cap, was hailed by universal acclamation as the swell. Very neat indeed, he looked and if Tommy's pluck had only equalled his elegance, there can be no mistake as to who would have been the winner on that day. He was the only one of the lot who felt that he was *quite* the thing and he commenced breakfast with a corresponding appetite. Very few men eat well who have a suspicion that their turnout is not all is should be, especially on a hunting morning. Boys are less susceptible to these *disagrémens,* but their attention was not diverted by the singularity of their costume from the hung beef, hot rolls, devilled kidneys, and split fowl.

"Now, young gentlemen, time's up. Let us be off to the stable-yard" said the Squire, trotting into the billiard room, in woollen cord breeches and top boots, with his neat broad-skirted black coat and white neckcloth, looking the picture of an old-fashioned sportsman.

"I suppose you know your mounts. Thornhill is to have the little bay horse Solomon; he's a capital fencer, and able to carry a little more weight. Then Wilkinson had better ride the gray pony Kitty; that's a good mount."

"She ought to win, sir," said Captain Thoroughgood, who lounged into the yard with one of his brothers, smoking a cigar. The captain was a great man amongst the boys, as all cavalry officers were before the universal adoption of a moustache and beard destroyed the most attractive distinction of the service.

"Who's going to ride Judy?"

"I, sir," said Russell, as he looked with an undaunted air at the labours of the pretty housemaid, and wondered whether the yokels would be taken in by the pearl buttons. She'll go into water, won't she?"

"Into it? Not she, if you ride her at it. Who told you that?"

"Thornhill said she didn't look as if she liked water any more than I did."

"Oh! Never mind him, he's only been chaffing you; he wants to win himself and he thinks that will funk you. You ride her straight; she can jump better than anything here, except Solomon, and he's not so fast as the mare. But come, get up; here's Dacre on the chestnut pony, shirt-sleeves and all," added he, as that worthy emerged from a stable door ready mounted, followed by the swell, leading a clever little roan mare that had been sent up from the dealer's to participate in the day's sport.

At the head of the cavalcade and surrounded by neighbouring farmers and tenants, with his own sons and guests, rode the cheerful little Squire. Happiness glowed in every feature, not only at the pleasure he was giving to others, but in anticipation of the fun he was preparing for himself, for giving a pleasure is no diminution of one's own and he almost broke out into a laugh. The gentlemen riders, each on his own mount, followed in due order and the whole was closed by such an assemblage of stablemen, helpers, and privileged labourers and servants, under the conduct of Mr. Gates, the stud-groom, as would have gladdened the eyes of a border knight on the advent of a speculative foray. Half an hour's gentle riding brought them all to a farm of Mr. Thoroughgood's where about two miles and a half of a steeple-chase course had been marked out by flags, so as to render the line as unmistakable as could be. The honest historian is bound to record the fact that a certain compromise had been entered into with the fences themselves, so as to put them all within reasonable chance of negotiation and in accordance with the presumed inexperience of the performers.

The Squire loved to see a tumble or two and thought falling gracefully one of the first accomplishments of a good horseman; but he had no wish to have the sunset of his life clouded or his pillow haunted by the ghost of a young gentleman of sixteen or seventeen years of age, with his trousers inserted into his Wellington boots, and a bloodstained waistcoat with parti-coloured sleeves. So the stiff timber was taken out, and the strongest blackthorns were laid a little low; and though the water was left wide enough for any juvenile glutton, it was carefully selected with a sound bottom, and not more than four feet in depth, so that the ducking might be complete without danger of drowning.

Another hour was spent in looking over the course and other preliminaries until the course and the starting post presented a tolerably lively scene. Notwithstanding the fact that the race was Squire Thoroughgood's private affair, an audience of half a dozen county carriages in which there were the bright eyed young ladies of the county; there were also a few flys, a mail phaeton, and a several gentlemen on horseback, all of which served to stimulate the nerves of the competitors. Having taken off their great coats and performed their preliminary canter, without which no truly sporting effect can be produced, even Teddy Dacre forgot the thinness of his shirt-sleeves. Bosville, indeed, was confident in the correctness of his get-up, and Billy Russell, regardless of the deficiencies of his own, took a nearer view of the bright eyes that were to recompense their exertions later in the day. But Charlie, naturally shy, kept aloof from the crowd of carriages till an awful knell, in the sound of a bell for preparation, smote upon his ear.

"Now, gentlemen, take your places, if you please," said the jolly Squire; "the captain's gone to the winning-post with Gates; here are three volunteers going as umpires, and there's Joey Sanders, the keeper, down at the brook, with a gaff to help out those that require his assistance. Never mind your breeches, Russell; they'll fit capitally before long, I know: they only want damping. Now, are you ready? When I drop the flag, and say 'Go!' you must go: and the devil take the hindmost; or 'Occupet extremum scabies.' You see I haven't forgotten my Greek, you young rascals.' Go!" And away they went, Billy Russell on Judy, with a lead a little stronger than he liked.

Three or four fences were safely negotiated without a fall. Charlie's harlequin jacket was not very forward, having been a little outpaced by the resolute Judy, who, by great good fortune, had the sturdy little Billy Russell on her back. Beyond an irresistible jerk at the first fence, which pulled him on to the shoulders and made his nose bleed, he was going pretty smoothly still in front. Teddy Dacre, too, was after him on the chestnut, and the swell – ignominious position! – brought up the rear. Wilkinson and Charlie were close together, playing at real jockeys remarkable well. Of course this amicable state of affairs was not likely to last and a few fences further on, little

Bosville spoilt the elegance of his costume by tumbling over the roan pony's head at a post and rail: whilst the Honourable Russell still led, sitting a little nearer the horns than usual. At the next fence Judy ducked her head, landing Billy on his back in the ditch, whilst she jumped over him and resumed the running on her own account. "Now then, Russell, you get out of the way, you're blocking up the gaps," shouted Teddy Dacre, who came next, and was really beginning to feel at home.

"You be hanged," yelped Master Russell, who was now up and standing in the fence, ready for an argument. "there's lots of room for you, only you're in a funk." The dispute was ended by Charlie making a fresh hole. In the meantime the ponies were caught straightway by the numerous touts and hangers on and restored to their owners, who were soon up and after their comrades. The cheerful little sallies which took place during the ride, especially at the fences, where little casualties happened, were quite refreshing, and robbed the rivalry of all sting. "Go it Magpie," said one; "don't chirp too soon," as Teddy Dacre cut a genteel summersault over a blackthorn. "Now then, Boots – well done!" said another, as Wilkinson landed side by side with Charlie in a muddy ditch, out of which, however, they managed to scramble without any inconvenience beyond the necessity of remounting; and giving occasion to the other three to make up for lost time, which they did somewhat at the expense of their ponies. And now came the water. Two-thirds of the course had been accomplished; and it was not till they had turned to come home that this formidable obstacle presented itself. Teddy Dacre was the only one of the party that had any experience in drowning and he had no fancy for a repetition. Charlie fully believed in a ducking, but never despaired of anything. Rather negative feelings accompanied Wilkinson, and little Bosville shut his eyes mentally and physically to the danger. As to Billy

Russell, he had not long become a voluntary agent, and scarcely realised the situation, but he made no doubt about getting over, if he could but sit on. They all charged it, however, manfully; Charlie got over with a fall, Solomon over-jumped himself; the gray refused, and blundered in and out again upon a second effort; Teddy Dacre turned on all his steam, and, though pretty nearly adrift of the saddle, went on with the lead. Judy, a little blown from previous exertions, landed Billy well into the water, who, as he was crawling out, was pulled back again a little unexpectedly by Tommy Bosville. The swell, when he saw the water, lost his nerve; and the roan mare, shooting suddenly round in the wake of Russell, alarmed at the melancholy failure of that hero, sent her rider flying over her shoulders right into the middle of the stream. He was but small; and not coming immediately to the bottom, he thought self-preservation, the first law of nature, should be obeyed. He saw no tails to a coat, but he saw a boot to a leg, and seized it. Had it been but Wilkinson, the boot would have come off: the Honourable William refused to give way, and they both fell back comfortably into the brook to find their own level. We need hardly say that when they found themselves safe within their depth they felt strongly inclined to quarrel then and there; and had it not been for the momentary absence of Russell, who had dived to the bottom in search of his whip, it would probably have ended in a fight on the spot. Luckily, the attention of both was called to the business in hand by Joey Sanders, who threatened to commence operations with his gaff, unless the young gents came out of the water, instead of standing there "a disturbin' of the fish." His remonstrances and the mighty weapon he wielded, had the desired effect; but the length of their controversy had put them out of the race. Dacre continued to lead; and the Magpie on the chestnut pony was becoming a strong favourite with the multitude. He had the foot of Solomon; but being a little nearer to dealers' condition, and not in such constant work as the Thoroughgood stable, there was still the ghost of a chance for Charlie. One more fence, and the run in: and with a laudable zeal for the ladies who had transferred themselves to the winning post by a short cut through a couple of gates from the start, the Squire had taken care that it should be a jump. Already Alice and Edith Dacre looked upon their brother as the victor. Already Teddy Dacre felt himself secure of the prize; already Wilkinson had declined, and Charlie began to think further perseverance useless, when the chestnut pony, which had hitherto been going well, declined the last fence and Solomon, pricking his ears and answering a somewhat emphatic kick from Charlie, cleared the hurdles and furze-bushes, and landed the "Dunce of the Family" a winner by some lengths. The gray mare Kitty, was a tolerable second; and after considerable persuasion the chestnut hung his hind legs in such an ignominious manner that Teddy felt compelled to dismount before he could be released. At an interval of a minute or two the missing competitors, Russell and Bosville, trotted up the course, still discussing in somewhat animated language whose fault it was that they were both of them wet through.

CHAPTER 11

A DINNER OF SIGNIFICANCE

There is no idea in the range of social life so beautiful as that of sisterhood. A single girl may remind us in her severity, if she be severe, of a Greek drama; if she be gentle, of a weeping willow. But two sisters are never too dignified for every day life, never too pliant. There is a golden cord of mutual obligation which unites them. That is why old Lady Trumpcard never knows which it is that young Scraptoft means to marry. How should she? He never knows himself. I do not know that this peculiarity extends beyond two. I rather think not. But unless two suitors present themselves about the same time, and each claims his victim at once, it is very likely to be a long game of haphazard and even then they have been known to change by almost mutual consent.

When Charlie Thornhill sat down to dinner at old Mr. Thoroughgood's, he saw around him a heterogeneous mass of excellent people; fast young women with palsied mothers and slow young women with dashing chaperones; unpolished country squires, boorish in appearance; with red hands and large feet – the former of which they were continually polishing with their pocket-handkerchiefs, whilst the latter reposed in uncomfortable inelegance beneath their chairs. It was just as impossible to overlook Dacre's sisters in such an assembly as to have overlooked the moon amongst the planets. They gave light where there would have been nothing but eating and drinking. Charlie Thornhill was a shy boy, naturally; he felt himself rather the hero of the day, which made him more shy: and he was of that age when the other sex had vast superiority over his. He found himself next to the one sister and nearly opposite to the other. For some peculiar reason, he was predeterminately attracted towards Edith Dacre. Charlie's indolent mind did not inquire the wherefore. "Blue-eyed and full of mischief" was the limited description he had had of her. Alice was seated beside him and was a "stunner".

It is just possible that the short description of these girls, by their brother Teddy, does not convey much notion of them to the reader. Attend then, whilst I somewhat amplify it. But not too much. Let facts attest their characters.

The soup being gone, Charlie Thornhill took courage to turn round to his left-hand neighbour, as less formidable than the turban and diamonds on his right. The first thing that struck him was the extraordinary smoothness and brilliancy of the coal black hair. Then he got to the eyes of the same colour, but softened in hue, as though some violet mingled with the black. The other features had no particular expression nor beauty, beyond the mouth, which was somewhat large, but well-formed and humorous, not laughing but capable of being made to laugh. The figure, which was not at present apparent, was well-formed and tall, but carried off by a corresponding presence. Charlie felt a little afraid, and much attracted. He knew Alice Dacre to be but a year beyond his own age: but she carried full three summers more in a simple but perfectly assured manner. Yet Alice was a little shy with strangers: perhaps proud. Towards the preserver of her brother's life she felt no pride, and towards schoolboys of seventeen but very little shyness. The great force of her character was in its truth and even the "Dunce of the Family" felt it at once.

Then he turned his eyes opposite and through the centre piece of spring flowers he saw his fate. Laughing eyes, soft brown hair, a beautifully-formed nose and mouth, every movement of which was a smile, and displayed the even, dazzling little teeth within: a complexion almost delicate but a matchless grace of budding womanhood. There was no deficiency of character in the features of form, soft and womanlike as they were. Alice Dacre could be dreamt of as alone, or as giving support were it wanted; but on first impressions of Edith Dacre, she appeared to be a more dependant character, that was her only weakness. Boy as he was, he saw nothing to fear, but something to cherish; and he thought the "chaff" about which Teddy had talked would be the most palatable food to nourish him.

A word on the Dacres themselves. Mr. Dacre was a man of high family, great pretension, and but moderate means; and had married a lady whose object in life was to appear in the world as a member of the *beau monde*. They went to the proper places at the proper seasons, were seen at the proper houses, and were unobtrusive in the world of fashion. He was tall, handsome, well-mannered, and slightly bald. She was stout, dignified, an excellent talker, and richly but darkly dressed. They were both a little above the average in point of brains: but made friends, and preserved them, by a judicious control of their intellects. They each had objectives in life. His was to obtain an attachéship for his son; hers to obtain eligible marriages for her daughters. Alice had come out. Edith was still in the schoolroom, if the embroidery of flowers, lessons in water-colours, and tea with Miss Wilkinson, whenever there was company at dinner, could be construed into that locality. They were pronounced by everybody to be a charming family: they were kind to the poor, condescending to their inferiors, tolerably civil to their equals, *obeisant* to their superiors, and distantly recognisant of the curate of the parish in which they lived. It would have been difficult to reconcile the visit of the girls to Mr. Thoroughgood's neighbourhood and table with Mrs Dacre's doctrines, but for one fact. They were under the charge of a lady whom it was not desirable to offend. Lady Elizabeth Montagu Mastodon was a great woman, in every sense of the word, and a relative of Mr. Dacre. Montagu Mastodon was a member for the county, enormously wealthy, and had no children. Lady Elizabeth, was the daughter of an Irish peer, whose estates had been sold under the Act[11] for £300,000, every shilling of which was long since squandered. She was the stoutest, vulgarest, the cleverest, and the kindest woman that ever walked, we might say rolled, upon two legs: and if Mr. Montagu Mastodon, with his iron and coal, found the money, she found the popularity for the county member. She went everywhere, did everything, and knew everybody: and hence the appearance of the Misses Dacre at the hospitable board of our old friend Thoroughgood.

"Lor' bless me, Mr. Thoroughgood," said the old lady in her own right, who had become more practical and more vulgar since her marriage, "I wonder you don't kill yourselves with your steeple-chasing. So that's the young gentleman that won today? It does you great credit, sir; whatever is done at all ought to be well done. Thornhill, Thornhill – ah! That's his name, is it?" said she, putting up her lorgnette, "His brother's at Christ Church with my scapegrace of a nephew, Carlingford. Do you know what the prize poem is this year?"

"I did hear, but I forget," said Charlie, blushing up to the eyes –

---

[11] We think this refers to the Encumbered Estates Act of 1849. (editors)

"something about eating in Africa," added he, after a moment's pause.

"What! The Africans? Eating? Surely that's not a subject for the Newdigate?[12]"

"I think it's eating or biting. I know it's about Africa, because my brother wrote to me about it."

"Bless my heart, so it is about Africa; no I recollect: it's about the Bight of Benin. Biting or eating in Africa, only not quite in the way you mean, Mr. Thornhill. Bless the boy! What a capital joke."

"Mr. Thornhill," said Alice Dacre, "I am so glad to have had an opportunity of thanking you for your kindness to my brother. Papa and Mamma often talk about you. We can never forget it; and they would be so glad if you could come to see us when the holidays begin. We can try and made you comfortable, though I dare say you love Thornhills: only we want to thank you. Do come!"

Charlie began to speak when to his infinite relief, Lady Elizabeth sent a meaningful glance to the old maiden cousin who had sat at the top of Mr. Thoroughgood's table since the death of his wife, pushed back her chair, and made preparations for rolling into the drawing-room. Alice rose too and as she held out her hand she said, "Goodbye Mr. Thornhill. I think the carriage will have been ordered before you join us in the drawing room." Charlie almost thought he could have tossed up as to which of the two sisters he liked the best.

---

[12] Sir Roger Newdigate's Prize for English Verse was founded in 1806 as a memorial to Sir Roger, fifth baronet (1719-1806) and Oxford university politician. The instructions to enter, if you can find them, are pleasantly odd: *"The length of the poem is not to exceed 300 lines. The metre is not restricted to heroic couplets, but dramatic form of composition is not allowed."*

BOOK TWO

CHAPTER 12

UNCLE HENRY

"Lerne früh die Kunst Geld zu verdienen."
Learn the art of earning money early.

Circa. 1854

Time is the steadiest traveller of my acquaintance. He stands still for nobody, and had not stood still for Charlie Thornhill who was now twenty with his majority less than a year away.

The London season had already begun. Tom Thornhill had left Oxford and was in town in great force, surrounded by bloodsuckers and lickspittles. He was saved from utter reprobation by the appearance in public of his friend Lord Carlingford, one of the richest noblemen in England. Sir Frederick and Lady Marston were at their own house, as usual, in Grosvenor Square, he for his parliamentary duties, she for her amusement: and staying with them was Charlie Thornhill, who always found a ready welcome with his father's oldest friends.

Lady Marston, a great reader, was in the library. Charlie had gone for a ride. Sir Frederick came into the room, and seated himself not far from his wife, with the paper in his hand.

"Have you seen the paper this morning, Kate?"

"No; not to day. Who is to be the new Bishop of London? I do hope we shall have learning or character."

"If you mean, by learning, a critical knowledge of the Greek article, and capability for editing a Greek play, I think we could do without the first: and I do not think any of the reverend bench can be said to fail in character."

"Humph!" said Lady Marston. "Cæsar's wife should be without suspicion; and that's more than can be said for all your venerable diocesans. As for learning, classical knowledge is better than none; and it demonstrates capability, you must acknowledge that my dear Frederick. But what was your news?"

"That miserable blockhead Feltham has married an outrageous woman with half a dozen aliases, after settling more than half his income upon her, and placing it at her own disposal; and old General Feltham, his uncle, with the rest of his family, has a commission of lunacy sitting to enquire whether he is capable of taking care of himself and the Feltham estates, to which the old general and his family are the heirs presumptive."

"But he is not mad any more than you are. He is vicious and foolish, but perfectly responsible for his actions, and consequently for the use of his property."

"It's a very bad case, however, Kate; and though legally capable, he is morally incapable of directing himself or his affairs. He'll be a beggar before another five years is over his head."

"Very probably, if the lawyers leave him anything to spend. But the family ought to have found that out before he disgraced himself and them by such a marriage. And if he spends everything now, the general will have the less to regret the loss of. Are you very busy?"

"No, Kate. What is it?"

"Charlie Thornhill."

"Ah! That troubles me, my wife. What's to be done?"

"Tell him the truth, the whole truth."

"The whole truth is not mine to tell. Besides, it's not a certainty and may come all right again. It seems that the purchase of the Irish property from Kildonald was not completed before Geoffrey's death and therefore the £4000 should have been returned to poor Geoffrey's estate. Although I cannot but suspect some rascality, the money certainly did not go to Geoffrey's banker nor his man of business but I cannot trace to whom it did go."

"His banker was Henry Thornhill, and he would not perhaps wish Charlie to know that the money had disappeared."

"The matter was arranged by a Mr. Burke, a lawyer in Cork, who acted for both parties. Poor Geoffrey was not only so little a man of business, but so culpably negligent in all matters connected with money, excepting the paying of his debts of honour, that neither I nor his brother can make anything of it."

"And from what you tell me, I am to conclude that there is little probability of Charlie ever having more than a pittance until his mother's death; he is not an absolute pauper, but he must have a profession." Here Lady Marston subsided into quiet thoughtfulness; it had a tinge of melancholy in it, as thoughtfulness for other people ought to have. At last she raised her head with a more cheerful look, and said, "Can I go to Pall Mall in the carriage to-day Frederick?"

"Certainly, my dear. Why should you ask?"

"Because I wish to see Henry Thornhill; and as it is on Charlie's account, I want to know whether you disapprove."

"By no means: but I fear you can do little to mend matters."

"We shall see; and if the worse comes to the worst, Charlie must make a fortune. After all, it is the more honourable course of the two."

It was a fine sunshiny afternoon when Lady Marston turned into Piccadilly out of Berkeley Square on her way to Pall Mall. Her equipage was faultless, her bonnet charming and she ought to have been the happiest woman in London. Indeed she was very nearly so, for she had a well-balanced mind which shook off light sorrows like "dewdrops from the lion's mane," as long as they only affected herself. She cared about other people and was always alive to their requirements.

Lady Marston drove in a carriage, with a fine, round, dignified coachman, well-powdered and silk-stockinged, who had never been asked to drive east of Temple Bar on the one side, or west of Kensington Gore on the other, and her footman was six feet two, and carried a stick with the air of a drum-major. The sensation created at the guard's club was not slight, and the young gentlemen at the Oxford and Cambridge were nearly frantic with curiosity. Her present object was a visit to Henry Thornhill, to see what could be done for the future advantage of the unwitting Charlie. That amiable youth at that very moment was making some scientific examination of a rather high-priced hunter, with a view to a first season on his own account, and wondering how far judicious cossetting would improve a rather questionable leg. St. James's Street was alive with dandies. Old General Bosville bowed from the steps of his club. 'What wonderful preservation!' thought Lady Marston. Then she stopped for a moment to speak to the Secretary of Foreign Affairs, who thought the government must fall if Sir John Plumper pressed his motion. The lady was not below politics nor above *petit point*. A very comprehensive mind was Lady Marston's. At the bottom of the street she caught sight of Carlingford and Tom Thornhill with two or three more of their set. She looked into the future and sighed, for she saw a long array of lost talent, misspent time, and a "sowing of the whirlwind," and she thought of Geoffrey Thornhill as she first knew him – not so young as that, but very like it. Within half a minute the barouche drew up at the dingy banking-house of Hammerton and Thornhill where Henry Thornhill himself appeared to her summons and courteously handed the sweetest woman in London into the very dingiest of back parlours.

Lady Marston had sufficient tact to know that time was more valuable to the banker than to her, and she was scarcely comfortably ensconced in a leather-cased chair before she proceeded to business.

"Have you seen your nephew lately, Mr. Thornhill?"

"Which, Lady Marston? For I have two."

"Charlie, I mean," said the lady.

"Indeed I have not. I wish I saw more of him."

"He's in very good company."

"If he's with you, Lady Marston," said the banker, who never paid a compliment. A disappointment in early life had shaken his faith in women. He saw the woman who was plighted to him walk up the steps of St. George's Church on the arm of her father, and return down them in half an hour on the arm of a wealthy earl. He knew she had been cruelly tortured, sorely driven, but he never forgave her, though he would have shed his heart's blood to save her from pain. His sense of truth forbade him to excuse her falsehood. His love taught him to suffer in silence for her, but his sense of justice condemned the sacrifice. He saw her almost daily on his solitary ride or walk from Pall Mall to Bryanstone Square.

"Charlie is with us: Frederick is very fond of him and we are anxious to see what can be done for him. This unexpected hitch about the Kildonald property, which we imagined was his, makes his case very different from what it was a year ago. He must have a profession."

"He must, indeed." And the banker seemed to think it was the best thing for him. He crossed his foot upon his knee, and looked at Lady Marston.

"Have you no advice to offer on the subject? With your experience, I think you might assist him. What say you to a mercantile life?"

"Has he any taste for it? Does he care for drudgery, toil, uncertainty, loss of caste, change of companionship, and a thousand little trials, of which he has no idea?" The banker thought about what had sent him into the back parlour of a bank instead of into country fields and pleasant places.

"What he may have a taste for I do not know; but I have thought of your profession."

"Mine is a trade, Lady Marston; more respectable, it is true, than many professions."

"And more lucrative." said Lady Marston.

"That's as it may be. But let me be sincere with you – and sincere as I can be on this point. He may go into my business, but into my house of business he never can come. There are reasons, insuperable reasons; and you know well, that if I thought I could serve him so, he might command me. But why not try something else – the army?"

"A commission in a marching regiment is all to which he could aspire." said Lady Marston thoughtfully. "But I think he should be consulted himself; he is old enough, at least, to have an inclination. What are his financial prospects?"

This was scarcely intended as a question, for Lady Marston, though truthful and earnest, was refined in mind. The banker, however, understood her train of thought and without apparent embarrassment answered –

"His mother's jointure, when she dies, but for the present, the money received from the uncompleted purchase in Ireland."

"And that is all? Financial security is only a distant prospect."

"It is. But he shall never want a home while I live. And Charlie seems to have no lack of friends, if all I hear of your own kindness and Sir Frederick's to be true. But he will never do in business."

"You are wrong, Mr. Thornhill. He is ignorant, and idle in the sense of learning; but he has high principles, common sense, and much determination. I should have thought he would have done admirably in your own ...."

"Trade, Lady Marston. Possibly: but I think not. You have great influence upon him which is more than valuable. Give him my kind love, and do all you can to impress upon him the value of independence. It will raise him in his own estimation as well as others, for it will place him above them. Believe me, Lady Marston, if he really wants to enjoy a fortune, he ought to make one."

That was the end of the discussion. A few minutes devoted, as usual, to the weather, the chances of the present ministry, the educational system, and Lord Shaftesbury and his bishops, finished the conference, and with the same courtesy, and with a cheek a little flushed, Henry Thornhill shook hands with Lady Marston and heard her give her orders to her coachman.

The banker was old for his years. Circumstances had made him so. English funds, and a contemplation of French pensions, American defaults, and foreign politics, make a young man old, though I believe they keep a middle-aged man in excellent preservation. Henry Thornhill had taken to business as a remedy against something worse. The battle of life is to the strong and people wondered why he was not in parliament. He knew himself. The vapours of political intrigue rendered the air of Westminster less palatable to the honest banker than to most men. He liked the life he led. He was unostentatious to a degree. One or two horses, a plain chariot which he seldom used, a good club dinner when alone, which was seldom, and an autumnal excursion into Scotland or Norfolk, to Homburg or Vienna, where he observed life with considerable amusement, of which, however, he was no participator. He had loved a woman; since then he had learned to love work and the dingy parlour at the back of those spacious premises in Pall Mall. He could give advice, even to Lady Marston, without offence. The accidents of his life, and his position, gave him an authority beyond his years. His memories, his sadness, the sturdy bachelor kept to himself; his experiences and his advice only for the friends, like Lady Marston, or his nephews, to whom he thought they were acceptable. He valued the influence exercised by a woman, like Lady Marston, upon his nephew. He knew such influence had a charm, a flattery in it, quite unequalled by any other friendship. It softened, it consoled, it ennobled, and it cherished the dying embers of a spirit of chivalry.

CHAPTER 13

RIPE FOR THE PLUCKING

When Lady Marston reached home, she found a note from her *protégé,* excusing himself from dining in Grosvenor Square. It rather disconcerted her plan, as she was dining at home and Sir Frederick was at the House to give her the opportunity of speaking to Charlie alone. It would have been an excellent opportunity for a chat about his prospects, and for urging the adoption of a profession of some kind or other. However, it was pretty certain that that young gentleman would make his appearance only to dress, and the subject was not one to be discussed in a five minutes' conversation on a second-floor landing, so she wisely determined upon postponing the business. There could be no doubt about an opportunity occurring within a week or two at latest, notwithstanding the multifarious engagements of a London season. So she took her drive, and her dinner, and went to the theatre to hear Grisi[13] for an hour or two, chatted sociably with half a dozen dandies, who amused her, and with one clever man who she amused, and returned comfortably to bed at

---

[13] Carlotta Grisi – a ballet dancer with a lovely voice.

a reasonable hour.

Whilst she had been talking to the worthy banker, Charlie had been spending his morning less profitably. Exactly opposite Cambridge House, he had been overtaken by his father's old acquaintance, Lord Dorrington, who hailed him with that good-humoured simplicity which is so flattering.

"Where to, Charlie?" said the jolly nobleman, who, beyond a tight boot (physically) and a twinge of '34 claret, knew no trouble, "Going my way?"

Of course he was, or any other way that suited; an idler or a more accommodating young man than Charlie Thornhill was not, at that time, to be met with; he had not even a pleasure in prospect to bore him. It was not long before he had confided to Lord Dorrington his intention of going to Scotland in the autumn, and from there accompanying Tom to Melton for the hunting.

"I must have two or three horses of my own, for Tom's such a good fellow, that if I don't buy one or two, he'll be increasing his number, and there's no necessity for that."

"There's a horse of Putney's at Tattersall's[14] now," said the noble lord "that would pay for summering, and that would just suit you; he's fast, and a capital fencer, but takes some riding, which I hear you can do for him."

Charlie blushed; but he knew Lord Dorrington to be a good judge, and Captain Putney to be a straight man so he sauntered on to the corner of Park Lane, where he took courage to say that he would go to Tattersall's and look at the horse.

Having made up his mind that "Ironmaster" (so called from his late owner) would be cheap enough at 120 guineas, he walked once more along Piccadilly till he reached Bolton Street. After hesitating a moment, he knocked at a gloomy-looking door, whose portals

---

[14] Bloodstock auctioneers founded in 1766 by Richard **Tattersall**

opened at the summons into a more gloomy-looking hall.

"Is Lord Carlingford at home?"

"No sir," said the man; "but Mr. Thornhill and Sir George Barrington are just come in, so that I dare say his lordship will not be long."

"Sir George Barrington?" said Charlie, half aloud, "Then I'll go up."

At the same time a groom of the chambers appeared, and Charlie followed him along hollow-sounding passages to a room on the ground floor. Nothing could present a greater contrast to the darkness of the passage he had quitted than the light and comfort of the room into which he was shown. It was a billiard room of very large size, made comfortable by the light from above, and by all the appendages which modern taste requires. There were books, pictures, armchairs and sofas of every description. Sir George was chalking his cue, preparatory to a stroke, and Tom Thornhill was lighting a cigar at the moment that his brother entered. Both stopped for a minute and welcomed our hero with the greatest cordiality. Sir George was not a favourite of Charlie's and he viewed Barrington playing billiards for money with considerable distrust. He knew him to be a gambler and, alas, he knew Tom to be one too. But he knew Barrington to be unprincipled, ungenerous, and licentious; living without means, save what he filched from his unsuspicious victims and this at the rate of some thousands a year. He was admitted into, or rather tolerated in, society; but mothers shuddered when they heard of him as an associate of their sons. He was adept at all games of skill and, it was reported, still more adept at games of chance. And he was a first-rate pistol shot, had already killed his man in a not very creditable fray, so it was pleasanter to say things about him rather than to his face. As for Tom Thornhill, he would as soon have believed in Sir George's lack of honour, as in his own. Charlie took a different view of the case.

The game proceeded. Thornhill had made a good break, but then proceeded to lose the game. Tom looked disappointed, not at the loss of the money, but the game. He was easily persuaded that luck was against him, and put on his coat with a reassurance that he could have won. Charlie watched the game narrowly, and knew better.

"Au revoir," said Barrington, as he took his leave; "I shall not wait for Carlingford," and the brothers were alone.

"What do you do tonight, Charlie?"

"Nothing particular. I was going back to dine at the Marstons'."

"Then come down to Richmond and dine with me. Here comes Carlingford; he or I will drive you down. There will be only ourselves, De Beauvoir, the Punter, and Barrington."

Lord Carlingford entered the room. He looked like a gentleman, but strength of mind was not his characteristic.

"How did you do with Barrington? – How do Thornhill?" added he on seeing Charlie.

"I lost when I was close to game."

Charlie hesitated a moment, and as suddenly consented to be made one of the dinner party.

"Well, then I'll call for you in Grosvenor Square at half past five." and Charlie took his leave for the present.

As he strolled slowly along Piccadilly towards Bond Street, his thoughts were on his brother Tom, who was his *beau idéal* of every perfection in man when he ran against one of those busybodies who love to astonish boys with their knowledge of all that is going on in society. Frank Tuftenham was five years Charlie's senior and was a clerk in the Foreign Office; he had a bowing and scraping acquaintance with everybody, and was intimate with nobody. He was a small, intrusive sort of man and Charlie Thornhill was a giant in every respect compared to this sallow official.

"Weren't you at school with Dacre, Thornhill?"

"What, Teddy Dacre? Of course I was. I should like to see Teddy again; I haven't seen him for a while. Where is he?"

"He's in Town. I thought you knew them very well; he always talks about you to everybody. But what a pity it is that that pretty sister of his is going to be married to De Beauvoir."

Charlie felt rather uncomfortable though Tuftenham was unconscious of Charlie's rising colour. The fact is, he was red hot to the roots of the hair and old Thoroughgood's dinner had inflicted a wound a great deal more lasting than the headache he had risen with the following morning. Still Charlie could not shake Tuftenham off and this disagreeable friend continued,

"I do hope there's nothing in that report that's going the rounds of the clubs about Sir George Barrington and your brother!"

"What the devil is that?" said Charlie, with considerable energy.

"Oh I beg ten thousand pardons – I ought never to have said a word, of course I concluded that you had heard all about it."

"Not I; let's have it."

"Well, they do say that Barrington has won five thousand from him, and two off Carlingford. Of course I only repeat what I have heard."

"I don't believe a word of it." but Charlie painfully recalled the game of billiards he had witnessed that morning. "Do you know Barrington?"

"He would rob a church I should think," was the official's reply. "He's about the greatest swindler in London. Adieu, Thornhill!"

Charlie Thornhill's reflections were sombre as he sauntered up Bond Street towards Grosvenor Square: he began to think there was something of truth in the gossip; he believed the De Beauvoir engagement was well founded so he could not altogether disbelieve the talk about Tom and Sir George Barrington.

"He is a thief," said Charlie to himself; "I am sure of it."

The drive down to Richmond was cheerful enough in itself. The charming spirits of Tom Thornhill, the quick stepping ponies – a new purchase of Tom's – the clanking of the pole chains, the sparkling river with its hundred boats, and hearts as light as its waters, the budding hedges, and the fresh air, all combined to drive away the gloomy spirits of Charlie. He could not help remarking on the way down, however, to his brother, that he didn't like Barrington.

"I know that, Charlie."

"How?"

"You're always so infernally polite to him, when *we* can scarcely get a civil word out of you."

"I mean to be so but they don't speak highly of him."

"Poor devil! – I suppose he's lots of enemies, like everybody else who hasn't money enough to buy a good opinion."

"He must have laid out some of his late gains, then advantageously; he ought to be pretty flush."

"I suppose some fool or other has been exaggerating the case, Charlie. A few hundreds aren't much for a fellow that's been plucked as he has." Tom was getting a little warm in his friend's cause, so Charlie reserved any communications he might have for another opportunity. A few more minutes brought them to the Castle at Richmond.

"Lord Carlingford come yet?"

"No sir, but his lordship's room is ready," replied the obsequious waiter, with a flourish of his napkin. "Dinner at seven, sir."

"Come, Charlie, let's go into the garden, and look at the boats," and in another minute they were lounging over the wall. The gardens were gay with fashionable men and well-dressed women, who strolled up and down, or sat on the wall, or occupied the seats scattered about. It was a pleasant scene; the lovely river, and the life that sparkled on and around it.

In a while the guests arrived, and Tom and his brother turned back to welcome them.

Lord Carlingford was chewing a toothpick, from which he seemed to derive considerable satisfaction, if not nourishment; even that exertion was almost too much for him after his drive. De Beauvoir and Sir George Barrington had come down together; the former presented an object of much interest to Charlie since the news he had received in the morning; and he was compelled to admit that even if De Beauvoir was a fool he was a very good looking one. His companion looked as *blasé* and washed out as any other naturally delicate gentleman who has lived upon nothing but excitement up to the age of thirty. The last member of the party was Cressingham, affectionately known as the Punter, he was a roistering, jovial, natural sort of person, of about five-and-twenty – very large, very stout, very loud in every way. He was not averse to having a punt when it came his way, but, with the exception of Charlie, was probably the least fond of the tables of any of the party.

I am compelled to state, with regret, that the dinner was not up to the mark. The Punter was the only person who felt really aggrieved; his jolly nature always attached itself to the present and he was an excellent judge of what he thought of as good food. The rest were scarcely competent to decide upon the delicacies of a French menu, not so common then as now and certainly Barrington had come to Richmond with other views than a mere dinner. The champagne was guiltless of the Champagne region or banks of the Marne, and the claret had to be twice changed before it was pronounced drinkable.

The conversation at a Richmond dinner is not always worth preservation: the evening passed cheerfully enough, if not very rationally: Charlie never talked much; he probably thought the more. He could not help looking at Barrington with a shade of suspicion; but before dinner was over it gave place to a pleasanter feeling, and he began to think that he might be mistaken, and that Tuftenham was but a gossip at the best of times. He was not *au fait* with all the subjects discussed, for Charlie almost despised the life he was obliged to lead during some parts of the year, and felt more at home in the Warren at Thornhills with his four-footed favourites, than in the middle of St. James's Street, amongst the fashionable acquaintances of his brother Tom. The next Derby, and the last fight, will not last forever as topics of conversation. The Opera, and the Oxford and Cambridge boat race had their turn. Carlingford's shooting and Tom's new hack did good service. By the time the conversation had arrived at the Chiswick fête, and the cricketing gentlemen and the players, most of the company was anxious for some more engaging excitement; and when Tom proposed a game of hazard[15], which he was quite certain to do sooner or later, no one but Charlie regretted it.

Why are we all gamblers – North and South, East and West; the most civilized, the most savage? The Malay, who runs amok after everything in the world that he has, excepting his clothing. The Frenchman or the Englishman, who, in running amok, loses his everything – reputation and honour not infrequently included. The former literally becomes the prey of his acquaintances and goes forth like a wild beast to kill or to be killed. The latter having stood to be shot at, takes his turn in victimizing his friends. The losing of many thousands seems to be an excuse or apology for every enormity. The Russian lights a fire at his heart, which burns as fiercely as the South American: and whilst the latter washes out his losses in the blood of his opponent, the former scatters his own brains upon the steps of the Kursaal at Wiesbaden or Homburgh. "Tom, Tom, would that warning might come in time!" thinks Charlie. There is a flaw in his idol, but he is none the less an idol for all that.

---

[15] **Hazard** is an Old English game played with two dice which was mentioned in Chaucer's *Canterbury Tales* in the 14th century. Despite its complicated rules, hazard was very popular in the 17th and 18th centuries and was often played for money.

So down they sit, and the rest look on. They begin with hazard.

"Seven!" said Tom; "eleven!" – and he wins. He throws the dice several times more, and wins a hundred. His blood is warm by the time he has thrown again, but is out.

"Five!" says Lord Carlingford,

"Seven to five!" cries Sir George Barrington; and five it is.

"Pass the box, Carlingford. Charlie?"

"No thank you". said Charlie. "I'll look on; I never play:" and they respected the scruples of a younger son. Before long the luck began to change, and, like a true gambler, Tom Thornhill clung to ill luck with considerable perseverance.

"More claret, waiter, and light those lamps on the mantelpiece," said his lordship. "De Beauvoir, what have you won?"

"A couple of hundred only," said the fool, "Barrington is the winner." And so he was as Tom continued to play the odds, and to bet them. He got more and more excited, and displayed an eagerness from which Charlie boded no good for that night

"Let's have some spareribs and a glass of champagne." Tom began to feel feverish. Lord Carlingford was limper than usual, and not disposed to risk any more money on himself or Tom Thornhill, who he had been backing; De Beauvoir decided upon going; and the Punter was fast asleep on the sofa with six new ten pound notes in his pocket, which he had won, and pocketed in the most jovial manner, without any regard to the pocket out of which it had come. The grilled bones and champagne, however, revived Tom who had vowed he would have nothing more to do with the dice five minutes before and now proposed a game at écarté[16] as a compromise between his conscience and his desire for play.

---

[16] **Écarté** is a two-player card game originating from France, the word literally meaning "discarded". It is a trick-taking game similar to whist, but with a special and eponymous discarding phase. Écarté was popular in the 19th century, but is now rarely played.

"Come, De Beauvoir, one game for a pony."

"Impossible, Tom, I must be off; there's my horse catching cold underneath that confounded portico all this time."

"I'll take a hand," said Lord Carlingford.

"And I," said Cressingham the Punter.

Barrington said nothing, but took the cards and a seat. His face was flushed with triumph; he looked confident, as well he might; to continue was the gamester's principle of backing his luck: écarté with such men as Tom Thornhill and Carlingford was Sir George's promised land.

Again the play was fast and furious. Tom began to hold cards. He got back some of his money from Carlingford, and would have recovered some of the ill-gotten gains of the baronet, who, however, was always ready to lay or take the odds, and by some combination of talent brought off the majority of his ventures. Time wore on, and Cressingham was again upon the sofa, having lost a trifle, and the peer had already sent for soda water and the bill. Still Tom played on, cursing his fortune and doubling his stakes, till the sum became serious. Charlie in the mean time had not been asleep. He was not given to admiring himself, but in the feverish silence of the two players and the drowsy stupidity of the non-combatants, he had taken to looking in the mirror, on the mantel-piece, and which was at the back of Sir George Barrington's chair. His attention was divided between his own well parted hair and a china shepherdess of the reign of George II, which formed one of the ornaments on the chimney piece, it was then he saw, what he had never seen in polite society before, the hand of Sir George Barrington secrete a card in the tail pocket of his dress coat, out of which peeped the corner of his cambric pocket handkerchief. Charlie's first impulse was to proclaim the fact, but Charlie was a thinker as well as a man of action, and decided to wait. Again he turned his attention to the game. Tom won: the stakes were raised. Sir George looked at his watch.

"Come, Thornhill, we must finish; one more game."

"What's to become of the card?" thought Charlie.

The game proceeded.

"Cards if you please?"

"How many?"

"Tout la boutique".

"The king", said Tom, who had taken to smoking and blew out a trail of smoke. Charlie had also lighted a cigar and stood on the right hand of Sir George, a short distance from the table. Still the game proceeded slowly.

"The trick," said Barrington: "Two to your one."

Again Tom scored.

"Even", said the Punter, with an ill-suppressed yawn.

Two deals followed in Tom's favour, and again he laid two to one. In the next hand the baronet held the king, and made the trick.

"Even again, by Jove! Your odds look badly, Tom," said the Punter, as he rose, and proceeded to uncork a soda-water bottle.

The time must be come, thought Charlie, who sucked at his cigar as if nothing extraordinary was about to happen, but he edged a little further round towards Sir George's right.

"You've laid me two hundred to one on the game, to finish up," said Barrington to Thornhill, who was no longer as collected as in the earlier part of the game, and chafed a little at the unexpected turn of events. Barrington repeated, "You've laid me two hundred to one; I'll accept that, if you like, Thornhill: it's now four all." The cards lay on the table.

"Done" said Tom.

The baronet suddenly stood in need of his handkerchief before turning the trump. Holding the pack in his left hand, he put his right hand behind his back, and drew out a perfectly scented and elaborately marked French cambric, as innocent of deceit, to all appearance, as the wooden horse of Troy. His hand had barely reached his hip, however, when with one stride and the quickness of lightning his wrist was seized as in a vice by the right hand of Charlie and the back of his collar by the left hand of the same individual. A violent struggle ensued of a second's duration, in which the lamp fell to the ground, which called Lord Carlingford's attention from his bill, and shot the bottle of soda water all over the Punter's shirt front.

"Charlie, you're mad!" said Tom.

"What the devil's the matter?" said Cressingham, coming to the rescue.

"Bring the light here, or bring us to the light: here's foul play. It's no use, Sir George," said Charlie. "I've not watched you to-night for nothinga" as Barrington struggled fiercely in the grasp of one of the most powerful fellows in Town. "It's no use: I'll have the card that's in your hand, if I tear you limb from limb."

"Speak, Barrington. What in the world is it?" at last said Lord Carlingford.

"I've no card in my hand; the man's drunk or mad."

"No, he's dropped it: his foot's upon it. Pick it up, Tom."

The Punter saved him the trouble. "By God, sir, it's the king of clubs!"

The announcement restored four of the party to their equanimity, the fifth stood pale, trembling, and discomposed. Lord Carlingford was quite himself again as he said, with the politest of bows, "Perhaps, Sir George, you had better order your carriage; mine will be round in a minute or two." And Barrington was gone.

The termination to the night's amusement was abrupt enough, though none too soon. The waiter announced Lord Carlingford's carriage and Mr. Thornhill's phæton in a few minutes, during which not one of the party referred to the transaction, excepting by an epithet not complimentary to the absent guest. They had already left the room, when Charlie returned for a glove that was left behind. The light was still in the room, and as he entered, between the door and the table at which the struggle had taken place, he trod upon something hard and sharp. As he moved his foot, he stooped to ascertain the cause, and found a dice.

"Waiter," said Charlie, "does this belong to you?"

"No, sir; I've just put the two pairs away that the gentlemen have been using this evening."

"Look again".

"Yes, sir, they're all there: they belong to the board, sir".

"Very good. You're quite certain?" He said under his breath "I thought I heard something drop." And he put the dice carefully into his waistcoat pocket.

"Good night."

"Good night, sir," said the waiter. In three quarters of an hour he was back in Grosvenor Square.

CHAPTER 14

TWO BREAKFASTS

"Falsley luxurious, will not man awake,
And springing from the bed of sloth, enjoy
The cool, the fragrant, and the silent hour."
THOMSON – *Seasons*

On the morning following the little dinner at Richmond, which had ended less pleasantly than it had begun, Charlie Thornhill was not up as early as usual. He was an early riser on ordinary occasions, but on this occasion he was a little late. He had an idea that the less said about the previous evening's occupation to Lady Marston or Sir Frederick the better. She was apt to ask inconvenient questions, and Charlie was a bad liar, so he kept out of the way.
Having delayed his shaving as long as he could and having taken extraordinary care in the selection of his clothes for the morning, a thing he was generally careless about, he reached the breakfast room some time after Lady Marston had left it and Sir Frederick had gone to his club. His appetite was remarkably good and he rang with intense satisfaction for more eggs and another roll or two: and –

"Jobson, just bring in the ham if there is any left; the one we had at dinner the day before yesterday." Charlie was a first-rate judge of ham.

"Certainly, sir," said Jobson, as he placed two fresh-boiled eggs in front of the latecomer, and put the "Times" on an adjacent chair. At the same time he poured out a cup of tea. Jobson was an excellent servant and as careful of his master's friends as of his master himself.

Charlie had just broken the crown of his second egg and was wishing the cutlets were made hot again, when a cabriolet stopped with a jerk at the door, and a loud and prolonged knock proclaimed a fashionable arrival thus early in the day. The breakfast-room door was not quite closed and an impatient, imperious voice was heard outside.

"Is Mr. Thornhill at home?"

"This is Sir Frederick Marston's, sir." said the footman; "Mr. *Charles* Thornhill is staying here: he is at breakfast at present."

"Take this card to him and say I will wait."

"Will you walk into the library, sir?" said the servant.

"A gentleman wishing to see you, sir," said the servant, presenting the card.

"Captain Charteris, 8th Hussars," read Charlie. "Ask if he is sure it is not my brother whom he wishes to see." Charlie had heard of Captain Charteris, but had no more idea of the reason for his visit than if he had been announced as the Emperor of China.

"Captain Charteris believes he has made no mistake, sir, and if you will allow him to wait until you can see him, a few words of explanation are all he wishes."

"Is that Captain Charteris's message?"

"Yes, sir."

"Then ask him to walk in here, if he will excuse ceremony."

Captain Charteris did walk in, without ceremony. He was a good-looking but dissipated man, some years Charlie's senior, dressed to perfection, and bearing evident marks of good birth and the habits of good society. Charlie apologized for the lateness of his breakfast, which was considerably earlier than the Captain's usual hour for that meal. He had been obliged to call thus early in consequence of the peculiar nature of his business.

"Excuse me, Captain Charteris; are you sure that it is not my brother you wish to speak to? If so he is in Grosvenor Place, I believe." Charlie was not anxious to hear what might be intended for Tom's private edification.

"I think I am under no mistake. May I ask if you were not at a dinner yesterday at Richmond? Sir George Barrington was one of the party." A light dawned upon Charlie; yet he never could be such a fool, thought he, as to send the man here.

"I was there, with my brother, Lord Carlingford, and some other gentlemen. Sir George Barrington was one of the party."

"Then, Mr. Thornhill, if I say that I come from him, you can be under no misapprehension as to the nature of my visit."

"Indeed, Captain Charteris, I am sorry to ask you to explain yourself, for I can hardly believe that Sir George can have asked you to call upon me for an apology or an explanation."

"I thank you very much for saving me an unpleasant task; it is the very reason for my visit this morning; but I am charged with no request for an apology, but for the name of a friend who may arrange a more satisfactory meeting at once. Personal violence admits of no explanation."

"You are Sir George Barrington's friend?"

"I am"

"You know him well?"

"I think I do."

"Excuse me saying, Captain Charteris, but you do not, or you would not be here this morning. I don't know much about these matters, though I suppose one always fights with gentlemen. I certainly don't intend to fight Sir George Barrington."

"Stay, Mr. Thornhill, I think I said Sir George was a personal friend of mine. I can allow no such insinuations against ..."

"I insinuate nothing; I state a bare fact: and though I give no explanation to Sir George, I admit one is due to you;" and here Charlie helped himself to an additional lump of sugar, and rang the bell.

"Send up to my dressing-room for a small paper parcel that the groom brought back from Bond Street an hour ago." He continued, " I detected Sir George Barrington in a gross act of cheating at cards last night, when playing with my brother – a card secreted in his pocket, and proving to be a 'king' at a rather interesting point of the game."

"That," said Captain Charteris, rising from his seat, "has been already satisfactorily explained to me."

"I regret to say that it has to be satisfactorily explained to others, as well, before any gentleman can consent to meet him."

At this moment a servant entered with the small packet, and gave it to Thornhill who said to Charteris, "Do me the favour of unfolding that paper, I have already seen its contents." The Captain deliberately undid the packet, and somewhat to his surprise discovered, under many folds, a loaded dice broken in two, in a most artistic manner.

"In the scuffle that took place that dice dropped from Sir George's pocket. Unfortunately for Barrington I found it." Here a loud knock announced another visitor – "I sent it this morning to be broken by Lady Marston's jeweller."

"Lord Carlingford," said the servant, throwing open the door, and that gentleman stepped languidly into the room.

"Ah Charteris! I heard you were here, or coming here, and I followed you. Thornhill can't fight him; the thing's impossible." Here the peer threw himself into an arm-chair, and smiled grimly. "I suppose you know all about it?"

"I know it all now," said the Captain, "and have to apologise myself; curse his impudence: to make me a cat's paw in such an affair as this: a cursed-----"

"Swindler, you would say." said Carlingford "You're right: now drive me back to St. James's Street, that's a good fellow, and ......"

"Wait a minute, Lord Carlingford, you don't know it all" – and here Charlie showed the noble lord the loaded dice. "Now, Captain Charteris, I must ask a favour of you. Keep this to yourself: if Sir George Barrington is out of England in four-and-twenty hours, I, for one, will say nothing of his part of the business, and I think I can ask the same of Lord Carlingford, and the men who were with us last night. But if I ever hear of his playing with any man in this country again, it shall follow him into every club-house in London. There's no necessity for further scandal: we are all well out of it. Some of us lost our ready money: he won't be bold enough to present his paper when he knows the terms of this interview." Here Charlie finished his cup of tea; it was the longest consecutive speech he had ever made. He was a man of action rather than of words.

As when a peacock, rejoicing in the sunshine, spreads his tail to the beams, and struts imperiously before the spectator, so had Captain Charteris disported himself on behalf of his friend; but as when some dark and unsuspected cloud dims the lustre of his pride, the same bird drops his feathers, and drags them on the ground, so did the gallant captain retire from the scene of his discomfiture.

In the course of the day Sir George Barrington received the information that he would neither be paid nor shot at, and he took the advice of his friends and left England never to return. In the course of a few days it was all over the west end of London, as the "greatest secret possible, not to be mentioned on any account".

* * * * * *

Some little time after this, when the season was on the wane and people were beginning to make those pleasant little arrangements for the autumn which are to be regarded as a rest from the fatigues of a London summer, Mr. Dacre stood looking on to the dusty leaves and parched flowers of Bryanstone Square, where he had taken a good-sized but moderately expensive house for three months. He was waiting somewhat impatiently for his breakfast, as might be seen by the manner in which he looked at his watch and the plain clock that ticked on the mantelpiece. In a few minutes, however, Mrs Dacre made her appearance and rang the bell for breakfast and as the breakfast appeared, in came Edith, and the three sat down, though two vacant places remained.

"Now, my dear, let me have some tea as soon as possible, for I am going to be busy this morning; I have to see that bay horse which Edward wants for the winter, if he's not too much money."

"I beg your pardon, we are so much later here than at Gilsland; and now that the girls are going out it makes a difference to us all; but I thought you were going to see Lord Tiverton?" said Mrs Dacre

"So I am, after the committee at the House, about the attachéship."

"Lady Tiverton was very gracious last night, and I think if she can do anything for Edward she will."

"She can do nothing in this matter. She manages everybody and everything excepting the foreign policy of this country; and is a most excellent but insincere person as you know, Isabel, as well as I; but where's Alice?"

"Upstairs, papa, dear; she'll be down directly; she's a little tired after the ball." said Edith smiling with that happy glow which is the indescribable result of good health, good humour, and the most becoming morning toilette. "Here she comes, and Teddy too."

Our old friend Teddy Dacre had become a great swell: he had lately passed an examination, in which it was ascertained that he could spell the words "despatch," "Mediterranean," and write a useful sentence, in which a "pedlar" and a "meddler," played a conspicuous part with a "medlar". Also placed before him was a test of the effects of fifteen years of Latin and Greek derivations, Sapphics, alcaics, elegiacs, and Greek iambics. Having passed this ordeal satisfactorily, with the one exception of the spelling of "achievement" he held up his head amongst the butterflies and late grubs who lounged in the Clubs and betted at Tattersall's; who rode on high-stepping hacks in the Park, and on neat ponies at Newmarket; and who spent their days in smoking and idleness. But for Teddy Dacre the fling was nearly over. Lord Tiverton was about to make him an attaché to be sent to Berne in Switzerland.

Alice walked steadily, almost gravely to her father, and kissed his forehead; and then to her mother, to whom she paid the same compliment on the cheek, saying at the same time: "I beg your pardon for being late. I see breakfast is half over but I was tired after the ball."

"How you can ever be tired, Alice dear," said her sister, "I can't think. You have all the best partners, wherever you go, all night long."

"Perhaps that's the reason, Edith," said Mr. Dacre.

"I'm sure I could dance for ever if I could get such men as Alice has."

"Who do you mean, dear?"

"Oh! I don't know if you don't," said the charming girl, and eyes, and mouth, and light-brown hair, and every limb laughed, to the tips of her rosy fingers.

"Who did you dance with, come, tell us, Alice?" said mamma, who, perhaps, had some better reason for asking, than mere curiosity.

Alice put up her head, and smiled only with her eyes. She blushed very slightly. "Well, then, mamma, I danced with Lord Claremont."

"That was kind of him, particularly with so many old women who wanted partners." Mrs Dacre had no mercy.

"Lord Claremont likes me; and he knows I prefer middle-aged men."

"We know you always say so, Alice," said her sister. "Tell us some of the young ones; surely they were not all on the shady side of forty."

"Captain Charteris, Lord Carlingford."

"Carlingford!" said Teddy, "what did he talk about? I like Carlingford."

"So do I; but his conversation was uninteresting rather like your own, Teddy. Then there was Charlie Thornhill."

"He's a misogynist," said Teddy Dacre.

"My goodness, Teddy!" said Edith, "what a dreadful name!"

"A misogynist, Edith, is a woman-hater," said Mr. Dacre.

"Then I'm sure Charlie Thornhill is not that," said Alice, with the slightest possible look at her sister, who didn't bear the scrutiny well.

"Go on with the list, Alice"

"You keep on interrupting one so: then came three or four more: I really can't go through the whole lot of them."

"Wasn't Mr. Tom Thornhill one? I saw him dancing with you, Alice."

"Yes he was;" and after a moment's hesitation, she added, "I like Mr. Thornhill, he's so cheerful, and so very natural."

"Is that uncommon, Alice?"

"Extremely so, sir," said she, turning her handsome eyes on her father. "The men give us but little credit for brains, or are sadly deficient themselves: now you know why I like middle-aged men, papa. Do you know Tom Thornhill?"

"Yes, he's coming this winter for a week to Gilsland from Melton, or wherever his horses are. He wishes to see our side of the country. Where are you going, Edward, today?" said Mr. Dacre.

"To Greenwich, sir, to dinner. The teams are going out, and I am going with Wilson Graves."

"What a pity! It's the Chiswick fête, and Alice and I are going with Lady Elizabeth," said Edith, "there will be nobody there."

"I don't think Wilson Graves is a very good companion for you, Edward," said his father. "I'm told he plays, and very high. I can forgive almost anything but that."

"I don't see how I can get out of it now," said Teddy, who was unable to defend his friend; "I promised to go down. If you do not wish it, I'll not do so again, but there will be no play tonight – certainly not at Greenwich."

"He was said, some years back, to have been the cause of poor Ludlow's death." said Mr. Dacre.

"I never heard that story." said Edward.

"Perhaps not. Fred Ludlow lost a large fortune gambling. He had determined upon leaving England. His passage was taken for one of the colonies. The remains of his once good property was in his banker's hands leaving him £5000 ready for a start in mercantile life. Wilson Graves met him two days before sailing; ate with him, drank with him, and took him to Crockford's: at five o'clock on a summer's morning he walked down the steps having given his last cheque to the croupier, with one sovereign in his pocket. A beggar is said to have held out his hat to him (Wilson Graves tells the story), 'Here's a sovereign, my man; I hope it may be of use to you, it's none to me.' He was found one hour afterwards by his servant in his armchair, having destroyed himself with prussic acid. I would rather follow you to your grave, my boy, than out of a gambling house." For a man of fashion, Mr. Dacre's notions of right and wrong were out of step with many in Society.

Alice listened to her father, on whom she doted. There was an unnatural brightness again in her eyes, but her cheek looked a little sadder and had lost its colour.

Later that day Mr. Dacre looked at the bay horse for his son, and did not think him short enough in the leg for a heavy country; he was also a little hot. He had a satisfactory interview with Lord Tiverton, who had not forgotten his promise. Lord Tiverton feared Berne was not so pleasant as St. Petersburgh, but it was not so cold, and not so expensive. He had heard a charming account of the Misses Dacre from Lady Tiverton, who was enchanted with them, and would leave cards for them on the first opportunity. Mr. Dacre had forgotten gambling and was a happy man.

* * * * * *

The season was drawing towards its close. The ministers were, of necessity, still in Town. But the West End began to look thinner, and Goodwood was approaching. The shrubs and trees in the squares and parks looked drier and dustier than ever. Already a keeper or two had been met, hurrying along Pall Mall towards the railway terminus, leading sundry setters, pointers and retrievers. The whitebait had grown perceptibly larger and nothing remained but a dinner or two at Twickenham or elsewhere, to which everyone was invited. Only one question was ever put to the afternoon lounger, "Where are you going?" and the answer, instead of being to Mrs Furbelow's or the Marchionness of Micklegelt, was invariably, "To Homburg," or "Scotland", "the Tyrol," or "the Italian Lakes". Whole strings of horses were leaving the jobmasters' yards daily. St. George's Church, Hanover Square, was open for wedding services every day, quite a number by special licence, and two or three bishops were seriously affected by the severe demands upon their time. The band was nearly over in Kensington Gardens and the theatres and the opera had long commenced their benefit nights.

In all the bustle of the dog days of that summer, and to Charlie's consternation, his favourite bull terrier, Rosie, had mysteriously disappeared on her way back to Thornhills.

One night late in July as the London season closed, Charlie went to Grosvenor Place, after the last of a series of dinners. "Good night, Charlie," said half a dozen voices, as he jumped down from his carriage, "See you tomorrow?"

"Probably," said he. "Good night."

"That near-side leader would make a hunter." he mused as he stood at his mother's door, watching the retreating team, and smoking the last inch of a very good cigar which he eventually threw into the gutter. He then knocked at the door of the small but very pretty house, whose balcony was adorned with flowers which brought the sweets of the country into London and spoke of a woman's care. When the door was opened, he missed the usual greeting from his bullterrier.

"Is my mother gone up stairs yet, Gregson?" said Charlie to the servant.

"No sir; Mrs Thornhill has not come home yet. She has gone to the Opera."

"Alone?"

"No, sir; Miss Stanhope went with her. She will be home soon, sir; Mrs Thornhill is always early on Saturday night. It's only half-past ten yet, sir."

"Then bring me a light; I'll stroll up and down here until the carriage comes."

Charlie lit another cigar and commenced his walk. A man cannot smoke and walk up and down a space of a couple of hundred yards without thinking: so he began to think. His meditations were not satisfactory. He asked himself who he was? Mr. Thornhill's brother. What he was? An idler in a false position. What had he? Great expectations, which might be disappointed; and many liabilities, which honest men discharge. What could he do? Literally nothing except ride well, shoot partridges and rabbits to perfection, shoot pheasants in cover not so well; drive – certainly; play cricket, tennis and billiards moderately; and – well it must be admitted, fight a little better than common. What did he know? One language – his own, very imperfectly, but enough to make himself understood; very little Latin, very little French, less Greek; multiplication, but was doubtful about long division and vulgar fractions; he knew the situation of a few places in England, and the capitals of France, Austria, Turkey, and Russia; the habits of some birds and animals, especially the dog and the fox: no history beyond the first seven kings of Rome and William Rufus; he could dance an ordinary quadrille, but not the complication of the dance called the Lancers. How did he live? On his mother, his brother, and his friends, who were numerous enough for anything. Had he any good in him? Yes, (and this question he answered hesitatingly) the love he had for Edith Dacre. When he had arrived at this point, and his calculations were becoming less methodical, his mother's carriage drew up at the door.

"Oh, Charlie! Are you come home? I am so glad to see you," said Mrs Thornhill, as she stepped out of the carriage followed by Mary Stanhope, a lady of fifty, commonly known as Aunt Mary by the brothers, but really a first cousin of their mother.

"Come in here, Charlie, I want to talk to you; never mind your cigar; Aunt Mary's used to it."

"Was the opera good, Aunt Mary?" said Charlie, who continued to smoke.

"Very; Grisi sang as well as I ever heard her, and they have a charming bass – what's the man's name? – a German," replied Miss Stanhope, who, though an eccentric of the first water, she had highly cultivated taste, and was fully competent to give an opinion on most things.

"Staudigl?[17]" suggested Charlie.

"Yes; I had never heard him before. What should such a dunce as you know about Staudigl?" said Aunt Mary.

"Cressingham heard him at the Grand Duchess's at Mannheim, some time ago, and said he had the finest voice he ever heard. My friends cultivate the arts for me – it saves trouble."

"Where's Tom tonight?" said Mrs Thornhill; "Is he coming home?"

"He's dining at the Mastodons: he said he should go back to the Albany to sleep tonight, as he had to leave town on Monday."

"Do you see much of Tom, now Charlie?" said the widow of Geoffrey Thornhill, with a sigh, as she thought of a time gone by.

"More than ever; every day."

"Where; at the Dacres?"

"Yes; not infrequently: I generally ride with him at five; I am exercising his black hack for him; besides we often dine together at the club."

"That Miss Dacre was at the Opera," said the widow, not to be shaken off. "What a pretty girl she is: but there's no money."

"I should think they'll marry without that; Miss Dacre is very handsome." said Charlie.

"I don't think it is Miss Dacre that I mean: she's handsome, with a great deal of intellect in her face, and a fine girl; I mean the other one."

---

[17] Josef Staudigl was one of the most famous bass singers of his age. He was greatly admired on the operatic stage, but was even more eminent as an interpreter of Lieder and as an Oratorio singer. Staudigl attended the school in Wiener Neustadt and, from 1825, was a novice in the Benedictine monastry. In 1827 he went to Vienna to study surgery there. On account of poverty he began to do some singing as a subsidiary enterprise, for he had possessed a very beautiful voice since childhood. He was already singing in London in 1842, when he appeared at Covent Garden in the German Company in the first English performance of *Les Huguenot* in the role of Marcel. In 1847 in London he sang at Her Majesty's Theatre.

"That's Edith," said Charlie; "some people think her the prettier of the two."

"So she is and Tom seems to be among them, from what I heard tonight."

"I fancy not, mother." Here Charlie emitted such a volume of smoke that Mrs Thornhill began to cough.

"I beg your pardon; I am sure the smoke is too much for you." And Charlie was making for the door, protesting that he would finish his cigar outside.

"You'd be better in bed, if you're only going to beat about the bush in that way." said Aunt Mary.

"Well then, Charlie, tell me, is there anything between that pretty Edith Dacre and your brother that is likely to lead to an engagement? Everybody talks about it, and I'm told he's always at the house."

"Nothing whatever, my dear mother; so make your mind easy on that score."

"Easy! Ah Charlie, if you knew my anxieties, you wouldn't be surprised at my wishing to see Tom married. And as to Edith Dacre, I could love her like a child of my own."

Mary Stanhope was tired of the conversation, and Charlie was not anxious to prolong it; he had quite enough love of his own on his shoulders, without interesting himself about other people.

CHAPTER 15

IN QUEST OF A DOG

**"One that I brought up off a puppy: one that I saved from drowning,
when three or four of his blind brothers and sisters went to it."**
– *Two Gentlemen of Verona, Act IV, Sc. 3.*

On the Monday after this conversation at about eleven o'clock am, a fine broad-shouldered young man, sitting on a magnificent black hack entered Stanhope Gate, with that charming negligence which speaks of the most perfect command of the animal. His shoulders were well back and squared, his elbows close to his side, his reins held at a tolerable length one in each hand, of both curb and snaffle, giving sufficient play to the horse's mouth without any loss of control. The feet were well home in the stirrups, and the legs easily bent at the knee, fell in a straight line from that to the instep, showing strength and power, as well as grace in every movement. His body swayed easily with the motions of the horse, which, proud of his burden, turned from side to side, occasionally breaking from his stately walk and exhibiting a valuable capability of bending his knee which would have been appreciated by every lover of a good mover. Very few men looked better on horseback than Charlie Thornhill; and though not strictly a handsome man, and certainly not to be compared with his brother, it was impossible to have passed him without admiration.

He was little aware as he rode along how many people were interesting themselves in his affairs. Sir Frederick and Lady Marston had already, that very morning, canvassed his chances of a commission in the cavalry, for which he was not too old, or a clerkship in the treasury, for which he was probably not well qualified. The days of examination had begun; and though not arrived at the pitch of absurdity to which they have since reached, they would certainly have found out Charlie's weak points. The Dacres had taken a great fancy to him and he had renewed his old friendship with Teddy, the boy whose life he had saved: it was not to be forgotten. At the same time, as a mother, Mrs. Dacre could not be blamed for wondering whether she had taken a prudent step in extending her autumn invitation to a younger son with doubtful expectations. She had no such misgivings about Tom: though I doubt whether she liked him the better of the two. His uncle, Henry Thornhill, had many a heartache over the prospects of the boy. And Lord Carlingford wondered much whether Charlie would be able to ride 12st 7lbs in the Aristocratic, for which he had entered a very good and resolute horse, which could race as well as go over fences, if one could but steer him straight.

His broad shoulders were espied in the distance by an early rider like himself; so, as he passed through the Park gate, De Beauvoir cantered up and joined him.

"Confound him," thought Charlie, "Here's one of Edith Dacre's handsome admirers." He had scarcely spoken to him since the Richmond affair. De Beauvoir, for his part, did not dream of a rival, having much too good an opinion of himself: so he touched our hero on the arm, and asked where he was going.

"To Tattersall's," said Charlie.

"So am I, to look at a cover hack for next season," said De Beauvoir.

"And I to sell; I shall ask Tattersall for stalls for the two horses I bought not long ago – I believe they're very good, and can carry a stone or two over my weight. I shall scarcely have time to hunt next season."

At Tattersalls the dandy descended from his horse and left him in the hands of a red-coated retainer at the Corner. "Gad, Thornhill, that's very nearly my own case: what with putting on one's breeches, and one's boots, and – and- galloping to cover, and jogging home again, 'pon my honour it does take up a deal of time."

Lord Carlingford joined them, as Charlie Thornhill left his horse in the hands of a man whose face he did not remember having seen there before. He was a shrewd-looking knave, in a worn-out hunting coat, and miserably clad in other respects; but he saluted Charlie with that ready assurance so indicative of the Emerald Isle, that the "noble captain" found himself with one foot on the pavement and the fellow holding his horse with one hand, and dusting his boots with an old rag with the other. At that moment Lord Carlingford called Charlie by name; the manner so assured a minute before suddenly changed. The obsequious hands trembled, the cunning eyes opened and fixed, and the face became pale and irresolute even to the lips.

"Mind the horse, you fool" said Charlie, "what's the matter? You'll let him go; here send somebody else, Jack; this fellow's afraid of the horse, I do believe," saying which he turned with De Beauvoir and Lord Carlingford to walk down the yard.

Half an hour sufficed to finish the business on which he went. He looked over a horse or two for Lord Carlingford, and gave a candid opinion of the capabilities of De Beauvoir's choice of a hack, which did not please that gentleman. He soon arranged for the sale of his own two horses for the following Monday and was returning when he was accosted by one of Mr. Tattersall's men.

"I beg your pardon, sir, but I think you lost a very valuable bull-terrier, as you set great store by, some time ago?"

"I did; a very valuable one. I should like to have her again."

"Yes sir; well there's a gent here as has got the promise of a pointer dog for the season after next. I think he is on the square, sir.""

"You seem to be up in the dog business, Jack" said Charlie.

"Well, we see a good many curious characters about here; there was one here last week as none on us know'd, was askin' if we know'd anythink about your dawg: I see the man about this morning. They're a rum lot they are, but I think the dog might be got at, sir."

"Was the man an Irishman?"

"Well, he did'nt talk altogether like one," said Jack, whose ear was pretty well accustomed to the brogue: "but he'd a man along with him as was a regular Irisher, I should say."

"Come to the top of the yard with me without saying anything;" and up the yard they went. Having looked stealthily down Grosvenor Place first, he then looked towards Piccadilly, and true enough the man leading the black hack proved to be the identical person in question, and in deep conversation with him was what Jack was pleased to call "the other cove". Charlie walked back to his horse put his hand into his waistcoat pocket, and having rewarded his temporary servant, was about to put his foot in the stirrup when he was accosted by the tall, black whiskered Irishman. After beating a little about the bush, the man freely admitted that he knew who had the bull-terrier. He also stated that it would cost money to get it back: the least he could say would be three pounds.

"Can you guarantee it for that? And how would it be done?"

"Yes, I think it could; but the how was the difficulty. Would you meet me this evening, and go with me to identify the dog, and pay down the money if it was all right?"

Charlie Thornhill hesitated. "Could not the dog be brought to me?"

"No, no; my pal had been done too often in that way. Would you meet me this evening at nine o'clock?"

"Where?"

"Do you know the sign of the "Lively Fleas" in Shoreditch?"

"No ; I don't know Shoreditch itself. However, there will be no difficulty about that."

So the black-whiskered individual, who seemed to affect something of the open and generous, and was not altogether so bad as the general run of these ruffians, gave a very lucid explanation of where the "Lively Fleas" was to be found: he only stipulated that Charlie was to be alone, and to trust him. He would take him where he could see his dog, and as he believed, have her back on posting the money. With this Charlie was obliged to be content and he rode off wondering what sort of a place Shoreditch was at 9 o'clock at night.

Having lunched with his mother and made a few calls, not forgetting the Dacres, who were about to leave town and the Marstons, to whom he imparted his intention of giving up hunting for this winter. He told them he was going only for the first week's shooting to Gilsland instead of to Thornhills; then he went to dine at the Club and prepared for his evening's excursion. The arrangement of his toilet was no easy matter. No hat, coat, or general vagabondism could be found sufficient to disguise his appearance and he gave up the attempt. His servant was summoned and instructed to seek a particular cabman from the top of St. James's Street. Fortunately he was to be found.

"Do you know an inn or public house called the "Lively Fleas," in Shoreditch?" At first the cabman seemed inclined to deny all knowledge of the "Lively Fleas". He shook his head, rolled it from side to side, and leered at Charlie with a very suspicious grin. At last he said, "Well, sir, I can't justly say as I don't."

"Which means that you do. Now, drive me there: and make it as soon after nine as you can."

At first the cab went reluctantly. It was loth to quit the fashionable quarter of the town, but as the streets became thinner and thinner, and the conviction forced itself upon the cabby that his fare was in earnest, he quickened his pace. The City, Fleet Street, Ludgate Hill, Cheapside, all looked gloomy and were beginning to be deserted. Shoreditch was emptied of all but miserable women and a few labouring men. Before reaching the "Lively Fleas" Charlie thought it was desirable to converse with his old acquaintance the cabman. He was a fat, lively fellow, summer and winter in jack-boots, and always with a flower in his button-hole.

"I am going after a dog," said Charlie. "I don't know the company and am inclined to think it's not over respectable. I must go alone with the man who meets me. You know my errand. Wait for me as near the public-house as you can. If I don't return in a reasonable time you'll know what to do. Are there any police about here?"

"Yes, sir, there are police, if they are werry much wanted – for a missing body or so, you know; and I think I knows where to hit upon a bobby, if needs be. But they ain't no ways so handy as in Belgrave Square and your parts, sir; I suppose the coves about here is so werry respectable there ain't no call for 'em. But I'm glad you told me, cos I'm blowed if there ain't some rum kens lower down. Here, sir, you take this," said the charioteer, giving him a railway whistle; "they don't like the sound o' that: and this here too," added he, presenting Charlie with a short life-preserver[18]; "they don't like the feel o' that. There's the "Lively Fleas", sir, as far as ever you can see. So if you like to get out and walk, I'll follow at a distance and wait till I sees

---

[18] Life Preserver – a weighted baton or club.

you again, or don't hear nothin' of yer."

After this very intelligible arrangement Charlie proceeded on foot, and at about one hundred yards from the "Lively Fleas" he was joined by the dark Irishman. "Follow me," said the man, as he turned short to the right, nearly falling over a child in a kennel whom he cursed, and proceeded at a brisk pace through alleys redolent of gin, tobacco smoke and pestilential fever. Charlie followed, mentally comparing his own chance with the stranger in a struggle for life and death, and almost thinking that he had run his head into a noose. But he was a cool, determined fellow, and marked well every house and turning as they passed them. At length they reached a low Elizabethan house, built of wood, with overhanging windows. Here the guide stopped, and pushing open a low door, they found themselves in a passage as dark as

Erebus.

The Irishman closed the door behind them; the ruffian was remarkable for nothing but his handsome, though bitter countenance, and a certain air of command. Behind the door they found themselves in total darkness and George Kildonald, for it was he, began to shout with a very audible voice, and no measured language, demanding a light. As Charlie Thornhill stood in that dark place he could not have known he was following George Kildonald, the very same Gipsy George who was one of his father's murderers.

"Now then, old Mother Skinflint, how long are we to be kept with a glim? What's become of the lamp?" This demand produced an effect. A door in the wall, on the left, half way down the passage, opened and disclosed a head more hideous than anything that Charlie had as yet seen. A scarlet kerchief surmounted a dark brown wig, at this time awry, and settling gradually over one of two eyes as bright and black and piercing as the other was bleared and innocent of vision. The face was sharp and hook-nosed, and the mouth gave visible tokens of the inroads of time. The lamp was held above her head, and as Charlie moved towards the door he had time to note these circumstances of personal appearance. Following his conductor, who steered by the light ahead, he found himself at once in a large but dirty kitchen, where a girl, evidently of gipsy blood, was frying eggs in a large frying-pan, whilest an unconcerned spectator, with a bridle in one hand and a heavy jockey-whip in the other, sat smoking his pipe in the chimney corner. The windows were strongly barred, and an old flint and steel gun, hanging at the roof, seemed the only ostensible means of defence. Opposite the fire, although a warm night in July, lay a ferocious-looking mastiff, active, sullen, and brindled. He showed his teeth at the new arrival, but resumed his couchant attitude at a sign from George Kildonald.

Charlie began to be assured, for though several sentences passed between the woman and Kildonald in a tongue quite incomprehensible to him, still there seemed to be no unfriendly feeling towards the newcomer. The girl, indeed, by a natural instinct, made way for him at the fire, though so warm, and he, by an equally natural instinct, smiled and thanked her as he declined the offered place.

"If you'll let me," said he, "I'll light my cigar." saying which, he took his case from his pocket, selected one with considerable care, and proceeded to smoke whilst waiting for further orders from his mysterious conductor.

"Now, if you please," at last said George Kildonald. "If you'll follow me I'll see what can be done. I suppose that's not the dog?" pointing to the one at the fire. Charlie could not help noticing that the man seldom made a mistake in speaking; and though his manner was utterly without respect for Charlie's condition, and assumed at least an equality with him throughout, he was free from that coarseness of expression or tone which is almost invariable, in one way or the other, with a man of that class. To Charlie, too, he had made use of no slang expression: his conversation with the old woman was evidently a language, and not thieves' *patter*; and he rightly conjectured that he was in a gipsy's London crib. This reassured him again for he reflected that if they were the least scrupulous, they had some redeeming qualities of generosity and courage. His was a race-course experience of that remarkable people. He saw the holiday side of them; and he forgot that if they had a negative feeling of good-will to himself, they were actuated by a positive feeling of regard for dogs and money, and would go to any length to serve their purpose when safe from detection.

At the further end of the kitchen, and away from the front of the house, was another door through this they disappeared, and descending four steps, they made their way, by help of a reflector in the wall, along a second passage of about five-and-twenty feet long to a room apparently detached from the kitchen. Kildonald opened the door which had an ordinary latch and said "Bide here. I'll wait for you in the kitchen."

By the very recent smell of tobacco-smoke the room had been lately occupied, and a rough arm-chair, one of the only pieces of furniture in the room, retained the impression of a sitter. There was a rough, round table heavily marked by stains from pewter ale pots, and a torn copy of "Bell's Life,"[19] some weeks old, had found its way into this den of thieves. The room itself was of a good size, some twenty-five feet by twenty. Over a battered-looking chimney-piece, now unused as a grate, there was a likeness of the celebrated buggy horse "Coventry, the property of Lord Ongley;" and round the room were some villainously-coloured engravings of celebrated pugilists. A set of gloves in one corner bespoke the occupation of leisure hours, and

---

[19] *Bell's Life in London, and Sporting Chronicle* was a British weekly sporting paper published as a pink broadsheet between 1822 and 1886.

some strong staples let into the wall here and there looked as if they were for bear baiting. In fact, it was a convenient place for the commission of iniquities, or for the promotion of sports peculiar to certain classes, and might be the scene of a murder or Sabbath-day's recreation for the neighbours, as the case might be. Charlie was allowed full leisure for the examination of the chamber and for reflections upon his folly in coming to it. He lifted up a dim light, afforded by a bad rushlight in a sconce, and examined the likenesses of Molyneux, Dutch Sam, Sambo Sutton, White-headed Bob, and the aforesaid Coventry. The chair was too dirty to sit down in, and the literary remains too filthy to read. A chorus of dogs, manifestly close at hand, kept breaking upon the ear, and the occasional clanking of a chain accompanied by a deep curse, reminded him of his errand. Surely that was his old favourite Rosie? He went to a barred shutter and listened. Somebody was quieting her, and undoing the chain from a staple in the kennel or wall to which she was fastened. In another minute he heard a smothered conversation: it sounded like a dispute. Then he heard steps of heavy boots, not as if intended for concealment, and immediately after a heavy door, which was on the opposite side of the room from that by which Charlie had entered, opened slowly, and another man made his appearance, leaving the door partially open, however, as though for communication, or more comers. As he advanced into the room Charlie saw a face which had gipsy blood stamped on it, with the peculiar fire of the eyes of that people. It had none of their beauty, for the other natural lineaments of the face were disfigured, swollen, and flattened by the exercise of the calling to which he manifestly belonged – that of a fighter. He was a hard-set man of about thirty-five, and had lost some of the activity and wire of youth. In his best days, science being equal, he would not have been a match for Charlie. He had neither his reach nor size across the chest, his length of limb, nor fine clean hips, indicative of activity. The measurement Charlie took of him was satisfactory, as the two men eyed one another – tolerably good specimens of their class, but the gentleman, physically, bearing the bell.

After a silence of about a minute, the man addressed him.

"You're come about a dog?"

"I am," said Charlie Thornhill.

"What sort do you want?"

"A white bull bitch, very handsome, and highly bred – almost thorough-bred, but with a greyhound mouth. She answers to the name of Rosie."

"I daresay she do. Leastways, I haven't tried her. We don't know anything about names here. You call her what you please. We've got a very nice 'un."

"Can I see her?" said Charlie, re-lighting his cigar, which he had allowed to go out.

"Oh! Yes, certainly; She's a very nice 'un, mind ye; she's a gentleman's dawg all over;" which was equivalent to admitting that she belonged to no one in Shoreditch, at all events. "Here, Bill," said he shouting through the door, "bring in the little bitch, you know, as we got from the sporting baker in Whitechapel."

Bill was not long in responding. A chain was heard, and in rushed Rosie, dragging Bill after her, making her way at once to Charlie Thornhill with every demonstration of satisfaction. Bill handed the chain to the gipsy and withdrew.

"Rosie, Rosie; down Rosie; be quiet, good bitch, down," said he. And she stood looking up at her master with every limb like alabaster.

"Well! I suppose you're convinced she's my dog?" said Charlie.

"We never asks any questions about whose dog she is, when she comes into our hands. We supposes as wants to buy a dog like this 'un here," said the man, quietly leading her away and fastening her by her chain to a staple in the wall at the other end of the room. "We'd as lief sell her to you as to any one else."

This was putting a virtuous aspect on a nefarious transaction: clothing poverty in fine linen with a vengeance. However, that was their look-out, and Charlie saw nothing very much to object to in this flimsy veil of honesty. The sight of the dog, too, had sharpened his affection for her, so he replied very simply – "Then I should like to buy the bitch. I am given to understand that three pounds – "

"Three pounds? Lore! There's hundreds as 'd give twenty. You can't buy a hanimal like this here for twice three pounds, not if she wur stole."

Charlie was losing patience. "Damn your impudence! Why, she *was* stolen. She belongs to me, I tell you. What do you suppose I came here for: to buy my own property again at its full value?"

"I don't know anything about that," said the man, sulkily, "but I ain't a going to part with that dog under twice three pounds; so if you ain't a mind to give more, there's an end to the deal."

During the whole of this time Rosie kept on whining significantly, standing at the full length of her chain, and straining her eyes and limbs in the direction of Charlie. He was becoming more determined than ever to repossess himself of his property, and the impudence of the robbery added fuel to the flame.

"Then you don't mean to give me back my dog?"

"I don't mean to sell this here bitch for less than six pounds."

"There are three sovereigns," and Charlie placed them in the palm of his hand, where they glittered temptingly in the surrounding gloom.

"They're no use: put 'em up again; why the collar's pretty nigh worth the money," and he pointed to a handsomely-worked steel collar.

"Why! You infernal scoundrel, there's my own name on it! I insist upon having the dog," saying which, with a firmly-closed lip, and a heavy determined step, Charlie moved towards the dog. But the gipsy anticipated his movement, and was there before him.

"Stand on one side." The man put himself into a posture of defence, and struck rapidly out; but Charlie stopped the blow with his left arm, and closed with him at once. Up to that moment Rosie had been quiet enough with the instinct peculiar to all the bull-dog kind, she no sooner heard the shuffling of feet, than her whole nature changed. She sprang violently to the length of her chain; she strained every muscle in her endeavours to free herself; her mouth foamed, her prominent eyes became bloodshot and her short bark changed into a prolonged and fearful yell. The chain almost yielded to her efforts, as she fell back at each bound in her frantic struggles. Charlie in the mean time had seized the neckcloth of his antagonist with his left hand, and the left wrist with his right hand. The struggle would not have been long, had they been left to themselves; already he was dragging the man towards the dog, who would soon have declared for her master, then he saw the gipsy's disengaged hand descend rapidly into his shooting-coat pocket and reappear with a glistening knife. Nothing remained to be done but to release his throat and get possession of the other hand. In a moment he had done so; but in that moment the man sent forth a shout for help, to which the hurry of steps told of a response. At the same instant, changing his right hand from the wrist to the throat, and placing his leg rapidly behind the man, Charlie threw him on to his back, his head within reach of Rosie. The dog seized him by the throat, whilst the frantic efforts of the gipsy were unavailing to free himself from the powerful grip of our hero. Charlie dared not let go. The life of his dog would have been forfeit. Easing himself, therefore, he placed his knee upon the fallen man's chest, bent upon forcing the weapon from him, when with a loud bang the door flew open, and he was seized by the collar from behind. Matters looked serious; Charlie remembered his whistle, and his life preserver. Relaxing his hold of the throat, and resisting the violent efforts that were being made to disengage him from behind, he dragged them from the side pocket of the old coat with which he had endeavoured to conceal his respectability. One shrill blast of the whistle which startled both his assailants for a second, and one gentle blow on the arm above the wrist with the weighted life preserver and the armed limb dropped as though it had been broken.

Charlie, still on his knees, turned upon the ruffian who held him from behind, and at the same moment George Kildonald and the old woman appeared upon the stage from the other door. "Hold hard," said he in a voice of authority, which so paralyzed the powerful fellow who still grappled with Charlie, that he was able to rise from his knees. As the only truly dangerous member of the group was still under the fangs of the dog, the affray was almost terminated. Fear kept the prisoner quiet. Kildonald approached the dog and was met with a low growl.

"Call off the dog, in God's name!"

"That's not so easy to do; besides which, your comrade still has one good arm at liberty, and a drawn knife by his side; one arm is disabled and if he moves the other," said Charlie, "I can't be answerable for the consequences. The quieter he lies the better for him." With that he picked up the knife. The old woman went to the fallen man.

"What, Giles, not blood enough yet?" Giles held his tongue, almost his breath. Rosie showed no inclination to let go.

"Call off the dog, if you can do so. Lie still, Giles," said the black-haired son of a gipsy girl and Arthur Kildonald, who had a curious expression of sadness stealing over his handsome features. Charlie went to Rosie and loosed the chain. With a few words he soothed the dog, which after a low growl or two retired to his heels, and the fallen man got to his feet.

"There, Giles, take your three sovereigns and let him have his dog; give him the three sovereigns, Thornhill, Now see him safe through the kitchen, mother. I owe him a life and I pay it." To Charlie he added " Take your dog, and be gone. Do you know your way?"

"Am I safe?" said Charlie, who began to realize the dangers of his exploit, as he handed over the three sovereigns.

"Yes; and if you're stopped before you get into the main street the sign is 'Cast off.' You're a gentleman – promise on your word of honour not to betray us. Your dog is safe from us for the future."

"I do promise;" and having leisurely brushed his hat with his sleeve, and shaken the dust from his clothes, Charlie followed the old woman, with Rosie at his heels, from the scene of his recent struggle. Once outside the felon's haunt, he traversed the alleys with rapid strides, doubtful whether, when he regained the street, he should find his cab. He was not long in uncertainty; he was still some hundred yards from the "Lively Fleas," which seemed to have a roaring trade, when he met his cab, coming slowly towards him. The man recognised him in an instant; he jumped in without a word, followed by the dog, and about five-and-forty minutes or something more saw him at the top of Grosvenor Place. It was now eleven o'clock, and having paid his charioteer handsomely and returned him his property, he strolled quietly down to his mother's door reflecting on his mysterious black haired guide's remark "I owe him a life and I pay it." He wondered what it meant.

CHAPTER 16

THE END OF THE SEASON

"Fire that is closest kept, burns most of all."
Two Gentlemen of Verona

"Where are you going, Charlie? I hear you have given orders for packing up; is it to Scotland?" said Mrs Thornhill on the morning following Charlie's desperate adventure. Circumstances made him look grave and Mary Stanhope was fond of thinking that he did not take sufficient care of himself. They were two devoted women; and the large black eyes and sallow skin of Aunt Mary concealed a whole ocean of love for the brothers, which was always overflowing in one way or another, sometimes in praise, as often in censure.
"No, my dear mother; but if you will have me for a month at Thornhills soon, I should like to go down. I've nothing between that and the Rhine, until September," said her son. "I am going to Bognor for the Goodwood week; Tom's already gone."
"And where do you go in September? I thought the shooting at Thornhills was good enough to tempt any one."
"To the Dacres: Tom won't be at home; he never begins till nearly

the middle of the month, and then the house will be full."

"I thought you liked a full house."

"So he does, Emily," said Aunt Mary, "but he's going to look after Tom's interests. There are two sisters you know, Charlie, and I prefer the eldest myself; so take care of yourself. When do the Dacres leave town?"

"Tomorrow. You're inquisitive, Aunt Mary."

"Sign of an inquiring mind, Charlie; you've no curiosity, and that's why you are so idle."

"I never trouble myself about other people's business."

"Thank you, Charlie – I do; and it's very fortunate for you and your dear mother that I have the taste for it; I don't know what would become of you all. So now tell me, where are the Dacres going? To Gilsland?"

"No, to some people near Chichester for Goodwood, called the Robinson Browns."

"Do you know who the Robinson Browns are, Charlie?"

"No, thank goodness; but probably you do, Aunt Mary."

"Yes, I do know something about them; I wonder a man like Mr Dacre should take his wife and daughters there. Robinson Brown indeed! What a name it is."

"It's a very good name in its way. He's not a Stanhope; but he has large houses, fine horses, magnificent plate, loads of ready money, and a large establishment," said Charlie, with a sinister smile.

"And large daughters and plenty of them," added Mary Stanhope, with considerable energy, "whom Mrs Robinson Brown wishes to marry to the best men in town. Do you call that reputable, Charlie?"

"Well! It's the way of the world."

"I hope your wife won't do so, whenever you have one. Your mother, poor thing, is saved from the temptation. I shouldn't have been much use to her here." And, true enough, she would not. Your average matchmaker wants a very peculiar combination of qualities – a mind capable of well-disguised dissimulation and an innocent simplicity of character which would have gladdened the heart of the great Lord Shaftesbury.

Mary Stanhope was a prejudiced old woman. There was no harm in Mrs Robinson Brown and her daughters. Her misfortune was that she did not come from a good family but she had the revenues of a duchess, or she might have pursued her schemes without society noticing. Besides her daughters, however, whom she was determined to marry off well, she had a son who had made up his mind to be guided by nothing but taste in the choice of a wife. This young gentleman had hit upon Edith Dacre as combining all advantages but one, that of money, and he proposed to remedy that deficiency himself. Hence the pressing invitation to the Dacres to join their Goodwood party; and as they were people who went everywhere, and knew everybody, there seemed no difficulty in accepting.

Anybody at all versed in old-maidenism will see with half an eye that Mary Stanhope – and I call her so, for I never heard her called Miss Stanhope by any one but the servants – was as good a soul as ever lived. She had that little vice which, on certain occasions, exalts itself into a virtue and, which we have already noticed, curiosity; but her motives were so good that nobody who knew her ever called her inquisitions into question.

The day before Charlie's departure for Bognor, she sat for some time evidently big with thought, and plied her knitting, the only work she condescended to engage in – fine, strong, warm, Welsh-woollen socks for her boys for the shooting season.

"Charlie, do you know a man I can depend upon to do a commission for me?" said the lady.

"Very few; but it depends upon what it is. Shall I do?" said the gentleman.

"No, not you; you know I never ask irrelevant questions. Is your friend the Honourable William Russell still in town?"

"I believe he is; why?"

"Well! I like the look of him better that De Beauvoir or Mr Dacre."

"De Beauvoir's an ass; Teddy's not a bad fellow, but scarcely to be depended upon for business. Won't the family lawyer, old Mr Sharpus, do?"

"Certainly not; he's no better than I am myself – an honest old woman."

"Then it must be little Billy Russell. If I can find him at the club this morning I'll bring him here. Aunt Mary, you're a regular Œdipus[20]."

"If Lady Elizabeth heard that, she'd say *you* were no conjuror; Sphinx, I suppose you mean; you're the Œdipus, you know."

"Ah, well! Good morning; I never was much of a hand at that sort of thing; I'll bring Russell back to lunch."

No sooner was Charlie Thornhill gone than Mary Stanhope was once more interrupted. Fortunately, knitting is not like the throes of composition, and will bear interruption. Mrs Thornhill opened the door and occupied her younger son's vacant seat. As she had the "Times" in her hand, you may be quite sure she came for conversation. Whenever I see a person seize the newspaper and

---

[20] **SPHINX :** A monster of Greek mythology with the face of a woman, the body of a lion, and the wings of a bird. She propounded a riddle and devoured those young men who could not answer it. The most familiar version of this riddle, is as follows: What walks on four legs in the morning, on two at midday, on three in the evening? When Œdipus gave the correct answer (man, who crawls as an infant, walks upright as an adult, and uses a staff in old age) the Sphinx killed herself in chagrin.
ŒDIPUS. In Greek mythology he was the son of Laius and Jocasta who had been brought up by shepherds since he was a baby. When he was grown a Delphic oracle warned Œdipus that he would kill his father and marry his mother. Avoiding Corinth in horror, he met Laius on the road and, not knowing him, killed him in an argument. He proceeded to Thebes which was then being ravaged by the Sphinx. After the Sphinx had killed herself when Œdipus answered her riddle correctly, he was offered the throne of Thebes and the hand of Jocasta. Later an old shepherd revealed to Jocasta that Œdipus was her son who she had not seen since he was a baby, and she committed suicide, while Œdipus blinded himself with her broach.

retire doggedly to a distant arm-chair, or to his own room, I know he or she means reading; but when I see them come into a room, already occupied, from another part of the house, newspaper in hand, I always assume that they mean talking, and prepare myself accordingly. A large sheet like the "Times" covers a multitude of sins.

"Mary," said Mrs Thornhill, spreading the paper upside down, and staring silently at it so as to hide her face, "What's the matter with Charlie?"

"Nothing at all, my dear, that I can see; he looks well enough."

"Oh! Yes; but he talks of reading for some examination, either for the army or for some government appointment; and he has ordered his horses to be sold. I'm sure he'll make himself ill."

"The most useful thing he has done, my dear, for years. Don't be at all alarmed about Charlie." Miss Stanhope liked nobody to spoil him but herself. "I thought it was Tom you came to talk about." This was a fib but certain authorities have dealt very leniently with this vice so that lying, upon occasion, becomes almost commendable.

"Tom! Oh no, poor dear Tom," said the widow, with one of her sweetest smiles, and a not very deep sigh, "he has but one fault."

"Yes; and that one leads to everything bad, and will end in utter ruin. Speak to him about his play before it's too late, Emily."

"*I* speak to Tom about his gambling!"

"Yes, you; who so fit as a mother? If he won't attend to you, do you think he will pay attention to me?"

"I'm sure he would," said the poor weak woman, "He's so affectionate. Oh! If he would but marry." Mrs Thornhill believed matrimony to be a sort of magic – a Morrison's pill-box[21] which any young lady could believe in and be sweetened by her son.

---

21   Mechanically operated wooden vase which accommodates a red wooden ball 1" in diameter. Removed from the vase, the ball vanishes, only to reappear inside.

"And who would you like him to marry?" Mary Stanhope, you see, had never learnt the Latin grammar. "There's Julia Brown Smith – oh! Robinson Brown, is it? Well, I'm always making mistakes about names, Emily, I know; but I can't help it. She's just as extravagant as he is, and hasn't half his sense. Then there's Lady Caroline Lambkin; a sick wife to nurse: he'd become more selfish than ever."

"I'm sure he's not selfish, Mary; he's the most liberal, kind-hearted, generous ...."

"Yes, dear, but not self-denying; and there's a great deal of difference between the two."

It is astonishing how sensibly Mary Stanhope could talk, and how foolishly she could act, upon occasion. She had petted and spoiled Tom; had given him all she could scrape together out of her own privy purse; had encouraged his extravagance at Eton, and had never contradicted him, except in trifles, and then only out of opposition. When a boy, she had bought him cigars, which he was forbidden to smoke; she sent him money to pay his childish debts of honour, when his father had refused; and then Tom, in the end, usually got both. Even now, if anybody but herself had suggested that he required correction, she would have put herself into a violent ill-humour, and refused to believe one word to his prejudice.

"Then there's that Miss Dacre, the pretty one, that we see everywhere."

"Well, now, Mary, what do you think of her? He's going there this season."

"Oh! She's well enough; her sister Edith is worth a dozen of her; the one that came to the Chiswick Fete with Lady Elizabeth what's her name? An antediluvian sort of name."

"Mastodon, Mary; that's the name. If he'd only fall in love with somebody, I should be satisfied. As to Charlie, there are no hopes of him." said Charlie's mother.

"That's a comfort; he'd better learn to keep himself before he thinks of a wife. He'll fall in love quite soon enough for his own good, and somebody else's too." Miss Stanhope chose to consider that she had had a disappointment early in life.

All good things come round at last, and of course luncheon-time with everything else. One of the accidents of luncheon today was the arrival of the Hon. William Russell, who, contrary to his wont – such is the force of example – ate a cutlet, some plum-pudding fried in slices, orange cream, a slice of cake, and finished with no end of brown sherry. I have no doubt it was all distasteful to him, but every man does it when he has nothing else to do. What gormandizers two-thirds of the men in London ought to be, say you; *au contraire*, their minds are so occupied with what they shall eat for dinner, that they can scarcely be said to be unemployed.

At length the last vestige of the meal was removed, and when the ladies ought to have gone upstairs Miss Stanhope remained behind. Russell had received orders, and lingered about the door, which Charlie deliberately shut in his face.

"Mr Russell," said Aunt Mary, not having the slightest idea that she bored the man to death, "I want you to do a commission for me; I cannot do it for myself, and when I say horseflesh is concerned, you will understand that I am in a dilemma, or something of that sort you call it."

Mr. Russell suggested "A fix?"

"Of course, that's what I meant to say, 'a regular fix'. You know Charlie has taken to reading, and I'm sure it will injure his health, so I ..."

"Permit me, Miss Stanhope," said Russell, "Charlie has not taken to reading, and I don't think he will injure his health."

"Do you know that his horses are to be sold?"

"Yes, Miss Stanhope, next Monday – one's a beauty."

"Is that his favourite?"

"Yes, it is: I don't know the price put upon the horse, but I should have thought twice about selling him."

"Will you buy him, Mr Russell?" said Miss Stanhope, eagerly.

"Well, that's not precisely the same thing, you know. A man may not be obliged to part with what he has, though he may not be in a position to buy what he'd like to have. No, I can't buy him."

"Could you buy him for a friend without letting Charles Thornhill know anything about it?" said Miss Stanhope, again.

"Yes," said Russell, dragging out his words deliberately, "I could do so, of course: but he would know some time or other who had bought the horse; he's too good an animal, Miss Stanhope, to be kept under a bushel."

"Under a good many bushels," said the lady, who was very matter of fact, and whose head was running upon the corn-bin; "but could you buy him for a friend, at a fair price, without letting Charlie know?"

"I must, in fact, buy him in my own name; that's easy enough."

"Do as you please about that; but I wish to buy him. Will you do this commission for me?" It was out at last.

"Certainly, I will ascertain the reserved price, and see what can be done to get him for you at as little money as possible."

"Don't do that, Charlie will get the sale money; don't let him lose a shilling by the transaction, whatever you do. Only let me be the purchaser; and, though I am a very economical person, I shouldn't like the horse to go into any other hands. I really feel exceedingly obliged to you, Mr Russell."

"All right, Miss Stanhope, your commission shall be done; shall I send him to your London stables or to Thornhills?"

"Oh! To Thornhills, if you please," said Miss Stanhope. "We shall be gone from here in another week at the latest; if I give you a blank cheque signed to fill up..."

"No, no, Miss Stanhope; that's too great a temptation: wait till you have the horse, or know that you are to have him: I'll arrange the cheque, and let you know the price in good time." After a few minutes more of unimportant conversation, the Honourable William took his leave.

* * * * * *

Of all the race-courses in England, there's nothing like Goodwood; and of all the empty-headed idiots that were to be found there at the end of July, 1854, there was no one equal to Mr Robinson Brown, junior. As usual, all the world was to be there. I mean, of course, the few thousands of happy mortals who put in a claim for that distinction. Out of that world there could have been no existence for Mr John Robinson Brown; or as he was more commonly known in his regiment, "dear Jane," or the "Heir Apparent," the latter sobriquet having been obtained from the preposterous exhibition of jewellery upon his person.

How he came to be Robinson Brown is simple enough. The Robinsons were respectable miners; that is, the grandfather and grand-uncles of "dear Jane." They amassed wealth by wholesome toil, unvarying honesty, an intelligence superior to their *confréres*, and undeviating luck. From excavating the ground when soft, and from blasting it when hard, from the pick and the borer, they raised themselves gradually, at a time when some mechanical knowledge was exceedingly valuable. They became tenants in fee simple of some land which proved considerably more productive beneath its surface than upon it, and the wealth of the three brothers centred at length on the only heir, the father of Mr John Robinson Brown.

The Heir Apparent's father Mr Robinson was one of the hardest, richest and vulgarest men alive. He was essentially a man of a vulgar mind. His wealth had brought him education at Harrow and Oxford, his incapability for the ordinary accomplishments of a country gentleman had given him his only redeeming qualification, a fondness for books; not poor men's books, but expensive medieval manuscripts, and richly-bound rarities, which could excite the appetite of the truly learned or the hereditarily noble.

As a young man, he married – not a woman, but money. Miss Brown, of Manchester, was undistinguished save as the niece of the richest of cotton-spinners; he was a good man, a clever man, but proud of the name and honest industry by which civic honours, wealth, and reputation had belonged to three generations of Browns. When he died he left his fortune, to his niece's husband, upon condition that he added the name of Brown to Robinson. It would have been better had it been Howard or Neville; but he went to bed one night Robinson, with five hundred thousand, and rose the next morning Brown, with a million of money to his name. Robinson Brown *père* had since then cultivated the peerage; and he loved a lord not for the good he did, but for what he was. His house was full of them now and amongst his favoured guests came the Dacres. He had seen, perhaps, his own mistake in wedding a Miss Brown of Manchester and he was anxious to remedy the defect in his son. His pride of purse was so great that he rather preferred a portionless girl to whose dazzled senses the brightness of his money might be more apparent. So he held divers conversations with Mrs Robinson Brown, who pumped her son very satisfactorily, and it seemed to be a settled affair between father, mother, and son, that the latter should endow one of the Misses Dacre of Gilsland with the ample resources but inane stupidity of a Robinson Brown.

Under the aforesaid trees in Goodwood there was, amongst other gay and happy parties, a circle as gay and as happy as any. Robinson Brown, to do him justice, had given every facility to his guests for enjoying themselves. All that excellent cookery, and the best champagne, well iced, could do, had been done. The weather, too, was propitious; and some of his friends had won a good stake or two. The selection of women did Mrs Robinson Brown great credit. They were very good-looking, *distinguées,* and had been got together without any of that jealousy which would have excluded rivalry to the Brown girls. Alice and Edith Dacre looked positively lovely. Tom Thornhill had just come back to the Stand and was receiving the congratulations of his friends on having won a good handicap. Charlie was seated on a drag[22] just outside the rails of the lawn and dividing his attention, between cold pie and champagne and the Robinson Brown party when an acquaintance sauntered up to him.

"Charlie, who's that talking to Dacre's sister, with lots of harness ... jewellery, I mean: the man with lank whiskers, and looking generally washed out?"

"Don't you know? Why the biggest fool in England – Robinson Brown."

"Don't say so? That's the 'Heir Apparent' is it? He's a very good-looking one."

"Oh! Come, nonsense, Truffles, you know better than that."

"And there's your brother Tom talking to the other Miss Dacre. What a pity they have no money. Had your brother backed his filly for anything?"

"Thornhill," said a jovial-looking young man, from the wheel of the drag, "come into the Stand a minute, that's a good fellow."

"What is it?" said Charlie, lighting a cigar at the same moment.

"They're talking about a match between one of your brother's hunters and a horse of 'dear Jane's;' they want to know if you'll ride,

---

[22] The **park drag** carriage was a lighter, more elegant version of the road coach park drag (or simply **drag**) was also known as a "private coach" and was owned by private individuals for their own personal driving. A park drag had seats on its top and was usually driven to a team of four well-matched carriage horses.

so do come down."

Charlie had been vacillating for some time between a little fit of the sulks and his wish to join the party with whom his brother was now talking. He slowly descended from the drag, stood ten minutes smoking and talking to Truffles and finally threw away his cigar and strode towards the Stand. With half a dozen nods to the men who he knew, and a cheerful five minutes' chat with Lady Marston, whom he met on the way, he joined the happy group.

"We have a match on between your brother's brown horse and Robinson Brown's mare, Reluctance, 12 stone, to be run in November, in Leicestershire or Northamptonshire. Will you ride?" Charlie hesitated.

"Do, Mr Thornhill, I shall back your brother, if you will ride for him," said Alice Dacre; still Charlie hesitated: he wanted a word or a look from Edith. He did not quite understand why he did not get it. She had shaken hands with him and was now apparently listening to the platitudes of Robinson Brown.

"Oh! I'm so glad you like steeple-chasing, Miss Edith, it is so delightful: so much ... aw ... aw ... fresh air and that sort of thing, you know."

"Dangerous, I think," said Mrs Brown.

"Cruel, I fear," said the oldest Miss Brown.

"Do you think it dangerous, Miss Edith?" asked Robinson Brown "Of course, you know, naturally ...aw ...aw ... I mean ... aw ... post and wails, and hairwy ditches, and that sort of thing. But ..."

"Some people's heads are thick enough for anything. I should think there was no harm in your riding, Mr Brown." said Edith. Here everybody laughed excepting Brown, who did not seem to know at what they were laughing.

"Oh, no! Besides I've widen before, Miss Dacre, and it's quite delightful. Did I win? No, no! I didn't win. I got into the bwook, you know. I got vewy wet; of course I was wet, you know."

"But some people are not born to be drowned, Mr Brown." said Edith and another cheerful roar greeted this second sally. "And what did you do in the brook?"

"Oh! I stood there and wung..."

"Your hands, I presume," said Lady Elizabeth.

"No, my pocket-handkerchief; it was so vewy uncomfortable; and then the man to whom the horse belonged, a howwid Colonel Somebody, came down and abused me for not winning: he said if I'd only holloed at him, he'd have jumped it like ... like anything. But I'd lost all my bweath by the time we came to the water, so of course I couldn't hollo. You know, Miss Dacre, a fellow couldn't hollo without any bweath could he?"

"Do you intend to ride your brother's horse," said Edith, turning suddenly round upon Charlie Thornhill. "Is he a very good horse? They all think he can win, if you ride him."

Charlie smiled, a happy, pleased smile: it was all he wanted and said: "Yes, he is a capital horse; he doesn't know how to fall. You had better back him; I think I shall win." The last was said *sotto voce*.

"I will back him, and I hope you may." She nodded her head gaily at the same time and turned to speak to one of the Misses Robinson Brown, who were paying her marked attention.

In the meantime Tom Thornhill had been receiving the congratulations of his friends. He ought to have been a happy man, but he was not. There was one voice for which he began to care too much, and that had not joined in the general expression of congratulations. Alice Dacre looked grave and held her peace. Love's eyes are prophetic of danger. She turned to Charlie, and said, "Your brother has won a good deal of money, has he not?"

"I believe so, but I never ask about his betting." Charlie was always communicative to Alice Dacre.

"Did you bet on the filly he ran?"

"No, Miss Dacre; I never bet, excepting a mere trifle. You know I can't afford it."

"Nobody can afford it, at least if reputation is of any value." Alice Dacre joined to a naturally acute and very truthful mind a great dislike to unequal associations for those she liked; and she heard and saw too much of the evils of the fashion for playing for high stakes to shut her eyes to its results. But what was it to her if Tom Thornhill ruined himself body and soul? She had no power to avert it.

CHAPTER 17

OLD ACQUAINTANCE

"Time is the old justice that examines all offenders."
'As You Like It'

A few months after the scene at Goodwood, Tom Thornhill had made further inroads into his fortune, but was as cheerful and happy as ever. John Robinson Brown was beginning to speculate on the chances of his success with Edith Dacre and was fearful of the match between Reluctance and the brown horse. Alice Dacre had had practice in steeling her heart against a gambler, and found how difficult it was to do so while Edith had had time to weigh the value of Mr Robinson Brown's acres against the most honest but least-confident love that could be offered her; and Charlie himself, finding out the real state of his heart and pocket, had made up his mind that if toil could win what he most desired on earth, then toil he must.

It was at this same time that Mr Burke sat patiently in the back office of a house in the principal street of the city of Cork. Pleasant images passed through his brain. He was prosperous, respected, unsuspected, had a good digestion, and suffered less from conscientious pangs than most men. He had thriven immensely since the perpetration of his great rascality. He had possessed himself of the title deeds of the little estate belonging to Kildonald; he had safe in his custody the receipt for the few thousands of purchase money for that estate which he had been about to send to poor Geoffrey Thornhill, whose fatal accident, however, had thus enriched him. He now sat happy in apparent prosperity, and in the respect of all good men and some very bad ones.

His office door opened, a shock-headed Irish clerk appeared with a pen behind his ear and a sheet of half-copied parchment in his hand.

"Here's someone to see you Misther Burke."

"What is his business?" said Mr Burke.

"It isn't conveyancing, I'll go bail, nor to buy the Ballymooney estate."

"What's he like?"

"Faith, he's no beauty then; but some of us is none the worse for that." Here Phelim, the clerk, stroked his own chin, which would have been the better for a razor.

"Send him in and be in the way, Phelim," and the respectable Mr Burke put on his most respectable look. It was rather thrown away upon the figure that now entered the room.

A sturdy-looking countryman in a frieze[23] coat, drab hat, gaiters, a black or dark brown wig, and large whiskers of the same colour, stood in the doorway and looked stealthily round. "May I come in?" said he, and without waiting reply, he turned the lock of the door and began divesting himself of his wig and whiskers. Having done so, he appeared to have light-coloured hair and red whiskers of no great size; the change brought Burke to his feet with a look of horror.

"In God's name, Mike Daly, where do you come from? Do you know your danger, man?"

---

[23] Freize is a coarse, shaggy woollen fabric with a long nap.

"No man better, Mr Burke, leastways if it's not yourself. It's a bad boat we've been sailing in," said Geoffrey Thornhill's murderer with a cunning leer.

"Nonsense," rejoined Burke, still standing and with his very lips of an ashen paleness. "Nonsense, Mike; what, in Heaven's name, brought you here?"

"Want, and a good will, sir. Money we must have, and will have."

"We! What's he doing here? George Kildonald, I suppose you mean?"

"Yes, George. We've been in London this six months, living, till I at least can live no longer, on what we can get. We must have money."

"Money! Silence, Mike! Do you know that I could hang you?"

"Maybe; but two can play at that; I think I could hang you. You've most to lose, Mr Burke. Consider what I say. Five hundred pounds down and we leave the country."

"You have done so once, and here you are back again. Besides, George will not go."

"I think he will; he doesn't like the ould country; there's no play for poor men."

"Where is he?" said Burke, knitting his brow and his fingers pressing his underlip.

"In London but will never stop in England; the climate don't suit him. Besides, you owe us the money, Mr Burke, and we want it."

"Want it indeed! So do many more; but what of Arthur Kildonald?"

"He's shot his last bolt and lost; I don't think he can rise again."

"If he does, it's only to go down again. Have you seen the "Hue and Cry?[24] You are not safe here for a day."

---

[24] In 1786 Sir Samson Wright, converted the *Weekly Pursuit,* a police newsletter informing the public of felonies and crimes, into more of a newspaper entitled *Public Hue and Cry*. By 1795 the title had changed again to *The Hue and Cry and Police Gazette* by this time the periodical was published every Saturday and was publicly

"Then give me the money; it's mine."

"Five hundred pounds! Where's it to come from?" asked Burke.

"We've nothing to do with that. We'll take care of where it goes to. We'll be drinking your honour's health before the month's past." As Mike rose in spirits, Burke rose in temper. Burke was not constitutionally brave, but circumstances made him so; and it was clear to him that vacillation with a man like Mike Daly was worse than useless, it was dangerous. Apparently while hesitating as to his answer, he tore one half of a sheet of paper, and going to the door, unlocked it.

"Phelim" said he, "get me a shilling stamp." In a few minutes he again opened the door, during which time Mike had again put on his disguise. His clerk presented him with the stamp.

"Now," said Burke, "this is a mere acknowledgement of a debt of £100 for which I can sue you the moment you are known to be in this country; such a transaction need compromise neither of us. Sign your name to that. Nay! Don't hesitate, Mike, for I can't afford to be robbed as often as you please for the eventual satisfaction of seeing you hanged."

"A hundred pounds!" laughed Mike; "nonsense, Misther Burke, the thing's impossible."

Burke took the key from the door and put it in his pocket. This was no place for a trial of strength, nor was Mike Daly's position well fitted for the encounter. The relinquishment of £400 gave him pain, but what was to be done? Burke stepped back to a small and unobtrusive cabinet, well secured with a lock, and opened it. When he turned round again he held a pistol in his hand. Mike's reliance had been in his moral strength. Now it wouldn't do.

"You have said that you and I sail in the same boat; I believe it, and I will not trust you. Sign that paper, take your cheque, and never let

---

available at the price of 3d.

me see you here again."

Mike looked at the pistol. "What will George say?"

"Never you mind what George will say. Sign the paper and when you set foot on Irish soil again, it shall go into the hands of the tipstaff, if needful. I would as soon be hanged in your company as live in the atmosphere of the canting hypocrites who surround us."

Mechanically then Mike Daly signed it. The pistol and the paper, with sundry other valuable documents were consigned to the strong chest again (a movement not overlooked by the astute client), and Mike went off to divide his spoil.

Two nights afterwards an entrance was effected into Burke's offices and before the police could arrive the offices had been ransacked and the cabinet had yielded up its treasures. Among other things taken, there was the receipt for £4000 which Geoffrey Thornhill had paid for the Kildonald estate which should have been returned to Thornhill's heirs.

CHAPTER 18

INDEPENDENCE

"Miserum est alienate incumbere famae" – *Juv, viii 761*

Lady Marston was a woman who had all the best and kindest gifts of woman's nature - constancy and truth, affection and tenderness, forethought and tact, and also the perseverance and active courage to act on behalf of her *protégés*. She was not, therefore, likely to forget Charlie Thornhill. She knew his necessities better than he did himself. She knew, too, how he could best help himself, for she had watched him from a boy. She knew his truth and his honest nature, his idleness and ignorance, and his strong good sense. But she knew how difficult it would be to help him in a world where everybody was fighting and struggling and cheating and bribing for self. Delicacy urged her to go to Mrs Thornhill but Mrs Thornhill, since her husband's mysterious death, had been out of the world. She had no political influence and no politics. Then Lady Marston thought of Tom and she found him willing to support his brother, to give him half of his fortune if he wanted it, in fact to do anything but seek the support of his friends who might know the Minister of the Home

Department, or the Foreign Office and might, therefore, be of help to Charlie.

"But, my dear Lady Marston, what can he want with anything to do? He's welcome to anything I have, you know. There's always a home for him at Thornhills; lots of shooting – the best bird season I have known for years; and there's my black hack for him to ride. And when my Uncle Henry dies, he'll have all that. And I only wish it was ten times as much for his sake."

"But you don't understand your brother's position, Tom. He ought to be independent of circumstances. Life's very uncertain; so is banking. Your uncle may live for forty years, or the bank may go tomorrow."

"Bless my soul! Lady Marston, how you frighten one! I hope it won't," said Tom Thornhill, laughing. "Let him come to Melton, and we'll put him up among us. You persuade him: he'll do anything for you." Well, of course this was useless. It was no use wasting time on his brother and approaching Mary Stanhope was not much better.

"Charlie at business! Why, he'll be ill in a week. Besides, what's he to do? He'd better marry somebody. I suppose he will some day. Why can't he go and live with his mother? That's the best place for young men now-a-days. They're always in mischief."

From such sage advisers Lady Marston turned to Lord Tiverton. The Prime Minister was a charming person, impervious to anything; always smiling or joking, *il se moquait de tout le monde*. He enjoyed the temperament of a duck's back. He was, however, a *beau garçon*, somewhat *passé*, and had a reputation for saying the pleasantest things in the world. A refusal was always a difficulty with him; to refuse Lady Marston an impossibility.

"A favour, Lady Marston? A pleasure to grant it. Anything I can do. Of course we must manage something for him." And on he rattled. "Remember his father? Yes, poor fellow; indeed I do. Rather crotchety about the Game Laws for current opinion, but a capital fellow, capital fellow. Can the son speak Spanish? Because I think we could manage something. What? Nothing but his own language? That's a bore. Now a little German or something of that sort goes a great way. Even if it's quite useless, and a man can neither speak it, read it, nor write it, still in these days, you know, public opinion must be considered. Perhaps he could *say* he knew something about it, and take his chance. He *might* satisfy the examiners. It's all great nonsense. I'm sure I couldn't pass an examination myself. Yes, yes, we must do something for him. Why doesn't his brother go into Parliament?"

It was very vague and Lady Marston knew the world too well to place much reliance upon it, so she turned her fascinations next upon Lord Thomas Charter. Little Tommy Charter, or little Lord Tommy, as he was familiarly called by the great unwashed, was brother of a Whig duke, the first statesman in England, the most popular of reformers, author of "The Life of Mumbo Jumbo", "The African Traveller" and "The History of his own Times," and everybody else's. He was a small, sallow, sharp-featured man, highly conscientious, and who stuck to his party through thick and thin, whichever it happened to be.

"Busy, Lady Marston? Indeed I am. But never mind, let us see what can be done. I suppose we are sure of Marston on the Episcopal Clearance Bill? The country gets more practical every day. There's the Sand and Blotting-paper Office; can't we do something for your friend in that? Examination? True, true; but it's very trifling. History of England – good knowledge of modern Europe, in fact, very essential – Italy especially; she's in a very peculiar position: couple of modern languages, say French and German: Latin absolutely necessary – a little of it; but no earthly use: a science or two and mathematics, of course. By-the-way, tell your friend to be well up in the provisions of the Great Charter. No man ever yet did any good in this world who didn't appreciate the efforts of Stephen Langton[25] and his fellows."

Lady Marston was not sanguine enough to imagine that Charlie Thornhill would qualify (as he would have called it) for this stake; but she could not but thank the great statesman for his kindness, and say that she hoped she should be able to write him a line in a day or two.

The next person to whom Lady Marston applied was the erstwhile Wentworth Jones, now Lord Silkstone. At Eton he was Bill Jones, rather a swell, high up in the sixth, and a very good fellow. At Christchurch he became Wentworth Jones, forgetting the Billy, and report said pretty truly that he had come into a good fortune as well as a good name. Then he went into Parliament, worked hard, had a ready wit and unfailing memory for other persons' shortcomings which made him an invaluable debater; for though deficient in knowledge he was never afraid to display his ignorance. Such valuable qualities could not be overlooked: he was taken by the hand by the Premier, and by the nose by Lord Tommy, who found him very useful for a time, and when he was in the way had him elevated to the peerage under the title of Baron Silkstone. From that day the little Joneses became Honourable Wentworths and their father became more polished, more civil, and less sincere than ever. He rode the neatest of hacks, had the smallest of grooms, wore the best-cut coats and the most lemon-coloured gloves of any man in England.

When he was first applied to on behalf of our hero he suggested at

---

[25] **Stephen Langton** (*c.* 1150-9 July 1228) was Archbishop of Canterbury between 1207 and his death in 1228 and was a central figure in the dispute between King John of England and Pope Innocent III, which ultimately led to the issuing of *Magna Carta* in 1215. He is also of note as being credited with having divided the Bible into the standard modern arrangement of books and chapters used today.

once the colonies. He was overpowered by his wish to serve so charming a person as Lady Marston. How he longed for whole hosts of governorships of South Pacific Islands, secretaryships of Pulo Penanga, commissionerships of Jungleguava, attachéships to the embassy of Owhyee, and half a dozen other ships of every line but the right one! And now, when pressed to say what he could positively hold out, he made a definite promise of a nice snug little sinecure on the coast of Western Africa, within easy reach of M. Du Chaillu's cannibals[26] and where Charlie would succeed a gentleman who had been eaten alive by a crocodile whilst performing his ablutions.

The charming smile, white teeth, and bland *empressement*[27] with which it was offered enhanced the value of this desirable post and it was with considerable difficulty that Lady Marston could refuse it in sufficiently polite terms.

"I am really exceedingly obliged, Lord Silkstone, for the interest you so kindly take in my friend Mr Thornhill, but the young man for whom I am asking the favour is strong and healthy at present, and might, if taken in his raw state, disagree with the crocodiles." I've never heard if one of the Honourable Wentworths were selected to fill the post vacated by the hardy bather.

Having waited a short time for something to turn up, and not hearing from either of her ministerial friends of anything more promising than the West African Station, Lady Marston consulted her husband. Sir Frederick Marston was a sensible, accomplished man; practical in all points; fond of the world in which he lived, in no bad sense; very

---

[26] **Paul Belloni de Chaillu** (1831 – 1903) was a French American anthropologist and traveller. He became famous for being the first European to observe gorillas in West Africa and for his work with pygmy peoples of Central Africa.

[27] Enthusiasm.

modern in his ideas, though not without a hopeful touch of chivalry in his nature. He married his wife because he loved her, but he was not the less happy to find that she adorned her station, and was exactly fitted to be "Lady Marston." The consequence of his appreciation was a happy mixture of deference and affection and that sort of intercourse which results from a mutual conviction of each other's capabilities.

"Well! Frederick, nothing has been done for Charles Thornhill yet."

"My dear, you seem to look upon Charles in the light of a pauper."

"So he is, to all intents and purposes. I can hardly conceive a more painful position than that of a man able and willing to work, but compelled to live upon the charity of others."

"Surely a mother's offering to a son's necessities is scarcely charity?"

"Up to a certain age, no; afterwards, yes. And what charms me with Charlie is that he feels it to be so."

"It's the case with half the aristocracy, where no provision can be, or has been made for the younger children. What's the use of a large house and a comfortable jointure?" asked Sir Frederick.

"Mrs Thornhill has not too large a jointure, Frederick; and though she can well afford a home and a few hundreds for a younger son, Charlie's view of his own position is the true one. So let us help him as far as we can."

"With all my heart, my dear; but that won't make him independent. There's very little real independence in this world; and if there were much, what a terrible set of savages we should be! The only really independent person of my acquaintance is my trainer, Turner; and he not only does as he likes with his own, but with mine too."

"Well then, independent or not, will you help him do as he likes?" said Lady Marston, checking her husband's inclination for a discussion, of which Sir Frederick was remarkably fond.

"Will a Government office suit him?" asked the baronet.

"I think not, if it means an examination without some preparation. And if he has that, he may as well go into the army, which he has talked of a hundred times."

"Well, an examination of some sort he must have: not very severe, I apprehend. Whether it does much good, I don't know. I think we shall have an inferior class of men, well prepared for special service, but not likely to make such good general servants. The education of a gentleman usually fits a man for any duties we have to put him to."

"Excepting in modern languages," said Lady Marston.

"No English boys can know much about them, unless educated abroad. And a comparison with us and foreigners in this respect is unfair: the Continent throws men of all languages together: there is both a greater facility for acquiring them, and a readier means for exercising them. But I don't think we're much behind them in essentials – eh, Kate? And you know I was a terrible reformer in that line once upon a time. No; Charlie will do best for a grenadier, or the household brigade."

"I almost agree with you; and if he reads for the one he will fit himself for anything that may fall out by the way. And now the sooner he is out of London the better. We must find a good tutor for him, who'll read with him and teach him to read for himself. That's rather out of my line, Frederick," said Lady Marston who was beginning to think she had entered upon a rather too masculine undertaking. "However, you and he can settle that between you. Only, if you have anything to do with it, beware of Gilsland, and don't let him get too near Melton."

With this sage advice Lady Marston started on some other benevolent errand and Sir Frederick went into committee on the Buffertown railway, and forgot, for a time, the very existence of his wife's *protégé*. Charlie, the person most concerned in these arrangements was, in the mean time, enjoying himself as we have seen but he was constantly visited with an anxious desire to do something for himself. He knew he was leading an unprofitable sort of existence, and envied hundreds who would have changed places with him: that's natural.

Charlie had little idea of what he might do but knew he had to do something. Hitherto he might have been described like some horses – he always had a leg to spare; he passed his time very comfortably but the thought was constantly recurring that he ought to be doing something more. I do not think that it ever occurred to Charlie Thornhill that the whole of the set were going downhill, or that there was anything actually wrong in wasting time, gambling, getting in debt, and the like. He thought it wrong for himself, because he individually could not afford it. Time was wanted to strengthen the growth of principles which seemed almost inherent in his nature, if such things can be. He seemed to have been honest by nature, thoughtful by nature, courageous by nature, chivalrous by nature: as yet he had tried to improve none of nature's gifts. He had a speedy way of administering rough justice of his own; he liked good eating and drinking; was an active enemy to poaching, vulpecide, and dissent, and had a horror of books; these were the gifts of his education. When he wanted a cheque he went to his mother; when he wanted advice or sympathy, to Lady Marston; when he wanted what he knew to be decidedly wrong, and what would be met by remonstrance from either of these, he went to Mary Stanhope.

He had a great deal of conversation with Sir Frederick, as much, in fact, as that legislator could find time for. He held out no great prospects in a Government official situation; besides which, the thing was in itself distasteful to Charlie.

Tutors are of various kinds. There is the well-educated University man, rather stiff and formal, whose ex-parochial existence is passed amongst dry tomes. There is the rough-and-ready, pipe-smoking, slovenly tutor. There is your respectable country clergyman[28] whose only qualifications are his former scholarship and his present necessities. An excellent man is he and as unfit to restrain impetuous youth as any man alive. Above all, there is your utterly incapable old soldier who having dissipated time and money on whist and sangaree[29], comes home to discover that there is only one profession still open to a gentleman. Knowing nothing, he nevertheless sets to work to teach it.

It was to one of these military tutors that Charlie was introduced before long, a man who was naturally urbane and also lived in the vicinity of Gilsland, and the latter point carried the day. Charlie went to bed in the consciousness of having done something for himself and Captain Armstrong retired to rest happy in having added one more to the list of his victims.

---

[28] The author was a country curate who had tutored young men.

[29] Sangaree, an old English name for the wine beverage sangria.

CHAPTER 19

TWO OF A TRADE

"Have more than thou showest;
Speak less than thou knowest" Lear, i. 4

To a dingy-looking house of considerable size, in one of the numerous streets which run parallel to Portland Place – be it Wimpole Street, Harley Street, or any other, matters not – I beg to transport my reader. There is a heavy respectability in the sombre darkness which belongs to this quarter. The carriages are of a heavy order with round, sleek, fat, pursy horses and family coachmen. Yellow chariots or long and low barouches stand about at 4 pm at intervals. Old ladies, with wondrous bonnets of flowers, feathers, or bugles and shaking ringlets, come creeping out on the arms of their footmen, and here and there a pretty girl, with airs, rustles down the doorsteps in attendance on dear grandmamma.

Here are the houses of millionaire merchants, who disdain the fashionable *quartier* and stick to their prejudices. Magnificent collections of water colours adorn the walls, expensive ornaments cover the ormolu and mosaic tables; costly wines, port unknown even in regal cellars, and choice Madeira of many a voyage, stock the cellars and a not inglorious hospitality is shared with men of their own time and weight, which is never under sixteen stone, and may be four-and-twenty. It is here that there is the abode of a prosperous banker; a junior in one of the great City firms – a junior only; for your chief of the firm chooses Piccadilly and the *beau monde*, has a stud in Gorsehamptonshire, and a moor in Scotland, where he entertains his West End clients. But the junior is rich and old, and will become richer and older for he loves nothing but himself and his money, and is alone in the world; his name is Roger Palmer.

He had quarrelled with his only sister years ago, for disgracing herself and him by marrying a handsome Irish scapegrace (at that time about town, but having since disappeared under the conviction of "nobbling" and some suspicions of manslaughter), called Kildonald. He had heard of her since, in a foreign country, in sickness and in want, but he had never relented towards her. He was nearly twenty years her senior and had once loved Norah and had taken care of her. But she left his house and he could not forget it; but he was proud to think that his prophesies of Kildonald had been more than fulfilled. He knew him better than she. Such is Roger Palmer of the firm of Mint, Chalkstone, Palmer and Co., Bankers of East Goldbury City, London.

Roger Palmer had treated himself to a little fire; the evenings, he remarked to himself, get cold in October and others remarked to themselves that Roger Palmer was getting older every day. He had eaten a good dinner, and was not so much out of temper as he looked. He was white, small, fragile, with pinched features and a very fair complexion. His mouth was very thin-lipped, and his forehead was low, but broad. He did not lack intellect, but was wholly without high aspirations. He loved money for itself, and his cold, silent, badly furnished rooms testified it. He was a childless widower, and he did not lament the loss of his wife so much as he rejoiced in the curtailment of his expenses.

Well! There he sat, over his little fire, warming himself and his bright, old toes; for he was scrupulously clean, and could not forget that he was of the firm of Mint, Chalkstone, and Co.; and by degrees odd matters assumed a form. The old man saw his sister as she was when he first took her to a small house in London, before he became a partner in the bank. Then he wondered whether her child had inherited her grace and beauty, and her self-will – this last thought was a little compromise. Then he thought of Kildonald, his good looking face, his bad reputation, his grace of manner, his latitude of principle, his turf practices, and the circumstances of his final disappearance.

"Thornhill! Ah! Poor Thornhill!" thought he; "But for his kindness what should I have been? Where would have been Mint, who never watched a horse race, and Chalkstone, who never played a rubber, and the Co.? We would all have gone under in the financial panic, but for the propping and bolstering by Henry Thornhill and his kind-hearted brother Geoffrey."

Two or three weeks after this soliloquy, Roger Palmer found himself in the little parlour at the back of the banking house in Pall Mall, face to face with Henry Thornhill. After a few minutes' conversation and leaning forward with his elbows upon the arms of the chair he occupied, Roger Palmer said,

"Thornhill, you know what we owe you, you who are occupied in the same pursuits, who have the same anxieties and I look upon it as an obligation that can never be repaid."

"Well, Palmer, be it so," replied the other; "It is long ago and I think you would have done the same by us. You attach too much credit to my personal share in that business. I am only glad that by means of poor Geoffrey I was able to help you."

"Help! God help you in a like case, my friend!" said the little miser cordially, and almost wringing his hands with the recollection. "It was life to us; we were gone – at our last gasp – the Thornhills saved us. Oh, how often I've thought of that Sunday night, which seemed to separate us from ruin and disgrace! But now I want another favour, Thornhill."

"There's no Geoffrey now, Palmer. What is it? Surely not money?"

"Yes, money, money; but a surplus. I want your advice. Will you be my executor? I must make my will; that's the load on my mind at present."

"What's become of your sister, Roger Palmer? You had one once. Where is she? What is she doing?" asked Henry Thornhill.

"No, no hush! I've sworn, never – not one stiver.[30]" and the old man frowned, and his lips closed so tightly as to disappear, whilst thick veins swelled in his forehead. "She laughed me to scorn; she ate of my bread and drank of my cup, and when the wolf came she turned to him in spite of the shepherd's warning. I might be generous, but now I mean to be just."

"Then be just and generous at the same time, and leave your money to your own relatives," said the West End tradesman.

"It's what you would do, I presume," rejoined the City magnate; "but you know nothing of the ingratitude of women, as I do."

"Of course not;" and a deep sigh was following, which Henry Thornhill suppressed with a strong effort; "Of course not. But if you do not leave your money, as I tell you, to Mrs Kildonald or her children, I'll have nothing to do with it. There, Palmer, we're old friends and need not quarrel; but you know my mind."

Henry Thornhill was too generous to add the repayment of an obligation to his advocacy of what was right. But Roger Palmer had

---

[30] A Dutch coin (stuiver), of the value of two cents, or about one penny sterling; hence, figuratively, anything of little worth.

done what we all do occasionally for ourselves: he had fashioned a course of justice in accordance with his own inclination, and intended to abide by it.

"And your nephews, your brother's boys, how are they? What are they doing?" asked Palmer.

"The elder is spending money, like his poor father; and the younger – well, the younger is thinking of making it on his own if he can; that's like you, you know." And Henry Thornhill smiled a grim smile as he clutched his friend's extended hand.

"Does he need it? Does he want a profession?" said the little man, eagerly.

"As much as any one that wishes to be independent, and is not so."

"Then why not take him in here? What an opening for him!"

"Humph! That's as may be. Perhaps he might be better with you." said the uncle.

"Oh, come, come, Thornhill, nonsense! Now think of what I've said."

"And you think of what I've said; and do as you ought to do with your money. When you've made up your mind to follow my advice, come to me, and I'll be your executor. Good-bye."

And Roger Palmer departed on his way eastward as Henry Thornhill sat down again to a ledger, but his thoughts were far away from the back parlour in Pall Mall.

It will be seen that there subsisted a considerable intimacy between these two men who were so different. Circumstances had thrown them together, and an obligation due, with a generous mind, knits the debtor more firmly to the creditor. Thornhill knew all he had done for Palmer; and with all his penurious hardness the latter had never been unmindful of it. In fact, he had gone to Pall Mall that day with the intention of leaving his money to a Thornhill. He had ascertained sufficient for his purpose and although he was prevented from announcing that purpose to Henry Thornhill, he had quite determined in his own mind that Charlie would be none the worse for his patronage and assistance. He liked what he had seen of him, and he had no particular wish that his wealth should go to replace an estate which was being, according to all accounts, rapidly dissipated.

In the meantime, our hero has carried out his intention honestly enough. Charlie was reading hard. The assistance he derived in all this from old Armstrong, as that gallant captain was called, was but small. Charlie, however, had a strong will, and for some weeks made considerable progress in spite of all difficulties. He had his pleasures too. Mary Stanhope's kindness had touched him greatly. He laughed at her fears for his health, but he accepted his favourite horse, and showed his appreciation of her liberality by riding him straight and well whenever he was fit to go. He had stuck to his first refusal to join his brother at Melton but he enjoyed a dinner and a bed now and then at Gilsland, though he was not always back so early the next day as he promised himself.

He was a mark for the arrows of the young women of the neighbourhood, which caused him a little trouble at first, as he hated writing letters of thanks and was not quite safe in his spelling. Miss Pilborough, the doctor's daughter, asked him to tea on pink paper, and in the name of her mother. The rector, old Cureton, went to the lengths of a dinner and a neighbouring squireen, who had heard of Charlie's brother and remembered his father's death, left his own card and his wife's, with Mr Thornhill's name in the corner, and an intimation that there was breakfast and the hounds at Topham Scrubs on the following Monday. But Charlie's horse was not fit and Edith Dacre continued to reign supreme.

* * * * * *

For some days after his interview with Henry Thornhill, Roger

Palmer was thoughtful, almost depressed even for him. But his affairs prospered and he got better. Norah, still alive and living with her gambler and roué, was dead to him; nor remembered as one on whom he would have lavished his beloved gold, even to the last farthing. Had she not preferred an empty-headed stranger, weak and unstable, without a principle or a shilling, to a brother and a man, strong and consistent with intellect, reputation and wealth? His long cherished resentment of Norah was still alive and she was paying dearly for her decision to marry Arthur Kildonald. He made up his mind to do the greatest amount of good to the Thornhill family as the least present sacrifice of his own feelings.

Banking, that is, prosperous banking, is a very pleasant amusement. The senior partner is usually a dignitary, a baronet (if not of James I's creation), an M.P. and a most influential authority on all matters, in and out of the Commons, connected with finance. So it was with the firm of Mint, Chalkstone, and Palmer. Sir Julep Mint was a very great man. If he had not been a banker he would have been Lord Mayor. He had the seeds of greatness in him. He was married to a lady in her own right, and was known by many as Lord Soapstone from the name of his place and the dignity of his manners. In a word, he was a pompous ass and a very low churchman.

Chalkstone was a much better fellow all over. He was a good hard liver; ate a dinner every day of his life and if he ever had the gout, had earned it. He drove off this enemy by horse exercise. He was not a bad riding man over a country and kept half-a-dozen first class weight-carriers in Essex; certainly the best provincial country in England and not far short of the shires. He was an easy man to deal with for though he said it in a blunt manner, he usually said what he meant.

One morning in December in a large, comfortably furnished room, at the back of the counter, and connected with it by large and handsome glass folding doors, sat the three partners, active partners, of the respectable firm of Mint, Chalkstone, Palmer & Co.. They had under consideration the feasibility of taking into partnership some younger man who would put certain capital into the business and work gratuitously for a certain number of years, until the seed he had sown should produce an abundant harvest. There were plenty of such young men to be found but there were not so many with thirty thousand pound notes and somehow or other, banking was not in its zenith. There had been a tremendous smash or two, especially among the low-church party, and it required time to give the public confidence. Again, Sir Julep had lots of daughters, but no son, not even a son-in-law. Those who were high enough to aspire to that happiness were too worldly, the rest were nowhere. Chalkstone was without children, and had a Caligula-like fancy for making his bay horse a partner. He often declared that the horse was the only one of his acquaintances that he could trust. I wonder whether Caius Caesar or old Boots had an equally sufficient reason for appointing to the consulship! Be that as it may, the two seniors being failures, the appointment fell to Roger Palmer. Much to the astonishment of his colleagues, he accepted the onus, guaranteeing the money, and only asking two or three days for some necessary correspondence. So reasonable a request could not be gainsaid. Due respect was had for the superior age and intelligence of the junior partner of the firm. Whilst he lived it was founded upon a rock; might his successor be like him?

"You propose to send him abroad to conduct the foreign business first, Mr Palmer; it's a great responsibility."

"Rather, Sir Julep, as a representative of our house; he must be a gentleman, if possible, of some position."

"Most undoubtedly, most undoubtedly; we are in your hands, my good sir, and it must be evident to our foreign correspondents that we can send out no counterfeit, no counterfeit in any sense. It behoves the aristocracy, in times of danger, like the present ... ." Here Chalkstone, in anticipation of a speech, interrupted the worthy baronet:

"Let's have a good fellow, Palmer, into the kennels, into the bank, I mean. Fresh blood, sir, is a grand thing in a pack of hounds – body of directors I should say; and I hardly know any kennel we could fall back upon, with any better chance of success, than our friend Palmer. A good, steady, true, old-fashioned, line-hunting, that is, an honest, intelligent, gentlemanly, young man possessing the requisite amount of industry and pluck and ... and ... ."

"Money," added Roger Palmer, with a little sigh, for he couldn't help feeling it, though he had made up his mind with the heroism of a Spartan.

"Are you going my way?" said Sir Julep, with one of his most polished and condescending bows; "my brougham is at the bottom of the street; I'm on my way to the lying-in hospital; the little help that Lady Elfrida can afford we are only too happy to bestow: I can put you down, and go on for her."

"Or come with me, Palmer, my cab's at the door and I should like you to see my new brown horse. I know you like a horse, although you pretend not to;" and Chalkstone almost pushed him out of the room before him.

"No, Sir Julep, thank you; no, no, Chalkstone; I can't afford to have my neck broken before this business is settled, you know. Let me walk home. It is but a step. I shall let you know, in a day or two, all about my nominee. The money's right enough; the money's right; and that's the great consideration." And away went the little miser, as quickly, and as jauntily, as if he had been a treasury clerk of five-and-twenty with four hundred a year. He knew that walking by himself was cheaper than riding with other men.

The result of this conversation was a letter to Charles Thornhill. It reached him at a time when circumstances made it more acceptable than usual. Charlie's military ardour had never been great. He had never been attacked with scarlet fever, or at so early an age that it left no traces behind it. It was the turning point of his life. All men have the turn; but few know it, and many neglect it. Verily, industry is a great thing, learning is a great thing, energy is a great thing, but *luck* is the greatest.

CHAPTER 20

A CATASTROPHE

Prepare him early with instruction, and season his mind with the maxims of truth.

"And who was the wife of Charles I, Mr Thornhill?" said Captain Armstrong, as he sat with his book before him, superintending a sort of morning canter through English history.

"Edith Dacre." said Charlie. "Oh, no! I beg your pardon, Captain Armstrong. I mean – let me see – 'pon my soul, I forget; but I was thinking of something else. How very stupid, to be sure!"

"'Charles was also engaged to Henrietta Maria, sister of Louis XIII.'" said the Captain very gravely, reading from the book. "'Just before this marriage took place James I died, March 1625.'"

"Of course – of course; I beg your pardon." And the lecture proceeded with no very satisfactory result, as far as Charlie was concerned. A reference to the book showed the Captain his pupil was wrong upon two or three points, of which he himself was not quite safe such as "that the area of a triangle was double its altitude with his base," and that "Edward II's widow was confined for life to

the Castle of Gilsland." If the reader requires any explanation of this ignorance it was to be found in our hero's left-hand waistcoat pocket. It had arrived that morning by post. It produced a greater sensation than the contents appear to warrant:
GILSLAND, Tuesday Morning.

Dear Mr Thornhill,
Mamma desires me to write, as she is much engaged, and ask whether you will give us the pleasure of your company from Friday till Monday next. The hounds meet at our cover on Saturday, and perhaps you can send your horse over on Friday morning. There is a stall at your service. My brother is here, as he is not yet gone to Berne. We hope you will be able to come.

Yours very truly,

"EDITH DACRE"

Charlie had dined before at Gilsland and slept there. He had been out hunting in his life often enough to have borne the news of the meet with equanimity and Mr Dacre's cover, though a sure find, was a very moderate one for sport. The fact is that this was the first time he had ever had a letter from Edith; and, though difficult to extract much from it in the way of great encouragement, he managed to pick out of it consolation enough to drive out all the effects of his previous day's studying.

Finding himself unfit for serious work, he lit a cigar and visited the stable. His hunter, The Templar, was fit. It was early in the season; there was no sign of frost in the air, he countermanded the nearby Thursday's meet and ordered his horse to be sent on Friday in good time to Gilsland. So much for the effects of a little scented paper and an invitation to dinner.

There was a goodly party assembled at the Dacres' on Friday, at seven pm: a heavy divine, two fox-hunting squires and their wives, a foreign nobleman who had a house in the neighbourhood for the winter, a dowager peeress, Mr and Lady Elizabeth Montague Mastodon, Mr Robinson Brown junior, Mr de Beauvoir and Charlie Thornhill.

A very meritorious impression has gone abroad that horse-flesh is never a subject of conversation before the claret appears. This is a simple misconception of the rules of good society, where people usually talk, as they eat and drink, of the things that please them best. Beer was not excluded from the table at Gilsland, nor was hunting proscribed. The divine had his say on the subject of tithes and the church rate, and Mr Mastodon introduced the subject of the duty on hops. The dowager peeress started on Paris, taking pity on the foreign nobleman, who was not well-up in English politics.

Charlie had not said much, for, having got next to Edith, and opposite to Alice, he satisfied himself with thinking. Edith never talked quite so much to Charlie as to other people; and Robinson Brown ran away with the conversation on the other side of her completely. Alice and De Beauvoir were discussing the charms of a certain picture by Millais in which the gentleman fondly insinuated a certain resemblance to the principal figure, but which Miss Dacre as strongly repudiated with very good reason.

"That's no compliment, Mr De Beauvoir; the woman looks as if she had been pressed in a mangle, and then ironed to get out the creases; and I hope you don't consider my hair bright red!"

"Iron," Lady Elizabeth was saying. "Demand for iron, of course there must be as traffic increases and populations in large towns becomes denser and gold flows in from these newly-found regions of which we hear so much, of course they'll want iron. We shall have an iron age again."

"I know that the consumption of metal must be much greater than formerly," said Sir Thomas Fallowtop with much dignity. "Though I presume it has not become dearer through the increased demand; for the farmers all round our country have taken to using it for fencing, and it's a most dangerous obstacle to crossing a country. Something must be done by the legislature. You ruin this country as soon as you put an end to fox-hunting." The old gentleman looked for a seconder.

"Of course – most undoubtedly – vewy, vewy true," said Robinson Brown. "Tewwible thing indeed, could wuin the awistocwacy's pleasures, and that sort of thing, eh, Miss Dacre?"

"I hope, Sir Thomas" said Edith " that we shan't go on to your land tomorrow then, for I am going out with the hounds. I've often been promised, and at last I am really going on horseback. I'm going to jump too – ain't I, Teddy?"

"The mare's a capital fencer," said Teddy Dacre, "but she's rather troublesome to ride. Edith has some peculiar opinions about gentlemen's hands, and she has insisted upon showing us how to ride tomorrow. Mind your neck, Charlie!" Charlie thought of somebody else's neck, and only said

"I don't think you ought to let your sister ride that mare, unless she's quieter than when I last saw her."

"Oh, how provoking you are, Mr Thornhill! Mamma and Papa set such value on my neck and your opinion about horses, that if you say much more I shan't go at all." Charlie held his tongue, which he found easier than talking; but he made up his mind to ascertain all about the mare, and act accordingly. He thought Alice might help him in the drawing room.

In the drawing room, the riding expedition of the next day was the topic of general conversation. The general feeling was against the qualifications of the mare for carrying a lady but Teddy Dacre laughed at the notion, and Edith declared she could ride her, had ridden her, and would ride her. Mr Robinson Brown offered a substitute and proposed to take the mare himself but Miss Edith declared that his mother and sisters would never forgive her if anything happened to him, and he had better reserve himself for his forthcoming race with Mr Thornhill. "Dear Jane" was accustomed to be treated with deference at home, and did not understand young ladies' chaff. Charlie had nothing to offer, as his own horse was quite unfit for any lady to ride.

" You know, Mr Thornhill, the fact is that I mean to ride the mare. Papa means to go with us on a hack, and I dare say you'll be good natured enough to keep an eye upon us." Charlie went up to blood heat, Fahrenheit. "Mamma would feel better satisfied." He was down at 32 degrees. Before bedtime, however, Alice had made him a participator, to a certain extent, in her own fears.

"The mare is very hot with hounds." said she, "and, though Edith rides very well, she has a great deal more courage than experience."

"Then I won't be far away," said he, and the ladies went to bed.

By eleven o'clock the following morning the hounds and servants with their master's horses; a score of second horsemen, farmers of every grade, shape, age, and character and about fifty county gentlemen who had partaken, or declined to partake, of Mr Dacre's morning hospitality, were assembled in the field on the other side of the sunk fence. Opposite the door of the house, grooms were leading the horses of those who had prolonged their morning meal. There was Mr Dacre's favourite hack, a neat looking animal fit to carry a thin gentlemanly old man such as he. There was also Robinson Brown's three hundred guinea Irish Birdcatcher[31] horse. Even now Edith ought to have changed her mind and the groom the

---

[31] Foaled in 1833 at the Brownstown Stud, in Ireland, **Birdcatcher** was by the Irish Thoroughbred stallion Sir Hercules, who lost only once at St. Leger in 1829.

saddles. There was a good, useful, not very expensive hunter for Teddy Dacre himself, and the mare which switched her narrow, blood-like quarters and clean-made thighs and hocks with her tail, now and then put back her ears and struck out with one leg. Then there was Charlie's young one, Mary Stanhope's present, a raw, lengthy, slack-looking horse, but with large limbs, good shoulders and great depth. His fault lay behind the saddle; but there was time as well as room for improvement there.

"Where to?" asked the Master of his huntsman, throwing himself into his saddle.

"That functionary touched his cap, "There's a fox lies down by the osiers, close against the river." And away he went in the midst of his hounds, preceded by one whip and followed by another, towards the supposed fox hole.

After drawing a blank in two or three spinneys on the road, which gave an opportunity to Charlie to superintend his charge whose mare fidgeted about considerably and had relieved her mistress of Robinson Brown's attendance by kicking the Birdcatcher horse above the hock, they approached the osier bed[32]. It was bounded by the river on one side, the upper part of it being dry lying, of blackthorn, at the end of which was a strong, almost impossible fence into a small meadow. At this end of the cover it was desirable that the crowd should assemble and the hounds were brought round and thrown in there, as the best chance of affording a run.

Charlie had taken his place at a corner of the cover. He had scarcely forgotten Edith for a moment until now, when his eyes and ears were straining for the hoped-for "gone away." The young lady, with more modesty than that exhibited by modern Amazons, had turned her horse back, and walking along the hedgerow, had ridden through a gate into the small meadow, partly to quiet her horse and partly to be

---

[32] A place where willows are grown for basket making.

out of the way. For a few minutes it had the desired effect, but when the hounds found, the rate of the whips, the cheer of the huntsman, or the sudden rush of horsemen to some favoured spot, again upset the mare. At this moment, standing in his stirrups, and straining his eyes to catch sight of fox, or hounds, or anything but Edith Dacre, he thought of her. He had seen her go back, and now, looking towards the meadow, through the fence, he was distressed to see the mare rearing and plunging wildly, as at every fresh bound she neared the river, swollen by autumnal rains. Edith kept her seat and her presence of mind, but she was deadly pale, and evidently her strength was going.

A fresh blast of the horn and a "tally-ho back" brought more horses up at a hand gallop; the mare seized the bit in her teeth, and plunged madly towards the river's brink. And now everybody saw the danger and the impracticable nature of the fence, and galloped, Robinson Brown leading, towards the gate, some two hundred yards up the hedgerow. Almost as they started a terrible shriek broke on the ear; the mare reared bolt upright; the poor girl caught tight hold of the curb-rein, and in an instant more they both fell with a crash into the river. The mare extricated herself immediately but there, on the waters, floated rapidly downstream the dark habit and brown tresses of that beautiful girl.

Charlie had quite forgotten the fox as soon as he perceived her situation on the bank; he hesitated only to calculate the possibility of clearing the fence, or of getting to the gate most quickly. The last scream and violent plunge of the mare decided the matter. His horse was raw, but fresh and resolute; the rails were strong, the fence pretty thick, but it allowed the pleasing vision of a broad, black ditch, and a second flight of timber on the other side. Catching hold of the reins in a grasp of iron, and sending both spurs into his horse's flanks, he rushed him at it. The result might be guessed: as Edith Dacre and the mare rolled off the bank into the water, Charlie Thornhill and his horse landed with a loud crash into the second flight of rails, which proved just strong enough to let them through, but with a heavy fall on the other side.

Charlie, amongst other accomplishments, had learned to fall well. He was seldom seen running after his horse over a ploughed field with tearful entreaties to his friends to "tie him up at the next gate." He never let go the reins, or was caught ignominiously endeavouring to soothe his cunning steed, who was standing grazing quietly after having given his rider a fall that shook every bone in his body and left him with scattered wits regretting his confiding reliance on the brute. The consequence was, that almost before he was down, he was up again; and with one short but heartfelt thanksgiving that *he* was not at this moment disabled, he dropped the reins which by instinct he held, and giving himself one shake, and one moment for reflection, he ran towards the river to a point somewhat below that at which Edith Dacre had just risen to the surface. He saw she was free from her horse, and that it was only a question of how long it would take to saturate her heavy riding-habit.

As to assistance from the rest, they were at this moment unhasping the gate which had closed again, and were some three hundred yards from the spot. Scarcely thirty yards separated him from the object he loved best on earth, or in the water, and in a second or two he was on the river's brink. In two or three vigorous strokes he was alongside Edith, and bearing her rapidly towards the angle formed by the fence and the osier-bed, where landing seemed easier than elsewhere. By the time he reached the spot, Robinson Brown, Sir Thomas Fallowtop, Mr Dacre, pale as ashes but covering his emotion with an assumed calmness, two young farmers who had been waiting out of the crowd with young horses, and about half a dozen labouring men and boys, were ready to give a hand or advice, as the case might be. Charlie accepted the former, and disdained the latter. Edith had already recovered in some sort her consciousness, and was pouring out thanks, with eyes that told too truly how glad she was to be indebted to her deliverer.

She clung to him as he held her for one moment to his heart and the next was in the arms of her father who uttered not one word, but who looked conscious of the narrowness of her escape, and gave one short but sincere pressure of the hand to Charlie, which assured him that his share in the transaction would not be forgotten.

Edith continued to shiver and shake, as well she might; and it became a question of how to get her home. Fortunately a groom was nearby riding a very quiet old horse of Mr. Dacre's. At this juncture Charlie made the inconvenient discovery that his horse was lame, the horse had struck himself violently on the fetlock when he fell. Charlie suggested that he should ride Edith's mare and Edith should ride the groom's horse so Charlie handed his own horse to the groom to ride home, saddles were changed and Charlie mounted the mare. He had but two regrets, that he had lost the run, and that Robinson Brown was escorting them home. It was a mixed feeling, but the last was by far the stronger of the two.

Gilsland was about two miles from the osier bed and Edith had begun to shake off her faintness after some sherry from Charlie's flask. It was proposed to jog on, as a means of keeping both Edith and Charlie from getting too cold and in this manner they arrived at the Hall and at once relieved Mrs. Dacre and Alice from any fears which an unprejudiced imagination is apt to attribute to a too early return from hunting. The young lady was dismissed to her room, where her mother, sister, and two maids insisted upon administering to her comforts.

Mrs Dacre's first idea was the true one, that Charlie and Edith had been in the water together; and she knew that was often a prelude to other misfortunes. She was very fond of Charlie but she did not like the idea of him for a husband for one of her children. However she found herself thinking more about Charlie's uncle, his fortune, its extent and his life. These are what she called his 'prospects': the fact is they were her own. Robinson Brown she could not endure; but she rather thought that it would be her duty to put up with a young man of such immense expectations, and who had certainly attracted the attention of several judicious ladies of even higher ton than herself. Alice had long suspected the state of Charlie's heart and she liked him for himself and the debt of gratitude she owed him for a brother and a sister.

Mr Dacre was an easy person, not given to emotion, excepting in very unexpected circumstances, such as we have detailed. He wrung Charlie's hand, as we have seen; wished he could provide for him (abroad perhaps!) and determined upon lending him the mare, or one of his own horses, until The Templar should be sound enough for him to ride. It was clear that Charlie would never lack a general invitation to Gilsland: that went without saying.

During the day the village Aesculapius[33], Dr Torrens, called. Nothing could be better for the young lady than "quiet; something light for dinner; a little soda-water, no wine, and the doctor would call again tomorrow." 'Doctor!' thought Charlie, 'what in the name of fortune does the doctor want here? Surely there's nothing the matter.' Then came the curate: he returned to his duties without being introduced. Charlie hoped he was not coming on the morrow too.

At that moment Mr Robinson Brown, who had also been disappointed by his day's hunting, without, however, the satisfaction which accompanied Charlie's disappointment, lounged into the room. Robinson Brown dabbled in polite literature, as he imagined, so he picked up a magazine, whilst Charlie looked out of the window,

---

[33] **Aesculapius** is the god of medicine and healing in ancient Greece.

struggling to get the better of a rather bad fit of the spleen. Alice was with her sister; and she was his only sedative in the house. The fact is that love, of which he had taken a dose, did not agree with Charlie's temper.

"Why, Thornhill, I thought you were gone to Van Dieman's Land, or Heligoland, or some land or other in Africa. I was quite agreeably surprised to see you yesterday at dinner." said Mr Brown, with a comfortable kind of patronage in his tone.

"No, not yet. When do you go?" rejoined the other, rather tartly.

"Gwacious! What a fellow you are! Why should *I* go to those outlandish places. I don't want to be eaten alive, my dear fellow," said the cornet.

"Oh! Nobody'll eat you alive."

"I don't know: 'pon my soul I don't know about that. I'm not so tough as you think, Thornhill." He was soft enough, to do him justice.

"No; but a man may be very soft, and yet disagree with a fellow," rejoined Charlie; and having delivered himself of this sentiment, he turned again to the window. He was not fated to enjoy his repose long, for he was once more interrupted by "dear Jane".

"You're weading, eh, Thornhill? Weading, I understand; and that sort of thing?"

"What? A garden or a stud? I've weeded the latter pretty closely."

"No, no; not weeding, but weading." said dear Jane: "Weading with a coach, you know." He made rather a violent struggle to make himself comprehensible.

"Yes; I am reading for a commission," replied Charlie, turning once more to the contemplation of the black clouds, which portended a wet ride home for the sportsmen.

"Aw – aw – yes – great baw weading, to some fellows. Now we never had any examination, or that sort of thing, when I went into the service; nothing of the kind." persevered Robinson Brown.

"So I should think," said Charlie, who saw it would be polite to say something.

"Our fellows are aw – aw – so ignowant: not bad fellows, you know, but so infernally ignowant."

"So I should have imagined," replied Charlie once more, who was watching a figure intently which appeared at the further end of the shrubbery, and which exhibited every appearance of one of the ladies of the house walking briskly to and fro. "So I should have imagined."

"Oh! You know our fellows then. Do you ever dine at the mess? Bad cook; and altogether – aw – aw - that sort of thing. Do you know Carnaby?"

"No, I only know you." And just as Robinson Brown was recommencing on some other subject, Charlie, feigning remembrance of something important rushed out of the room in search of the shawl, which had once more disappeared round the shrubbery. It was Alice Dacre.

Charlie was not a bold man, but as soon as he saw that it was Alice Dacre he testified an invincible desire for news of Edith.

"What a morning it has been for us, Mr Thornhill." began Alice, who exhibited very recent traces of tears, which did not escape the discriminating eyes of Charlie.

"Poor Edith! It has been too much for her; and, now that the excitement is over, the reaction is very painful. And what do we not owe you?"

"Don't let that burden you, Miss Dacre."

"It does not burden us; but ..." And here poor Alice blushed, for she knew one whom it did burden painfully who hugged her burden closer than was good for her. Alice Dacre was very thoughtful for others

"Oh! Mr Thornhill, I could say so much. If you knew how we have lived together and what a blessing you have restored to us all by your courage," and here a large pearl did run over. But she soon brightened again, for she saw that the conversation was painful for Charlie, who was not inclined to magnify his own exploit.

Alice felt a strong inclination to ask after his brother but as the words rose they stuck and she only asked him where he was going to spend his winter.

"I scarcely know; I presume at Thornhills. But, you know, I am reading for a commission, and must work hard at Scampersdale; for I hope to have one before long."

"Yes, we heard of that; but you did talk of going to Melton."

"I did; but I have not the time. What hunting I do I must do in this neighbourhood. However, I must be a prisoner for a fortnight or more. I lamed my horse."

"And papa proposes to send over one of his, or the mare Edith rode today, if you think her worth riding."

"I hope we shall see Edith at dinner." said Charlie.

"No, not dinner today. Tomorrow the doctor proposes calling early; and I hope she will be much better. But, tell me, when does the steeple-chase between your brother's horse and Mr Robinson Brown's "Reluctance" come off? Edith will want all the news."

"Not immediately, it's postponed. And as I am to ride, I should like to have got through my literary difficulties before I risk your sister's gloves; for I know she has backed the horse. But," added he encouragingly, "I think we can manage to win."

"I hope so or poor Edith will be ruined in gloves. I heard her backing you to her last penny; so I beg you win."

"You say we shall not see her at dinner today? You fear not. But is anything the matter? Tell me, tell me, Miss Dacre." And here, seeing how far his feelings had carried him away, he became suddenly cold, and hoped it was nothing but fatigue.

"Have they much opinion of your doctor?"

"Oh! Yes; certainly. He was to see Edith tomorrow; and if she had a good night she would be better, no doubt." And with this Charlie was obliged to be satisfied. But the next morning Edith was much the same. She was to lie in bed and keep to her room throughout the day. Excitement and cold had been too much for her.

Sickness in a house full of guests is always very depressing. Nobody seems to know what to do. There is a vague listlessness about the visitors, breakfast is a scurry; luncheon is not cheerful, and lacks the plans and proposals of healthier times; as to dinner, you have to sit down with a vacant chair or two. Then one drops in, then another; everyone has come from the sick chamber. You feel your insignificance and uselessness. You can do nothing, and are plainly *de trop*. Such was the party at Gilsland. So on the Monday morning Charlie returned to work; but he had the happiness of seeing Mr Robinson Brown depart before him, a woe-begone object of simulated tenderness.

CHAPTER 21

LIFE IN THE SHIRES

"Things sweet to taste prove in digestion sour." – *Richard II*

Charlie found himself at Captain Armstrong's once more involved in the intricacies of English spelling, French dictation, the square root, and simple equations; and why called simple he had some difficulty in understanding. He had received a note from Alice Dacre three days later, which gave but a very poor account of Edith's recovery; and when he rode over on Saturday morning to inquire after her, ostensibly to see his young horse, it was impossible to conceal the fact of very severe illness. In truth, she was attacked by low fever, the result of cold and excitement combined; and a summons for a more reliable opinion than that of Dr Torrens confirmed Charlie's fears of considerable danger. Three weeks of much suffering, alternating between life and death, he was as little able to pursue any efficient study; and it was not till the fourth week that his mind was made easy by an assurance, on a repeated visit, that all danger was completely over, and that beef-tea and champagne were doing the work of the doctor in curing, not killing, as might be supposed.

Leaving Edith to get well, and Charlie to recover his lost ground, I take this opportunity for a reflection or two, which the reader can miss, if he likes, but which is as much the necessary ingredient of a novel as pepper is to a rabbit-pie

It will have been observed that Edith Dacre was a lively, cheerful, high-spirited girl with many lovable qualities. Her anxiety to ride an unruly mare arose mostly from sheer animal spirits. A good ducking would have been sufficient punishment but a fever which reduced her to a skeleton, frightened her family, nearly killed her lover with anxiety, and deprived her for a time of a valuable head of hair seems to have been more than adequate.

What shall we say of the young ladies of the present day, who are not satisfied with a modest exhibition of themselves but who are either so desirous of display, or so wedded to the charms of manly exercise, as to take a pride in the successful negotiation of stiff timber or fourteen feet of water? Their conversation has become a mixture of the stable and the schoolroom and whose fantastic dress ranges between the collars and pea-jacket of a Whitechapel gent and the picturesque conventionalities of a rope dancer? What is the reason for all this? Who or what are the ladies who have introduced all this to the most lovely, the most delicate, the most womanlike of the women of this world? Whoever heard of them thirty years ago, save at some unholy bacchanalian festival?

And what of Tom Thornhill all this time? He was at it, body and soul. A dozen horses at Melton; a house that befitted his ample means; and companions that drank deep of his cup. There was nothing but pleasure before him, and he revelled in the prospect. And in that prospect one stood out and that was Alice Dacre, with her glossy hair, and soft deep violet eyes, and truthful serenity. But there she stood in Tom Thornhill's picture of future happiness, bright and glorious, for whom he would have sacrificed himself, but not all and not his passion, his devourer, his god.

There is but one thing that no fortune can resist: the gaming table. Tom loved play, and he loved to play high. He had backed horses with a recklessness that was the result of strong prejudice or ignorance, and had already suffered. At this game he stood no chance of winning, excepting by accident. He was always playing a game which they with whom he played, knew better than himself. He betted honestly and paid as readily, and with the same good humour as he did everything. But he did not always get paid. He had already been borrowing money; and it was clear that in a few years he must be in the hands of the usurers, who had their eyes upon him, as one of their daintiest morsels. They saw no fish so ready to take the bait as Tom Thornhill. Already they counted their 60 percent, and something tangible – Thornhills – to fall back upon.

"Who was that we left swimming about in the Whissendine today with our second fox?" asked Captain Charteris of Lord Carlingford, as they sat in Thornhill's drawing room in their hunting things before a roasting fire, with no other light but its ruddy and cheerful blaze. "He looked to me as if he stood a good chance of being drowned."

"Only Wilson Graves," said his lordship; "He went very well up to that. But I could see his horse didn't mean to have the water; he became exceedingly shifty as soon as he caught sight of it, and I heard him go in just as I landed with a desperate scramble; and when I looked round, I saw nothing but a hat and one top boot above the water. I presume they belonged to him. I suppose he got out?"

"Yes," said Charteris; "I pulled up a moment and he scrambled to the bank. The water was not above four feet and a half deep there, so he was perfectly safe. Is he the man that broke the bank at Homburg the year before last, and got out of the window with twenty thousand dollars from a Broadway billiard room, whilst the indignant Yankee was sharpening his bowie-knife at the bottom of the stairs?"

"So they say," rejoined Lord Carlingford;

Tom Thornhill, who had just come in from the stable said "He's coming to dinner today. I've given him a bed, as he hunts on this side tomorrow and it saves him a ride back to Leicester."

"By-the-bye, Thornhill, has anything more been done about the race between your brown horse and Robinson Brown's mare? It ought to be coming off soon."

"It's postponed by agreement for another month. Charlie thinks he shall ride so much *lighter* when his examination is over, and Robinson Brown's mare wasn't fit, I believe. So he wanted to have it later in the season. My trainer writes me word that the brown horse never looked better in his life. I believe they will lay 3 to 1 on him before the day of the race. But I didn't want to rob the poor devil, if his mare wasn't fit to go." Thus spake Tom Thornhill, with the spirit of a gentleman and a sportsman, but with more of the innocence of the dove than the wiliness of the serpent. "If you fellows are going to dine here today, I should advise you to go and dress." And with that he walked out of the room.

The conversation at dinner between Lord Charteris and Wilson Graves was about to take an unpleasant turn when the dining room door was thrown open, and Mr Robinson Brown junior was announced. Now be it known to the reader that Robinson Brown was not a favourite with Tom Thornhill, nor, indeed, with any of the men who were present. But Tom was hospitality itself, and could no more do an unkind action, or allow anyone to think himself aggrieved in his house, than he could fly. So down sat "Dear Jane" with a hearty welcome as if it had been Charlie himself.

"Where are you from?" "What horses have you with you?" "Where are you staying?" "Seen any sport?" were questions poured in upon him as fast as the claret was poured out for him.

"I'm just come from the Dacres." said he, with considerable pride at the announcement of a name which gave him a favourable status in the present company.

"The Dacres? By Jove!" said Tom. "Any news? Old Dacre pretty well? Capital fellow 'pon my soul! ... And the girls?" Added he, after a pause, not liking to appear over anxious "Who had you there?"

"Oh! Yes, all very well, excepting Miss Dacre: she's ill of a howwid fever." He had no time to finish the sentence for Tom was on his feet in a moment; and fortunately for him, down went the claret jug which attracted immediate attention, whilst he had time to collect himself. But the effort was a strong one, and left Tom burning hot, with a very uncomfortable degree of fever himself, whilst his informant added "Yaas, the younger one, Edith. Charles Thornhill fished her out of the water ... fell in near Dacre's osier bed the end of last week; your brother lamed his horse. Vewy unfortunate altogether, wasn't it?" And he really felt as much as he was capable of feeling: for he had managed to get up what he called a good wholesome passion for the little Dacre. Tom's colour had subsided and by the time the butler had brought another bottle of claret the excitement was over, though Tom continued to repeat, "Poor girl! 'Pon my soul, sorry to hear that: very. And how's Charlie?"

"Your bwother? Oh he's vewy well. Wather sweet in that quarter, I should say." And here Mr Robinson Brown lapsed into insipidity. It was getting late, and as no one took any more claret, they adjourned to the drawing room. Here Carlingford yawned; Robinson Brown stretched himself on a sofa; Cressingham hummed an air out of a new opera of the last season; Charteris picked up the "Racing Calendar". Wilson Graves feigned sleep in an arm-chair and Thornhill himself walked straight to the card tables.

"Anybody for a rubber?" Nobody answered. "Graves, have a rubber?" And the game was made, at which Tom Thornhill won. So far, so good. Then they tried hazard. This was not so good for Tom, who began to lose, and, like a true gambler, backed his bad luck.

Brownsoon took his leave after having succeeded in backing his mare for the race. The day was then fixed for it to come off, and the riders were declared. Mr Robinson Brown would steer his own mare, and Mr Charles Thornhill would ride for his brother.

By degrees the men moved off, Carlingford to his rooms, Cressingham to his, and all to give orders about the morrow. And then, instead of going to bed, Tom Thornhill would play. His iron constitution seemed to know no fatigue. His indomitable passion was only roused by losses. Nor was Wilson Graves the man to thwart his purpose. One word might then have checked him: but there was no one to say, "No, hang it, Thornhill, we've had enough for tonight; let's go to bed." The devil had taken possession of the room, in the shape of a dice box and his prime minister was Wilson Graves. So they went to it again, the one with well dissembled satisfaction, the other with unfeigned enjoyment – an enjoyment which never appeared to diminish with the loss of hundreds. But at last the game did flag, from a sort of inherent deference to received opinion that men ought to go to bed before three who have to start for the cover side again at half past nine; so they took up their flat candlesticks, and prepared to go, leaving behind them a curious testimony to the housemaid of their evening's occupation; empty soda water bottles, the ends of cigars, three or four packs of cards, a backgrammon board and a dice box.

* * * * * *

"Do you know that brown horse of Mr Thornhill's, that he has matched against Reluctance, Mr Robinson Brown's mare?" asked Wilson Graves the next morning finishing off a neat and successful tie, and looking his servant very straight in the face.

"The big brown 'oss, as Mr Thornhill rode last year, and hung up the field at Gopsall Park paling? Oh yes, sir, I know the 'oss well enough. He's down at Sam Downy's in training for this match; leastways, I hear so."

"Very likely. Do you know Downy?" And here Wilson Graves dropped his voice to little above a whisper.

"His son and me was schoolfellows, and in service together, when I lived first with Lord Ambulance, sir; and I generally go down to the old man's every year for a day or two, just for a change of air and a little quiet or so, after the season here, see his osses out, and help him a bit with the stud."

"Can you give him some advice about the brown horse then, Jacob? I know you're a clever fellow, and can do what you like. That horse mustn't win; in fact, he can't win: the mare's the one to back." And here Mr Wilson Graves condescended to look again at his groom in a very peculiar manner which said, "You know which horse the money is on now, so do your best to bring it off."

"The Downy's are uncommon sweet, sir; they love the brown 'oss like theirselves: and as to Squire Thornhill, they love him almost as well as the 'oss."

"And I tell you what they love better than the brown horse, or the Squire, and that's money." Graves judged the world by his own standard: he loved money's worth, and cared little how he got it.

"I don't know, sir; you know best: but it's a dangerous game among that lot." Jacob looked preternaturally solemn, and as innocent as a dove.

"It's not the first time we've had to deal with danger. Pull the string strong, and they'll all dance. It's time to be off; give me my coat, and send round the hack at half-past nine."

"Set a thief to catch a thief!" So it was with Wilson Graves. His retainers were not selected for their honourable antecedents; and, as their work was sometimes dirty.

Graves cared very little about those his people robbed, as long as they let him go scot free. Jacob Ritsom, his groom, was selected because he was clever, unscrupulous and walked about with a noose round his neck, and his master knew it. He was therefore his very humble servant and understood a hint as well as most men whose apprehensions are quickened by the fear of a halter. It was not quite so bad as that, however; still men have been hung for the same and for less. He had once poisoned a horse; and the proofs were in the hands of Wilson Graves. Good heavens! What a life to lead. I do not speak of either as an absolute pleasure, but better far would it be to be hanged at once, honestly and like a gentleman than to go through the world the slave of such a man as Wilson Graves.

Whilst Tom Thornhill was enjoying himself, hunting, losing money, making good resolutions and breaking them, and Wilson Graves was profiting by his lengthened visit in Melton, Charlie had three things on his mind which caused him considerable anxiety. The first was his examination which, as it approached, presented its difficulties in gigantic proportions; the second was Edith Dacre about whom and whose love he felt as most modest men in his position would have felt. So he made himself uncomfortable, to his full satisfaction; which he need not have done had he known all that I know.

The third care was not a heavy one, for his confidence here was as great as in the other matters it was small. This was the steeplechase between the brown horse, which went commonly by the name of Œdipus, and the mare Reluctance, the property of his mortal enemy, Robinson Brown. He was very jealous of that young man – not without cause. For when we take into consideration a fashionable lisp, or whatever his peculiarity of pronunciation might be called, a quantity of first-class jewellery, the whitest of hands, and neatest of feet, a tall, delicate figure, his tailor's very best attentions, and the enormous fortune to which he was heir, what young woman could resist him? Yet Edith Dacre managed to do so in a very decided manner. And whilst Charlie was fretting under a whole suit of flannel and three top-coats every morning, to get his weight down to the requisite 12st 4lb with the saddle and bridle, John Robinson Brown, the heir apparent, was smarting, not from rejected love, but injured vanity. Charlie Thornhill's dashing performance, and consequent rescue of Edith Dacre, with the very warm feeling which was exhibited towards him by every member of the Dacre family, had so roused the dormant energies of "dear Jane", that he was determined to formalise matters with Edith.

No sooner was Miss Edith's health perfectly re-established, which it was in a few weeks, from the excellence of her constitution and the invincibility of her spirits, than she determined upon riding again. She began with the old pony, and prudently confined herself at first to the road. It was not long, however, before a lovely morning, such as we have only occasionally in the winter, tempted her to hunt again. Her father and Mr John Robinson Brown were her escorts. The latter of the two rode one of his very best looking horses, Captain Bobadil, and was altogether such a pattern of perfection as no one but the best of tailors and the most skilful of valets ever sent out. Edith's charms at the breakfast table, her lovely figure, the glow of renewed health and the simple beauty of her unaffected toilette had completely upset her suitor. Mr Dacre was held up on his way to the Meet by one of his turnip-growing friends, who had got him fast upon the subject of swedes and parsnips making admirable soup, and the relative proportions of saccharine matter in the one or the other. The horses were at a foot's pace as the gentlemen rode their hunters and accommodated themselves to their fair companion's humour. She and the millionaire were about a hundred yards behind and their conversation had taken a turn on general affairs and affairs of the heart in particular. Never was such a chance, thought the knight.

She was just then wondering who he was describing as "weally vewy much ... aw ... aw ...positively quite unable ... aw ... aw ..., one of the most wwetched, or the most fortunate ... aw ... of beings, sufferwings, and that sort of thing quite widiculous, mawwiage, and so forth, difficult to expwess his feelings." When, leaning gently forward, he ventured to place his own ungloved hand on the lady's pommel of the saddle, occupied already by the tightly gloved one of Edith Dacre. At that moment a cheerful little bird in the hedgerow (a "wobin in fact," as he afterwards described it) who had heard every word and understood it – which was more than you or I could have done – flew out with a twitter right in front of Robinson Brown's horse. Captain Bobadil, who was fresher than usual (and he had an awkward way of putting up his back sometimes) gave one lurch to the off-side, as the gallant cornet was leaning down a little too tenderly, shot out his hind legs with a peculiar twist of the back and sent his master right into the mud at the pony's feet. Having done this, he trotted on in magnificent form to join the turnip-crushers in front, who were thus made aware of the little accident behind. If Robinson Brown wanted an answer to his remarkable proposal he found it in an uncontrollable fit of laughter, which the poor girl nearly strangled herself in her endeavour to stifle. The only result to him was the kind inquiries of his friends at the cover-side, whether he had been larking on the way to the meet and some sapient remarks that when he was older he'd know better. The robin evidently knew all about it for he saved Edith Dacre, what is always a painful performance to a good-hearted girl, the necessity of refusing like a lady a great ass. How she would have got through it she has not the slightest idea to this day. He never began again.

Of course the thing was not mentioned by the two parties concerned. We can scarcely conceive Mr Robinson Brown publishing his own defeat. I can answer for Edith Dacre's silence. In the beginning of

December, however, there was a four days' frost and men came up to town.

"By Jove, Lurcher, how d'ye do?" said our old acquaintance, Tuftenham, of the Foreign Office, walking into the Reform Club one morning, and tapping his friend on the shoulder. "What sport?"

"Fair; not very first-rate." replied the other, "We've killed about twenty brace of foxes. Payne has had some capital sport in the Pytchley country. Any news in town?"

"Not much," said the Government clerk. "You know Robinson Brown, the man in the 103rd Dragoon Guards?"

"The woman, you mean" interposed Lurcher.

"He proposed to Edith Dacre, out riding. You know the Dacres, Teddy's sisters? And she knocked him off his horse."

"I beg your pardon, Tuftenham." said young Balderdash of the Blues. "I had it from the man who saw it. They were going to cover when it happened; and Charlie Thornhill who thought he had insulted her in some way, pulled him off his horse. The thing was hushed up because of the girl. By the way" added he, lowering his tone confidentially, "don't mention it, for it was told me as a great secret and it might create a row if it got wind – fellows are so deuced particular about that sort of thing."

"Certainly not," said Tuftenham; and off he went to the "Tag and Squeamish" to retail his pretty piece of gossip. Of course it did not come round to Charlie in this form, as it underwent many more additions, modifications and perversions before it reached him; but he ascertained pretty surely that the gentleman had received his *coup de grâce*, and he was happier for the intelligence. The robin and the frost were to blame.

In the meantime most things went on quietly and consistently in the sacred grove in which Captain Armstrong instructed British youth, including Charlie Thornhill, in the mysteries of military science.

CHAPTER 22

STRONG OF THE STABLE

"An honest man is able to speak for himself, when a knave is not." – *Henry IV*

Charlie Thornhill had just finished, what in racing language is politely called his last sweat, and was lying in his room preparatory to another attack upon those eternal logarithms, when a knock at the door summoned him.
"Man below wants to see Mr Thornhill," said the servant.
"What's he like?" said Charlie, through the door.
"Looks like an Irishman. I think he is one, sir."
"Why so?" again demanded our hero.
"Talks like it, sir and says he's so thirsty."
"Where does he come from; and what does he want? Not a gentleman, is he?"
"Oh! No sir. Won't give no name; and says he can't leave the house till he's seen Mr Thornhill."
"Well, then, take care of the hats and coats and I'll be down in five or ten minutes. I dare say he wants money."

"Most of 'em do, sir. I'll tell him to wait in the hall."

Charlie rose, completed a rapid toilette and descended.

"I think you want to speak to me; my name's Thornhill."

There was no one in the study so thither he conducted his visitor. The man did not answer immediately and Charlie had time to run him over. He was evidently from the Sister Isle: it did not require him to talk to recognise that fact. He had a quantity of shaggy brown hair, a thick beard, with which his eyes and the general colour of his face were at variance. His high cheekbones and ferret-looking eyes gave a character of cunning to him. His dress was peculiar. He twisted a low-crowned hat in his hand. His clothes were well made but rather shabby. A shepherd's plaid shooting coat and a waistcoat; a scarlet woollen neckcloth, with the ends hanging down; a pair of brown trousers, very tight and terminating in three buttons over the rough and thick highlows he wore, completed the suit. What was he? A helper; a wandering conjuror; a pedestrian attendant on a pack of hounds; or a Newmarket tout out of season?

"Now then, what is it, my man? Where do you come from?"

"I come today from Mr Downy's"

'Oh! Oh!' thought Charlie 'Something wrong about Œdipus? Now I suppose he wants to see my brother.'

"Are you engaged in the stable?"

"No, sir; not exactly."

'One of those rascally touts,' thought Charlie. 'It's about time honest men cut the turf.' And indeed Charlie was right about that.

"Well, then, you know something about our horses. Now, out with it like a man. Let's hear what the information's worth, and you shall have it."

"Faith, then, your honour's right; it is about the horses."

"Which of them?" said Charlie.

"Well, it's not Kathleen, nor the two year old; them's all right: and I seen Jonathan Wild the day before yesterday. Oh! he's the picture." During which speech the man continued to turn and twist the rim of his hat.

"But there's the big brown horse, your honour knows, as isn't quite clane-bred; and ... and ... he's more of a steeple-racer or whatever your honour calls 'em."

"Œdipus, you mean; the horse that's engaged in a match?"

"Well, Captain, I wouldn't engage for the name," said the Irishman. "I don't well know about them foreigners, but that's the horse that I mean."

"Is there anything amiss with him?" said Charlie, rather nervously, for he knew how heavily Tom had backed him. "The horse was all right a week ago." Here Charlie looked closely at the man, and a sudden idea that he was not unknown to him set him thinking where he could have seen him.

"He's right enough now, and will be so, maybe this week or two or whenever the match is; but he won't be right the day before, nor the day itself. But I see your honour don't belave me."

"If what you tell me is true, you've some object in telling me," said Charlie, who was still endeavouring to recall the place in which he had seen his companion.

"'Deed, I have, then. It's to save yer money, and, maybe, yer horse; but I'll be murther'd if it's known that I told yer honour anything about it."

"You havn't told me anything about it yet. What is it you fear?"

"What is it I fear? I fear I'll be murther'd," said the Irishman, taking thought for himself.

"No, no; I mean what do you fear for the horse?" said Charlie,

"For the horse? Sure it's poison."

"What makes you think there's any danger of that? Do you know the trainer, Sam Downy?"

"Do I know Sam Downy? 'Deed do I. He's done a queer thing or two, but he won't do that: he's right enough. It's the boys."

"Then why didn't you go to him at once?"

"He's a good man, is Sam Downy; but he's not a real gentleman, Misther Thornhill: he hasn't the blood in him. Wouldn't he think I'd be lying to him; with his own boys, and all? But it's true as gospel; and ye'll belave it, if ye lave the poor beast and then you'll see." This seemed a very conclusive condition, but Charlie was too English to enter into it. So he said again: "This may be true; but I can't test it. How do you know this?"

"Faith, I do know it. I heard it."

"Men hear more lies than truth in this world."

"Your honour's right this time. So your honour will send for the horse away?"

But Charlie was too staunch to his point to be shaken off like this, so he said again, "Not unless you give me your authority. I won't move a hand or foot in it unless you do. Take your news to Mr Downy."

"You won't? Then, sir, by Jakers, it's just Jacob is my authority; divil a soul else." This was said with a sort of obstinate energy, which impressed Charlie somewhat with its truth.

"And what did Jacob, as you call him, tell you?"

"Just nothing at all. What for would he tell me? Faith it was the lad as looks after the horse, as he told it to. Says he, 'Jim,' says he, 'it must be done' and he showed him the money. 'That's your own' and he spreads it out. 'And you'll have a handsome trifle put on for ye besides.' and the boy said something about the Squire, maning your brother, and how he loved the horse. And then the blackguard promised that he wouldn't hurt him, only make him safe. And he's to have a key the night before the race; and if the money given for it is anything, it'll be a golden key that unlocks the stable door."

"And where were you when you heard all this?" said Charlie.

"Wasn't I asleep in an outhouse, and they two was talking to one another all the time about Mr Thornhill's horse."

"And what Jacob is this, that you seem to know so much about?"

"He's Jacob Ritsom; I knew him when I first see him: for we were together, maybe fourteen or fifteen years ago. He was always a bad'un was Jacob. They do say as he's groom to a gentleman – Misther Graves, they call him, a great sporting gentleman." This threw a new light on the subject, and made Charlie pause. He knew Wilson Graves; he knew his character and he knew that, for some inexplicable reason, he had been laying against the horse, by commission, up to the very day.

"And your object is to serve me?"

"It is."

"And how have I deserved that at your hands?" said Charlie, who, being one of those men who acted upon some sort of principle himself, expected others to do the same.

The Irishman looked down, with a foolish look, as though not understanding the question. At length he raised his head, and ignoring the previous question, he said, "Then ye'll look afther your brother's horse, sir; I never saw a finer beast. He's a grand horse altogether."

"Listen to me, and never mind about the horse. I want to know what I ever did to or for you that you should be anxious to serve me. You must have a reason." As Charlie spoke he rose from his chair, and placed his back, apparently with no purpose, against the door. The movement was not lost on the Irishman, who looked nervous and again resorted to a vacant stare, whilst he appeared to ponder the last question.

"What ye ever did to me? Sorrow a thing ye ever did to me. Maybe ye'll mind the puppy ye lost ...."

"And got back again. My good man, I'm not likely to forget it in a hurry. Did you hold my horse at Tattersall's that morning?"

"Well then, your honour, I won't decave you. You're too quick for the likes o' me, anyhow. How'll the dog be? I heard that ye had her back."

"She's upstairs at this minute, and well. But why did you come here to me today?"

"Och, yer honour, it's Misther Downy, sure, I was thinking of. Ye see, your honour, I've been a bit in the horse line myself, and, though I'm out of luck, I know a trifle about them sort. They're not the same as a gentleman-born." And Mike Daly, for it was he whom we had met previously on the heath where Geoffrey Thornhill met his end, and nearer at hand in Mr. Burke's office, began to feel quite comfortable at having put Charlie off the scent as to the motives of his information. He was wise enough to hold his tongue, a thing few people can do. At length Charles Thornhill looked at him steadily and said,

"Supposing this information to be true – and I shall take care to see whether it is or no – what is the price? You haven't travelled with it here for nothing. What do you want?" And Charlie resumed his seat by the fire. Mike stared for a moment and then drawing up with a certain dignity, which assorted badly with his tight brown trousers and highlows, said,

"Faith, it's no fault of your honour's that ye can't understand me. I was better off once, and I'd a good name to the back of me; but it's a long time ago. I haven't a rag on me now that wasn't given to me; and it's not proud that I'd be, under the circumstances of the name I'd get if I'd my deserts. But I'd rather walk barefooted to the next jail, or, what's harder fare, to the parish workhouse, than I'd rob one of your name for doing an honest action." Mike burst into tears, the first he had shed for many a long year; and before Charlie had recovered from his astonishment, he was out of the garden-door, and into the road, on his way home.

No sooner was he gone, which Charlie ascertained beyond all doubt, by looking after him out of the gate, than he began pondering on the strange occurrence. It was not odd that a man should wish to tamper with a horse in training: such things had happened before. But it was odd that the man who did so had no more sense of shame or obligation than appeared to be the case with Wilson Graves. What, too, brought the Irishman here to tell him? He looked like a scoundrel; doubtless he was one (for appearances are not always deceitful); and yet the man took a journey and refused money, two things that none but a madman would be guilty of, instead of participating in the robbery. Charlie's doubts resolved themselves finally into three distinct propositions. When once that happens with a man of his character we may look for a speedy solution of difficulties. For, if not over sharp, he was exceedingly honest; and a sort of useful common sense assisted a conscientious view of right and wrong. His first impulse was to take the matter in hand himself; but a moment's reflection showed him that that had its problems, the simplest of which was that he had no sort of authority whatever to do so. The horse was not his; the stables were not his; the money was not his. He possessed nothing but the information.

Should he go at once to Tom? After all, he was the person most concerned. But prudence told him that if it could be disproved he might as well spare Tom some very uncomfortable sensations. Charlie was loth to believe that Wilson Graves was concerned in such a nefarious business; still, appearances were against him. Should he see Mr Samuel Downy? The only real objection to this was the recollection that he had not secured the cooperation, nor even the address of his informant and therefore the injustice he might be doing to an innocent stable boy. Still, it was eminently Downy's business to know about his lad, and to fathom it; and if he knew it already, as the Irishman had hinted, the sooner his owners knew it the better for the interests of the turf. One cigar, and a turn in the garden, settled his deliberations in favour of meeting up with Downy. He put it into practice at once.

Mr Samuel Downy was one of the best trainers in the business and as he had risen to its heights from its lowest depths, through all the gradations, he fully comprehended its details. He had that grand virtue, that whilst he was in dignity of carriage, redness of face, the superintendent of his establishment, he was not above descending to the minutiae of his own stable boys. It was the making of him as it had been of the great Duke and some other remarkable persons. Sensual indulgence unhappily produced gout, and gout infirmity; otherwise Mr Downy would have been an active man; as it was he was a very clever one. He was placed in a situation of much temptation, which he resisted so successfully that his reputation was unblemished.

It was about nine o'clock at night: the low, snug room which Mr Downy called his own, and in which he smoked his evening pipe and drank his evening glass, was warm and well lighted. Downy smoked in silence and Mrs Downy did the talking at intervals. Then they heard a clatter and a knock on the outside door and after wondering whether it was some half-dozen possible but unlikely people, Mrs Downy attended to a second appeal by snatching up a candle, with "Lor love the man, he's in a hurry, whoever he is," and going to the door.

"How do, Mrs Downy?" said Charlie as soon as he got inside; "How's Mr Downy? I hope I haven't disturbed you; and it is rather late to come down without writing. However, I want to have five minutes' conversation with Downy, if he's up;" and here, having been subjected to Mrs Downy's scrutiny, she recognised the speaker and opened Mr. Downy's door.

"Bless me, my dear, if here ain't Mr Thornhill; who'd a thought it at this time o'night?"

She proceeded at once to ring for another glass, more hot water and what Irishmen know as the "materials." Charlie was not averse to the arrangement; mixed himself a tumbler of whiskey and water, and accepted a cigar, which had been a present from his brother to Sam Downy.

It was not long before he made Sam Downy understand the exact state of his suspicions with regard to Œdipus. As he progressed with his story, he might naturally have expected some remark, some affirmative or negative grunt. Not a sound relieved or assisted him. Slowly and methodically Sam Downy puffed away at his pipe; but a little more prolonged expulsion of smoke betrayed an increased interest in the story. Charlie finished; and Sam puffed away and looked steadily into vacancy. At length, stopping his pipe with his little finger, and taking a gulp at his whiskey and water, he turned slowly round to Charlie and said,

"Oh. That's the game is it? Do you believe it?"

"I can scarcely say that I do. I haven't told my brother but I thought it right to come here." Charlie had been so reassured by the trainer's coolness and he really now very much doubted the truth of the story. After another half minute to the question,

"No! I do not believe it."

"I do!" said Sam, emitting a cloud of smoke which spoke volumes.

"Any reason?"

"Half a dozen." Here Charlie waited for one of these half-dozen reasons; but he was doomed to disappointment for Downy continued to smoke in silence and then 'He drank and smoked, and smoked and drank and smoked again.' Charlie was too prudent to interrupt his meditations with rash enquiries. After, however, a considerable pause in the conversation he ventured to ask, "What sort of a boy is it that looks after the horse?"

"Jim's a very good boy; good as most, better than most."

"Do you suspect him then?"

"Yes."

"Why?"

"Because he's a liar and a coward. They go together."

"Then is that your idea of a good boy, better than common, Downy? What an experience of youth yours is!"

"There's only one out of ten that wouldn't be too bad for the Old Bailey if you could know half the truth. The boy's been lying to me lately about a key, and his being out at night. I've had an eye on him; the horse is all right, and you'll say tomorrow it's all over but the shouting if we can circumvent this rascal Jacob, whoever he may be."

Charlie turned his cigar in his mouth, looked at it attentively without seeing it, and asked "But how to do that?"

"Leave it to me. I shall write to Mr Thornhill tomorrow, sir; and if he'll put me on sixty pounds to forty, I shall be much obliged to him. I'll guarantee him all he's laid upon the horse against anything going wrong now."

"Well, then, good night Downy. I'll be with you tomorrow about nine." And Charlie walked off to the Stapleford Arms.

"Now, Sally, let's have that rasher in directly. I begin to feel a bit peckish." Mr Downy still dined early.

The next morning dark clouds lowered ominously above; and there had evidently fallen much rain in the night. Charlie was punctual for his appointment.

"That's a nice colt, the one we've passed." said Charlie; "Good useful legs and feet, and big thighs and hocks."

" By Orlando[34] out of Durandarte." replied Downy; "Great turn o'

---

[34] **Orlando** (foaled 1841) was a notable British Thoroughbred racehorse, best known for winning the Epsom Derby. He was a leading sire in Great Britain

speed." This was said almost in a whisper.

"Strip that Oaks filly, Ned." And the boy, slipped off the clothing."
"That's a nice filly, Mr Thornhill;" and he ran his hand approvingly over the mare's quarters. "Quiet!" added he, as she lashed out with one leg; "Quiet can't ye? This way, sir."

Charlie turned from his inspection into a dark doorway and Mr Downy, putting a key into a lock, turned it and they were in the presence of Œdipus. "Now, where's Jim?"

"Here, sir," said a good-humoured looking youngster about eighteen or nineteen; not very strong minded to all appearance and mischievous but not malicious.

"How's the horse?"

"All right, sir." Jim stripped him in a minute, and wiped him down with an old piece of silk handkerchief. The trio stood and surveyed him. He was a good-looking horse and his appearance told no falsehood. His coat had been singed down closely, but looked glossy and well. He was a long, low horse, able to carry about 13 stone and though, as Mike Daly had said, he was not a "clane-bred 'un," still he looked it all over. He had a fine, intelligent head, not too small, well set on to a rather muscular neck. His shoulders were beautifully laid, but a little thick and weight-carrying to a fastidious eye. Good legs and arms in the proper place; and hardy of feel and appearance. Behind the saddle he was beautiful; and his length from the hips was very great. His hocks were well let down, and under him; and with the exception of the blemish from which he took his name[35], he

---

and Ireland

[35] Œdipus the infant eventually came to the house of Polybus, king of Corinth and his queen, Merope, who adopted him as they were without children of their own. Little Œdipus/Oidipous was named after the swelling from the injuries to his feet and ankles.* The word **oedema** (British English) or **edema** (American English) is from this same Greek word for swelling: οἴδημα, or *oedēma*. Apparently his injuries were from having his ankles and feet pinned together as a baby because his father

appeared to be almost faultless. His performance over a country was as perfect as his symmetry; and he required nothing but skilful steering to render victory pretty certain.

"Is William ready with the old Saucebox to lead?"

"Yes, sir," said Jim.

"Then on with the cloths directly; you shall see him gallop sir." And Charlie saw the horse walk and gallop; and he never saw him look or go better. So he wrote a letter to his brother as soon as he reached Armstrong's, telling him of his journey, its object and satisfactory termination and he trusted to old Downy's sagacity to defeat any plots, if any existed, fully confident that the man was as honest as it was possible to be, living in an atmosphere of so much temptation.

[for some unknown reason] did not want him to crawl.

CHAPTER 23

A FIRST VISIT

"Utere convivis, non tristibus utere amica."
Spend your time with company you enjoy: spend it with your sweetheart.

There was a frost at Melton – indeed in most places. In vain the after-dinner zealots kicked the heels of their boots into the ground; in vain they looked at the thermometer; in vain they inquired after the moon. The frost would not go, so they did: some to London; some to shooting quarters; some to agreeable country houses. The horses remained in Melton to make echoes on the hard roads as they passed to morning exercise, slipping and sliding, here, there and everywhere; their riders loading the morning air with the thin clouds of their tobacco; their masters lounging in bed, and impatient at the weather which made them thus inactive.

"When are you going, Thornhill? This is the third day and it looks like lasting. Everybody except you and me is gone to town. They were all off yesterday."

" I'm off today." replied Tom Thornhill, but he did not think it necessary to add "where." Either it was not sufficiently important, or far too important to be mentioned. The assumption was that he was bound for London; the fact was that his road lay to Gilsland. He was not a man to make himself unhappy about a frost and the Dacres' invitation, which had been accepted conditionally, was regarded now as a boon. So Thornhill ordered his valet and his valet ordered the post-horses[36]; and having sent over a groom with a couple of hacks to the Dacre Arms, and having left orders for the stud to be forwarded in the event of a sudden thaw, he himself started about four o'clock for Gilsland.

The house was not full, but there was a good sprinkling of men and two or three women. A dowager to assist Mrs Dacre in her hospitalities or schemes; and a dear friend or two of the girls, without which no young woman of well-regulated mind seems capable of going through life. They write an infinity of letters, always have a breakfast confidence though they may have slept in the same room and wear the same coloured neck-ribbons. It is but fair to say that Alice had fewer weaknesses of this kind than most girls. She was superlatively true. Edith Dacre was less qualified to fight against that interesting partner of unmarried life, a "dearest friend." She was more inclined to lean upon somebody. It is but justice, however, to say that she had a limit to her amicable relations and had mentioned not even the name of Charles Thornhill nor Robinson Brown to Lady Lucy Trevanon, the supposed friend of her bosom, the depositary of blighted affections and of rejected addresses.

Tom Thornhill was in time for dinner. He stayed many days; and as he was in love when he got to Gilsland, and had had the symptoms on him ever since the end of last season, it is not singular that the malady should have broken out upon him in full force during the frost, which lasted more conveniently for him than for foxhunting.

---

[36] Post horse – a horse kept at a post house or inn for use by post riders or for hire to travellers.

The life in an English country house is much the same everywhere. There was shooting for the men and an occasional day with the rabbits. The covers at Gilsland, were good enough. Thornhill was an excellent shot. He was an excellent sportsman, which is widely different from a mere gunner. Whether he walked over the turnips and stubbles, whether he accompanied the keeper to the common at the end of the park, or whether he was posted at the warmest corner of the cover to make slaughter, he won golden opinions. All the men in the house talked of him. The ladies' maids heard all about him. He was referred to and deferred to daily at the table, when questions arose amongst the men, and it is not extraordinary that the women caught the epidemic.

Then they went to an election dinner. The local papers reported Tom Thornhill's speech, and all agreed that it was the most amusing, if not the most erudite of the evening. The "Times" condescended to make an extract. Eloquence always finds its way to the hearts of the women. They skated, Thornhill admirably; and he insisted upon a sledge on the ice for the ladies. They had some impromptu charades; he was the life and soul of the *corps dramatique*. He was not much in the library, but he seemed to be more or less *au courant* with the literature of the day thanks to the periodicals.

Guests went and came. Still Tom Thornhill remained. He had promised himself and Mr Dacre a week's hunting round Gilsland, and the latter would not be denied.

"Mr Thornhill must find it very stupid here," said Mrs Dacre. Next week, to be sure, they expected Harry Stapleton back; General Martinet was coming, Baron Hartzstein; and the frost looked like going. So Tom stopped on, nothing loth, and sent for his horses; and the frost did go, which is not usually the case when you send for your horses; and the guests came, which is not usually the case when you particularly want them; and everything was *couleur de rose*.

Meanwhile the Dunce of the family was making up for lost time. He had put everything pretty straight at Downy's. He had told his brother all his suspicions, who had poo-pooh'd them of course, and amongst Charlie's multifarious employments he had almost forgotten the subject. He had made up his mind to get through his examination.

Charlie Thornhill was not one to give up a thing he had once taken in hand: so he worked away every morning, indulging in a walk during the frost every afternoon, and pulling out of his pockets, at intervals, the dates of the Stuarts, the battles of the Wars of the Roses, George the Third's Ministers, the men of letters of Queen Anne's reign, a list of the British dependencies, the principal ports in Ireland, and the military stations of Hindostan. One thing, in the middle of it all, Charlie did not do. He did not go so frequently to Gilsland. "Only let me get over this examination and the steeplechase, and then we'll see all about it."

"You had a good run today, Mr Thornhill?"

"Not at all, Miss Dacre; what made you think so?" said Tom smiling, lounging into the hall in scarlet, covered with the mud which accumulates on a thaw.

"You look so happy and I concluded it was the run," said Alice.

"One can scarcely be unhappy here but I'm not so wedded to the horse and hound as you imagine. It really pains me to think that I can be so far misjudged." At the same time Tom looked brighter than ever and not at all pained.

"Misjudged? Oh! Mr Thornhill. No one misjudges you; but ..." here Alice felt the colour beginning to rise. Tom waited for the fruit of the "but".

"But, but, with all your love of ... of ... of" (Alice would like to have said "play") "hunting and racing, it is odd that you should find much pleasure in our quiet home." Here she thought she had said too much, so she added:

"Unfortunately, my brother is gone to Berne; but General Martinet comes tomorrow, with Lord and Lady Dunningfield, and then you will be better amused."

Here Thornhill's servant crossed the hall with clothes, hot water, etc and it was necessary to say something.

"Martinet, Martinet. Oh! He comes tomorrow," said he, in a quick, unmeaning sort of tone. "Oh! Ah! Well! Yes! Capital fellow, Martinet. You know him well, Miss Dacre, of course? He'll talk of nothing but horses. He's forgotten the army almost. Just recollects one circumstance; when he had a horse shot from under him. Miss Dacre, you never hunt?"

"Never," said Alice, with a rather determined but good-humoured face.

"That means never will."

"You read countenances well, Mr Thornhill. Surely one sportswoman is enough for a small stud. Besides, we have had our warning."

"Ah! I beg your pardon for reminding you of... " here Tom stopped suddenly.

"We never need to be reminded of it: it is a pleasure to remember our obligations to your brother. He has become very intimate here lately."

"So I hear. I envy him the leisure and the distinction." Tom began to think almost that Alice was in love with Charlie.

"As to leisure, he hasn't much: the distinction, if it is one, is well deserved. We owe him two lives out of the three."

"Charlie's a good fellow, Miss Dacre: too good to go out of the country. I can't understand why he should go," rejoined Tom.

"I think I can," said Alice; "but it is not everybody that would understand your brother."

"Quixotic?"

"Not the least in the world: never was good common sense so strongly exhibited: I love his independent spirit. You see he has made a *confidante* of me."

'How like Lady Marston she is,' thought Tom. And so she was, but stronger. She had lived less in the world, and was less a woman of it. It was quite clear she was not in love with Charlie.

* * * * * *

An evening later after dinner with the newly arrived guests, Tom Thornhill was not in the drawing-room, nor in the billiard room. He was at that moment in Mr. Dacre's morning room in an armchair sitting in gloomy silence running over the best days of his boyhood and making some sombre reflections on his present career, his coming match, the news of Œdipus that he had received from Charlie, and his heavy Newmarket betting involvements. At length Tom rose, shook himself free from his cares, and sauntered towards the drawing room. The sight of Alice would cure him. The room was deserted. What! So late? Eleven o'clock? All the women gone to bed? No! They are in the billiard room. General Martinet and Harry Stapleton playing a game.

""Is the General giving you lesson, Harry?" said Tom at the open door.

"Yes; it's not very dear: a pound a game. We've just finished. The ladies are waiting for you to play."

"I can't play tonight." And for the first time in his life Tom was proof against persuasion and odds. He took a seat by Alice Dacre, who had never found him so agreeable.

There was a smoking room at Gilsland to which men retired after the ladies, and Dacre (who never smoked) or those of antiquated notions about eight hours' rest, were gone to bed. Here was whist, a little higher than in the drawing room; here were betting books compared on the Leger; here were the racing *on dits* of the day sifted; and, above all, a considerable deal of handicapping and match-making for the next Meeting took place over cigars and hock and seltzer water.

Tom Thornhill had had a bad time of it. During his stay he had sat late, and played high, not with success. Now and then Tom looked his position in the face and saw a very deep gulf in his once ample resources. But his lawyers had never failed him yet and had not even talked of a mortgage. Still it had been a ruinous winter. That night he turned on one side of his pillow and he saw in his mind's eye Alice Dacre. He could not be indifferent to her. A thousand trifles had assured him he was not. He'd go and live at Thornhills and make his mother happy, and take her home a daughter she could love. How the two women at Thornhills would rejoice. He saw their approving faces through half the night. And then he turned over on his pillow and saw Dacre of Gilsland, stern and sad, and he thought Alice was very like her father about the eyes and mouth. Would he give his child to a gambler?

CHAPTER 24

ANOTHER OFFER

"I like thy counsel; well has thou advised."
Two Gentlemen of Verona

On the morning of the day on which Tom Thornhill was to leave Gilsland, as good or ill luck would have it, he walked into the library, where he found Alice Dacre turning over the pages of an old periodical. It was quite clear she was not reading them. He was in most things a person of impulse and it was just possible, notwithstanding his feelings that, but for this accidental meeting, Tom would have left unsaid what he had to say. An ominous silence reigned for a minute or two, when Tom Thornhill looked up from the paper he was pretending to read and said in a low voice,
"Alice."
"Mr Thornhill."
"Excuse the abruptness of my address. It must have been evident to you during the few weeks I have been here that my happiness, everything I have in life, is dependent upon you. If I have been unable to impress you with this I have indeed failed." and here Tom

took a passive hand in his, and proceeded to declare his love of her, perhaps a trifle incoherently.

Alice regained possession of her hand, and rising to her full height, placed it for support on the back of a chair. A blush rose to her cheek and a tear hung on her eyelashes; and if she ever looked perfectly lovely, it was now.

"Forgive me if I have hurt you by what I have said." Tom continued in surprise and mortification. "I was foolish, and flattered myself; and now I have been rash and impertinent to the only being ..."

"No, no don't say so;" and one single tear glistened a moment and dropped.

"Are you then not entirely indifferent? Oh, Alice, if a lifetime of devotion could assure you how sincerely I love you, give me the opportunity of proving it." Maidenly reserve and truth struggled for a moment in Alice. She almost immediately saw that they were consistent the one with the other.

"It would be unkind to let you remain under a wrong impression until we meet again. You have surprised me into this admission. But we have seen so little of each other. My whole heart, without one single doubt, one single scruple, shall be given, but it shall go hand in hand with respect and esteem. Are you satisfied with my honesty?"

"Yes, Alice, I presume I must be."

"Then let me say adieu to you here. Good bye; God bless and protect you!" she held out her hand, smiled through her tears, and hurried from the room. Tom stepped into his carriage an hour or two later; his feelings were difficult to define but altogether he was a happy man.

Charlie remained at the Armstrong's house working with a savage determination only known to military candidates.

"Come in." said one of his fellows to a knock on the common room door one afternoon.

"Second-post letters," said a boy in buttons and not dirtier than they usually are. Why do not the middle classes employ female labour for all domestic offices? Cleanliness, good humour, and good looks, instead of dirt, idleness and impertinence.

"Here they are," said Smith, the ex-Harrovian, taking them from the willing hand of the youth, who retired: "There's one for you, Fothergill, and two for Thornhill; and here's 'Bell's Life' of last week and 'Bailey[37].'"

The party were instantly immersed in their letters or their newspapers; and Charlie's contained something which startled him. The first was simple enough: it was from Sam Downy, and gave the latest intelligence in the fewest possible letters.

'HONOUR'D SIR

"The 'orse is well. We know all about it. Mum's the word, as we want to ketch the rogues. More by-an-by.

Yours to command,

S. DOWNY

The next letter was less expected: it was from his uncle, Henry Thornhill, from Pall Mall. It also went the shortest way to its object.

HAMMERTON & Co, PALL MALL.

MY DEAR CHARLES,

A friend of mine is very desirous of seeing you in London on business of importance to yourself at Mint, Chalkstone, Palmer and Co's bank, East Goldbury, City. Ask for Mr Roger Palmer when you send in your card. I believe his business is very important to you. You can call on me afterwards if I can be of any use; and you will find your friend, Lady Marston, in town, who will be glad to see you. Adieu.

---

[37] Bailey's Magazine of Sports and Pastimes

Yours affectionately,

HENRY THORNHILL.

PS Your father was a friend of Roger Palmer's and once did him a service almost irredeemable.

That evening Charlie Thornhill was in London at his old quarters, Sir Frederick Marston's, where he underwent a little badinage on the subject of his military knowledge. Charlie was on his way to East Goldbury by twelve o'clock the next day and reached it at about half past one. He was not kept waiting. Roger Palmer sat in a comfortable inner room with "The Times" over his knee, and warming himself by a good fire. He rose to salute Charlie, offered him a chair, and again sat down.

"Mr Thornhill, I have no personal acquaintance with you, but your poor father was once the means of doing me so essential a service, at some risk and inconvenience to himself, that it will add sincerely to my pleasure if you can entertain the proposition I am about to make you, for my partners and myself. You'll take a biscuit and a glass of old Madeira?" Here he rang the bell.

"How did you come here?"

"I walked from Grosvenor Square." Roger Palmer gave a satisfactory grunt: it was indicative of energy, one of his own virtues. He then detailed to Charlie, that from the large Continental business they were doing, it was considered necessary to send a gentleman to Germany, not as a mere clerk, but almost as a partner. A knowledge of French and arithmetic would be necessary, and German should be added to it as, on the return to England, the youngest partner would have the Continental part of the business to transact. Every facility would be given, as it was proposed that the gentleman to go out should be a bachelor and reside in the family of the senior correspondent in Frankfort. That a handsome income, increasing according to circumstances, would be given; and that at the expiration of a certain term of years, the gentleman would be received as a partner in the house in England without any further premium or advance of money in any way.

"In short," said the little man – and he had a struggle about telling or concealing it ... "the income and the partnership will be yours by right, as I have myself advanced the needful. There, sir," said Roger Palmer, wiping his glasses, which had become a little dim, "there's a fortune for you, let me tell you, such as your ancestor may have had when he first bought Thornhills."

Charlie was so astounded by the unexpected nature of the proposal, that he could do nothing more than stammer out his thanks; but after a minute's hesitation the money part of the transaction seemed the most incomprehensible. He was anything but a man of business; but he knew quite enough to be well assured that such an offer was not obtained without a very large sum of ready money paid down; such a sum, indeed, that he could not accept it from the hands of a stranger. He had a very proper pride, and the expression of it only endorsed Roger Palmer's determination on his behalf.

"Then you can't or won't see that obligations may arise between men which renders any future relations between their families quite extraordinary?"

"I don't say that; but I have not lived, even to an age, Mr Palmer, not to know that the obligation I place myself under to you is immense, and that I, at least have no claim upon your bounty. There's my brother."

"You brother, sir, ought to have enough; besides, the 'wind bloweth where it listeth,' and I desire to confer this, not as a present, but as a recompense for the work you will have to do, and the benefit we shall derive from it. Come, look on it in that light."

"I can't look on it in anything but its true light – a sense of obligation to a stranger. Excuse my saying so; but you know what I mean."

"You are proud, young man."

"Perhaps I am." said Charlie.

"Will you reserve your answer for three days, and consult your uncle and your best and most intelligent friends?"

Charlie hesitated, looked at Roger Palmer's face, and said, "I will."

"Then take another glass of Madeira, and adieu."

" Bless my soul alive," said the banker, as Charlie descended the steps of Messrs Mint, Chalkstone, Palmer and Co., "I've more difficulty in getting rid of thirty thousand pounds than I ever had in making double the money."

Charlie called in at Pall Mall. He detailed the whole conversation to his uncle.

"Can you translate French tolerably?"

"I think I can now."

"And do a sum in arithmetic?"

"Certainly."

"And don't care about being a gentleman and a dependent on your family for the next forty years?"

"If coupled, it would be singularly distasteful to me," said our hero.

"And you came here to ask my advice with a view to weighing it?"

"Most undoubtedly, my dear uncle." Charlie laughed.

"Well, you know, very few people do. Then you shall have it. Accept his offer."

Lady Marston and Sir Frederick dined at home. Charlie gave a succinct account of his visit in the City.

"And now, Sir Frederick, what am I to do?"

"I know the circumstances of the case and you need have no scruples in accepting the partnership, or anything else. They owe their existence to your father's generosity and confidence. They were at their last gasp when your father, with scarcely a hope of saving them, and knowing full well their position, ordered every farthing he could command, besides a large sum which he borrowed, to be paid into their bank. It stopped the panic, and was the means of saving them. Accept it by all means."

"Frederick, nonsense – impossible! I've been down to the Horse Guards and had a long chat with General Bosville; and he has promised me the first cornetcy in the household troops for Charlie. I shall break my heart if I don't see him in uniform. I meant to have taken him to the drawing room in your place – you know you dislike it – and now he's to be a banker. Never mind, Charlie, we'll have you in Parliament. It's absurd throwing away six feet two and so much common sense on a back parlour in Lombard Street."

"Then I'm still to be a soldier, Lady Marston?" said Charlie, laughing.

"Well that depends entirely upon your own inclination. If you like a life varying between Windsor and London and all the pleasures which accompany a charming mess, the most intellectual conversation, champagne *bien frappée*, the idolatry of the Queen's balls, parades, operas, clubs and bachelorhood, by all means. But if you desire to put yourself in the way of doing good work, or following a useful calling; of assisting your fellow creatures; of becoming a really valuable member of society; and of bringing up a family after you, also to do the work properly that God sets them upon earth to do, then..."

"Ah! I see; I must go to Frankfort: so I accept tomorrow."

* * * * * *

It was three weeks later in the year, and Charlie was to start on his new career shortly. Arrangements had been made and he was to open his life at Frankfort-on-the-Maine under the auspices of Herr Meyerheim of Winkleman and Co., and in the house of the former. But there was still a task to undertake, and it was to this end that on a dreary, drizzling afternoon Charlie took his seat in the train for Dunham Heath Lodge, the residence of Samuel Downy. The crisis was come and in three days' time the great race between Œdipus and Reluctance was to be run. The horse was to be moved across the country tomorrow or the next day. Tonight the attack must come.

When Charlie arrived he found one of the boys at the station to carry his bag, with Mr Downy's favourite hack at his service. That gentleman thought it best to remain at home under the circumstances. When Charlie reached the lodge it was quite clear that good counsel had been kept. Even Mrs Downy herself knew nothing about it. Her cap, or pagoda, or structure of whatever kind, was as brilliant as ever; her smile as unfettered, her buttered toast equally good; and the roast fowl and egg sauce got expressly for Charlie Thornhill, was not the cuisine of a lady tormented with doubts, or ill at ease in her mind.

"The horse looks beautiful, Sir." said she. "Lor! What dangerous work that steeple chasing is, to be sure. One day here, another there. Perhaps the poor thing may kill hisself, for all his good looks. Downy often says he wishes you gentlemen would stick to the flat. He says that's a duty you owe to your country, but the other isn't."

Downy was evidently big with the cares of state; and well he might be. He had one policeman locked in an empty stable on one side, well supplied with beef and beer. Another policeman in an outhouse on the other side, also revelling in beef and beer, of which Downy himself had the key. And he had a third policeman, who had already partaken of hot gin and water, who was waiting in the little thicket at the back of the box in which Œdipus stood. All this had been done without Mrs Downy's knowledge. What a clever fellow was Sam Downy!

"The time is to be midnight, Mr Charles. We've made the boy safe; and as there's a little moonlight just then, we shall be able to see enough for our business." With this Sam lit his pipe, Charlie his cigar; Mrs Downy brewed some hot whisky and water, and then took to knitting, which shortly ended in a comfortable nap. Her better half soon followed her example. "My dear," said he, waking suddenly up, "I think you'd better go to bed." and to bed she went.

At half-past eleven Sam Downy led his guest mysteriously across the yard. First he unlocked Policeman One's box, then Policeman Two's box, proceeding cautiously to the rendezvous with Policeman Three. "There, sir, they won't show fight; but you'd better take the life preserver, in case of accidents. Rogues are always cowards."

They had been in their hiding place not more than half an hour when they heard stealthy steps crossing an open patch of heath at the back of the stables. Just then a cloud cleared away from before the waning moon, and they saw three figures, a boy and two men, crouching along the ground towards the yard, which was here open to the heath. They crept slowly forward, passing within the shadow of the copse. Charlie longed to give a war-whoop and be at them, but was restrained by Downy, who rightly judged that "ketching the rogues" was of the first importance. They allowed them, therefore, to continue their serpentine path along the side of the building, until they had turned the corner; they then followed them just as stealthily and reached the angle in time to see the key applied to the lock. It turned without noise, and silently the two men entered, whilst the boy remained without. At that moment a policeman appeared on each side; the boy became a willing prisoner; a very dim light scarcely shone in the stable; and Charlie, Downy and their companions had already their hands upon the latch, when a fearful scream woke the silence of the night, and pushing open the door, they beheld a scene of terror, which we reserve for another chapter.

CHAPTER 25

PREPARATION

"Shall I not take mine ease in mine own inn!"

Three days later (and the winter was far advanced) the silent little town of Sedgeley was all alive. Sedgeley was one of those places that had been spoilt by a small aristocracy. A potent lawyer, a real physician with an Edinburgh diploma and nine daughters, a rector who had been senior proctor, two medical practitioners and a wealthy banker, who combined with his usury the advantages of chief linen draper of the place – all had set their faces against railway intrusion. The consequence was that a thriving town of four thousand inhabitants with a roaring trade in penny whistles, came to nothing and Sedgeley had become eminently dull, save on one or two occasions.

Whenever the hounds met within two or three miles (for Sedgeley was in one of the best hunting counties in England,) all the idlers became busy. The landladies put on their best caps, and the ostlers were ready for any little odd jobs that might turn up on such an occasion.

The present occasion was not of that sort. Something more than common brought Mrs Bustleton down into the bar at four o'clock with a wonderfully smart cap. It was neither a funeral nor a wedding that produced a ringing of bells and a rustling of chambermaids with cherry-coloured ribbons on this sombre afternoon. When Ramsbotham, the saddler, rushed into the inn yard with an old but very good-looking saddle on his arm, to which he had been doing something, quite a crowd of inquisitive boys and lazy apprentices surrounded the gateway of "The Saracen's Head".

"Well, Margaret," said Mrs Bustleton to her sister, between mouthfuls of hot muffin, "I wonder the gentlemen don't come in. It's past five, and I'm sure they can't see to hunt."

"P'raps they've gone the other way, you know, and then they'd have a good ways to come home. I heard Tony say there was a good many 'orses already in; and I dessay the place will be quite full tomorrow."

"Yes, we must have supper in the big room, after the race. The Squire must take the chair, and Mr Thornhill and Mr Dacre must sit on each side of him I suppose. The rest must sit as they can."

"I thought the other gentleman, Mr Somebody Brown ought to sit the other side."

"Bother Mr Somebody Brown, Margaret; how you talk! He don't belong to the county. We'll have Mr Thornhill and Mr Dacre, if he comes, or some of our own people, and Mr Charles Thornhill all up at the top ... Lor! There's the fly." And true enough, after paying the fly and the driver, a tall well-made man in rough coat and comforter, opened the door, and stood unceremoniously in the badly-lighted corner of the bar-parlour.

"Why, bless me! It's Mr Charles." said Mrs Bustleton, colouring and wiping her hands on her handkerchief.

"Right, Mrs Bustleton," said he, stretching out a hand and advancing to the fire; "Let me warm myself a moment. I hope you are quite well, and the children?"

"All well, thank you sir; and Mrs Thornhill, and your brother, sir? We don't see so much of you as we did once, when you were boys, and used to ride over on your ponies. How's Miss Stanhope too sir? I hear she's a great deal with Mrs Thornhill. Your room is ready, sir, with a capital fire: isn't there, Margaret?"

"Thank you." But Charlie stood with his back to the fire, a little preoccupied. "And what time do we dine?"

"Seven o'clock, sir. You'll take a biscuit and a glass of sherry, Mr. Charles?"

"How many was dinner ordered for, Mrs Bustleton?"

"Six, sir, I understood. There's Mr Tom, and yourself, and Lord Carlingford and Captain Charteris, and Mr Stapleton and someone else; but I didn't hear who. P'raps you'd like a cup o' tea, sir?" Here Mrs Bustleton made an attempt to squeeze the pot.

Charlie looked down thoughtfully. "Is Mr Downy here with the horse?"

Mrs Bustleton rang a bell, which summoned the one-eyed ostler. "Tony, is Mr Downy here with Mr Thornhill's horse?"

"No mum – lestways, sir," said Tony, first to his mistress and then to her guest. "No, sir, he's coming this evening. The head man's here."

"Send him to my room." And Charlie, having picked up his overcoat and shawl, walked out of the bar, ushered by a tallow candle and bunch of cherry-coloured ribbons. On reaching his room which was warmed with a fine fire as promised, he took his coat off and there was a knock at the door.

"Come in." said Charlie and William, Mr. Downy's head man, entered.

"How did the horse come?" Charlie asked.

"He never was better, sir. It's my opinion he can't lose, if he don't make a mistake."

"But they do make mistakes sometimes – all of them: however, that's as fair for one as the other. How's the country?"

"A little sticky, sir; just suit the old horse, I should say."

"I don't know: the mare's a thoroughbred one and can stay."

"Well, Œdipus must be thoroughbred too, sir."

"He's not in the Stud book. But how's the poor fellow who was so horribly injured?"

"Not so well, sir. He's been a bit delirious – talks a bit, sir. They couldn't keep his bandages on last night. The man's bandages, you know, sir."

"But they are not seriously worried about him?"

"Oh! No, sir; I didn't hear as they were." Here William scraped himself out of the room.

Charlie Thornhill followed William out and went to the parlour. It was a comfortably furnished room, with a good fire, and a dinner table laid for six. He remembered it well. It was the room in which he and his brother met on the day of their eventful journey after the death of their father. He had been several times at the hotel since, which was only ten miles from Thornhills, but he had never been in that identical room till now. He looked at the pictures. They were the same. There was the famous American trotter, with the wonderful dog-cart, which looked like a wheeled spider. There was a picture of the late Mr Bustleton, a short, red-faced man in a dress coat and waistcoat with his hands by his side; and across the room facing him was the most extraordinary painting of his brown horse, Solomon, the most striking points of which were the biggest head and the shortest tail in England. There was the Prodigal Son, with a hole in his hat, with nothing on but a shirt and a pair of knee-breeches, being welcomed by his father in a flowing wig and a court sword. His brother looks on in gloomy silence, while a groom in a blue livery leads a couple of saddle horses up and down in front of the house.

The butcher in the distance is sharpening his knife ready for the fatted calf, which has not yet left her mother's side.

The door opened, and the same cherry-coloured ribbons appeared with a lamp. Mrs Bustleton was followed by a heavy footstep and the smell of tobacco. Tom Thornhill came in, and shook his brother by the hand heartily. Then came Lord Carlingford and a young man called Harry Stapleton.

"Charmed to see you, Charlie. How are the nerves?"

"All right, thank you. What sport today?"

"Very moderate. We found at Dodford and went down to Norton: it's wretched scenting country. We got on better terms with him after crossing the Sedgeley road, but we lost him at Driffield. I suppose Œdipus is all right, notwithstanding the reports in town?" said Stapleton.

"What reports?"

"Oh! I don't know exactly; but they offered me three ponies[38] to one against him yesterday. I was such a fool as not to take it, thinking there might be something wrong; and then we got the newspaper account of the scrimmage. I suppose you had a horrid row at Downy's place? They've committed the villains, I hear." said Stapleton.

"Well! Yes, we had, rather. Tom, dinner will be up directly and you fellows need to dress." And they all four adjourned to their rooms.

When they met again, Charteris and Baron Hartzstein had joined them. They sat down to a soup, leg of mutton and beefsteak pudding sort of dinner. They washed it down with some warm sherry, and ordered up some claret.

"Bye-the-bye, Thornhill, you were going to tell us about the row at Downy's and the attempt on your horse." Asked Carlingford.

"Charlie knows all about it; he was there: not I."

---

[38] A pony is bookmakers slang for £25.

It must have become evident by this time that one of Charlie Thornhill's besetting sins was his modesty. If he had to tell a story of which he was the hero, he made nothing of it. He loved a short cut to anything, and would gladly have said nothing more about the business. He seemed perfectly content that the horse was safe, and the perpetrators on the road to punishment.

"Let's have it, Charlie," said Tom. "I've hardly heard it properly myself yet."

"Oh. It's nothing particular. We found out that something was going wrong, so old Downy set a trap for the fellows and caught them."

"But wasn't there something about Œdipus eating one of the fellows?"

"Well. Not exactly: Œdipus is quiet enough. It seems that Downy had got a new boy, who mistook his orders. The boy ought to have changed a savage horse called Homicide to an empty box: but he made a mistake, and put Œdipus into the empty box and Homicide into our horse's place. They're not very unalike; and when Downy went round he never saw the mistake."

"Well! But what happened?"

"Oh. Nothing particular," said Charlie, helping himself to sherry; "we followed the men into the box without their knowing it. The horse was loose; and before we could get into the place, he rushed at one of the fellows, knocked him down, and seized him by the side with his teeth. Luckily, Downy was there, and got him off, by one or two violent blows on the nose; but the fellow was picked up half dead. He had broken several ribs and his side is terribly lacerated; but I hope he'll get better. The other fellow is remanded and will be committed of course."

"Where's the wounded prisoner? He won't get off, will he?"

"Certainly not. There's a policeman sleeps in the room. But he can't be moved; and Downy's man says he's not so well today."

"So nothing at all happened to your horse? What a fool I was to let those three ponies slip, to be sure;" and the recollection seemed to make a profound impression on Stapleton, who asked for the claret.

"And what are they going to do with the horse, Homicide?"

"Make a watchdog of him, I should think," replied the dunce of the family.

Tom Thornhill rang the bell and ordered some cards and a backgammon board. Before long he and his friends had dealt some hands and the Devil had once more got possession of him.

"Come, Charlie, will you play?"

"No! No!" laughed Charlie; "not I. You know I never play. Besides, I'm going to bed." This was a wise measure for a fool.

"Bed! What at ten o'clock? Smoke a cigar: here's a capital one."

"No, thank you: smoking at night's a bad thing for the nerves; and I've got all your money on my shoulders. You'd better let me go to bed."

"He carries Caesar and his fortunes. Well! Good night; and good luck tomorrow."

"Good night." And the play went on more and more furiously.

A gambler never understands ruin till it stares him in the face, and then he strives to stare it out of countenance. We all harden in time: but there's no fire like the dice box. Wife, child, self, soul are all too light to put in the balance with the turn of a card. Oh, Alice! Alice! What an intuitive knowledge of the world for one so innocent and so young!

CHAPTER 26

THE WALK OVER, AND THE RACE

"Si sors ista dedit nobis, Sors ipsa gubernat."
'If we like the hand that destiny has dealt us, destiny is indeed our guide'

Charlie slept well (it was his custom, once he got rid of his waking dreams about gambling.) There was always one figure which occupied the principal part of the picture. Tom was changing: not to himself, nor to his mother but still he had become capricious in his moods.

In the morning they were all off to look at the course that had been set for the race. It was four miles from Sedgeley, on the Croppington road, equally convenient for Robinson Brown, who had a box for the season, not half a dozen miles off, and for the Thornhills who lived in the county, ten miles from Sedgeley.

Charlie drove out in a fly with Charteris, Lord Carlingford and his brother. He intended walking the course. Robinson Brown was there before them, with a couple of hacks. Lord Carlingford's man had horses there for the others. Three accepted them, but Charlie adhered to his opinion and his legs. He was essentially a shooting-boot style of man. Robinson Brown was patent leather all over. A man's character almost always resembles his boots.

The course was already marked out with flags. It was plain and broad, as another path is said to be. A good four miles of it.

"The riders will keep the flags to their right hands, if you please," said the course judge. "It will be found a fair hunting country. You can choose your course as you will but only to the left of the flags."

Two or three gates let the horsemen in, whilst Charlie surveyed them on foot with a critical eye. The first four or five were good hunting fences, with nothing remarkable, and as easily seen from a pony as any other way. Then came a cramped place – the ground a little raised before taking off.

"Not to be ridden at too fast," said Charlie to himself; "and to be sure to get close up to it."

"That's an easy fly," said Robinson Brown from his hack. "A donkey could do that."

"Here's the water, Charlie. It's a fair jump everywhere; but the banks are rather higher in some places than others above the water." said Tom.

Charlie stood between two willows, and measured it with his eye. "What's the width, Tom?"

"Width? Oh. 'pon my word, haven't the slightest idea. You'd better ask the depth, Charlie. It looks quite big enough to get into."

"Not with Œdipus. I think I could jump it myself."

"Very likely," said Carlingford; "but that won't win the match. Come on. There's nothing but grass up to here, and the next field is the only bit of plough in the race." And on they went, smoking and laughing, till they came to a ridge of rough plough. It was almost like the sea but the way out of this difficulty was over a good stiff double post and rails. There was no room to land between; and it must be done at a leap.

"A place for a cropper," said Charlie again to himself.

Robinson Brown was chatting away with his friends, and surveying the scene with considerable *nonchalance*, seeing that he was going to play a prominent part in the drama to be enacted shortly. Either he had great confidence in himself, or his mare, or his luck: for the course was a decidedly stiff one, nothing short of a fatalist could have regarded the last field and fence with indifference.

"Brown, that's a big 'un," said Wilbraham, a good sportsman, and one of the leading men with the county hounds.

"Wather; y-a-a-s. A-should say, a wegular yawner."

"What did you think of the water? I suppose the mare's pretty good at that?"

"Water? Oh? Ah! The bwook. Ya-a-s: to be sure."

"Yes, the brook. You saw it, I suppose? Because you'd better canter back if you didn't."

"Ya-a-s, I saw it. I call it a wavine. It's a jump."

"Jump; indeed, it is a jump!" added his backer, in hopes of reviving either his spirits or his attention. "It's not unlike a family vault. You won't get out in a hurry if you once get in."

"Jump or vault, Weluctance will do it, Basset, *'Wise from the gwound like a feather'd Mercury, And vaulted with such ease ...'* Your hundwed's safe enough." And on they went. Beyond this the fences were fair hunting fences – timber occasionally; a thick bullfinch here and there, interspersed with a little child's play; and a second arm of the same brook, but by no means a formidable place. They were nearing the finish, and had passed about five-and-twenty fences, when a flag, placed on a high bank over which it was impossible to see, attracted universal attention.

"Charteris. What's this?" shouted the owner of Œdipus.

"That's a bank," said the Captain. "A new railway line is coming. If they don't like it, they can go round. We were ordered to pick four miles of hunting country and we agreed that that railway embankment was an obstacle which could present itself whenever the hounds run across here. It is about thirty feet high. Besides it's as fair for one as the other and if they don't like the embankment they can go round it further along."

The remaining fences had been inspected and approved of and as the course was arranged so as to form a semicircle, it was not a difficult one for the spectators. A large pink flag was carefully placed in every hedgerow, and the top of the bank was so conspicuous an object that it served for an excellent landmark for at least a mile beforehand.

The time was getting on – 1 o'clock – and the start to take place at two – or as soon after that as our gentlemen can get into their breeches. They all turned towards the little village inn from which they had started where carpet-bags, portmanteaus, horses, flys, grooms, and the various types of the fine old English farmer, had collected in great number.

"Well, Charlie, what do you think of the course?" said Tom Thornhill, whilst his brother pushed himself into a thinner and tighter pair of breeches than usual, and proceeded to pull on the very neatest pair of tops possible.

"Very good course. That's a sticker, that bank, you know. I suppose we shall both go round." said Charlie.

"Most likely."

"It is a hunter's course and I dare say many a horse would get round safe enough. Shy us that boot." said Charlie

"Don't put that jacket on; here's a purple and white stripe," said Tom again, tossing him one from a chair-back in the room.

Charlie then went downstairs slowly, as men must in boots and spurs, covered over with a light greatcoat of approved fashion. He found half the county ready to shake hands with him. It was a non-hunting day, and everybody within distance had come to see the race.

The crowd below was thick and anxious; and the heroes of the day were not likely to be more than an hour late at the starting-post: in fact, it was only half-past two o'clock, and they were already on their hacks, and starting for the post. To judge by the crowd that accompanied them, and the crowd that was already gone before, steeple-chasing was in the ascendant in the neighbourhood of Sedgeley. All the farmers' wives and daughters were there in flys, four-wheelers, dog-carts and carts, taxed and untaxed, of every description.

The member for Croppington was there too, on a clever hack; and the Master of the Hounds. Upon this occasion they were on the most friendly terms: as a rule, politics divided them. A goodly company planted itself at the brook and I must confess there is something sublimely pleasant in seeing another man get a ducking. The post and rails was also a pet place: it numbered some of the ladies, who are always kindly and tenderly placed at the spot most favourable to accident.

Besides the county families, the members of the neighbouring hunts, and the farmers and sporting tradesmen, there was a strong London division, who were peculiarly interested in the affair. In a word, for a private match, not supposed to excite particular interest out of the county, it was the most marvellous success that had been known for years.

We have already stated that Tom Thornhill's colours were purple and white stripes; Robinson Brown sported all white. Œdipus was a magnificent dark-brown horse, of great power but he has been already described. Reluctance was a racing-looking mare, a good golden chestnut, showing vast speed; she was low and long. They were both capable of crossing any country, and their condition was exceptional. Œdipus was the horse for choice on this ground; the mare was just a little too fine. She had, however, a great turn of speed. In addition there was a good field of amateur riders, but Œdipus and Reluctance were attracting the money.

They are off! Charlie would willingly have made the running at his own pace: he could depend upon his horse to stay, and he suspected a turn of speed in the mare. Reluctance, however, was too fresh to be steadied at once, at least by Robinson Brown, and the running to the first fence was in his hands, or, I might say, out of them.

Charlie watched him, as did many more. Away they went, the mare lurching at her bridle, and her rider sitting a little uncomfortably, to all appearance. Now her head was down, now up, and his hands were evidently full. Œdipus was fresh, but was held together in a manner that told him pretty plainly he had his master on his back. Charlie had the inside and steered close to the flags. He remembered every fence, and knew pretty well where to have them. Robinson Brown was not a bad man on a good horse, a hunter; but the mare was fresh and he was up in his stirrups and obliged to go faster than he liked.

The first fence was nothing extraordinary; but he went at it faster than he ought to have gone. Charlie sat down on his horse closely. His power over his horse was manifest. "Steady!" said he as the horse became excited by seeing the mare in front, and hearing the crowd behind. Crash, smash, flop, went the amateurs in the rear.

The fourth field was ridge and furrow, and the mare began to settle. Robinson Brown is no great favourite of ours; but he was not a fool in the saddle, and began to be more at ease. He still had to look back for Charlie, who kept his own line, at six or eight lengths behind. They were coming to the cramped fence with a suspicious slope in front. "I thought so," said the Dunce to himself; "steady Œdipus!" and he dropped his forelegs just in the right place, and landed well, as Reluctance pulled her hind leg out of the ditch, and shot Robinson Brown a little too forward to be elegant. There was no fall, however, and by now they were again side by side. "Well saved," said the crowd. "She's a quick'un" thought Charlie "and won't fall for a want of a leg to spare."

The horses now went stride for stride by one another; and the riders eyed each other. Like two of Homer's heroes, they looked for a hole, but the joints of the harness were well riveted; no weak spot was perceptible. The crowd was silent enough. No incident, no fun, nobody down yet. The ponies and hacks had turned aside and sought a shorter and safer cut to the water or to the finish. The pace had been good; but both horses held their own. The line of willows appeared in the distance, and Œdipus crashed into the rotten wood of an old pleached fence, with the ditch on the taking off side. The mare cleared it all, and was a length into the next field before Œdipus. "Bravo! That's the way to do it," said a warm-hearted tenant of old Robinson Brown, from the bough of a tree, who owed a half-year's rent, and wanted a new barn; "the young master wins for a hundred." Nobody took him. "I'll lay you five shillin' on the squire's brother, Master Chanticleer," said one of the Thornhill party. "Lor! Bless you," added the old sportsman, "see how he handles his horse: he's savin' him for the water; we ought to ha' been there."

In the meantime they were nearing the brook and a low fence and ditch brought them into the very field. Charlie marked his spot at once, and Robinson Brown, in advance about six lengths, diverged a little to the left, looking at what he imagined to be an easy place. It was not so big, but the ground was low on the taking off side, and the water was shallower having fallen over an artificial dam.

The mare put back her ears, and swerved. The first refusal; but no blood drawn. Robinson Brown held on by the bridle. Charlie kept the upper ground, and squeezing the old horse, sent him at it, where the bank was highest. The place was wide, but sound, and he landed well on the other side. The white handkerchiefs went up in the carriages, with a little buzz of applause.

Just then he heard a shout and hoped his competitor was in. Robinson Brown was just getting on his legs, the mare was already up but they had both fallen on the right side of the brook. Once up and mounted she was pulling double and seemed all the fresher for her fall. Brown looked positively cheerful, and Charlie never liked him better than at that moment. He really could ride, and had plenty of nerve. It was only even betting still. It was anybody's race now, and they were entering the ridge and furrow field before coming to the double post and rails; Charlie was well in advance and Œdipus was going up and down like a pony. Reluctance surely could not go over the ridge and furrow like that. But she did; and Robinson Brown raced to catch him. "Not a symptom of distress raced in either." said Charteris, as he sat on his mare, to some ladies in a carriage beside him; "but Charlie looks like winning. What a horseman he is!" The take off was not good, and Charlie knew it; so catching the horse tight by the head, and putting all his heart into it, he sent him at the most favourable place he could see. There's never a great deal of time to think when once in the air, and a faint shriek from a spectator was the first intimation that he had smashed twenty feet of stiff timber, and was down. "Lucky I held him tight," thought our hero, as he jumped on to his feet, almost as quickly as Œdipus and, shying the reins over his neck, threw himself into the saddle. He had just time to see that the mare had done it all safely and was well to the fore, when he set his horse going. His situation was precarious and he knew it.

Wherever Charlie went he carried his head with him. They were three-quarters of a mile from home, the fastest horse of the two in front by about a hundred yards and a heap of other people's money was on the event. There were five more fences, and whoever was round the bank first must win. "Round the embankment? There is but one chance for it, and it must be done." thought Charlie. Reluctance still went on with the lead, and though the horse never slackened his pace, the mare didn't come back, as Charlie intended she should have done. He began to shorten the distance by only a trifle. Yes, by Jove! She's getting shorter in her stride and here's the plough. It's a sticker at the end of three miles and a half; and Charlie looked for a furrow full of water. Robinson Brown kept straight on. Splash, splash went the horse; but still he gained; he entered the next field about sixty yards behind the mare. And here was the bank, right in front, which separated them from the winning field by a single fence.

Crowds of people lined the ridge, even to the right of the pink flag they extended. What will the rider of Reluctance do? Robinson Brown neared the obstacle and glanced back, then he gauged his mare, then he looked at the people. "It's all over," thought he; "he can't do the bank and I won't risk it." He turned away to the left and steered straight for the gap that let him through to the opening in the proposed railway line. As he reached the gap, Charlie steered straight for the embankment holding his horse firmly and jogging him up the ascent, the people in suspense cleared a road, and shouted applause. Straight over the bank he went. Slide, slither, slide! But with his head perfectly straight towards the winning post. Œdipus came towards the bottom of the descent; and just as he looked like falling, within ten or twelve feet of the bottom, Charlie jumped him over a low post and rails into the course. At the same moment Reluctance in full stride, appeared beyond the edge of the bank within forty yards of the horse, and right abreast of him. "It's a race! It's a race!" shouted the people. And it was. But Œdipus was galloping straight for the fence before him, and the mare came diagonally towards it. They both jumped together, but the mare had shot her bolt; and as Charlie turned round to look at her he slowed his horse gently for a couple of strides, and cantered in a winner by about six lengths. Time eleven minutes and a half, and Robinson Brown quite pumped.

"You'd better wipe those scales," said Charlie at the weigh-in; "they're covered in dirt, and these colours of Tom's are quite new."

Later as he was riding slowly off the course, an open carriage ploughed its way solemnly through the grass; it was stopped near Charlie by the crowd, and the well-known voice of Lady Elizabeth Montagu Mastodon, of whom we have lost sight for a time, was heard in congratulation.

"The first time we ever met, Mr Thornhill, was after a steeple-chase, but I little expected we should ever meet at another one. However, my friend Edith Dacre is too much of a sportsman to stay away; and as Mr Mastodon is not enough of a sportsman to come, I have been doing penance. Let me congratulate you on your success. If it's worth doing at all, of which I'm very doubtful, it's worth doing well. I suppose you've made a fortune."

"You forget that I never bet," said Charlie, taking off his hat to Edith, and longing to get round to that side of the carriage, but wondering at the same time, what everybody would think.

"Bless me! No. Your brother does that for both of you. We've not seen him for an age."

Charlie apologised for Tom and himself. They had both been away, but he would ride over tomorrow or next day to take leave. He was going to leave England for some time. Charlie looked at Edith's face as he spoke, and he saw a sparkling smile which gave him hope.

When he got back to Sedgeley, Mrs Bustleton had a note for Charlie from Sam Downy who said he had been summoned to the room of the wounded gipsy, at the moment he was about to start for the steeplechase. The injured man begged Mr Charles to come over; there was something to divulge, and he would tell it to nobody but Mr Charles Thornhill. He could not live; he was injured internally, and in his spine. The letter begged him to come quickly.

Charlie went as fast as his powers and the train could take him to Durnham Heath but it was too late; the poor fellow was dead. Tom Thornhill followed in the morning. They went into the chamber of death, the two brothers. The woman drew aside the cloth from his face, and there was the Gipsy George, the Whitechapel Dog-stealer who was also, unbeknownst to them, Arthur Kildonald's son.

And then they heard from Mrs Downy, and the nurse, and the police, of a mixture of names which seemed to startle, as a roar of a very distant thunder: a storm that had passed away – Kildonald, and Burke, and Squire Geoffrey Thornhill, and the meeting on Bidborough Heath – a terrible night, and never mentioned amongst them; buried, forsooth, in profound mystery; and now, for the last time, as it seemed in the grave. How soft, placid, and beautiful the face of the gipsy was, as he lay in his long last sleep! His matted hair clustering round his white forehead, and his long eyelashes lying on the cheeks from which all colour had at last fled. How little symbol of his noisy and criminal existence remained behind! Have we buried all his evil with him, or no?

A few days later Charles Thornhill rose from a seat in the drawing room of Fossils Thorpe Park where he was a guest of Lady Elizabeth Mastodon.

"Good morning, Lady Elizabeth. I must say goodbye," said Charlie, looking round the room, however, as if he missed something which ought to be there. It was getting dusk, and he had a sharp ride to Thornhills before him, as he justly remarked.

"Miss Dacre will be sorry to have missed you; though, as she returns home next week, you may see her at Gilsland before you leave England." Here her ladyship held out her hand cordially, for Charlie was a favourite, and said, "You must ring for yourself, or walk round to the stables; I get so very lame, Mr Thornhill."

Charlie preferred the latter, and retired. In crossing the hall, Edith Dacre met him; she had just returned from a walk in the park. I know nothing so becoming to a girl's face as the roses gathered from the fresh air of a fine winter's day. Summer roses carry the seeds of their own failure in the heat that produces them; but hibernal bloom tells of health, vigour, animation, life. So thought Charlie at the moment that Edith recognised him; and he stopped, absolutely perplexed by her beauty. It was nothing new to him to be perplexed, it is true. Still he floundered and faltered, till she fairly turned round, and walked towards the hall door. It opened on to a terrace which, at any other time than a raw winter's afternoon, might have invited a walk. Her bonnet was still on, and very becoming.

"My dear," said Mr Mastodon, half an hour later, "who is the gentleman whose horse was just now being led out of the visitors' stable?"

"Just now? If you mean an hour ago, it was Charles Thornhill."

"Of course it was; the white-legged chestnut: but he is only this moment gone."

"Then he'll have a very cold ride of fourteen miles, scarcely be in time for dinner. I suppose he's been admiring something."

"But it's pitch dark."

"Perhaps he admires somebody. Did you see Miss Dacre, my dear?"

"No, Lady Elizabeth. That's an imprudent idea. He hasn't a shilling."

"He may not be the worse for that. I don't like monied men – at least usually they're not all like you. Besides he may make a fortune – one of his ancestors did."

CHAPTER 27

SWEEPING UP CRUMBS

Now leave to talk of love,
And humbly on your knee
   Direct your prayers unto God,
     But mourn no more for me.
    Ballad

In one of the wings of Gilsland were three rooms *en suite*. They belonged to the Misses Dacre. There was a common sitting-room, shared by both, and a bed-room opening from it, on either side. It was their option to share the same or to retire to separate rooms.
They had dismissed their maid and sat in demi-toilette before a fire which lighted up the warm-looking carpet and winter curtains. Edith had that day returned from Fossils Thorpe Park, and was resting her head on her sister's shoulder. There was no lamp, but a small flat candlestick was, so to speak, thrown into shade by the fitful but fine glare of the Derbyshire coal fire. There were tears gathering fast on her lids, and her cheek was flushed – at least as much as could be seen from the luxuriant folds of her rich brown hair.

"Oh, Alice dear, what a weight of happiness in all this uncertainty!" said she, as she let a tear fall upon her sister's hand.

Alice kissed her kindly, and then said, "But why make a weight of it, darling? You must love him dearly. Who could help it?"

"But papa and mamma. Dear mamma; what a disappointment!"

"Come, courage! Edith. I know papa better than you. Act as you ought to act. Have no secret from them. All will go well."

"Ah! If I had but your courage, dear Alice. But you have no secret such as I; you have no trouble, dear. So it's easy enough for you to advise." And here Edith was getting a little out of temper, and becoming by consequence unjust.

"And how do you know that I have no secret and no trouble, Edith?" said her sister, colouring to the temples but making a bold effort to look her sister in the face. It was unnecessary for Edith only buried her face deeper in her sister's shoulder, and sobbed louder.

"I have a secret and a trouble such as you." Edith raised her head, and her tears ceased to flow, surprise had dried them. Alice did not need to bury her head whilst she made the confession of her love.

"I fear no confession to my dear father, nor to my mother, darling; but I fear to make it to myself. I have not told them what he said to me, nor what I said to him, for I have not accepted him; and it is his secret as much as mine. But I tell you; and you must be cheerful and happy yourself, and help me to be so. Mine is a worse burden than yours, dear: yours will be light enough in time, but mine will grow heavier every day." And here the stronger leant against the weaker, and took comfort from their mutual helplessness.

"Then you don't love him, Alice, as I love Charlie?"

"Why not?"

"Because you don't trust him."

"Does a mother love her child less because she will not trust him when wandering on the brink of a precipice?"

"Then reclaim him, as the mother reclaims her infant."

"You shall have no secret tomorrow, dearest. We'll both confess together. Tonight, God bless and direct us both."

The scene now changes to Thornhills, and it is after tea.

"Nonsense, Emily!" said Mary Stanhope to Mrs Thornhill. " Why in the world should you be in such a hurry to marry off your elder son? You always talk of it as a universal panacea."

"It would be in his case. And how are you to know anything about it?"

"I think I know quite as well as his mother what's good for him, at all events," rejoined Aunt Mary. "You've always spoilt him: and now you want to punish him for your self-indulgence." Aunt Mary was given to warmth of temper as well as heart.

"Spoilt him, indeed, Mary Stanhope. That's rather good of you, who never allow him to be contradicted."

"Well! He is coming here tomorrow; and, from all I hear, he's not very well disposed to take his medicine."

"Tom would be much oftener here, if we asked someone to meet him." said Mrs Thornhill.

"He would if you filled your house with card sharpers and gamesters and ...." retorted Mary Stanhope

"I shall write and ask the Dacres tomorrow: he was at Oxford with Edward Dacre and I dare say he'll enjoy the pheasant shooting. As Charlie won't be here, they'll want another gun."

"Charlie's worth a dozen of him, and much fitter to be married than he." said Aunt Mary.

"I hope it will be to Miss Robinson Brown, unless you intend to support them." and here Mrs Thornhill shook out the voluminous folds of her dress and prepared for further combat. But Aunt Mary would not go on. She looked at her cousin with considerable temper and ringing the bell unceremoniously, she retired for the night, without a salute.

"How stupid Mary Stanhope is! She thinks she knows everything, and is always giving her opinion about Tom's extravagance. I'm sure if he only got a good wife, he'd be the best husband alive. I shall certainly ask those Dacre girls for the shooting week." Here the soliloquy ended; and, ringing the bell, she followed the example of her cousin Mary, and went to bed. She thought, too, that a mother's prayer would not hurt him.

* * * * * *

The pleasure of writing a novel has its drawbacks. The necessity for going back, as the only means of getting forward, is exceedingly troublesome. But it must be done. We seem almost to have taken leave of some of those with whom we opened our story; and we never know the value of our friends, nor our creations, till they seem to have left us forever. This is just the case now. We would willingly leave everyone to tell his own story in his own way, more by ethical than by historical development: but before we can do so, we must retrace our steps; just to make the place tidy we will sweep up the crumbs.

After the strict investigation, and hopeless mystery, which succeeded the assassination of Geoffrey Thornhill, Arthur Kildonald had disappeared from the scene. Circumstances had placed him in so questionable a light, that many persons were not without their suspicions that he was directly or indirectly concerned in that affair. Those, however, who were best informed, entirely exonerated him. The whole circumstance, the intended duel, his return to Henry Corry's house, and information of the murder, the improbability of the thing altogether, and his uniform explanation, served to acquit him in their eyes. His absence from England immediately after the final dismissal of the case could easily be accounted for. He could show his face no more amongst his former companions. The Clubs, St. James's, Newmarket and Melton, were henceforth closed to Kildonald as thoroughly as if he had been the archfiend; and there were none behind as bad as himself. He had committed the unpardonable offence of being found out when he held Marston's horse back in that fateful race. The Jockey Club pronounced on the case with a zeal and honesty of expression quite edifying, and made such a raid amongst the suspects of the betting fraternity, that no one was found out again, until very nearly the end of the season.

However, Kildonald got his ill-earned money from Burke, and retired to that Paradise of Sharpers, the Continent.

Kildonald was a man of quick impulses: some generous ones; and not all bad. His errors had been those of upbringing, strong temptation with an inability to resist. The loss of his property, and the ties he had contracted – his false position in the world, and the evil influence of a man like Burke, who, as we have seen, held him by some secret power – were the rocks on which he split. He had never felt his position before this time: he had done much that was dishonourable, but it had never recoiled upon him, as his present disgrace.

Geoffrey Thornhill's death affected him very seriously. It made him think and the Tyrol, not then so *recherché* as it has since become, is a great place for solemn reflection. So he carried with him the money, the price of his dishonesty and lived quietly, cheaply, and unknown, not far from Saltzburg. There are many like him. His reasons for this seclusion were manifold, and did credit to his head and heart. It was not expensive: it was out of the world: was not unlike the wilder parts of Ireland, on a larger scale; afforded good, but inexpensive education for his children; and was not so unpleasant for his wife, as a life of exile might have been.

When he left England, his wife, Norah Kildonald, whom he loved very sincerely, had decided upon going with him. During his hours of prosperity she had borne his absences without complaint, under the impression that he was happy. In a season of adversity, when the world frowned, she insisted on her right to comfort him: what woman does not?

She came: and the household of Mr and Mrs "Donald" was small, but gracefully administered – after the fashion of a woman. She brought her son and her stepdaughter. She had never inquired further than the fact, which she had learnt piecemeal, that her husband had made an early and imprudent marriage. Kathleen was the sister of Gipsy George.

For a length of time they grew old together. But by degrees Kildonald pined for the world, not exactly of London, nor of Paris but for an approach to its suburbs. He had forgotten his peccadilloes, as easily as the world had forgotten him. He did not want to continue to be boxed up in a Tyrolese village, Norah and Kathleen never saw a soul, and the boy wanted to see something of society before he went into the Prussian service!

"What's the matter, Arthur? You look tired," said his wife kindly.

"Tired? I'm ill, Norah. This place doesn't agree with me. I can't stay here any longer. I should like to get back into Germany."

After some discussion, Frankfort was fixed upon. Here, in an obscure street, not far from the Jewish quarter, they rented a small flat. Kildonald was pleased for a time: then a run to Wiesbaden or Homburg was easy, and on one or two occasions he came back smilingly – occasionally the reverse happened. His means of subsistence to you and me was a mystery. Norah believed in the old Kildonald estate. The facts are simple.

Some money he had. It did not last for ever. Two years after his expatriation he heard of the losses on the Kildonald property, by reason of the non-completion of the sale to the Thornhills. He certainly had had no money, nor was he receiving the rents of the estate. He applied in Cork, by means of friends, for a statement or a settlement. He got money, when he wanted it, doled out at intervals, by Burke. He understood that Burke was receiving the rents, and claimed the greater part of the estate by taking out a mortgage upon it. He was not a man to be forced into explanations, at any rate by Kildonald. To say truth Kildonald cared but little for anything, if he could gratify his passion for gambling, which had only lain dormant for want of opportunity. Each year in Frankfort had seen them on a downward course. Norah tried hard to stem the tide; but the devil was too strong for her, and ruin was running its course. Norah was a woman and as her husband sunk in her esteem, he seemed to have risen in her love. What could she do? She began to teach in Frankfort. An English governess, resident in the town: so charming a manner; so sweet a face; always a smile to cover that aching heart, could not fail to make friends. But teaching is not highly paid anywhere, least of all in Germany: a few florins monthly, which could have helped her boy, Hubert, who was at Dusseldorf, or Kathleen, who was not old enough to help herself, found their way to the gambling table.

Kildonald was not himself – there was always some evil influence behind him: silent, unknown, but secretly felt. Norah felt it, knew it: Arthur was so changed: it was Ireland over again, with the weight of years added to its pains. And so we have brought them down to this present time: and the evil influence is again upon the stage.

There had been great doings at Mainlust Gardens, Frankfort. It was a fine evening in autumn, and the gardens had been full to a late hour. There had been music and *weissen wein,* and *rothen wein,* and smoking and flirting. It was very late, and all good and quiet citizens of the free city had left long ago. There lingered some ladies of the old town, some noisy visitors from Heidleberg, and two or three officers, finishing their last bottle. They were not all. At a corner of the gardens, not now so well lighted by the coloured paper lamps as half an hour previously, sat two mysterious-looking persons, smoking, not drinking, and conversing in low tones. They were not Germans, still less Frenchmen. The one was thickset, short, vulgar; without beard, but portentously whiskered and singularly overdressed. The other was tall, thin, pale, and iron-grey. Aristocratic-looking, prematurely old: he wore a drooping moustache and large beard. He was remarkably quiet in his dress and, but for a certain nervousness, would have been equally so in his manner. It would have been difficult to have recognised in him the former man about town of London, and the finest horseman of his day. They rose at the same moment. The one saying, with a vulgarity of Irish accent somewhat rare in society.

"I wouldn't have known ye anywhere, Kildonald. Sure, you're a changed, man!"

"And you, not at all. I should have known you, Mr Burke, if I'd met you in the streets of Pekin or – or – or Cork."

Burke winced under the allusion to his native city, and was silent for a minute ... "How much did he know, or how little?" thought he.

"Shall we be going?" at length said he.

"Certainly" rejoined Kildonald.

They took their way from the gardens, along the quay as the last waiter extinguished the last lamps and carried away the last empty bottle. It was a warm night, and they walked slowly, distrustfully, without the cheerfulness of friends, or the energy of open enemies. They were useful to each other, mutually suspicious, and mutually fearful.

"Which is your way tonight?" asked Kildonald, assuming an air of coolness, and turning a cigar in his mouth.

"To the Mayence railway."

"You have come the wrong road – it lies the other way."

"I have an hour to wait for my train, and will accompany you home."

"Impossible! My lodgings are not ... not exactly ..."

"If there's a chair to sit down upon, I'm content; faith, I know what roughing it is, since we knew one another before."

"But it's ... there are reasons ..."

"Pooh! Pooh! what, an old friend, Kildonald? Come, bedad, we must talk the matter over: between us, sure, there's no ceremony." Kildonald stopped at a turning which led on the left towards the Romerberg and the Cathedral; he hesitated a moment, and seemed suddenly to make up his mind: then said deliberately.

"You forget that Mrs Kildonald is with me, and my daughter – let us turn towards the station."

"And pray, sir, have you forgotten to whom you're indebted for that same lady, whom you call Mrs Kildonald?" Kildonald turned pale; he felt it, and his companion must have felt it too; for he as suddenly added, "But there, man, let us talk of something else. What about the young Englishman? When will you come to my house?"

"I cannot assist you further than I have done," said Kildonald.

"Then thank you for nothing; you've found our fox, which any one might have done; but I can't kill him alone," rejoined the other.

"Without hounds, I suppose you mean to say," and the tone in which Kildonald spoke had a bitter irony in it.

"Perhaps I do: but at least we hunt in couples.... I share the risk ..."

"And take the whole of the profits." said Kildonald sourly. "You must find another dog to bear you company in this matter, for I cannot."

"Say ... will not. But, come, Kildonald, you throw fortune away from you at the very moment she is at your feet. Listen; there's enough for us both to be got out of this wealthy Englishman, this Carlingford. He plays high, and eagerly. He wants no persuasion, has no skill, not even common prudence. Sure you or I may profit by our knowledge: we've bought it."

"And I have paid for it, Mr Burke: it costs you nothing. Have you one soul to drag down to infamy besides your own? Have you a wife, a son, a daughter? Yes, I repeat it, a daughter; for she's as dear to me as the rest – who might live to curse the infamy of a father who sold them all to misery and vice, because ... because ..."

"Because he wouldn't see them starve. Where's the infamy? We play as thousands more. We are successful. Why not? Are we accountable for the losses of a young fool who thrusts himself into the way of danger? Come, you take this too seriously. What is it? The whole of these rascally pettifogging foreigners live by gambling. What they call play – some half-dozen florins a day. The young earl does not care for the tables: they're not quiet enough, nor high enough for him. He likes hazard. Lord Carlingford can bleed enough in one night to – what shall I say? – to enable you to – ay! To pay me the whole of the debt on the Kildonald property. With good nursing it can be made to pay twice its present income; and you may return to Ireland, be yourself again, and leave it to your boy ..."

"Saddled with his father's dishonour," and the sigh was one of decreased resistance.

"If it was so, bedad, I think he wouldn't refuse the offer," said Burke, who saw that he had made an impression, and became less guarded in his brutality.

"What!" said the other, hoarsely, "with the education of a gentleman and a soldier ..."

"What are you speaking of?" asked Burke.

"Ah! Stop, Burke; true, true. You remind me, cruelly, very cruelly." He tried to be dignified, but a strong sense of degradation, a weight of previous necessity, kept him down. At last he said, "I'm not well this evening; tomorrow, or the next day, we may meet again: but pray leave me now."

"Then dine with me tomorrow, Kildonald? No? The day after, then. Come; and bring Mrs Kildonald and your daughter. It will do them good to have a run into the country to the Mount" (The Mount was the name given to a cottage in which he lived half a mile from Wiesbaden.) "I'll invite Lord Carlingford."

"Yes, the day after. There. Good night." And, as if fearful of further parley, he turned round and disappeared up one of the narrow streets leading from the river.

Burke turned away, and returned by the riverside. "I have him safe enough." thought he. "With Kildonald's assistance we shall manage Lord Carlingford admirably. He's not half out-at-elbows yet. Lords never know when they are ruined. There's been a few of them through my hands."

The street up which Kildonald turned was one of those very old, picturesque parts of Frankfort which have been enlivened by Prout and Roberts[39], but which, without the bits of bright green, blue, or scarlet, never seen in the original, are brown and dingy-looking enough. The houses overlap one another, and the upper stories overhang the lower, so as to render it very artist-like, but dangerous and dirty in the extreme. The confusion of his mind, the conflicting hopes and fears, his anger, and the necessity for restraining it, battling in a not-over-strong frame, had a very painful effect upon him.

Though perfectly conscious of it, he suddenly found that he could not prevent himself from reeling. Once he stopped short, as if about to fall; but he recovered himself again and proceeded towards his own house. It was in a mean back street, not far from the cathedral – between that and the river. At that moment he felt a hand on his arm, and a good-natured voice said, "Excuse me; I followed you from the quay, and seeing you were a countryman, and evidently

---

[39] Artists of the day.

unwell, I thought I might offer you an arm. Lean on me."

The assistance was very timely, and too kindly offered to be refused. Kildonald took the stranger's arm; and, after a silent walk of a few minutes, he halted at the corner of the street in which he lived. He thanked the stranger gratefully for his assistance.

"And are you certain you require no more?" asked Charlie Thornhill, for it was he.

"No, thank you, I feel better. A sudden faintness overcame me. Besides, I'm at home. Adieu; and many thanks for your kindness."

"I wonder how much of our conversation he heard?" thought Kildonald

"Well, that was a dismissal, at all events." thought the good Samaritan. "Now who, in the name of fortune, is he? And who was the man I saw by the water-side? They were after no particular good, by the little I heard. This fellow looks like a gentleman. Confound these streets, how dark they keep them!" However, he was soon home and let himself into a handsome house with a latch-key.

The next day Kildonald was ill of stroke paralysis and it was many weeks before he left his room.

CHAPTER 28

"HE'LL PAY DEARLY FOR THIS!"

During this time Burke was not idle. His career thus far had been chequered. Sudden suspicions of his honest dealings had been followed by heavy losses, the estrangement of friends, and the attacks of enemies. He was observed to be uneasy and absent; his once flourishing business became less respectable and less lucrative. Some transactions connected with the turf, and some heavy speculations in the money market, helped him on his downward course. His vulgarity no longer stood for honesty, his brusqueness for talent. He had therefore decided to quit Ireland forever, comparatively a ruined man – if so great a scoundrel could be ruined in a world where there are so many fools. He had not been very unsuccessful, however, at the various gambling tables to which he resorted: he only felt his inferiority in private houses, where his grossness of manner and vulgarity of appearance were against him. When he had accidentally met with Kildonald a few months previous to their last conversation, he was not too blind to see that Kildonald would be a most valuable ally.

Lately he had begun to suspect that his hold upon Kildonald was looser than it had been. But Kildonald was one of those men who could not face want; and Burke, however unjustly, held the purse-strings in his grasp. Impaired as his own fortunes were, he contrived to live well and ostentatiously, wherever he was. Strange to say, whether with ulterior views or from fear of detection should his victim be driven too hard, he also contrived to supply Kildonald with a pittance at intervals, and with some regularity. This was always supposed to be a portion of the Kildonald rent-roll, the rest finding its way into Mr. Burke's pocket.

Another force besides the fear of want, however, had, up to the present, kept the suffering Kildonald quiet, and induced him at least to offer no strong opposition to the schemes of rascality of his countryman. Now Burke was positively generous. He came frequently to Frankfort – always apparently with inquiries for his old acquaintance. He did not always come empty-handed. He appeared to force on the sick man's wife a more liberal allowance. He talked boldly and blusteringly of the pleasures of doing good, as the roar of the wild beast before an attack. The wife and the mother's heart was gained. Kildonald's son, Hubert, was home from Düsseldorf and Burke was loud in his praises of his fine figure and his noble appearance. Perhaps his admiration was sincere for the boy was all he said, and more too. The mother's culture had not been thrown away.

There was another member of the Kildonald household, too, whom he had seen once or twice, but whom his bold, bad gaze had sent blushing from the room. This was Kathleen. She was just bursting into womanhood and, though not the daughter of Norah, she had so much acquired her look, her manner, her softness and simplicity, that the face was imperceptibly being impressed with a great likeness. But she was brighter, gayer, and less regular in feature than Norah: she had wit and intelligence; she had a well-cultivated mind, as far as her seclusion would allow it to be so. Her eyes were large and lustrous; her hair abundant and glistening, of a dark brown; her nose only piquantly *retroussé*; her mouth full and dimpling, not very small, but very characteristic of her country; her figure was perfection – not tall and stately, but light, active, of middle height; her very step denoted vigour of purpose, the companion of high health and physical development. She had a charming smile, and was an impersonation of dimples and blushes. Such was Kathleen Kildonald at eighteen years of age.

The winter was gone: Kildonald's health had improved, but he had grown prematurely old. He had scarcely quitted the house in the cold weather, but an early spring and the pleasant sunshine of a brighter day than usual strengthened him. He began to move more like himself again. He walked more upright, and he was beginning to be as careful of his dress as heretofore. Norah had nursed him well; and, despite the necessity for economy, had even managed to afford him comforts and some luxuries. Burke seemed to have left the neighbourhood for a time. Letters from England arrived during Kildonald's illness which had interested both him and Norah; and though they contained some intelligence that could scarcely be called cheerful, they relieved him of a great anxiety. He learnt of the death of his unhappy son, George, who had been fatally injured by the savage horse, Homicide. He also learnt of the wreck of a vessel in which George's mother had sailed for Australia and in which all on board had perished, freeing him, to a great extent, from Burke's thrall.

When Kildonald was a young man, under age, he had fallen in love with a beautiful girl much below him in rank, and of no very good character, called Mary Connor. A secret marriage, through fear of his father, had been arranged between them, and George and Kathleen had been the results of this connection. Whether by his own neglect, or the woman's depravity, she had proved false to him. She left him taking with her, her son, then a boy of four or five years of age, and had sunk by slow degrees into nothing more nor less than a common tramp. The girl had been preserved from a similar fate by accident. She had been educated by his friends as a child; and when he was married again to Norah she was taken to his home, and had had the same affectionate care bestowed upon her as his son, Hubert, the only fruit of his second marriage. By the management of Burke, his first wife, then still alive, had been bought off by the payments of periodical instalments; and caring nothing for Kildonald, but fearing the loss of her means of enjoyment, moderate as they were, she had felt it to be in her interest to keep scrupulously to her promise of secrecy. It was this power which had given Burke his influence over Kildonald. The fear of exposure, whilst in the world, had made him a willing instrument in the hands of the lawyer; and though time and distance, and his absence from society so long, had weakened the bond, still the pain that the knowledge would have inflicted on Norah, who he sincerely loved, as far as his selfish nature was capable of loving, made him anxiously fearful of an exposure. The death of mother and son so far lessened the chance of detection that he felt almost at ease on this score. The only remaining evidence was that of Burke himself; and although he would not have provoked it heedlessly, he felt himself at liberty to assume an independence of his tyranny. The question of the money and estate Kildonald now thought might be submitted to the lawyers with some hope of successful issue.

The summer passed slowly on. The pittance forwarded from time to time served to keep them from want, and to purchase some luxuries needed for a convalescent. Norah was, as ever, patient, unflagging in kindness, and self-sacrificing to the whims and caprices of the sick man. He recovered slowly. His native air was recommended. He answered, drily enough, that he "didn't think his native air would agree" with him. Kathleen was increasing in beauty daily: all that could be spared was spared for her education; and, amongst other advantages, good instruction is cheap enough in the Hanse Towns. It had been almost decided that she should seek employment in Frankfort by way of meeting the increasing expenses.

When Autumn arrived, and with it the usual locust herd at the German baths, the tenor of life in Frankfort changed. The English, Russian, Viennese, Parisian (I mention the two latter municipally, for I do not mean Austrians nor French), all who had lost money, and would retrench, and many who had a few thousand francs to spare, visited the town. The Hotel de Russie was always crowded: and the celebrated Johanisberger wine, at seven thalers the bottle, seemed to be almost a widow's cruise. It was always going. In due time Burke re-appeared.

He was not long in seeking the humble street in which Kildonald lived. He had the same game in view as last autumn of plucking the wealthy and unwary in partnership with Kildonald, and his previous disappointment only sharpened his appetite. He hoped that as Kildonald now used the name "Donald" and was greatly changed in appearance, he was unlikely to be recognised by his countrymen. He might perhaps have found another and more tractable accomplice; but he could have found few so fitted for his purpose. His objective was, therefore, to make a favourable impression: and he had paved his way by some pecuniary advances more liberal than usual.

"You have been seriously ill: you don't recover as you should," said he, after a few ordinary expressions. "You must take rooms at Homburg, or Wiesbaden, Mrs. Kildonald. Have you no influence? It's not fair on you for Kildonald to insist on looking so old." Burke was self-satisfied.

"The baths are fuller than ever; but you'll, maybe, get rooms a little way from the town, which will be better for your husband. He'll get some fresh air and a little society." Here Burke appealed to Kildonald himself, who sat nervously turning in his arm-chair. Now and then a spasm seemed to pass across his face, and a peevish "pish!" was the only answer he gave to each new suggestion.

The room in which they sat looked uncomfortable for an invalid. A strip of carpet did duty for a whole one: the polished boards underneath were very clean, and very cold. The stove was not yet on in the room. The piano occupied one side, or rather end; and the size of it, and the old-fashioned, but handsome cornices, gave it an air of cheerless grandeur. Kildonald sat at a table, on which were many letters and papers. Of books there were none but a few of the Tauchnitz edition of English novels, and some German and French schoolbooks, which belonged to his daughter. After a little time Mrs Kildonald left the room.

"Letters from the ould country?" asked Burke.

"They are," replied Kildonald, with a cold and distant manner.

"They bring no good news, I'll go bail. There's nothing but ill luck there; and as to that estate, faith, I'm entirely out of pocket by it this two years." Burke spoke deprecatingly.

"It's a misfortune that my family has been accustomed to for longer than that." said Kildonald. " It would be satisfactory to know what does become of the rent. The tenants must be in clover." And here the speaker turned round and looked Burke in the face.

"I own I – don't quite – understand, Kildonald."

"Probably not, Mr. Burke; but it's hard to find comprehension – "

"Oh! Here's Mrs Kildonald." said Burke, as the door opened, and she and Kathleen entered. The latter, however, seeing her father engaged, stepped back, and Mrs Kildonald crossed the room, and went out by an opposite door. They were alone again; but the interruption enabled Burke to evade the former discussion, and he continued; "But come, you want something to do. Your health will be the better for the change. *I* want money Kildonald; and if I want it, you will want it."

"Then I must continue to want it if you depend upon my assistance; but, at least, you are in receipt of my property."

"At present I'm in receipt of nothing. I've lost my last florin; but I've borrowed a hundred. Share it with me. Come to Wiesbaden. I've a goose there that lays golden eggs." And Burke chuckled.

"And I'm to be the decoy duck. You assign me an honourable post."

"Decoy-duck? Nonsense! Come, come, be reasonable. You were not so particular once. We've rowed in the same boat too long to upset it now. It won't be many years before we shall be doing a little racing here: the foreigners are very keen about it. It will be well to keep your hand in whenever you get a chance."

During this speech Kildonald had slowly risen: he appeared to find a difficulty, and sat down again, whilst a bright flush lighted up his pale cheeks, and his still handsome eyes nearly flashed fire. As Burke, however, ended with the allusion to his hand, Kildonald rose suddenly, and resting his left hand upon the table, he drew the right suddenly from his bosom. "Hand, did you say, hand!" and he held up, to the astonished sight of his visitor, a withered and useless limb. "There, sir! Is that a hand to deal a card, or to pull a horse? Is that, sir – answer me – a hand to help you in your tricks of leger-de-main[40], and to transfer gold from one pocket to another? Would to God it had withered before it ever lent its aid to your schemes of villainy and fraud – the hand that has made me an exile and a byword! Ay, look at it! You may well stare! Would to God it had been employed in digging the acres it has striven to secure, but which have slipped from its grasp, and if it had always been thus weak and powerless! Look at it! And if prayers could restore it, its first act should be to avenge

---

[40] Sleight of hand

itself upon the cowardly miscreant who fattens upon the blood of his victims! I know you, sir; and I'll unmask you." Whilst he was yet speaking Norah had opened the door, but he had not heeded her. She stood still, and he continued: "I fear you not, now. Do your worst. Your secret is worthless."

"Oh! Mr. Burke, Mr. Burke; heed him not: it is his health – his irritation. He does not know what he is saying." And Norah stepped between them as Burke's face assumed the passions of a demon about to spring upon his prey. "Leave him, sir, to me – to his wife – I beg,"

As Burke turned to leave the room Kildonald threw himself into the arms of Norah – sobbing – "Yes, my wife, my wife!" and sank fainting upon the floor.

Burke was already gone; and as he walked slowly down the wide, but dark staircase towards the street, he clenched his hand and muttered, "He shall pay dearly for this! But, first of all, how much does he know?"

CHAPTER 29

DANGERS LURK

As Burke closed the door of the house in a narrow street between the Cathedral and the Schur Gasse, Charles Thornhill threw open the folding door of a large banking house in Zeil, and took his way to the left in that confident manner which proclaimed him perfectly at home in the city of Frankfort. Englishman as he was, and looked (for he reserved to himself the sacred privilege of a clean chin), he was neither looking for the Hotel de Russie nor examining his "Murray" or foreign "Bradshaw". He was not in search of the Juden Gasse, nor even of the Ariadne, and no *valet de place* addressed him with the hope of employment. He walked sturdily and steadily forward with a rather business-like air, and attracted no notice from anyone, excepting that universal admiration which is given to size when accompanied by grace and good looks. It is almost two years since we had anything to do with Charlie. He has employed them well; and with the exception of a short visit to England on business in June last, which he made one of pleasure also, he had stuck to his work with a perseverance which confirmed the judgement of his friend, Palmer.

He was about to cross the street to his "mid-day" dinner at the house of his chief, Herr Meyerheim.

"Dornhills, by Jove! My goot fellow, how are you?" The inquiry proceeded from an old acquaintance, the Baron Hartzstein. Having had a very successful season in England, he was bent upon a little foreign gambling.

"Well, Baron," said Charlie, who was always amused by his friend, though by no means holding him in great respect: "Tired of England?"

"England for me is London, and London is gone away. That is to say, come abroad: and who's here?"

" Who has lost his money, or his wife, or his digestion? You can get them all back somewhere in the black forest, or on the Berg Strasse." said Charlie laughing.

"Yees! You have right. And you – you go to Baden, or Homburg?" The baron not conceiving that any of his acquaintance could be at Frankfort for any other purpose.

"Neither: you know I am a banker now – in Meyerheim's house: delighted to hold your winnings for you Baron: safer with us than you."

"Ah! I see: you will hold the money what your brother spends. But why not go to drink the waters? Waters is very goot."

"Wine's better; besides, what would our clients say?"

"Say! Nothing – no! My friend, Baron Goldstock, the great banker of Vienna – bless my soul, Dornhills! He's alvays breaking the bank; and then he breaks my sleep. I live in his hotel, and am not so lucky: so I go to bed, and at two in the morning he wakes us all up to tell us the news; and the next day all the world send their moneys to Goldstock and Co., of Vienna."

"I think I should close my account. Have you been long in Frankfort?"

"Last night only. I have been in Wiesbaden. There is an Englishman there, a man with a scarlet face and whiskers, who plays very high – and he wins: one Burke."

"Burke, Burke," said Charlie, soliloquising: "Where have I heard that name?" and Charlie rubbed his nose, and smoothed his chin.

"Yes, Burke! He is a friend of one Donald; but Donald I never see: he was to come to dinner, many times, but Providence befriended him. You know I am strong. But I have seen you yesterday."

"Really! And where?"

"At the Thier-Garten: and, come, Dornhills, who was your pretty friend?"

"Some German lady, probably; but I forget at this moment."

"No, no! Not of my Landsleute. You English cannot dress, and you have no manners; you sing not, and you dance almost on what you call all-fours; but ah! Gott bewhar – you have lovely women, and long-legged horses. I could add some of both to my collection: but come, you will not tell me?"

"Yes, I will, Baron," said Charlie, who had no great fear of the Austrian's powers of fascination. "That was the governess of the two little Meyerheim girls, and the other was Madame Meyerheim; but I think she sat down whilst we walked about."

"Oh! The governess!" and here the baron meant to be intelligible. "What! Of my good friend Meyerheim? I must bank with Meyerheim and Co. I shall keep a large balance. Madame shall ask me to her evenings. Come, Dornhills, you shall introduce me at once."

"But I am not going back to the bank at present. I am going home to dinner. I am become quite a German."

"So much the better: you shall present me at once to madame."

"No! Baron – that's out of the question. She doesn't receive."

"Then take care of yourself. You are jealous. You know I am sceptic about women. They are all bad, that is, good, when there is a 'rapport.' You believe in magnetism; mesmerism. No?"

"I believe in honour among men, and chastity among women. And if your intentions are as serious as you would have me think, don't forget that this is an Englishwoman. Adieu." and Charlie crossed the street.

The baron continued his walk: and the beautiful English girl, whom he had seen with Thornhill, became a settled idea. It took its place with dice and the Derby winner. Nothing of this sort presented difficulties to Baron Hartzstein.

"Mr Thornhill," said Madame Meyerheim, in German, "We almost gave you up: we are sorry to have begun, but Miss Donald and the children are going out after dinner, and we are anxious not to be late. The band plays at Mainlust today." Charlie apologised good-humouredly, and took his seat opposite Miss Donald, by the side of little Bertha; Mr Meyerheim was at the other end of the table.

"Where's Heinrich?" asked Mr Meyerheim, looking up from his soup.

"Gone for a ride on one of Mr Thornhill's horses," said Mamma.

"You'll make him quite English; you are too kind to him: and he'll want to go to London, whenever we lose you."

"I shall be glad to help him, whenever I can," said Charles Thornhill; "but I don't know that I shall be wanted in London this year at least – but we must talk English now for the children."

And accordingly they did so.

Mr. Meyerheim himself was the best and mildest of continental bankers. He was more simple than a child, which is strange when we take into consideration his knowledge of business, and the opportunities presented to him of studying rascality in its happiest garb. He was one of those good men, who, from the deep well of worldly hardness, avarice, and scepticism, saw nothing but the blue sky above him. He loved Thornhill because he was honest and true. He did not know how he found it out; but he felt that it was so. Charlie was originally like him. The clay, the humanity of both was the same.

Madame was an excellent person. Stout, fair, with good hair and blue eyes. The best housekeeper in the world: a practical cook, and not ashamed of it. She was an admirable housewife who religiously collected the table napkins after dinner, and ordered them to be pressed and put away for the morrow. A reader, and a great philosopher on the science of the education of women; she was a little speculative, which was to the credit of the Bourse; but not excessively so.

"You are going too soon, Mr Thornhill: another glass of Marcobrunner?"

"Work, Mrs Meyerheim; your husband sets me a good example."

"But it is a model you have improved upon," said he.

When the bank closed Charlie went at five o'clock to Mainlust. He found the children and Miss Donald. He smoked his cigar, and chattered cheerfully with them, until he was joined by Baron Hartzstein. That gentleman joined in the conversation with an indomitable energy which repelled all coldness. He would take no denial; and though not formally presented, he made the acquaintance of the pretty governess by force of eloquence. Charlie was not a talker, so the baron had it all to himself.

The following evening the banker's lady had an "at home". A few friends dropped in, and Charlie remained at home to help to entertain. About nine o'clock a very gay gentleman in a white uniform, Comte Degenfeld, had the honour to present his friend, the Baron Hartzstein of Vienna.

* * * * * *

London society had not much changed since Charlie Thornhill had left England. Sir Frederick and Lady Marston dispensed their usual hospitalities in the country, and participated in the pleasures of legislation in the town. Lady Elizabeth Montagu Mastodon was as great, as vulgar, and as good as ever and continued to revere the mighty master whom she had married. Robinson Brown, pére et fils, were as gorgeous as ever in their separate lines: the former, the solemn and gloomy larva, the vital principle of the latter that useless and tawdry butterfly. There were the same balls and the same people at them night after night. The same opera, and the same singers. The Rotten Row was more rotten than ever. The same Newmarket, Epsom, Ascot, and Goodwood, and the same horses, four years old instead of three. A few men, supposed to be good, were gone, gone to the bad: others, long supposed to be bad, were still to the good. Wilson Graves had never been heard of more: his servant Jacob was amusing himself in the penitentiary. Lord Carlingford told everyone he was ruined, and had gone to Rome to retrench. There were drawing-rooms, and levées, as usual; and a few new scandals. Here and there rarely a man or woman had gone overboard, but the great vessel of the state passed on its way. Excepting by Mint, Chalkstone, Palmer, and Co., Charlie was nearly forgotten. Tom still kept his head to the wind, and breasted the opinions and innuendoes of the British public. And what did it say of him? That he was almost ruined. Impossible! Listen, however, to excellent authority. Scene – Punter's Club at 2 a.m.

"What's Thornhill lost this season?"

"Five-and-twenty thousand."

"You don't say so" the speaker who had not twenty-five thousand to lose, sighed.

"Fact: Thornhills is mortgaged all over. Came from old Stamp the lawyer: Tom goes to Como at the end of the season."

"Sorry for it: he's a capital fellow, and always stands a rattler on a good thing. Is there any truth about him and Dacre's elder daughter?" Here the speaker looked at his own person, boots especially, by the flaming gas-light.

"Not a word: their mother did her best, but caught the younger brother instead, which wouldn't do at all. I should think they're sorry they let him go now: he's the best spec. of the two. He's gone into Mint and Chalkstone's house, and he'll have all his uncle's money." Mrs Dacre was, and has been, in piteous plight. Both husband and daughters thwarted her schemes and ruined her hopes. Mr Dacre would not see the miseries of a match with the younger son; and supported Alice in her semi-rejection of the elder. Tom Thornhill with a clear unencumbered estate was a man of his county. Tom Thornhill, deeply in debt, with a worsening reputation and a passion for gambling, which not even the heaven-born beauty of Alice Dacre could subdue; Tom Thornhill of Thornhills, unable to live on his estate with the place coming under the hammer and his affairs in the hand of Stamp, the great family lawyer and agent to half the nobility; Tom Thornhill, on the steps of Crockford's, cursing his fate, or sitting dolefully in his rooms in the Albany, was a different man to the Tom Thornhill the world beheld at St James's; at the Clubs; at Tattersall's; on the Heath: or in the field. There he was cheerful, generous, charming and no man saw the invisible spectre that walked arm in arm with its prey.

The only one to see that spectre was Alice Dacre, and she wished she had not. From the earliest day of their intimacy she had seen it all. It was the vice that most shocked her as incurable. Alice had great faith in her father; and Mr Dacre deceived neither himself nor his daughter. So Tom Thornhill proposed in form, and was formally refused.

The misfortune of such a case is this – that no one can bell the cat.

No one told Tom Thornhill why he was rejected by the woman that manifestly loved him. Peasants would have known the truth: but it's not the way of the great world. So he turned and went away sorrowing but bitter. She was capricious, cold and incomprehensible. At Gilsland he was an idol, debased, broken, prostrate, but he was an idol still.

And then Alice grew sad and thoughtful; her eyes grew dim, and her figure more pliant, she was evidently bowed. And she sought not counsel, but love, from Edith; and the tree began to be supported by the tendrils that had clung to it in earlier times. There had been a grand ball at St. James's – the last of the season. The Dacres were returning towards Grosvenor Street. Near the top of St James's Street the crowd of carriages had become great, and a dead stoppage ensued. The place was alive with gas, illuminations, and people: it was as light as day. The girls were looking anxiously at the crowd which scarcely separated to let their horses through, when they heard two young men of their acquaintance beneath the carriage window, in close conversation.

"No, no: it was about a card, I tell you; they were playing piquet, and he laid him five thousand to one. I think that fellow Hartington took an unfair advantage, as Tom threw down his cards, considering it a certainty. However, what was to be done? He wrote him a cheque for the money, and wouldn't hear of a drawn game. Thornhills must go, and it has been in the family ever since James the First."

"Charles the Second," said Herbert Cardstone, whose baronetage dated from the former monarch, and who was a little tenacious of any unjust encroachment on the privileges of that most pedantic and eccentric king. "What a charming place it is! I should like to become....." At this moment the companion caught sight of the Dacres' carriage, and stopped the conversation abruptly.

Alice looked up, and at that moment, on the steps of the most notorious gambling-house in Town, she saw the haggard face of her rejected lover; his whole air was one of dejection and faded excitement. His handsome features were drawn, and his eyes had assumed an unearthly size. He was looking without seeing, laughing without a smile, whilst his companions talked rapidly. Alice had not seen him for some weeks, and he had aged ten years. Edith followed her sister's eyes and as she took Alice's cold hand in hers, she felt the silent tears drop noiselessly upon her naked wrist. From that day they talked no more of the ruined gambler. By the end of the season, Thornhills was on the market and its owner was alone at Como.

About the same time Charles Thornhill sent for an English groom but got the next thing to it, an Irish one and his name was Daly.

CHAPTER 30

THE BETTING BOOK POINTS THE FINGER

Charlie's life at Frankfort continued to be exceedingly pleasant. He was one of those men who, without any personal regard for comforts or luxuries, had lived in society where such things become second nature. He wore good clothes without knowing or attaching the smallest importance to it. He liked good dinners without caring to go in search of them. He rode good horses, and he expected his saddles and bridles to be well turned out; but it never occurred to him that they were so. I think, if Charlie Thornhill had been born in another rank of life, he might have been a sloven: he was now only indifferent, and it gave him a very high-cast appearance. There were few men of his age altogether better looking, and few so utterly free from personal vanity.

To persons who understand German society, I need hardly explain that the domestic comforts, the manners, and the *ménage* are very different from those of the same class in England. Herr Meyerheim had with difficulty been persuaded by correspondents in England to accept Charlie into his house. He was well off, had every comfort, and he had prevaricated about Charlie for a long time, on the score of anticipated fastidiousness. Private friendship for Roger Palmer at length prevailed, who was anxious that his nominee should have the full benefit of a good commercial training, and do credit to his discernment whenever he should be recalled to London. The arrangement was made for one twelvemonth. At the end of that time Herr Meyerheim himself placed his rooms further at Charlie's disposal for as long a period as he should feel it convenient. This was too flattering to be overlooked and though Charlie Thornhill decided upon removing to some commodious rooms within a few doors of the Meyerheims, it strengthened his intimacy and enabled him to regard his old quarters as a home. In fact, he lived as much in the one house as the other.

I am obliged to admit a truth which, I hope, may not militate against Charlie. He was attracted to the Meyerheims not altogether by his admiration for Madame, who was as remarkable for her good pastry as for her beauty, nor yet by his sincere regard for Herr Meyerheim, whom he saw daily in his official capacity on the other side of the street, but by the beauty and grace of his country woman, Kathleen Donald, in whom he felt an indefinable interest. Something drew him towards her. Probably her helpless condition. Enough was known of her to conjure up an obscure and dingy home: parents, probably vulgar, certainly living in poverty or disgrace: her expatriation assuredly necessary from some cause or other, unconnected with herself. To a man of Charlie's age the self-assumed protection of a beautiful girl is always dangerous, however delicately paraded; and it is seldom that either escape from the fire unscathed: never both. Strange to say, however, Charlie never thought of her without associating her with Edith Dacre. "Ah!" said he to himself, "how I wish Edith could see her; she's just the sort of girl she would like."

And perhaps he was right. She was a very pretty girl indeed – with a simplicity of mind, but clever, imaginative, warm hearted, Irish, attractive herself, and easily attracted by kindness and attention from others. Charlie Thornhill saw all this, and he saw its dangers to her. He had been long enough on the Continent to know the general want of principle of most foreigners. He saw the girl flattered by the attentions of Hartzstein, and he had difficulty in persuading himself that his interference would be quite disinterested. There was a great deal of truth in Charlie.

As occasion offered he had been two or three times to England. When there his visits had been chiefly with his intimate friends, the Marstons, his mother and Tom at Thornhills, Roger Palmer, of course, and to his uncle, who always received him with the greatest affection. Henry Thornhill was beginning to show age. He was unostentatious to a degree, lived very substantially well, and gave his friends the best dinner and wine that could be put before them. But he had no luxuries for himself; a simple brougham, and a good hack of the cob sort. People thought it odd in a man of his temperament and antecedents: but he kept his own counsel; and the most that could be said was that he was laying up a good purse for his nephew.

Charlie's relation with the Dacres was not altogether a satisfactory one. It was scarcely an engagement; and yet no two people could be more conscious of this position towards each other than Edith Dacre and he. This is not very uncommon in society when circumstances tend to render a positive betrothal imprudent and a positive rejection cruel.

It was evident to our hero that Tom's career had been madly reckless of late. So much he learnt from the Marstons. Lady Marston indeed spoke of his rejection by Alice Dacre as the turning-point of his life.

"He was too good, Charlie, to be turned adrift in such a stream," said she. "I'm not one of those who like experiments upon *roué* ; but your brother is a man who might have been guided by Alice Dacre: he wanted delicate treatment - an arm of iron with a hand of spun silk; and if ever I saw such a woman, Alice Dacre is the one."

Charlie knew what she said was true, and grieved over it sincerely. He lived in such a world that it never entered his head that Alice had a reason for her refusal beyond want of affection. Such is the blindness of those who, unlike Alice Dacre, love and do not wish to see.

During a visit to Sir Frederick Marston some conversation led to the opening of a subject which had a mysterious charm for Charlie - the possibility of bringing to punishment the murderer of his father, and the ascertaining of the facts connected with the Kildonald property. One remarkable trait in his character was tenacity. He was slow in adopting views or suggestions but once adopted, he held to them with a steadiness remarkable in everything but an Englishman and a bull-dog.

The facts are simple enough. Sir Frederick took great interest in his farms, and, holding some grasslands in his own hands, was in the habit of superintending the haymaking himself. As he rode round his fields, or strolled about with Lady Marston, he recognised again and again certain Irishmen whom he had engaged from year to year, and who, as a mark of grateful remembrance, brought a trifle or two as a present to his honour and the lady. Not infrequently a couple of bottles of Irish whiskey, such as even Sir Frederick's cellar could not produce, or a bit of Limerick lace of wonderful workmanship, which had been wrought expressly for the occasion. Lady Marston took much notice of these poor people, and did what she could to make them comfortable in the neighbouring village during the hay harvest on her husband's land. There's a great deal of good in the great world of which the little world wots not.

Not long before the time of which I am writing, a poor fellow called Peter Daly had been taken ill on the Marston estate, and died. He had been uneasy as his end drew near, and a Roman Catholic priest, who had been sent for from the nearest town, had failed to make him quite easy under the circumstances in which he was placed. He was still very anxious to see Lady Marston once more. Now, Lady Marston was a fastidious person in all things connected with personal comfort, and no fonder of a peasant's dying chamber than you or I, or anyone of my politest readers. But Lady Marston was a woman as well as a lady, and no more to be daunted by foul smells and wretched sights than Florence Nightingale, and some thousands of women all over the world, when the strong light of duty beckoned her to come on. By the time she reached the dying man his mind had become weakened and his speech incoherent. He muttered some thanks, and his happiness in seeing her, and then with a strong effort proceeded to make what might have been a confession, but for his evident intention that it should be acted upon. Lady Marston's mind was easily led back to a time which had never been forgotten by her or her husband. She now heard a confused account from the dying man of one Burke, and the Kildonald property; of certain forgeries; of an old man, a former clerk to the aforesaid Burke; of his own brother, Michael Daly; but all incoherently and without any sort of chain which could connect it in Lady Marston's mind with poor Thornhill's death, or with his title to the Irish property in question. There was one word which sharpened her curiosity: "The book, my lady: och! It was the book I've been draming on to tell you this many a day."

"Book, Daly! What book do you mean? The wine and water quick, Mrs Gray." Here Mrs Gray administered the draught.

"The pocket-book; we sent it by the mail: there it went safe, my lady, to the direction, Sir Frederick Marston. 'Tis the mail: I gave it myself. More by token, Misther Burke bid me be careful. He sent me away afterwards: but I knowed it all by the papers. The murder, and the search, and the book, an' all: but I was in foreign parts; and now I'm come back to die."

There was very little more to be got out of poor Daly. He never rallied; and his father confessor never came again. Lady Marston took her way thoughtfully to the Abbey. She walked up the steps of the portico, turned round in the hall to the right, and entered a small room, where she hoped to find Sir Frederick. She was not deficient in good sense, and had enough to know that she could not consult anybody better than her own husband. In the present case she was certainly right. I wish all my female friends would adopt her views. If wrong, which might happen once in a hundred times, they could console themselves with having done the right thing, or with having no one to blame but themselves in having chosen a noodle instead of a man. So the weaker vessel rang the bell for a servant.

"Is Sir Frederick in?"

"No, my lady; he is gone into the park with Mr Thornhill."

"With Mr Thornhill?" Lady Marston felt, without expressing it, a considerable surprise - "Which Mr Thornhill?"

"Mr Charles." And whilst Lady Marston stood up at the window, and looked out meditating many things with herself, the servant left the room. Charles was a valuable ally if anything was required to be done: and his unexpected arrival was useful.

At dinner the three met. It was a comfortable meal in autumn; when one dines by daylight in the country, and finishes with a mysterious twilight. Candles were not brought in on this occasion. There was nobody else in the house; and the subject was discussed without the exhibition of painful feelings, which daylight or candlelight must have evoked.

"Yes, Emily, I recollect the book well enough: it was not a pocket book, but your poor father's betting- book, Charlie." Here he turned to his guest: "He backed a horse of mine very heavily, called

Benevenuto; and he would have won but the race was fixed. A man called Kildonald …"

"Yes, I remember, Sir Frederick: it's long since I heard the story, but I have never forgotten it;" and Charlie clutched the stem of his claret glass, and drained it. The bottle was with him, and he filled himself a bumper.

"And now what's to be done, Frederick. The poor fellow died this afternoon. You know the substance of our conversation. Can anything be made out of it to justify further steps?"

"Everything. We have Burke, Michael Daly - you're sure of the name? - and the old clerk, if he's alive. I wish we had his name; and Cork must be the basis of our operations." Here Sir Frederick paused, helped himself, pushed the bottle to Charlie, and added, half soliloquising, "Yes, we must try Ireland itself."

"I'll go at once," said Charlie, still attacking the '34.

"Take our lawyer, Diver, Charlie," said my lady.

"I don't like law, Lady Marston. I shall do better alone."

"I think not." said Sir Frederick "Besides, what time have you?"

"A good fortnight,"

"That's something. But you can't do without what is called 'a legal adviser.' You'll get into some scrape, Charlie; and if you once alarm them, the opportunity will be lost."

"If you knew how I have it in my head. I've thought of it for years, and never forgotten a single thing you told me, when I first left old Gresham."

"I believe it," said Sir Frederick.

"Then let me go. Poor Tom's abroad; and it wouldn't suit him."

"Then take Diver," again urged Lady Marston.

"If you wish it, I will."

And then Lady Marston rose from the table, and her husband opened the door with a grace and kindness that would have done credit to the first week of their honeymoon.

"How's the stud, Charlie?" asked Sir Frederick returning to his chair.

"Not large, but very good for Frankfort. I've a neat Arab, and a good English horse that I bought at Barton's sale when I was over here at the end of last season."

"No racing I suppose, about Frankfort, or within reach of you?"

"Paris on one side, and not very far off Baden Baden. They've taken to it very kindly. It's at present too much in the hands of English legs. But the young French world is so fond of it, they must succeed."

"They won't" said Sir Frederick.

Sir Frederick could just see to pour out one more glass of claret. "Shall we ring for candles?"

"No, thank you, I love this light."

"Or want of it?"

"Whichever you please. I can't talk by daylight."

"Is that a great deprivation, Charlie?"

"Sometimes. When I'm interested, I'm generally able to say what I mean; but I often envy fellows who say it so much better."

"Ah! You're an admirer of eloquence."

"I've no self-confidence."

"Then, don't go to Ireland without Diver."

Lady Marston was pouring out tea at a small round table in the drawing room. The room was glowing with light: a sudden change. Charlie buried his long body in a fauteuil near Lady Marston, while Sir Frederick took up a pamphlet and prepared to read.

Lady Marston looked at Charlie and gave him his tea and said carelessly enough,

"Have you seen or heard of the Dacres lately?" The question was simple, but Charlie felt like a ship on fire. Some men, poets probably, would have said that his colour came and went: the truthful historian is compelled to declare that it only came. There was no "go" about it at all. He got redder and redder as he answered truly, "I came from there yesterday."

"How are they all? Alice looked ill through the season; and when she was at Thornhills she was exceedingly unwell."

"Thornhills is damp in the autumn, it is so surrounded by trees." By this time Charlie was getting a natural colour again. He ventured to look at his questioner.

"I'm glad they go to Thornhills. Since Tom has been on the Continent the place is lonely for my mother, and she seems to have taken to the girls." Charlie swallowed a little confusion in his tea which, being hot, made his eyes water.

"Where is your brother? Does he think of coming back?"

"He was at Naples last winter. Carlingford persuaded him to go there from Como. He'll not come back to live at Thornhills, I fear."

"I've no patience with Tom," said Lady Marston, viciously biting a piece of thin crisp toast, which gave peculiar force to her verdict. "He might have been anything or have done anything: he has thrown away too many chances. As a country gentleman, six years ago, he was the man of his day. Why doesn't he get into Parliament?"

"He says politicians are so dishonest," said Charlie shyly.

"What's that?" inquired Sir Frederick, looking up from his pamphlet.

"Oh! I beg your pardon; it's only Tom's idea of politics. Of course he knows nothing about it but he says political integrity is 'all my eye.'"

"Well, perhaps he's not far wrong. Does he find men more scrupulous on the turf?"

"He says they're nearly as bad, but that he's prepared for it there. Have you any horses, Sir Frederick?"

"None in training: I've given it up. I breed a little for amusement; but the turf is very different from what it was when your poor father and I went on it thirty years ago. Talking of the turf, what has become of Wilson Graves?"

"He went abroad after the match between my brother's horse and Robinson Brown's mare." Charlie said nothing more.

"I heard he lost a great deal of money; and something was said about his trying to get at the horse. Of course nobody believed that, men do tell such wonderful falsehoods."

"What's become of young Robinson Brown, Lady Marston? I've not seen him since the race."

"He's going to be married to Lady Susan Trumpington. He has been most liberal about the settlements, and the Trumpington property is unembarrassed once more. Is there any truth in the report that your mother is to leave Thornhills? We have a place in this neighbourhood that would exactly suit her and Mary Stanhope."

"I think not. All sorts of stories were about, I've no doubt. When my brother went abroad and it was supposed to be on the market Tom wouldn't have her disturbed as long as she wanted to live there and it wouldn't have been very easy to let it."

"Have you seen your mother yet, since you came from Frankfort?"

"Not yet," said he sheepishly "No one but you," he added, flatteringly.

"And the Dacres. How goes on the banking?"

"Very flourishingly. I'm glad I took your advice. It's better than soldiering."

"Now take some more. Go and call on Roger Palmer. You owe him a visit; and your uncle Henry: you have no better friend in the world. And now, Fred, if you and Charlie want a cigar, you'd better have it. It's growing late. Good night."

In three days' time Charlie was steaming from Bristol to Cork, in company with Mr. Diver.

CHAPTER 31

FOLLOWING THE FOX

"The thicket is best, he cannot 'scape"
Two Gentlemen of Verona: Act V, Scene 3

The voyage to Cork is at no time a pleasant one; and when, after about six-and-thirty hours of intolerable pitching and tossing, Charlie received a reply to a natural inquiry as to their whereabouts, that "Faith, his honour was *on the say,*" he managed to climb out of his berth, and nearly wring the neck of the cabin-boy. He was a shock-headed young ruffian, and so appreciative of a joke that he had already been thrashed for this one no less than five-and-twenty times. Charlie scrambled upon deck in time to catch the first glimpse of Cove and the Black Rock. In a few hours more they were in Cork.
If this was about the beginning of the second volume of a fine old-fashioned half-bound marble-covered affair, instead of being, as it is, near the beginning of the end, I should delay my reader to carry him on a tour through Ireland, or at least a certain portion of it. I recommend him, if he wishes to know anything about it without the trouble of going there, to apply to some of the numerous tourist

volumes, headed Killarney, or Glengariff, or Bantry Bay, which about embraces the parts traversed by Mr Diver and our friend. As regards the going there oneself, that's a matter of taste. I liked it, but then I'm fond of scenery, character, fighting and general excitement. I don't dislike roughing it here and there. Can do without feather beds, carpets, a valet, or a fireplace; can sleep with my window open or shut, broken or whole, with my door locked or unlocked: am a convenient height, say 5ft 10 ins, so that I can wear anybody's clothes of reasonable size; am 11st 8lb, so that I can ride anybody's horse of reasonable weight. I am equally handsome, with or without a beard, having tried both, am lavish with money when I have it, and can make a shilling go as far as – twelvepence (and there's an enormous difference) when I'm hard up. I prefer truffles, and clear turtle, and cliquot sec, with every conceivable delicacy of the French cuisine; but I can live upon bread, beer, whisky, Swiss cheese, and Dorsetshire draught cider, which latter drink I take to be the nastiest thing in existence.

"Now, what's the first thing to be done, Mr Diver?" said Charlie, as they sat over their breakfast the following morning.

"I've a friend, or old acquaintance, once a lawyer, now a magistrate, who may assist us in this business." said Mr. Diver.

Nicholas Corcoran lived in a handsome house near the centre of the modern town, south of the river Lee. He was the last of the pigtails, wore black breeches and well-blacked boots up to the knee; a square cut, straight-collared blue coat, with metal buttons, a very soft and voluminous white neckcloth and a long striped waistcoat of buff colour. He was a shrewd, clever old man – handsome, delicate-looking in figure and feature, with sharp grey eyes and dark lashes and brows, which contrasted sharply with his white hair, which was thinly scattered on his brow and grew more thickly and wavily on each side of his temples. He was a good judge of law and claret and dispensed both with equal hospitality. His reception of Diver and Charlie was distinguished by great urbanity and a determination that they should dine with him that day. In the meantime what could he do for them?

"Did I know Burke?" said the old gentleman after an explanation of their visit had been laid before him, as far as was needful. "Indeed I did: sorrow a gentleman in Cork that didn't know him, for he robbed us all. But he was the best sportsman and the greatest scoundrel I ever saw; and they seldom go together. If he's not dead, he's surely up to no good now."

"You've heard of an old clerk he had, who..."

"What, Phelim O'Brian? He is in Cork still, and a greater scoundrel than the other. If there's anyone can tell you anything about Burke, it's Phelim. He's been accused of forgery and every other crime in the world, short of murder, since Burke's absence, and might have been guilty of both."

"And where shall we find him between this and six o'clock?"

"You must cross the bridge at the bottom of the next street to this, and that leads to the old town on the north side of the river. But stay, the streets are narrow and irregular: don't be afraid of dirt or misery, Mr Thornhill, my servant shall put you in the way." After many thanks, Thornhill and Diver withdrew.

Mrs O'Brian, the mother of Phelim received them. She was eight-five years of age, and looked a hundred. She was muttering a low chant over a small turf fire, on which was a kettle; she took but little notice of the strangers and when asked for her son, pointed upwards – whether she meant in heaven, or only upstairs no one knew. The two men only guessed that it was not the former, so chose the latter alternative. They ascended and there found Phelim and a long-coated terrier.

Below stairs nothing could have been more wretchedly miserable than the whole appearance of things. It divulged the last stage of poverty prior to absolute starvation. Upstairs things were more cheerful. Phelim was a miserable-looking object himself – lean, lank and dirty and bearing a strong resemblance to his mamma. But he was surrounded by business in the way of writing materials, chairs, a table, a bottle of whiskey, though it was early in the day and a pipe which he laid aside on the entrance of the visitors.

"Maybe I'll be able to do something for you gentleman?"

"Nothing at present – much hereafter, if you can only inform us where Mr Burke is to be found."

Phelim looked up with a scared look and then, recovering himself, asked if it was "Mr Burke of the Blackwater Villas, or of Tivoli, on the river, a little way out of town?"

It was neither – and this led to an explanation of *the* Mr Burke in question. And then he knew nothing. And no one knows the immovability of an Irishman's determined stupidity, till he has tried it. He almost forgot the name; nearly denied his own identity; and, when compelled to admit that he had been Burke's clerk at the time of his quitting the country, pretended never to have heard of him or from him, from that day to this.

"There's an estate called the Kildonald Estate. Who receives the rents.?"

"That's Mr Burke himself that receives them." Here he looked uncomfortable and a gradual tremor crept over Phelim O'Brian.

"But he's not been in England for years; and yet the rents go somewhere."

"Is it the rents? Sorrow any rents we get. It's the agent in London – he comes down twice a year."

"What's his name, Phelim? Come, don't be afraid. It will be a fine thing for you, when the business is righted. You'd like a little agency round here." (May Mr Diver be forgiven – Charlie allowed him to lie.)

"Indeed, it would suit me, and the ould woman downstairs."

"It's possible Phelim; but where's Burke?"

"How would I know? Didn't he go to Australia, and then to America? Leastways they say the New Yorkers was puzzled quite. I'd thought he'd ha' met wi' his match there, anyhow."

"But where is he now?" said Charlie, putting an obviously leading question.

"Honour bright, I don't know. I wish I did."

"What would you do?"

"By my soul, I'd make him curse the day ever he cheated Phelim O'Brian out of a year's wages."

"But you don't know where he is?"

"I don't, yer honour."

"Leave us together and I'll see you at dinner." muttered the wily lawyer to Charlie.

Louder he said "Well, Thornhill, it's no use – he knows nothing, so we'll be off. Good morning, much obliged." He got thus far, but no farther, for no sooner had Phelim O'Brian heard the name of Thornhill, than, rising suddenly from his chair, he repeated the name three or four times and, resuming his seat, seemed with difficulty to restrain himself.

Charlie who had sense enough to know that Diver was the proper person to hunt the fox, obeyed him implicitly; and, though he fully comprehended the value of this exclamation, he turned round and made his way down the ruined staircase without eliciting a remark from the old lady in the chimney corner. He was no sooner gone, than Mr Diver brought his artillery to bear; it was evident that Phelim O'Brian was to be bought. Burke had left him in the utmost need.

Money and safety were the two grand things for which Phelim stipulated. The first was a certainty, the latter nearly so: for the best of all reasons, he seemed to have known very little and acted entirely under Burke's directions. Of the papers connected with the Kildonald property he knew nothing, excepting that they had been stolen from the office on the night of the robbery. There were others whom it was absolutely necessary to find before much could be made out of the business. There were two Dalys. One was dead, we know, the other was nobody knows where. There was one Gipsy George, too, an illegitimate son of Kildonald's as they said. He knew something about Burke, but not very much. One thing only came out and that was that Burke had deliberately forged the date and the name to several deeds, drawn up by Phelim himself, after the death of Geoffrey Thornhill. To prove this it was necessary to secure Phelim, and Charlie very wisely left it to Mr Diver to make use of his professional knowledge for the purpose.

When Charlie left Cork he had enjoyed some good dinners at Mr Corcoran's table; he had seen something of the beauty of the Cork ladies. He had tested their inflammability to a certain extent, and found them as soft as gun-cotton, and equally combustible but he had made no progress in the discovery of his father's murderers and went back to England more determined than ever of purpose.

Of course he went down to Thornhills. His mother was all affection as usual, but while she talked to him and of his prospects it was evident that she was thinking of Tom. Mary Stanhope thought they had both been spoilt; and as to Tom's folly, it was perfectly incomprehensible.

He forgot neither his Uncle Henry nor Roger Palmer. The former he found, as usual, in Pall Mall in the midst of business. Everything had a prosperous look about him but the man himself. He looked worn, prematurely aged and overworked - a dull stone in a gorgeous setting. He was to Charlie the same as ever; touched lightly, but kindly on Tom's extravagance and hoped Thornhills might be saved. He could not buy it, or he would.

"If ever you have the chance, Charlie, don't throw it away." Charlie walked off thoughtfully enough. If his uncle did not put it in his power, who would? By this time he had reached Roger Palmer's. The old man was delighted with everything his *protégé* had done. His services would be very valuable at home in another year or so.

The first person Charlie saw on his return to Frankfort was his new groom. He looked very steadily at the man, and then began to wonder at his own stupidity. If everyone was as honest, what an admirable world this would be! He recognised him directly. This was the man who had held his horse, who had stolen his dog, who had sent him to Whitechapel and who had called on him when studying at Armstrong's. And now he saw the difference. The one character was that of a cunning looking, half ferocious sort of person with a bullet head, ragged whiskers, unkempt and unshorn. The other was that of an active, cleanly, close-shaven, practical groom. Not the fine gentleman who spent one half of the year at Melton and the other between Newmarket and London but there was something still in the man's eye that recalled his former characteristics at once.

"How are the horses, Daly?" said his master.

The man jumped round as if he had been shot. All colour left his cheeks and then, as suddenly recollecting himself he said,

"I ask yer pardon sir; did ye spake?"

"I asked after the horses, that's all. Is the brown English horse all right?"

"Yes sir, they're both right enough; and his feet's improving anyhow. I kept his heels nice and open and I wouldn't let 'em even cut away his frog. Baron Hartztein's man wants the master to buy him."

"If he is big enough to carry me, I may as well keep him as sell him."

"He's the horse that can do it yer honour. He's near thoroughbred and has great hocks and a good back. He'd make a steeplechaser if he knows how to lep."

"I'll ride him at half-past three" saying which, Charlie turned from his stables and made his way to Madame Meyerheim's. "I think we know where to put our hands upon Mr Daly when we want him." thought Charlie and he entered the *porte cochére*[41] and rang the bell.

"What Miss Donald all alone? Well, I hope you are all as I left you. But you look unwell yourself" added he, after a pause, in which he stood looking at the pretty eyes of his compatriot.

"Miss Donald," said little Bertha Meyerheim, "is very naughty, I'm sure."

"Why so, Bertha? What makes you think so?" said Charlie encouragingly.

"Ah I know, but I won't tell. I know she is because she's just like me." Bertha was a flat-faced, blue-eyed little girl, with flaxen hair.

"Not much Bertha, I should think."

"Yes but she is. She's always crying now; and I only cry when I'm naughty."

Charlie looked round and Kathleen jumped up and left the room.

"Well, Bertha, and what have you been doing since I went away? Who's been here to play with you?" And Charlie drew the child towards him.

"Oh! There's another gentleman been here instead of you and he goes to the Tier Garten and to Mainlust and…, and … but I don't like him so well as you, he talks funny English." Little pitchers have good ears as well as long ones.

"Really, that's kind. And what's his name?"

"I don't know his name but he came here with Comte Degenfeld." Charlie changed the conversation, and after chatting with Madam Meyerheim, he took his leave.

Charlie's Irish groom was not exactly what he seemed. His life had

---

[41] The carriage entrance

been a chequered one. He was well brought up, for a cotter's son. The priest and the squire had stood his friend when a boy and had sent him to school. More than that, they saw that he learnt and had half-a-crown in his pocket. But he took to evil courses. He took to poaching and horse-breaking instead of quill-driving in Burke's office, for which he was intended. Then he began to wander further a-field. He became a vagabond frequenter of race-meetings and Burke discarded him. Presently he returned; starving, begging and want drives out honesty. Burke had something for him to do, which he did, unscrupulously and effectively. And the two had a hold on one another, but the rich man's grip was tighter. Poverty was a lying look when confronted with wealth. By-and-by he got more honest and tried to work but it took him a great many years to do so. He was a tout, then a stable-boy, then he became a helper in some large stables and when he got the chance he became a groom. He had not been so happy since he was a child in his father's house on the Kildonald estate and the name of Thornhill had a mysterious charm for him. He had been of service to Charlie before this and we love those we can serve.

A few days later, Charlie was smoking in the stable, a reprehensible but not unpleasant practice, when Daly said to him,

"Baron Hartzstein was looking at your English horse, yer honour. He wants to buy him."

"He may have him. I've seen one belonging to a Hungarian gentleman." Charlie looked very indifferent.

"The English horse goes well in harness. It's a grand horse he is in leather." said Daly

"It's just what he's fit for. If he wants any information the baron can ride and drive him and the price is eighty pounds."

"I'll be puzzled entirely, faith, with the pounds. It's about francs and florins he's always axing. Maybe I'll tell him too little."

"Then say two thousand francs: that's about the mark." The next day the horse was sold.

Charlie sat in a brown study a day or two dater, about three o'clock, smoking a German pipe. It was rarely that he indulged in that way but his cigars were getting low and he had no fancy for the produce of Bremen or Hamburg in lieu of the Havannah. So he took to a pipe. "Come in," said he and there entered a not frequent visitor or two: Degenfeld, de Weiller and Hartzstein.

"Herr Carl becomes quite the German," said Degenfeld.

"How's the pipe? Tastes he good?" said De Weiler.

"Middling, thank you, baron," replied Charlie. "There's a cigar for you. Hartzstein, those are some of Tom's: you'd better take one,"

The two barons helped themselves, and the Comte followed their example. Charlie rang the bell. "Bring up a bottle of Steinwein."

"Do you go to the ball given by the grand Duke next week, Mr Thornhill?" said De Weiler, who was not an old acquaintance and consequently more formal than Hartzstein and Degenfeld. "I hear some of your countrymen are coming over from the spas."

"Yes, I have an invitation and intend going."

"And your pretty countrywoman?" said Degenfeld: "Hartzstein raves about her."

"I agree with him," said Charlie, "But she's not quite a countrywoman. She's Irish."

"Irish or English, will she be there?" said Hartzstein.

"I hardly think so." said Charlie

"The Meyerheims are going I presume, but I should not like to propose it to Madame Meyerheim..." Hartzstein said.

"I should not like to propose it to Madame Meyerheim, myself." interposed Thornhill. "If I were the Grand Duke's most intimate friend, and I don't think the Baroness Hartzstein would feel complimented if she were placed in the same situation as Miss

Donald." Here the conversation dropped and Charlie inquired what the Baron thought of his new purchase. He liked him much: the horse rode well and was good in harness; a capital match to the one he had brought with him from England. Young Phelps, the *attaché* to the Embassy, had offered Hartzstein a hundred for him. Before the three gentlemen rose to go, Degenfeld drew nearer to Charlie.

"Mr Thornhill, I expect an Englishman to dine with me and our friends here, next week at the Hotel de Russie privately. Will you join us!"

"Certainly, with pleasure."

"What day will suit you? We can make it any day."

"Say Wednesday then. Adieu, adieu!" They all shook hands and parted. Two of their sabres clanked downstairs and they sallied into the Zeil. Charlie finished his pipe and went to the bank.

"Confound that fellow Hartzstein's impudence," thought he. "These Germans are the most impertinent fellows alive. When an Englishman means wrong, or does wrong, he is seldom proud of it. But these fellows are as fond of their vices as a North American Indian of his scalp. Poor girl! I wonder what old Donald and his wife are like. Upon my soul, she stands in a very awkward position. Meyerheim is as good as gold and so is his wife. But they know no more about fellows like Hartzstein than I do of astronomy. It certainly is no business of mine. I wonder whether Degenfeld knows anything about it. What's every man's business is nobody's business. It's every man's business to protect a poor girl from an unprincipled blackguard like Hartzstein. If she wasn't so good-looking I'd do something towards stopping it myself but someone would say I was in love with the girl." Such were Charlie's meditations as he sat on a three-legged stool, staring vacantly and no man can deny that, though slow and old-fashioned in his notions, they were tolerably just.

The day before the intended dinner at Degenfeld's Charlie sat at his desk in an inner room of the bank. He had had letters from England, detailing the course of events in Ireland. Diver was in full cry and hoped not only to secure the testimony of Daly but the person of Burke himself. The latter was and had been alive and living under his own name not twelve months ago as the rents had been received from the Kildonald estate, and receipts signed by his agent in his name. That gentleman had not yet appeared: doubtless he would be found within a month of the next rent day. Burke had been traced to America and there, finding the aborigines as barbarous and the settlers as unprincipled as himself, he had disappeared. Charlie was requested to be as quiet as possible and to awake no suspicion of the intended investigation.

The letters from Lady Marston and one from Mr Dacre who occasionally wrote to him, were full of English gossip or family news. Tom's affairs were better than had been expected. His mother and Mary Stanhope were at Thornhills for the winter. Lord Audley had proposed and been rejected by Alice Dacre and Robinson Brown was going to be married to Lady Susan Trumpington; lots of blood for the money as the Piccadilly Phenomenon might observe. Both letters spoke of the rapidly failing health of Henry Thornhill who was gone into the country for a change of air and Mr Dacre seemed to think that they might pass the next winter in the south of Italy - he did not say for what reason.

"A letter by private hand for Mr Thornhill" said one of the clerks, opening the door of Charlie's office. He placed it on the table. The edging was black as well as the seal and the hand-writing was unknown to him. It had a lawyer-like appearance. Charlie was but mortal himself, so he turned it and twisted it, and looked at the crest and made a dozen conjectures. He never guessed right and with some fear of undefined calamity, he broke open the letter. When he opened it he did not look at it for a minute or more and when he did, the truth was told in a most unceremonious fashion. His uncle had died without a warning and without a struggle. Henry Thornhill was no more. Enclosed was a letter, the last that had been written by the deceased, addressed to Charlie and to be forwarded to him as soon as circumstances permitted. As its contents concern no one more than the recipient and may well remain undisclosed until the requirements of the story bring them to light, I shall try the reader's patience if he feel any curiosity to know them.

CHAPTER 32

INTENTIONS

Charlie digested the last words of Uncle Henry. "He was a good fellow," said Charlie to himself; "I hadn't a better friend in the world, I believe, excepting my mother, and Lady Marston, and Mary Stanhope, and ….. Well! There are lots of 'em when you begin to add them up. Why in the world did he make Roger Palmer one of his executors? And why must I talk matters over with him? The two men are so different. I should like to know what there is in that other letter which I am not to know at present. Here, Daly, take this note to Comte Degenfeld's: there's no answer."

The young Englishman expected to dine with Degenfeld was Teddy Dacre, so that they had a narrow escape of meeting; and Dacre did not know that Charlie was in Frankfort. Dacre was on his way to England, on leave from the embassy in Berne.

That's a very pleasant life, that attachéship. When I see the gallant young fellows at high jinks at the Variétés, or the Palais Royal, disporting themselves at the bal masque, shying champagne corks across half a dozen little tables to the charming Iphigénie and her dear Duc, who are fighting aloud over the leg of a pullet, and shocking the respectable company between them, then I see the advantages of our diplomatic system, and admire the pertinacious determination of our rising Talleyrands to acquire a correct accent. Teddy Dacre had done all this, and was now acting the sterling character of the virtuous young English gentleman to the edification of his co-attachés and the distinguished circle of which an attaché is always a segment. He was very fond of Charlie, and Charlie of him; and I think, had they met, Charlie might have employed his diplomatic talents on a special mission of some importance to him.

* * * * * *

"What the deuce has become of Henry Thornhill's money?" said Sir Herbert Cardstone to his friend De Beauvoir, as they walked steadily over a turnip-field on the estate of the former.
"Aw-aw--speculated--speculated. Lost every shilling. Mysterious case altogether. Very sudden: only ill two hours." (He had been ill of bronchitis one fortnight, and eventually died of inflammation of the trachera.) "- hard on Charlie Thornhill, I call it."
"Why so?........ That brown dog of yours is drawing."
These were old-fashioned, middle-aged sportsmen, and used dogs.
"Confound the dog: how wild the birds are. What right has a fellow to die in that way, and leave nothing, when the only reason one could have an uncle banker is to inherit his money? A banker without money is an ….. anomaly…. There goes another brace."
"Have you ever seen a regular driving day?" said Sir Herbert.
"Lots of 'em. Day at Bedfont. Gad! I believe you. My old governor was a regular member of the club as one might call it." Here it occurred to De Beauvoir that he had changed foxes – at least he and Sir Herbert were not following the same one, so he pulled up.
"I mean driving partridges: we do it down here sometimes late in the season, without dogs." explained Sir Herbert Cardstone.

"Oh! Partridges? To be sure. By Jove! We had a grand day last year at Thornhills. Tom Thornhill was there, and the Dacres, and old Dorrington, and Corry, and one or two men. We walked in a line over all the turnips in the two parishes with six or seven beaters between each of us. Capital fun it is, too. Only Tom walks such a pace and shoots so quickly that no one has a chance with him."

"Who has Thornhills now? Tom's away." said the baronet.

"Mrs Thornhill and Miss Stanhope are living there. Tom talks of coming home for the shooting in December; and Charlie, I fancy, will be over again – unless this death of his uncle makes some change in his plans."

"I should like to have Thornhills better than any place I know," said Sir Herbert Cardstone. "But what difference should his uncle's will make to Charlie's prospects, except the loss of the money?"

"Charlie," said De Beauvoir, who was not a bad fellow, but a club gossip, "was supposed to be engaged to Edith Dacre, and the prospects were brightened, but dimly, by his expectations from his uncle. The light was very small, you know, but it was bright enough to keep up – what you may call it – hope, as the poet says, and now Charlie's light is out altogether. I don't think the old lady will stand even Charlie without something more than a bank salary, which is all he has at present."

"Why, De Beauvoir, they used to talk about you for one of those girls."

"The world's given to lying, Cardstone; and you're quite old enough to know it. You've been married a hundred times, only you didn't hear about it, that's all. I quite think a man might do worse, and not burn his fingers much. They're both charming girls."

"Why doesn't Tom Thornhill marry? There must be lots of girls with a few thousands that would jump at him," said Cardstone.

"Thornhill is very young, but is almost fit for nothing but a racecourse or a card table. The worst of it is, that he's hardly bad enough for the former, and too good for the latter. If he'd been anything but a gentleman, gad! What a fellow he'd have been! But I should like to know where the girls with a few thousand are: one of them might do for me." said De Beauvoir.

* * * * * *

There was a neat looking horse in Frankfort called Kosciusko, with a bad character, which, I am obliged to confess he deserved. At least, so said half the manège riders in the city, and all the horse breakers and regimental riding masters, most of whom he had managed to place on their backs, either in the barrack school or at exercise. He was a pretty, well-bred Hungarian horse, not very deficient in power, and of most undeniable pluck. He was not vicious, but playful and it seemed only a question of how long you could hope to sit on his back. If he got tired before you, you had mastered him for the day; if not, you would have to return home with or without him, as the case might be. It is but right to say that, having succeeded many times in his efforts, he had become emboldened, and this made the mastery of him difficult. This horse Charlie Thornhill set his heart upon and he was not many hours in Charlie's hands before he was ambling about the streets of Frankfort, with apparently as much good humour as if he had never had his own way at all. It was a fine sight to the lovers of good horsemanship to see the two pacing gently along the Zeil, the young Englishman sitting closely down in his saddle without effort, and giving sufficiency of liberty to his head to enable him to play with his bit, and turn from side to side, instead of that alternate urging and curbing which had made him the plunging performer that he had been.

Some little time after he had reclaimed Kosciusko, he had given Hartzstein a mount upon him. Owing, probably, to the fact of his change of masters, he took to his old tricks. The baron resorted to his old form, spurs, and the curb, and though by no means deficient in pluck or experience, he was pitched off in the kennel, exactly opposite Herr Meyerheim's and in a state of insensibility, was taken in there. In one week, with the exception of his collarbone, he was again well; but it was sympathy or the natural goodness of a woman's disposition, which disposes her to love everything which she can protect, it is certain that Hatrzstein made much progress in the heart of Kathleen. That she was flattered by his attentions it is natural to suppose; and day by day, as he prolonged his stay on some frivolous pretext, she became more in love. As to Hartzstein himself, his passion gained strength hourly; and he vowed to himself the possession of a girl whom he could not regard as fitted for the wife of a Viennese noble.

In the mean time to say that the death of Henry Thornhill affected Charlie very seriously would not be true. With the contents of his letter, and his solicitor's explanations, he was satisfied, but he failed to understand entirely his uncle's position. He had been his favourite nephew, he knew, but he had not been intimate with him, nor had his house ever afforded him a home. Under these circumstances, he got over the loss pretty quickly, but was obliged for the sake of propriety, on the day of Comte Degenfeld's dinner, to absent himself altogether. We shall see to what important results it led. There was no other absentee, and Teddy Dacre found himself side by side with the Count, and on the other side the Barons Hartzstein and de Weiler, in a private room of the Hôtel de Russie.

A day or two before on a dark, warm night in autumn, or now just verging towards winter, three men stood in a small, well furnished room with folding doors. There was in the room a round table, on which were two packs of cards scattered about and a dice-box and backgammon board. On the small table on one side of the room was a tray with some half-emptied glasses and two empty bottles, one of champagne, the other of a labelled Rhein wine, and a stone bottle of Seltzer water.

Burke and Baron Hartzstein were smoking cigars after a night of high stakes. Their fellow players had left, one of whom had been very pale and much poorer. After some preliminary conversation, in which language asserted its right to conceal meaning, Hartzstein seemed suddenly to grow tired of beating about the bush.

"You say you know the father and mother; and can assist me?"

"I can and will," said Burke, with a fierce vehemence. "And now I'll tell ye why, - Because I hate him, and all connected with him. You say you are prepared to go to any lengths to attain your object. There is no risk; no danger, set about properly; but there must be money; and I ...."

"Anything you want."

"Your carriage and horses: hired horses create suspicion."

"Everything is at your service. Take my servants; and when you have arranged your plan, let me know, and we'll fix the day. The girl is well enough disposed for the journey, could I but once get her away from other influences. Do I make myself understood?" The baron spoke in German, which Burke, with the natural facility of an Irishman, had easily mastered during his residence abroad.

"Perfectly. And my services, baron?"

"Cannot be esteemed too highly." The baron took his leave, and strolled slowly down the hill, ten minutes walk to the middle of the Spa."

As Burke shut the door of "The Mount" and prepared to lie down in the inner chamber, he thought with malicious cruelty on one topic for some time. "Now Arthur Kildonald, we shall see how you like the tricks of sleight of hand in which you have taken no part."

* * * * * *

One morning Charlie Thornhill took his hat and strolled leisurely along the Zeil. Turning up three or four steps on the left, he found himself in a flagged passage, with a small window barred with brass wire and closed: below it was a small door. "Hier darf man nicht rauchen!"[42] So Thornhill threw away his cigar, and knocked at the little door.

A gruff, broad German face, with stiff blue frock coat, and a strip of yellow braid on each shoulder, presented – no, not himself, but his moustaches at the door.

"Can I see the Chief of the Police?"

"If Monsieur will take the first door on the right, and ring." So Charlie took the first door on the right, and rang. On answering the summons "Hierein." he was admitted into a large room, the chief furniture of which was a few chairs, a round table, a side table covered with papers, a stove, a bird-cage, and plenty of sand. The walls were covered with posters in various languages, otherwise they were quite white. A man was seated in the room; he was petting a kitten and smoking a pipe which seemed the grossest violation of the rules of social propriety. Yet when Charlie answered to the summons, "Hierein!" such was the employment of the man that received him. Over fire-place, were some strong fetters.

"I believe I address the Chief of the Police?"

"Is there anything we can do for you?" He neither answered the question nor deserted his cat, but he rose politely, and offered his visitor a chair.

"I have a servant." started Charlie. Here the chief laid down his pipe.

"The name and address of Monsieur?" said the man politely. He was tall, florid, stout, with straight, hard features, but good looking.

"Thornhill, of Meyerheim's house, and Number 361, Zeil."

---

[42] No smoking allowed here.

"Good; we know all about Monsieur."

Some men might have been flattered, Charlie was not.

"Circumstances render it desirable that a close watch should be kept on my servant." Charlie continued.

"His name and country?"

"Daly, I am told; Ireland."

"Monsieur, is cautious. Has he been guilty of anything whilst with Mr. Thornhill?"

"Nothing whatever; and is an excellent servant. Still there are reasons."

"We understand, Monsieur," said the Chief of the Police. "He will not escape. You are sure his name is Daly, and his country is Ireland?"

"Of the first, no; of the second, decidedly – yes."

The chief then took up from the table a paper, letting the cat fall gently upon the ground, stroking her at the same time, and calling her poor little pussycat, as though loth to part with her. He read aloud: "Five feet eight; flat face, very slightly marked with small-pox; whiskers lately shaven; strongly built, but not large; consigned as groom to Mr. Thornhill; character good; antecedents, suspicious; answers to the name of Daly – supposed to be fictitious.' there, sir is that the man?" said the chief, looking up from his papers. "Not much chance of escape there, I think. 'He has a scar on one thumb, and has lost his two eye-teeth and one molar; age, about forty.' I fancy that's your man sir. He's one of the best servants in the town. 'Strict surveillance,' I have added to his name. Will that suffice?"

"Amply. I wish you good morning, Herr Diebnehmer, and am much obliged by your kindness."

And Charlie heard him say, as he turned to go out, "Poor little pussycat, come den, come. Biedermann, has that fellow had his breakfast yet in cell 36?"

"No sir."

"Then stop it. He wants a change of diet, or we shall have him a kicking. I manage the municipality. Another flogging will do him no harm."

"And this is your kitten lover and canary fancier.," thought Charlie. "I wonder Herr Diebnehmer is not suffocated by the mask he wear."

CHAPTER 33

FRUSTRATED

A nice little dinner is a charming invention of the enemy of mankind to dispel serious thought, and to deaden comprehension. A large heavy turban-and-feather business is quite another matter.
Listen in!
"You must have Lord Alfred, dear, on Tuesday week."
"Why so, love? He is terribly stupid, and as deaf as a post."
"Because he owns three parishes in the southern division; and if your brother is to be returned again, you mustn't forget him."
"And what am I to do about Sir William? There's no room for him."
"Gad! You must put on another leaf, and ask old Mrs Perrywinkle to meet him. They're old friends; and his covers will be shot the beginning of next month, and it won't do for him to forget us."
"Do you care about my asking Adelaide instead of Mrs Perrywinkle?"
"Oh! I can't stand Adelaide Tempest: by Jove, she's worse than old Lord Alfred: she talks as much, and,...... What's worse I can hear every word she says."
"Well, then, all I have to say, dear, is this: you won't get your gardener's son into the Omnilogical School at Dunderhead, for

Adelaide can do just as she pleases there." Then ensues, not a quarrel, but a matrimonial difference of opinion, in which both fight, and give way, and Adelaide and Mrs Perrywinkle are both asked, and the dinner becomes more oppressively stupid than ever.

I therefore like a little dinner. It is but fair, however, to admit that ideas of a little dinner differ as much as anything in this world can differ. One man means an atrociously bad beefsteak, and a still worse pudding; another, half a dozen badly-cooked dishes, including cold, thick soup, soft fish and a dingy table-cloth; a third delights to satisfy the cravings of his friends with a roast fowl and a boiled leg of mutton, with what he calls a nice head of "sallery", and a glass of newly-concocted port. A suckling-pig, a green goose, and a welsh sheep are all excuses, at one time or another, for a little dinner.

But these little dinners are a national facility. They require a minute attention to detail, which Englishmen expend on what they call higher objects, as if any object could be higher than one's daily bread. As a nation we are not, therefore, a good light-dinner-giving people. The heavy and pompous we do to a turn: it is characteristic of our maritime, political, and commercial greatness. Commend me rather to the French. The Germans are utterly out of court with their vegetable diet, green pickles and stewed pears so Charlie Thornhill lost nothing by his absence from the table of the Lieutenant Comte von Degenfeld.

"Have you seen Dornhill's new horse, de Weiler?" asked their host, producing some cigars, and tendering them to his guests.

"Not yet; but he is said to be dangerous. Is he the horse that hurt you, Hartzstein?" said de Weiler. Hartzstein blushed as he acknowledged the mischance. De Weiler was not remarkable for tact. "He is a dangerous horse." said Hartzstein, "or rather was when I rode him; but he is become quiet with Charles Thornhill."

"Thornhill? Charlie Thornhill?" repeated Dacre. "Ah! I remember now. Charlie is in Frankfort. I quite forgot. He is banking here. I've been away from England, and not heard directly from him lately. Is he here now?"

"Certainly," said Hartzstein. "I saw him yesterday. He was to have dined here today with Degenfeld. By the way, I spent a few days at your father's Mr. Dacre, with Charlie's brother Tom, the last time I was in England."

"So I heard," said Dacre. "They say Tom Thornhill is nearly done. He's a fine fellow; but I know Charlie best. He saved my life at school, and my sister's the season before last, out hunting."

"I have been told so; but I never heard the particulars."

Teddy related them, and concluded by saying, "Talking of his riding, you never saw such a place as he jumped at the corner of our cover. However, he was always considered one of the best men in the midland counties. What's the horse he has now?"

"Oh! An incorrigible brute, a Hungarian stallion who has half killed half the men in the regiment. But Thornhill has quieted him. He came back to Frankfort, and bought him on purpose to practise some trick he learnt from your American Rarey.[43] What did you think of him, Dacre?" said Hartzstein.

"Rarey? I liked him very much. He's a clever fellow with horses."

"Said to be rather a charlatan, wasn't he?" inquired Degenfeld.

"You know," added De Weiler, "that something like his method has been practised here, and in almost all cavalry schools, for years past."

"The same *method*," replied Dacre, who was unwittingly led into the defence, "but not the same principle."

---

[43] The Original Horse Whisperer - John Solomon Rarey (1827 - 1866)
Briefly, the technique consisted of hobbling one of the horse's legs with a strap enabling the trainer to completely control the horse and quickly tire him out. The trainer could then make the horse lie down, then stroke and gentle the subdued animal, even lying down on the animal, until the horse was thoroughly convinced, in the most peaceful way possible, that the trainer was master.

"I don't understand the distinction exactly," said one of the three.

"Let me endeavour to explain, then. It was customary, occasionally, to put horses down in our own country, but no reason given for doing so, nor was it supposed to be part of an organised system. Rarey's is. That's a very fine glass of hock that M. Sarg has given us."

"And what is the principle involved in Rarey's practice?" asked Degenfeld.

"Complete subjugation without active violence, succeeded by kindness."

"Is the horse capable of comprehending that? Women are not. They don't forget the process of subjugation." said Hartzstein.

"You speak as if you had had considerable practice, Hartzstein; however, horses are naturally good, entirely good: women, like ourselves, have a leaven of malice and wickedness, and don't always forget the struggle, whatever may be the struggle, whatever may be the result. Beware of a first quarrel!"

"But the horse fights, like the woman," said the baron.

"Yes; but from fear, not from vice. A young horse is mischievous from ignorance; but whatever vices he has have been contracted from bad management. I think Rarey's system would answer with children, though they seldom feel confidence where there has been too much or continued strictness."

"And was Rarey usually successful?" asked Degenfeld.

"Invariably," said Teddy Dacre, "and with very bad horses."

"They became restive again, though," said Hartzstein, "when the restraint was removed: women all over."

"Now and then. And remember that in those cases the habits of vice were confirmed; and he had no fair chance of frequent repetition. The management of women is like the bitting, rather, of horses. Every horse can be ridden if you get the right tack on him, and a woman only wants the right man for her lord and master." said

Teddy Dacre.

"I wonder whether your friend Thornhill is as clever with the one as the other," said Hartzstein.

"I should think he gives himself very little concern about the latter; but he's just the sort of person to obtain a very strong influence. He has all the qualities women most admire, and the strongest will I ever knew." said Teddy.

"And what are these qualities?" inquired De Weiler.

"Great firmness, manliness, self-respect, and chivalrous notions of their rights, with an utter absence of any vanity. He has a heart and arm of iron, with a silken hand."

"He's keeping them in practice with a very pretty Irish woman at present," said De Weiler. "I saw them together yesterday with Meyerheim's children."

"Who is she?" said Dacre, to whom Frankfort scandal was new.

"She is the governess at the house of his chief, with whom he formerly lived. She is said to be a woman of family, whose parents are needy, and who have left England from necessity." Degenfeld repeated only what he had heard, which was not far from the truth for a report.

"Then she is safe from Charlie Thornhill, I lay my life," said Dacre.

"Why so?" asked Hartzstein, abruptly.

"Because he's a gentleman," rejoined Teddy, who had very pretty notions on the subject for an attaché, and whose theory was excellent, whatever might have been his practice. "He's more likely to protect her than to take advantage of a very helpless situation."

"You seem to have studied his character," said Hartzstein, rather insolently.

"I have," replied Dacre, not noticing the tone of the speaker, "and he is someone I greatly admire though I know no one whom I should less desire for an enemy."

"Why so, again?" demanded Hartzstein.

"Because, though slow to move, he is perseverance itself; and though not a man of quick apprehension, he is singularly tenacious of an idea when once it has taken root. What is the name of the lady?"

"I forget," said Degenfeld. "Hartzstein can tell you; he's rather in love with her himself."

"She calls herself Kathleen Donald," said Hartzstein, thus appealed to. "The report goes that her father left England for some betting transactions years ago; and that that is not his true name. The Meyerheims know nothing of him, but they describe the girl's mother as a lady. Of one thing you may be quite certain, that Thornhill is paying her very marked attention; and from your account we must credit him with good intentions. Now, Degenfeld, you'll excuse me, but I'm going to dress for the ball."

The little dinner was finished with a cup of coffee and a cigar, and the guests separated, each on his own business or pleasure, as the case might be.

Hartzstein went to the ball, as did Degenfeld and De Weiler. The scene was gay and glittering as foreign ballrooms are wont to be. The Meyerheims were there. Hartzstein paid his sweetest compliments to the banker's wife; but he saw no Kathleen Donald, as indeed he presumed would be the case, and Charlie Thornhill had not arrived. "But Englishmen are always late," said he to himself.

We will not stay to analyse the sincerity of the smiles, or the truthfulness of some of the hearts there that beat beneath white satin and diamonds.

It was about three in the afternoon that Degenfeld and his friends had sat down to dinner, and three of the clock also when Charlie Thornhill ordered his horses. They were short of work, and he desired his servant Daly to ride the Arab, he himself mounting the once vicious Hungarian. They rode slowly out of the town, and being indifferent as to the route, he turned towards the left bank of the Lahn, on they rode to Wetzlar. Charlie was not given to blue devils, but he had some reflections which were not the most cheerful in the world. The mystery connected with his uncle's will, and his ignorance of his affairs, affected him more than he chose to acknowledge. Brought up with the expectation of benefitting by his uncle's death to a very considerable extent, whenever it might happen, then this frustration of his hopes, made him seriously consider his position. It was not for himself alone. He had been accustomed for the last few years to think of his future prospects in connection with Edith Dacre. His sense of honesty did not permit him to indulge the same happy reveries now, and he was only wondering what ought to be his course of action with regard to her and her family. Missing the dinner of Degenfeld's was unlucky; had he only seen Edward Dacre, it might all have been easily settled. Of Edith herself he had no misgivings; but whether she ought to be asked to share the moderate income of the foreign correspondent of Messrs. Chalkstone and Co. was another matter.

I am reluctantly obliged to admit that as Charlie rode along he took no notice of the magnificent view which broke upon him to the west. The sun was sinking; and there stretched the chain of hills called the Berg Strasse, with Mayence in the middle distance, and the beautiful slopes of Wiesbaden. Magnificent prospect! And redolent of German knightly chivalry. He was himself eminently chivalrous, if honesty and the defence of the wronged formed a material part of the creed; but of poetry or romance he had nothing, and cared less; and as for every woman these knights rescued, he firmly believed they probably carried some of them off to their own strongholds, so he may be excused for his dubious admiration of the Middle Ages.

The time of year, as I have already implied, if not said, was middle autumn. A beautiful day was about to be succeeded by heavy banks of clouds in the south-west, which came up, louring, with the wind. The sun was darkened, and the moon, which was near its full, was hiding her light. In the distance lightening began to play, and gradually the landscape had a turbid look, inky, streaked with sullen red. Charles Thornhill's horse had been a little troublesome, but he had sobered down again: but as he heard the distant rumbling of the thunder, he began again to fidget and lash his sides with the quantity of tail that English taste had left him. He was some distance from Frankfort when the storm began; somewhere in a region unknown to English travellers of these railway days, but hallowed by the book "*Sorrows of Wherter*"[44]. Charlie knew nothing of that. It was not in his way, and, I confess, the book is dry enough to stagger a better man.

"Daly, do you know of a public house anywhere before we get back to Wetzlar?" Daly rode up along side of his master.

"Sorrow! There is a public house I know along here, sir. We passed one half an hour ago, coming out of the town, on the right-hand side; but it looked like a poor place, your honour." And Daly saluted his master respectfully.

"Poor or rich, it's better than nothing; and I rather think we shall upset this Hungarian's temper if we get into the storm." Just then came a terrific clap of thunder, which certainly irritated Kosciusko, whilst the lightening which preceded it made him start as if he were shot. Mr. Rarey's system had not yet taken into his consideration a thunderstorm. Charlie played with the horse's mouth, and after some handling induced him to settle. They turned towards the inn and proceeded at a good trot, the Arab cantering after them towards the roadside public-house, the lightning and thunder continuing to roar and behind them, and the rain coming up in gusts.

---

[44] ***The Sorrows of Young Werther*** (*Die Leiden des jungen Werthers*) The book made Goethe one of the first international literary celebrities. Towards the end of his life, a personal visit to Weimer became crucial to any young man's tour of Europe.

After ten minutes' sharp riding, and just as the floods descended, they pulled up at the little roadside inn. It was a mysterious-looking place, not the resort of good company. The windows were broken in places, the carriage entrance was old and worn. The front of the house was guiltless of paint, and not a soul seemed to be stirring. On their arrival Charlie jumped from his horse, and threw the reins to Daly, at the same time calling loudly for "the house!" A fine big, good-humoured-looking fellow came to the door, pipe in hand, clothed in a blouse, and with a species of foraging cap on his head. He wore a light moustache, and a pointed beard, uncommon in those parts: he had an indifferent air, but the sight of Charlie's groom and horses roused him into attention, and he welcomed Thornhill in a good-humoured manner. Charlie rather liked him, though devoid of anything like obsequiousness, he was civil enough, and ordered Fritz to go and show the gentleman's groom his stable. He remarked on the badness of the evening, and the loneliness of the road; he complained that the railways had spoilt his trade. Charlie ordered a bottle of wine, which the landlord had recommended, and Daly was accommodated in the kitchen. Charlie lit a cigar; and by this time the storm stood over the village, and spent its fury on the road beneath. Both master and man were glad to be indoors.

In the course of half an hour it began to abate, and Charlie went out to the stable-yard to see about resuming his journey. His servant had already commenced tightening the girths, and getting ready the manes and tails of the horses, which required a little straightening after the buffeting of the wind, when the noise of wheels was heard, and there dashed into the yard a carriage and pair of horses, which pulled up suddenly at the carriage entrance. Charlie, impelled by some unusual curiosity, returned towards the house in time to see the door of the barouche opened and the steps let down, while from it descended a strongly-built powerful man, with red whiskers and beard, lifting rather than leading a girl, more dead than alive, as white as marble, and down whose cheeks the tears rolled rapidly. I have said that it was become dark; the house was scarcely lighted, yet, as she passed beneath a lamp in the passage, near the door, Charlie was enabled to see a part of a face which he thought he could scarcely have mistaken. Still, how and why here under these circumstances? Could it be she? And what was it to him? What was it to any man situated as he was? Was he the investigator of adventures to the forlorn damsels of Frankfort? Suppose, too, he should have made a mistake!!!

"Sir, bedad here's the bay horse, looking all the worse for his gallop."

"What the deuce do you mean?" said Charlie, abstractedly.

"I mane that the bay horse is here, sir – the one you sold to Baron Hartzstein; and he isn't improved by the leather."

"Are you sure it's the horse? Here, landlord."

"Sir. Excuse me, but you're an Englisman," said the landlord.

"I am. But ....."

"There's a lady of your country upstairs has just arrived. She's in great distress. Is there anything wrong? Because, if so ...."

"Listen to me, landlord. You know nothing of this?"

"Nothing upon my honour," said the landlord.

"Nor the name of the man?"

"No."

"Nor the name of the lady?"

"Certainly not."

"How many are there with her?" asked Charlie.

"Two; the master, and his servant, who drove them; both are armed."

"How?" asked Charlie.

"Pistols," replied the Landlord.

"It looks bad. If I can convince you it is as you suspect it, will you help me?"

"I will," said the man.

"Have you any firearms – a pistol, for instance?"

"One, at your service."

"Have you a boy that can ride to Wetzlar for the Gendarmer?"

"Yes, but no horse."

"Let him take the Arab it's as quiet as a child. Daly, stand by the door of the room we shall show you, without breathing; the landlord will be ready to help: but let us have no scandal, if we can help it. Give me that hunting-crop you have in your hand. Now, landlord, take my card to the lady, who speaks German as well as we do, and ask her to see me."

The landlord ascended the stairs, and Charlie followed. The landlord entered, and closed the door. A smothered conversation ensued, of which, however, Charlie heard but stifled sobs, and a coarse, broad accent, which said, "You know your promise, and you know mine. Your father's life, as well as your own, depends upon it. No, landlord," added he, "the lady cannot see the gentleman." As the landlord opened the door to retreat, Charlie Thornhill, however, stood before them.

"What is the meaning of this intrusion?" But, before he could answer, the girl, Kathleen Donald – for it was she – threw herself between them, and seizing Charlie's hand, entreated protection in moving terms. "Save me! Save me, Mr. Thornhill! Thank God, I have a friend! I have been deceived into the belief that my father was in danger; that he had sent for me; that I could save him; and, knowing how he needed it, I trusted myself to this villain, who has disclosed himself as the agent of another. Is it possible that he too could mean me this wrong?"

"Who and what are you, sir, that you have dared to entrap an English girl into these meshes? Are you so low as to be pander to the Baron Hartzstein whose horses I recognise?" and Charlie approached nearer to his opponent, while he supported Kathleen with his other arm.

"How much do you know and by what right do you interfere with the journey of this lady and myself?"

"Nonsense, sir. You hear what she says. Relinquish your claim, and go hence in peace. Avoid further scandal, or it may be the worse for you."

The man then drew deliberately a pistol from his breast, and looking at Charlie said.

"Sit down, then, young lady, or it may chance that I put my threat in execution. Leave the room, sir. And, faith, be glad ye leave it alive. You have interfered in a most unjustifiable manner in what does not concern any one but this young lady and me. Be advised, and interfere no further."

"This is a matter, sir, that concerns every honest man. I know this lady, and her relations with Baron Hartzstein. She claims my protection, and she shall have it. Put up your weapon, and listen to me. The landlord is aware of your business; already the police have been sent for to be used if necessary. My servant waits without; and your own, who I see there and recognize and can be identified in Frankfort. Daly!" The groom entered the room, and Charlie Thornhill continued: "Order the horses to be put into the calèche[45] that drove in here half an hour ago; leave the Arab here with the landlord, and attend us on the Hungarian horse. I hear your servant, sir, is armed; weapons are useless, as he is to drive us back to Frankfort. He will therefore surrender his pistol. Your master will be better pleased that this business should be hushed up at once."

The scoundrel also understood that three honest men and a hostile woman are more than a match for two rascals, though one of them was bold villain enough. Charlie's terms were therefore complied

---

[45] barouche

with at once; and the betrayer threw himself into a chair with a dogged air, whilst the more humble ruffian placed his undischarged pistol on the table.

"Right," said our hero. "Now go and help the landlord with the horses. When they are ready, we are. What are you staring at, Daly?"

"B-u-r-k-e!" found its way slowly from between his lips.

"Yes, it is Burke; and I'm not the first man who has been cajoled by a woman. Faith, I give ye joy of your conquest, sir."

The landlord announced the horses; and Charlie, offering his arm to Kathleen, proceeded slowly down the stairs followed by his servant. The carriage was at the door; the night was again fine, and cooler than before. Daly mounted Kosciusko, and Hartzstein's servant the box; and thus they drove quietly towards Frankfort.

Arriving in that city, Charlie took his charge at once to her father's house, where they were received without emotion; Mr. and Mrs Donald imagining only that their daughter was still with Madame Meyerheim. This rendered explanation more difficult than ever. So Charlie, after essaying in vain to render the business intelligible, and not himself quite certain how far Kathleen had acted with imprudence, was at length obliged to give up all attempts at explanation, and to leave the girl to satisfy her father after his departure.

The facts elicited speak for themselves. Kathleen had received a letter from Burke, hinting darkly at calamity impending over her father. The name of Burke, not unknown to her, gave sufficient force to the warning. It prayed a meeting on the evening in question, at a late hour, though not yet in darkness, to suggest remedies in the hands of the girl herself, for some known ills. She had been easily deceived, and went without misgiving. A pretended letter from her father was given her in the twilight. Burke was a practised forger, and again she was deceived. Once in Hartzstein's carriage, she was not aroused to the real danger of her situation till she was out of Frankfort. The reader knows the rest. Her accidental meeting with Charlie, and Daly's recognition of Hartzstein's horse saved her from danger. Hartzstein was merciless, and away from other influences, he would have added her to his other victims.

CHAPTER 34

TWITTERINGS, LITERARY AND DOMESTIC

The escapade related in our last chapter had not been so quietly managed but that it had not given some cause for scandal. Little, however, of the real truth was known; and perhaps the most prevalent report was the intended elopement of an English governess with a young English banker, now resident in Frankfort; but that they had been caught and brought back by the girl's father. At all events, this version found its way to England; and some time later, Charlie Thornhill was half annoyed and half amused by the necessity of enlightening Lady Marston, which he did not do, however, quite in time to save his own reputation.

Like all Germans, or young men living in Germany, Charlie had no cook of his own at his rooms; he had contracted to have a permanent place at the *table d'hôte* of the Hôtel de Russie. It had many advantages, not the least of which was the occasional meeting of an old friend, and the hearing of some English news, in which he was interested. At the present season such things happened daily. Whole families seeking health, education, or economy: single men, new scenes, or repose from old ones: women, blue stockings, ready to rush into print, or adventuresses into matrimony; and both seeking a foreign subject for the exercise of their powers. Charlie liked to observe at them all.

Today he took his seat, according to custom, near the top of the table. A Russian general officer, who spoke four languages and drank oceans of champagne, occupied the post of honour at the head. There were the habitués of the place, like Charlie, and many English visitors. All the girls were more or less good-looking and excited attention as they entered. Their brothers emerging from the chrysalis state of Oxford or Cambridge, a regimental mess, the Guards' Club, or the Marine Parade, were insipid, straight-nosed, and gentlemanly. There was one exception to this rule, and he was placed next to Charlie. Our friend was attracted by the stranger who poured floods of sporting intelligence over the dinner table.

"Know him, Gad! I should think I do; he knows how to run a bye as well as most men," said he to a bald headed old gentleman, who had been imprudent enough to mention the name of an English nobleman. "There's not a leg that wouldn't have been broke if he'd won the Derby last year." Here the wife of the bald headed man dropped her knife and fork, and gazed with silent horror at the speaker. The gentleman, however, feeling called upon to say something, replied "God bless my soul, you don't say?"

"Oh! But I do. What a pot it was; he'd have boiled 'em all." Here the company looked up in general, and one or two of the younger members sharpened their ears to see if anything was to be learnt from so distinguished a professor of turf slang.

"Here, Kellner," added he handling a bottle of Rhine wine, which he had ordered at the instigation of the waiter himself; "there, that won't do at all, it's infernally nasty: now, what is really good?"

"We think our Hockheimer a superior wine, sir; or if you would try the Johannisberg –"

"By all means, a bottle of Johannisberg, and mind it *is* good."

Charlie ventured to look at the speaker, as soon as he got his Johannisberg. He found him to be a stout, short, pasty-faced, unintellectual-looking American with red hair and whiskers, and an imperial[46], which he stroked with an air of superiority over the rest of the company. He had large hands, without energy in them; and a hurried manner of eating, as though he was not accustomed to much time for his dinner. He was, in other respects, a vulgar person and yet talked of everybody of note, always speaking of titled people without their titles.

"Do you know Beaufort?"

"I haven't had the pleasure," replied Charlie, and he manifestly fell in the estimation of his new acquaintance. Here many of the diners rose to leave the room, seeing that, unless they put an end to the dinner, the dinner would certainly put an end to them. Charlie took out a cigar, the stranger did the same, and proceeded to qualify the bottle of Johannisberg with tobacco.

"You know that part of the country?" again said the man, with American perseverance.

"I have hunted there occasionally, two or three seasons ago. You seem to be well acquainted with it."

"Indeed, I am: charming neighbourhood, and beautiful places all over the country. Now to my mind, Gilsland is one of the finest: but perhaps you don't know Dacre?"

"Slightly."

"Ah! Capital fellow, when you know him intimately. Of course you know Robinson Brown is engaged to be married to one of the girls?"

"Who the devil can this fellow be?" thought Charlie.

"Nothing but his racing propensities, and the dollop he dropped to Thornhill on the match, they say, postponed it. Dacre would have it

---

[46] Lavish moustache or other facial hair 'fit for an Emperor'

at any price. That is the *on dit*, but between ourselves, I know better."

"Oh!" said Charlie, with considerable astonishment; and it was all he could say.

"The fact is, the match was a sell: there's no doubt the mare could have won. Of course it wouldn't do to say that; but I wrote a devil of a leader the next week in the 'Evening Gammoner,' which, of course you saw."

"I beg your pardon –"

"Not at all: very likely you didn't see it; but it was the talk of London for the following week. I gave it to them most tremendously about the light-weight handicaps, and the present system of roping."

"And did you see the match yourself?" asked Charlie innocently.

"See it; bless you, no! not I. I just went down to the club, and picked up what I could about it. I really know no more about it than you, except by hearsay. But, you may take your oath what I say is true."

"Undoubtedly," rejoined the other; "and – and – do you write much on these subjects?"

"Yes, every week; almost daily. I'm quite knocked up, really in wretched health; but it's a great thing to lead public opinion. I'm *'The Sphinx'* "

"Really," said Charlie again, who hardly testified the surprise at the great man's proximity which might have been expected, but which probably arose from his never reading at all.

"Yes, *The Sphinx* of the 'Evening Gammoner.'"

"The Sphinx! That's all about Œdipus, I remember, thanks to Gresham's teaching at school."

"Yes, well .." said the American doubtfully, but continued " I'm *Œdipus* in the 'Cockfighter's Chronicle.'"

"What's the use of that?" said Charlie.

"Well, between ourselves, we are able to give one another a lift: and, as we are both prophets, we predict four horses instead of two: and when *Sphinx* is wrong, it is hard if *Œdipus* isn't right."

"That's a good idea," said Charlie, impressed more strongly with the wit than the honesty of the proceeding: "I would never have thought of that."

"I dare say not. It don't much matter what a fellow writes, as long as he makes it strong enough. The worst of it is that the 'Chronicle' is a tremendous paper for light weights, short distances, and two year old races; and 'The Gammoner' goes in for the breed of horses; the Beacon Course, eleven stone and all that sort of thing. Kellner, give me another cigar. Well, but what do you think about it?" said the American "because it seems to me that 'The Gammoner' is right. Racing doesn't do much for the breed of horses, except in quantity."

Charlie was so amused with his companion that he took out a second cigar, and offered one to *The Sphinx*.

The American continued. "You see, I know nothing about the merits of the thing; and it can make no difference to me. All I have to do is to keep my ears open; and, unless it's a very bad case, I go for the nobs."

"And what line do the nobs take?" asked simple-minded Charlie.

"They're always honest enough when they haven't a good thing on themselves; and they're boys to halloo when other people are throwing stones. But the truth is, they've done so much in the dairy of late years, that there's no more milk to be had for love or money; and, I think, I know a gentleman or two that daren't look a calf in the face again." Here *The Sphinx* took a silent pull at his cigar, rolled it round with this finger, and looked inquiringly up at his interrogator. Charlie began to think he had been undergoing the milking process himself, only in a different form.

"Might I ask if you are resident in Frankfort, as you seemed to speak German exceedingly well at dinner?" asked the American.

"I am residing in Frankfort, but I dine at this *table d'hôte* daily."

"You're a bit of a sportsman too, I perceive."

"I was when in England: here we have no opportunity."

"I'm going for a little tour, and then to Baden. They rather expect the races to be something out of the common."

"Baden! Races at Baden! So there are. I shall be able to get away about that time," said Charlie rising; "and then, I trust, we shall meet again: at present, I must wish you good morning, Mr. - Mr. -?"

"Smith, my name's Smith; but everybody knows me."

"And mine is Thornhill. I'm a brother of the Thornhill you mentioned." Smith turned blue: "Good God, what a fool I am!" said he as, Charlie walked quietly down the steps of the *sale à manger;* "that's the very fellow that rode the race: I thought I'd seen him before."

"What a pretty blackguard that is to direct public opinion, as he calls it," said Charlie to himself. "I thought I'd seen him before."

A few days after this, it occurred to Charlie that he ought to inquire after Miss Donald. If he had not been rather conscious of liking her, he would have done so before. Since the evening when he had returned with her to Frankfort, she had not been at Madame Meyerheim's and her health was the natural excuse but Madame Meyerheim had unbounded faith in Charlie, and refused to believe even the gossip of her most good-natured friends. What is still more extraordinary, she dared to form her own opinion on the case of her children's governess, and had not yet sentenced that delinquent to unqualified dismissal.

"Now, Mr. Thornhill," said Madame Meyerheim, on the day in question, blushing a little, as being altogether too young and good-looking to put such a question, and yet owning, even to herself, a considerable advance on Charlie's time of life, "Now, Mr. Thornhill, *sehen sie mal,*[47] will you tell me the truth about my governess, Miss

---

[47] *Sehen sie mal* – look here.

Donald, whom I love almost like a daughter?"

"What! They've been talking about it then, have they?" said Charlie, and his good humoured face looked as coolly unconscious as if he had been talking about American freedom, or any other nonentity to which the world had given a name.

"Of course they have: that's not very remarkable. But I want to hear the truth; and perhaps I shan't get it if I listen to the women."

"Possibly not, madam;" and, as Charlie was rather shy of his own voice, he blushed too, but he managed to tell his story, and to exonerate the girl entirely, which indeed, was not difficult to do.

"I'm glad to know the truth: poor girl!" and the good natured lady dropped a tear on her black silk dress, which she carefully wiped off the next minute. "What a pretty story Baroness von Holtzäpfel would make of this if she knew it: she's jealous of Kathleen, and in love with Hartzstein herself." Then Charlie took his hat, and his leave, and his way towards Römerberg, and the dark street behind the Cathedral.

When he reached the house he was left to find his way to the door on the second *étage* by himself; and here an inferior looking servant, with nothing neat about her but her hair, opened the outer door. Charlie found himself almost at once in the presence of Mrs Donald and her husband. He was kindly received, but with evident restraint. "Miss Donald was not well; her nerves had received a shock but in a few more days she would return to Madame Meyerheim, who was kindness itself, and had written the nicest note, giving her any length of absence necessary." Donald himself was evidently a great invalid. Charlie looked at his handsome, delicate features, which bore the marks of suffering and irritability: and he saw with pain, his attenuated frame and hands, one of which seemed almost useless, and it lay passively along the arm of his invalid chair. He had a way of stroking it with the other hand, whether from hope of alleviation or mere habit it was difficult to say. Donald had hitherto failed to recognise in Charlie the handsome stranger who had given him a helping arm on the night of his encounter with Burke. Charlie had suspected his protégé on the previous visit, though hurried, short, and by candle light, now he was sure of him.

"Did you say Thornhill Norah – Mr. Thornhill?" asked he, and a curious shadow, almost a spasm of a painful recollection, passed over the invalid's face.

"Yes, Arthur, Mr. Thornhill, of whom you have heard Kathleen speak so often, but to whom we scarcely expected to be under such an obligation! Ah! Sir, my husband's health is not what it was, or we should have thanked you more heartily, as poor Kathleen would have wished." Mrs Donald rose hastily to conceal her tears, and left the room. There was a dreadful sense of oppression on Charlie's mind. The circumstances of the case came painfully upon him but, more than all, an appearance of poverty and suffering, which seemed to be unusual, and unfitted to the aristocratic manner of the man he knew of as Donald and the beauty of his wife. The room was bare of furniture, more even than is usual in the larger cities of Germany. A few books on a side table and a piano constituted its whole ornamental arrangement; and an empty stove, in lieu of a cheerful English fireplace, is not calculated to give an impression of cheerfulness where other adjuncts are wanting. So Charlie sat for a moment, bearing the somewhat inquisitorial glance of his host.

"Thornhill – Thornhill; yes certainly like, but not strikingly so. But -. You're Mr. Thornhill of Thornhills? Forgive my abruptness; but there are circumstances connected with that name which attract me irresistibly, and – and – I'm sure you'll forgive me." Donald spoke with some hesitation of manner, as though anxious to say something, and yet not knowing how to begin.

"My brother is Mr. Thornhill of Thornhills."

"You must have been young; very. Excuse me; but may recollect, you must have heard something in connection with – with – the melancholy circumstances of the late Mr. Thornhill's death?" Here Donald turned away his head, and the colour mounted to his temples.

"Everything, I believe," said Charlie, who thought this the safest termination to what might be a disagreeable revelation.

"You know me, then? Ah! I was to blame: I was mistaken. We all have much to regret; but I was in a net. My eyes have lately been opened. I thought Geoffrey Thornhill was my enemy; I was my own. I would have slain him, sir, in fair fight, it is true, but not like a dog. There has been foul wrong done – forgery; and both families have been robbed by that scoundrel Burke." Here the sick man rose, and the flushed face and trembling limbs told of energy too great for an enfeebled frame. "If there's a god in heaven, he shall suffer for it. I was duped, deluded. I was persuaded that your father had taken my birthright and I thought myself justified in my revenge. But I have since learnt all. And forgive me, Mr. Thornhill."

"You're under a delusion, Mr. Donald."

"Kildonald sir, is my name; Kildonald. You must have heard it. I would have killed your father, and you have restored to me my daughter. That's Heaven's retribution. And how – "

Charlie rose. "You refer to very painful subjects. I have heard much of what you say. I believe punishment awaits the guilty man, even in this world, and at this distance of time. But excuse me if I seek no disclosures, but such as can be, and will be, used unscrupulously and unconditionally." The fact is, that Charlie was so unprepared for the outburst he had just heard, that he was by no means certain how far Kildonald intended to incriminate himself.

"Stay, Mr. Thornhill; there are some things you must hear still." Here the flush passed from Kildonald's cheek; he collected himself, ran his hand over his forehead, and appeared to think for a minute or two; then became more quiet; and finally relapsed into apparent indifference. He spoke of the property which had been bought by Mr. Thornhill, but which had never been paid for. He admitted the injustice he had done Charlie's father in believing Geoffrey Thornhill to be his debtor; later events had shown that Burke was the recipient of these rents, and he had defrauded both parties. He hoped to be able to prove it; but his information was vague and his energies gone. Charlie replied to these confessions by inquiries which assisted his own views, but he received no confirmation of his own suspicions, so he kept them to himself. He had little doubt that the mystery would one day be cleared up, and he did not feel inclined to risk anything by premature explanations. He kept his own counsel: not always an easy thing to do.

Kildonald was a vain man, not a proud one, and his mind was weakened by illness. This induced him to tell Charlie a certain amount of truth. He was to blame in his quarrel with Geoffrey Thornhill; but few men could have humiliated themselves sufficiently to have confessed all. He satisfied his conscience and his gratitude by a half-measure of justice; but he did not say, "I hated your father because he was acute enough to detect me, and bold enough to denounce me; and I would have shot him, because he was a bar to my advancement in fashionable life." He did not detail the miserable transaction with Benevenuto in which he had been involved, and which led to the quarrel; but he placed all to the account of his hatred of the man who would have bought his estate and supplanted him in his reputation and position as a landowner and a gentleman. Two men only could have told the truth, and nothing but the truth – the sincere penitent, or the utterly degraded; and Kildonald was neither the one nor the other.

In a few days Kathleen Kildonald, as I may now call her, was back at the Meyerheims' and Charlie was occupied, as usual, at the bank. No one who had seen and conversed with that undemonstrative gentleman, would have imagined the match he carried about with him ready to light the fuse he had laid. In England, indeed, in certain circles he became a subject for club gossip and dinner table conversation, and did not shine in so amiable a light as could be wished.

"Well, Towler, that's a rum go of Charlie Thornhill's in Frankfort; such a deuced quiet fellow too; much more like his brother Tom." The speaker stood on the steps of the Guards' Club house and addressed himself to a brother officer of remarkably doggy appearance on the step below.

"Demme, it's always your quiet fellows that do the mischief. Look at me." Whether Mr. Towler meant that he was a quiet mischievous person, or an example of irregular but irreproachable virtue, is not known.

"But dash it! Fancy bolting with the governess, and being brought back together in triumph by the lover, who rode beside the carriage, with a loaded pistol to his ear. Besides, I thought he was engaged to one of the Dacre sisters?"

"Oh! That's off long ago. He was scratched as soon as they found he'd got no money from Henry Thornhill," chimed in young Foozleton. "They want money; the market's tight at Gilsland."

"What became of old Thornhill's money, do you suppose?"

"Left it all to the Lying-in Hospital, because Tom wouldn't give up racing."

"It's not true that the girl is the daughter of the man that murdered his father, is it?" said the first speaker.

"No, not exactly that; but there was some story about his being under the surveillance of the police some time back. Hartzstein saw him coming out of the Polizei, or whatever they call the place, with a gens-d'arme after him."

"Poor Charlie!" said Towler; "that's more mysterious than agreeable." And they went their way.

"Mary Stanhope," said Mrs Thornhill, "what is this story about Charlie that they say Edward Dacre brought from Frankfort about some governess?"

"Probably some horrible falsehood, if it's found its way about London. The truth remains so long at the bottom of the well that it gets drowned altogether."

"But what is it that they said at Lady Sarah Screamersdale's?" persisted Mrs Thornhill.

"Nothing that you need fret about. Only that Charlie has fallen in love with a beautiful girl, a governess in Frankfort, and that ….. Well, the natural consequence had ensued."

"And who said that, I should like to know?" said Mrs Thornhill, who honoured chastity in man as well as woman, and was most unfashionably angry. "I don't believe a word of it. I suppose it was that scandalous old Mrs Barnacles whose own son carried off that poor girl from Lady Hemingford's. Anything else, I wonder?"

"Yes, plenty; they finished the story satisfactorily. They said that he was seen in the carriage with her in the evening then she had mysteriously disappeared, and had not been heard of since; and that he takes long rides out of Frankfort every evening."

"And do you believe a word of it, Mary?"

"Not one syllable," said Mary Stanhope: "he would rather cut his hand off. So let's go to bed dear. Come along." And they did not believe it; but there were others who did.

The truth is that Edward Dacre was not very strong minded, and, though a very good fellow, had unwittingly done some mischief. First, knowing nothing about Charlie's *penchant* for his sister, beyond that of a boyish fancy, he told a friend of hers of the pretty Irish girl at Frankfort, and of Charlie's attentions, as insinuated by Hartzstein and De Weiler. Then his friend mentioned the staid Charlie's peccadillo, as something of a laugh at the club. Then two or three old chums of Thornhill pretended to be much amused by it, and carried the news home to their wives. These wives told other wives, until it came round to Mr. Dacre's ears; and Teddy was fain to admit something like the truth of Charlie's attachment in the presence of his sisters. The position of Edith and Charlie was just of that nature that nothing could be said upon the subject to her; and yet nobody's mouth was stopped by it. She was a sort of *fiancée* by courtesy among her intimates; but it was not a courtesy which a man or woman was bound to respect. It affected her spirits to a certain extent; for one thing, and one thing only, startling enough in all conscience, it led her to believe in the possibility of his desertion. She anticipated the death of Henry Thornhill as altering her position; but when it came unexpectedly, she had a right to expect that her lover would have claimed her openly, and would have acknowledged their engagement before the world. She knew nothing of the circumstances of the case, and her conjectures were natural enough. And now she was beset on all sides, and if not an unbeliever was, at least, perplexed.

But Charlie had a firm friend at court. Alice Dacre knew him, and upheld him. "Don't throw away your happiness upon idle reports, Edith. Depend upon it, there is something of which we know nothing. Charlie's character is worth a great deal of London gossip; and according to Teddy's own account, he didn't even see him."

"But why hasn't he spoken to dear papa? And how long does he expect one to wait, now that there can be no further need of delay?" And Edith Dacre pouted a little.

"Never mind. If you love Charlie Thornhill, trust him."

"Ah! It's all very well, dear Alice, to say 'Never mind; but you don't quite understand the feeling."

"Perhaps not," rejoined Alice with a very heavy sigh. "But I won't give my troth till I can trust; and then mountains should not shake me."

Charlie himself was at this time unconscious of the construction to be put upon his silence. He argued simply thus - if I propose now, I have nothing to offer; and I don't wish to risk a refusal, which her father would be fully justified in giving. He was, besides, quite honest, in leaving her to accept any other offer. But Charlie was little versed in women. One other motive deterred him – the obligations the family, and especially Teddy and Edith, lay under to him personally. And though he knew the value of such honest love as his own, he would not put Mr. Dacre in the awkward position of saying "Yes," from a sense of gratitude for the preservation of his children. Charlie believed in Edith; and he would take his chance and wait.

About the same time there came a bundle of letters and papers from England. Diver had done wonders and with the assistance of the police, was hunting his foxes beautifully. It was hard work when their lines diverged, as they had done, one in London and the other in America; but the lines were coming together again, and pretty quickly. Charlie had been wisely silent, excepting to the right people, and his conjectures had proved conclusive. Burke was still wanted. So Charlie put the finishing touch to his previous information by writing as much to Diver of his own adventure as he thought fit, and some portions of his conversation with Kildonald. Mr. Diver was not long in getting that excellent hound Bradhall, the detective, upon the scent; and that gentleman appeared in Frankfort itself before very long, as we shall see.

Amongst the newspapers was one which Charlie opened with some degree of curiosity, "The Cockfighters Chronicle," not because he felt particularly interested that week in the Liverpool weights, or the last deposit of Mace and the Unknown, or the explanation of the last

Deerfoot's swindle, or Billy the ratdog, or Captain Jones's testimonial as the great amateur runner of the day, but because he saw a paragraph streaked with black marks for his especial information. It was signed "*Œdipus*," though, as that interesting *litterateur* was on the Continent for the good of his health, it could hardly have come from him. "Something pleasant, however, from some d------d good-natured friend, I suppose," said Charlie, lighting a cigar. And sitting down by an open window, he read a startling announcement.

It exceeded the ordinary gossip of one of the most talented reporters of the sporting news of the day. After relating, with considerable humour, his visit to the various horse studs of the Continent, his opinion of the modern system of French breeding, and making many pertinent remarks on the men and manners which were by no means new to him, he proceeded to speak of the various fashionables who were at that time enjoying themselves, and wasting their time and their money at Homburg, Wiesbaden, Spa, and Ems; and he, naturally enough, and without the slightest malice aforethought, but rather in a cheerful, gossiping manner, arrived in Frankfort. The pleasure of introducing Charlie was too great, and he finished a very excellent article with the following memorable words:-

"*We were so fortunate as to meet with Mr. Charles Thornhill, a sportsman of the very first water, and so celebrated as a horseman in our own country. It will be no mean gratification to the friends of that gentleman to learn that there is no truth in the reports which were so prevalent of his compulsory absence from Frankfort, but that he is about to be united to a lady of ancient Irish family and of great personal beauty. We can only trust that one so capable of adorning society will return to his own country, of which his brother, Mr. Thornhill, of Thornhills, is so distinguished an ornament.*

Œdipus"

At the perusal of the first part of the article, Charlie was inclined to be much amused. Then he got to the conclusion, and saw himself.

Where in the name of fortune did these reports come from? Curious suspicions took a more palpable form as he watched the eddying wreaths of smoke that curled slowly from his mouth, and he felt called upon to determine on some course of action, he did not very well know what. He was not impulsive – that we know – or he would have written to Edith Dacre a denial of the whole business. His ideas, at length, resolved themselves into two courses. He wrote a letter to Lady Marston, and he swore to horsewhip Mr. Smith whenever he could catch him; and Charlie was to be accounted a man of his word.

CHAPTER 35

THE MODERN SQUIRE'S TEMPTATIONS

And what had Tom Thornhill been doing since he left Como and Naples? He had been living on good intentions in half the capitals in the world, and occasionally indulging in the luxury of high stakes to make up for lost time. It seemed as though a card, or a bet, or a speculation had for him an addictive fascination. "You must come to me, sir; you can't resist; come you must." And then you saw the veins swell, and the hands fixed, and the muscles rigid; and just as you begin to delight in his resistance - behold! The muscles relax, the feet are loosened, and the patient does not walk or stagger, but rushes with frantic violence towards his master tempter. In Paris on one occasion he had shut himself up for days, and debarred himself of all possibility of temptation but then miserable and out of spirits, he strolled from the Hôtel Bedford to the Boulevards. "Hallo Carlingford, how came you here?" and in one moment he was the Tom Thornhill of Oxford, of Melton and of London once more. He became the noisiest of the noisy, the universal favourite. On another occasion, indeed, he was found (upon a short visit to London to raise money, when no one was in town, and when Arlington Street was up, pavement and all) to have steeped himself in a great city speculation in molasses which collapsed in a fortnight with a loss of ten thousand, which had to be raised on the estate.

Vienna was even worse than Paris. After weeks of dissolute nights, pretty women and reckless high stakes, he met Carlingford again.

"Thornhill! You need a change of air. Why not come to Baden." enticed Carlingford. And here the noble lord took a pinch of Prince's mixture, a vice of a bygone aristocracy.

"Baden? So I will. I shall go mad if I stop here. When shall we start? Tomorrow?"

"Not exactly; but we'll be off next week, if you like."

"Very good: the sooner the better." And so to Baden they went, via Antwerp and Heidelberg.

I need hardly say that rumour was not silent as to the course of profligacy on which Tom Thornhill had entered. His debts and embarrassments had long been the talk of the clubs; and, though everyone spoke of them with a sigh, nobody seemed inclined to settle them. Thornhills was deeply mortgaged, but his mother continued to live in it with Mary Stanhope. Tom himself came down with a party of men occasionally for a few days shooting; but he had forgotten what he once so loved to dream of, the responsibilities of a country gentleman.

The breaking up of his stud was supposed at least, to have curtailed his racing expenses considerably, if it did nothing towards diminishing his passion for the turf. Never was so mistaken a notion.

"Thank God, Tom Thornhill has at length been persuaded to give up his racing establishment!" said old Dacre to Corry, whom he met on the steps of White's as he was sauntering down St. James's Street in the spring of the year.

"Ah! His poor father was very much like him, but married young, and it saved him" replied Corry. "But don't imagine that your friend

Tom is cured of his mania. He's just as enthusiastic about his friends' horses as he was about his own; and what's worse, he hasn't the management of them. I have just heard him back a horse of Carlingford's for the Derby that has no more chance of winning than you or I. He certainly is the most inveterate gambler I ever knew. The night before he went abroad he told us all, rather solemnly, that he had given up play of every kind and that he had determined upon never betting another hundred as long as he lived. We were bold enough to doubt his self denial, upon which he at once offered to lay 500*l*[48] to 400*l* about it instantly, and did not seem to consider his offer as a singular entry in the first line of the new leaf he had just turned over."

Corry had no idea of Dacre's feelings, or the interest he felt in the subject of their conversation, or the former might have withheld his information. But an English gentleman withstands anything from a tight boot to the surgeon's knife, and old Mr. Dacre bore it as one of his order. But he went home sorely oppressed and he swore again a round oath that, with his consent, Tom Thornhill should never have his daughter; he would rather see her in her grave. A broken heart is not the common termination to a fashionable career, and unsuccessful love in the higher circles is met by so many remedies, that the most virulent form of the disease is seldom fatal. They take it lightly in the Upper Ten Thousand, whether from early inoculation or from the coolness of temperature to which they are habitually subject, I cannot say. Still, broken hearts are known; and Alice Dacre was fighting a cruel fight on the side of her principles.

In the midst of it all, nobody saw that Tom was older: they saw nothing but the same cheerful spirits which had made him the life of every society into which he went. They never watched him half an

---

[48]500*l* – Five hundred *livres* - £500 in today's money, although valued at some seven times more..

hour after old Stripp, the steward, had been with him, or after a long deferred interview with his man of business, or when he was calculating how far short of forty percent interest his last 10,000*l* was borrowed. They never saw him throw himself into a chair opposite the dying embers of his fire when, with his usual good nature, he had ordered his valet not to sit up for him. There he sat watching, in his mind's eye, the form of her he loved, and knew that every day placed a fresh impediment and a greater distance between them.

Alice Dacre said nothing, not a word. To whom should she talk? Edith could not have understood her. It's a sad thing to worship a broken idol, and to know that it is broken. Her head was not bowed; but nature asserted her sway, and she was declining. Still she struggled on. A warmer climate was recommended, and the Dacres started slowly for an Italian winter. Tom had her heart, and he was breaking it. But shall not a man do what he will with his own?

At about the same time in Frankfort Charlie sat reading the "Allgemeine Zeitung", that is, pretending to look for the money column, when the door opened, and the servant introduced a person without a name; but, understanding each other, the ceremony was omitted by mutual consent. The individual in question was only remarkable as to be the very least remarkable person in the world. I never saw anyone so utterly undistinguished from hundreds of others as Mr. Bradhall, the detective   He was neither short nor tall, plain nor ugly, well dressed nor badly dressed and no one would have recognized him under a third or fourth visit. How his mother ever recognised him, I do not know and there lay the great secret of his success. This characteristic *inidentity* extended to his clothes. His hat was like every other hat; his clothes were just no way extraordinary. His nose appeared straight. I don't know that it was not slightly *retroussé* after all. I never met anyone who could tell whether his hair curled or not! And his eyes – oh! By the way, his eyes had a peculiarity, and Charlie Thornhill discovered it: they did not blink.

"Pray sit down, Mr. Bradhall," said Charlie. Mr. Bradhall did sit down, but not precisely on the middle of his chair: at the same time he dived cautiously into a breast-pocket of his coat, and produced a letter, which he handed over to his host with as much care as if it were a cocked revolver.

"This must be from Mr. Diver," said Charlie. "Your's is a hard life, Mr. Bradhall."

"Sometimes. The present job has been tolerably easy, but we have suddenly missed our man from Baden or Frankfort, and without any apparent reason."

"And you are led to believe that I can assist you!"

"You or your servant;" and Bradhall drew from his pocket again a small note-book. "He is under the surveillance of the city police. By whose order I am unable to discover –"

"If you mean my Irish servant –"

"Just so, sir; Mike Daly."

"I spoke to the police myself."

"It does you infinite credit, sir. He is one of those men who once committed, or assisted at, a great crime, and it frightened him: he's been quiet enough for years; but he's not the man we want: he's perfectly safe, and to be had at any moment."

"Then who is it you do want, Mr. Bradhall, if the question involves no indiscretion?"

"We want Burke, and we must have him. We shall put you to some inconvenience, for we must take Daly when the time comes. We are not quite clear what part he played; but he knows enough to make a valuable witness and we would like him to become king's evidence. Can you help us any further in the matter of Burke?"

"I think I probably can. Word has reached me that he goes to Baden race course this day fortnight and goes to ride a fine horse, Glacier, who must win if fairly ridden, but Burke goes to lose the race." Charlie then told Mr. Bradhall of his own adventure, in which Burke figured so conspicuously; his servant's accidental recognition of him, and involuntary pronunciation of the name; his own conjectures and of his information given to Diver; of his suspicions of Daly not destroyed by his uniform honesty and good conduct, and of his precaution in placing the Irishman under the eye of the police.

"And now should you like to see him?" asked Charlie.

"It would be desirable," said Mr. Bradhall, "On more accounts than one."

Charlie rang the bell, and desired Daly to be sent up with a small tray and a bottle of niersteiner. He could then give his orders about the horses.

"There," said he, when his orders had been obeyed, and Daly had left the room "That's the man."

"I know him now; and how long have you suspected him of being concerned in the unhappy murder of the late Mr. Thornhill?"

"Since my last visit to England."

"And you've held your tongue; and he suspects nothing?"

"Nothing whatever."

"Excuse me, sir, but what a detective you would have made!"

CHAPTER 36

BADEN BADEN

"Ich habe genossen das irdische Glück
Ich habe gelebt und geliebet."

I have enjoyed the luck of the Irish.
I have lived and loved.

I regard it as a privilege to have seen Baden in the winter – in her undress, in fact. It cost me neither the bowing and scraping employed in approaching the private boudoir of a great lady, nor the hard fighting in the waiting rooms of St. James's Palace to the reception room of my sovereign. Still it is a privilege. I suppose those linden trees never occur to the ordinary visitor as sometimes laden with glittering, diamond-like icicles, or some of the beauties of those hanging woods round the Alten Schloss as heightened by the chaste covering of winter.
Nothing of this kind occurred to Charles Thornhill as he entered Baden Baden on a lovely afternoon in September, 1856.
"Rooms here?" said Charlie, alighting from a yellow barouche amidst

a flourish of whips from his yellow coated postilion. The waiter feared not.

"Send the landlord to speak to me." Herr Tischtuch appeared.

"Have you a room for me here?"

"Not a hole in Baden. Most distinguished English lords have been sent away, and the Furst von Bolsöver is just gone on in despair towards Darmstadt."

"Has Mr. Thornhill arrived? I expected to meet him."

"Not yet; but we have rooms for him – two bedrooms and a salon."

"Well, then, take off the luggage. I am his brother, and the second room is for me." Charlie opened the door and jumped out.

"Monsieur will show his passport" and he did so.

"That is good; and the Herr Brother will arrive?"

"Today," said Charlie. "My horses are here: my servant came yesterday."

"Ach! Forgive me, of course. Your horses are here, and all is right." At that moment Tom Thornhill drove up, and as Charlie's empty carriage made way for more flourishes of the whip, the brothers greeted one another affectionately.

"Looking so well, Charlie; banking agrees with you – does with most people. Money passes through your hands; that's pleasant enough: still better when it sticks." These disjointed fragments were the most commercial Tom had ever been known to utter. "Now let us go upstairs. Waiter, send up those portmanteaus. Dinner at seven, Herr Tischtuch. How are your daughters? And don't forget the ice."

"Young Mr. Thornhill don't want icing: he looks cool enough." And Tischtuch trotted off bent on obliging a favourite customer.

Tom and his brother dined *al fresco*, or nearly so, under a roof, but with open doors and windows looking on to the cheerful gardens, rippling stream, alleys, and hanging woods. Now, at seven in the evening the whole place was studded with tables of various sizes.

Here and there longer tables were laid, where a mixed company – half a dozen men of the fast Parisian lot, and a couple of young ladies whose toilettes were as loud as their manners – were discussing men, women, and racing, past, present and to come, with some gusto. The constant popping of champagne corks, and the snatches of song from the mellow lips of a beauty of the Palais Royale, mingled with every dialect of every tongue, from the purest Gallic to the most sonorous Gaélic, French, German, English. A bow window added considerably to the general confusion, where it was understood there was an English milord, who was always borrowing money off the croupier, and breaking the bank with it, while old Tischtuch and his waiters rushed in and out and up and down the steps of the alcove, in a state of perspiration and bewilderment as if the house was on fire.

"Good hock, Charlie?" inquired Tom

"Excellent, if that fellow had not iced it. But he's a Frenchman. They understand nothing but champagne, which is very like themselves."

"You don't like the French?" said Tom, draining his glass.

"Not much, I confess. What a noisy set they are! Look at that woman, Tom, and that idiot sharing her plate, and wearing her hat."

"That's one of the first men in Paris, Charlie – a rising man at the Chamber, and one of the best fellows out: that's De Clermont."

"And what's the man on the other side of that pretty woman, shying pellets of bread across the table? There'll be a row in a minute or two."

"That's – oh! I forget his name - attaché to the French Embassy at Vienna."

"He looks a diplomat. France must have great confidence in him," said Charlie, as the young Frenchman, decorated with a bonnet, commenced waltzing with one of his male companions. Charlie rose from the table and lighted a cigar and as he and Tom strolled down the steps in the twilight, a buzz of admiration and unsuppressed "Who's that?" followed them as they went their way over the little bridge towards the Kursaal.

"Come, Mademoiselle Eugénie you know well enough, you hypocrite."

"Parole d'honneur," said Eugénie, jumping to have another peep.

"There, don't excite yourself, and I'll tell you. But he won't do for you: he cares for nothing but play. You'd be jealous of the ace of spades in a fortnight."

In the meantime the object of attention and his brother reached the Kursaal.

The walk in front of the rooms was crowded to excess: every chair and table was occupied. Some were drinking coffee, some wine; and the fragrant air, the balmy night breeze, was laden with the wreaths of – of – what shall I say? – bad tobacco. Long pipes, short pipes, and cigars, Pernambucos, Tordesillas, Cabanas, and all the growth of Lubeck, Bremen, and Hamburgh had nigh smothered the pretensions of the true Havannah. The huge globes of gas in front of the assembly rooms were blazing in full light, and under its portico, or leaning and sitting in every variety of posture, men and women discussed the all-important subject of tomorrow's racing. Every nation seemed to have contributed its quota to the whole. Russians, with highly dressed and delicate looking women laden with jewellery, strode straight towards the tables; Germans of all types – the Austrian, the Prussian, the proud and handsome Hungarian noble; the Pole, forgetful for a moment of the barbarity of his masters, contrasted favourably in intelligence and civilization with his rulers. Paris sent her motley groups, and England hers. Here the highest type of Norman or Saxon aristocracy strode regardless of criticism or consequences of the questionable company in which it was playing its part. Vice there was in its most attractive garb.

The inner rooms, opening from the great room, were devoted to play. Everybody at Baden is supposed to gamble: almost everybody does so. Some with a nervous, anxious look, and an uncomfortable twitching of the fingers, and an expression of face which says nothing but "Gold, more gold:" such men always back their ill-luck. Some with a cold, glazed look, which watches night after night the heap grow less, and feels the heart grow harder and harder: true, but unsuccessful gamesters. Others, with a wild reckless impatience betokening nothing more at present than a love of excitement, a bold, buccaneering sort of gambler, who loves to throw down his rouleau, and leave it on the colour. A few pettifoggers at florins and five franc pieces; your respectable city dweller from Balaam Hill, who counts the florins to his wife and daughters, which he has brought away the night before, and holds his tongue about the three Napoleons[49] which have mysteriously disappeared on the previous occasion. The tables live by these men, and there are half a dozen who live very badly by the tables.

I think that even in the matter of gambling, Charlie Thornhill exercised a sort of influence over his brother, and Tom did not play that night.

* * * * * *

The sun was rising next morning and had already drunk in the morning mists which settled about the valley of the Oos, when Charlie found himself dressed, with nothing to do. Since he had applied himself to business it was a novelty, and he seemed to have lost that facility for engaging zealously in nothing which is such a talent for a pure idler to possess. When, therefore, I say that Charlie Thornhill was dressed on the following morning by seven o'clock, his

---

[49] Probably a 20 franc coin 6.45 grams (gross weight) and 90% pure gold.

brother Tom was soundly sleeping.

Being dressed, it was desirable to do something; and if breakfasting on trout, and smoking cigars, and looking at prospects, and drinking and eating in general, be anything, then Baden Baden is quite a commercial city, for it goes on all day. Charlie knew this and the difficulty was to do these things most satisfactorily. Besides which, if he had nothing to do he had plenty to think of and that could be best compassed further back from the footlights of the world's drama than the Hôtel Stéphanie. The thing was now to consider where to go for the trout and cigars in question. To the Alten Schloss, the old château that frowns like an aged seneschal[50] keeping watch over the town, and rebuking it for its worldliness and frivolity.

Charlie lit a cigar, and turned towards the Alten Schloss. For the first time in his life it occurred to him that he had wasted a great deal of his time. What had he done at Gresham's? What afterwards? Nothing. Then he thought of Tom: what a clever fellow he was, and how much beyond him in most things. This had always been the received opinion while they were boys, and it must be true. "And yet," said he to himself, "I'm always fidgeting myself about Tom." The fact is that Charlie was really uneasy. Tom had been so reckless and his late habits had taught him that a very few years would utterly cripple an estate like Thornhills. He climbed higher, on through the dark pines, and caught here and there a glimpse of a magnificent prospect. "If I could but save him! Or it! Or both!" He emerged from the dark pines at the base of the castle. There was that magnificent view stretching away into the far distance: fainter and fainter it became, until the silvery, serpent-like Rhine was lost in the distant hills and the blue lines of the horizon mingled imperceptibly with the atmosphere, and lost all definite form. And so did Charlie Thornhill's thoughts. For a time they reverted to his breakfast;

---

[50] The chief steward or butler of a great household.

delighted he was with the food which was set before him, nor till he had well disposed of it, did his mind again wander. He was not given to idle musings. It was quite impossible, however, to shut out all castle building; so he went on from his brother Tom and his extravagances to his mother and Mary Stanhope; and then to his uncle, and his curious will, and the explanation to come from Roger Palmer; and then he thought of himself, and what he might have done had things turned out differently. Had his uncle's fortune come to him, as expected – had he got the few thousands from the Kildonald estate, which seemed even now not impossible – had he made a fortune if not inherited one – had he gone to visit or written to Edith, told her and her father his plans and hopes, as far as he could, and asked for time – had he, in fact, ascertained beyond all doubt how far he might calculate upon the forbearance of the girl that loved him. And did she really love him; and how many of her best years was he worth? Had she seen "A Cockfighter's Chronicle," or not? Or had her brother told her of the mysterious or damning paragraph in the article by *Œdipus*? Ought he not to explain? Or had he any right to enter upon the question? Certainly he had; and a straightforward policy, when practicable, was the best. And now, when should he see her again? They were gone abroad: report said to Italy; Lady Marston said "she didn't know where;" so it might be months, and might be years, before he had the opportunity. But there was a post, and, much as he hated writing he would write tonight. Confound it, if one of those Italian scoundrels with their soft Southern voices, handsome eyes and silky beards, were to see her …. "But that's absurd. I know she'll never marry anyone but an Englishman. Still, to make sure, I'll write tonight." As he came to his determination he turned from the broken old tracery of a window through which he had been watching the winding stream in the far distance, leading this train of thought much after its fashion, when right in the low doorway opposite he saw Edith Dacre.

"How dare you smoke so in the presence of ladies, Mr. Thornhill!" she said

"I only see one, the last I expected to see here," and he came and shook hands with her.

"Mamma is outside looking at the view, and Papa is with her."

"And Alice?"

"Is not well enough to climb so far. You hardly seem to know the state of her health?" At that moment she looked less cordially at Charlie, or so he thought.

"No, Edith, I did not. I heard she was unwell, but not seriously. She is in Baden?"

"We are all on our way to Italy for the winter."

Mr. and Mrs Dacre were soon found. Their greeting was cordial. News from England occupied a half hour more among the ruins. Lady Marston and Sir Frederick's health and Charlie's own pursuits, came in for a share of attention. Beyond the fact of his presence in Baden the Dacres did not allude to Tom. Charlie noticed the omission and before long the party began to descend.

Is it very extraordinary that after a short time Edith and Charlie should have found themselves a little in the rear of Mr. and Mrs Dacre? And that when Charlie proposed to show them a short cut through the wood which, he was sure came out close by the Neuen Schloss, or new château, that Mr. and Mrs Dacre, being older than their own children, as we know they were, should have preferred to continue along the road? Or that Edith Dacre, at Charlie's request, should have allowed herself to be persuaded? Charlie's natural eye to the country must have stood him in good stead, for he could have known no more about the Baden woods than the road to Jerusalem.

During that short walk those young people said much – much that it was well to know for both of them. At first their conversation was monosyllabic, but it progressed towards an intelligible sentence or two towards the end. Edith found out that it was no ungenerous motive that had prompted Charlie's silence since his uncle's death; and Charles Thornhill made a clean breast of it by exposing the difficulties and uncertainties of his present position, and his fear to ask her to share with him a want of luxury so different from that of her own home.

"And so sir, you thought I should have said 'yes' if you had asked me?"

"I've thought so a long time, Edith, and that was the greater reason for not speaking."

"And what made you speak now, Charlie?"

"Your appearance here. I was thinking of you all the morning. I could endure the uncertainty no longer; and at the moment I turned round and saw you, it was with a determination to write tonight; but I shall ask your father today."

"And he will say, 'Wait'. I know him so well."

"And you love him so much, Edith; so I shall say 'wait' too."

"No, Charlie, that's not necessary. But you must listen to papa, and – and – Charlie," said she, looking up at him, "I shall never doubt again. Alice has taught me never to mistrust you; but you know I – I – did – just – hear about the Irish lady. And who *is* that Mr. Œdipus who tells such stories?"

"Œdipus? Oh he is Mr. Sphinx; but I don't think I need to horsewhip him now."

There were several pauses in the walk that morning. Both looked down, and then up, and their eyes met, and Charlie's smile reflected the innocent happiness of his darling. Now she could see no difficulties, and feared no hindrances. Charlie had spoken, and she dare tell the world that she was his affianced bride. Charlie saw difficulties and delay, but none that he did not promise himself to overcome.

"You are ambitious, Edith. I know you are."

"Very, of a vast possession."

"What is it? A house in Belgravia, an opera box, a mail phaeton, or a park like Thornhills? What is to be the size of it?"

"Can't you guess?"

"No."

"What is your height and weight, Charlie?"

"Exactly?"

"Yes, I must know exactly to a fraction."

"Six feet and half an inch, and twelve stone," said Charlie.

"Then now you know the exact extent of my ambition. Listen, sir, and don't be conceited." Edith tried to smile, but a bright tear or two ran over the lid as she said, "You once saved my life, Charlie, and now you have made all its happiness." She put up her face as she spoke, and when she took it down there was a blush of colour in it.

They ran down the next few steps to the Neuen Schloss, and found that the elderly folks, who had been round by the road had only waited twenty-three minutes.

"I thought you didn't know your way, Thornhill, as well as you fancied." said Papa Dacre. "You seemed rather puzzled when you started."

Within one week from that time things had changed. Dacre had given a conditional consent to the engagement between Charles Thornhill and Edith. The first day's racing at Baden had taken place. Tom Thornhill had broken the bank and was the talk of all Baden. He had also been finally rejected by Mr. Dacre; and Alice silently acquiesced in a decision which she knew to be right, and felt to be unmerciful. She was fighting bravely against a malady which the south of Italy could not cure. Cold had nothing to do with it; and the bank had not suffered alone; for Tom Thornhill had half broken the truest heart that ever beat for a man. The Dacres, however, were now gone to Italy. Charlie had been recalled to Frankfort, as soon as his furlough was up. Mr. Bradhall had matured his plans by the arrival of an important witness. And Baden was impatiently awaiting the principal day's racing and steeplechasing on the morrow; the Baron de Finance named a horse called Glacier to be ridden by an 'Englishman' whose name, mysteriously, did not appear on the bill.

CHAPTER 37

RACE AND CHASE

Driving to the racecourse in the duchy of Baden along a flat but interesting valley with the beautiful chain of the Black Forest in the distance, were carriages of every description. The Russian drosky, the American dog cart, the Prussian or Paris Berlin, and the Hungarian aus-spanner – every sort of hired vehicle, from the four horsed barouche, with its yellow jackets, long whips, big boots, and post horses of official stamp, to the most humble coupé, were all there. There was the eilwagen[51], and an English four-in-hand, with the most elaborate harness, made to look as little like a coach as possible. There were the handsome carriages of the royal party, and here and there a Baden hack or two, carrying a Heidelberg student and a young woman evidently out for the day. If the equipages were bad, the bonnets and toilettes were charming; and the women made up for in drapery, what the conveyances wanted in paint.

The course stretched away on a fine, open, common-like piece of ground, surrounded on three sides by forest-trees and sloping sides

---

[51] Express coach

of hills, dotted with villages and castles. It was admirably marked out with white posts and rails nearly all the way round. The enclosure for the horses joined the stand, and in the centre was a covered platform which commanded a view of the whole course and country for miles. The immediate neighbourhood was a flat, open country; here and there with enormous dykes, but utterly fenceless. It was very heavy going, and there were standing crops of wheat, maize, potatoes and patches of vegetation and vegetables, such as pertain to poor allotments in our own country.

The Thornhills had ridden and Daly and Tom's groom had already secured a stable for their horses. The former, however, was still on Kosciusko, Charlie's Hungarian bred horse, who was too fresh to be trusted in a crowded stable, and since his subjugation, was too valuable.

"Who's that cantering down the course, Tom?" said Charlie, as a tall, thin man went down alone on a chestnut horse.

"Finest horseman of his day, Charlie. That's Duncan Græme. He's gone down to start them."

Just then a remarkably quiet man, but considerably altered from the Mr. Bradhall whom we have seen, by the addition of a drooping moustache, and a small order of merit in the buttonhole of his frock coat, looked at Charlie. He was still unlike himself, but exceedingly like everybody else. Charlie and he exchanged a few whispered words.

"It's the next race, I think, Mr. Thornhill."

"It is."

"He's here, sir. I've seen him dressed and weighed in. It's all right. Be at hand, and have Daly here."

"I will. There's Daly on my bay horse. You know him?"

"I do sir. We will make sure that Burke won't ride today and save him from a fresh robbery. Be here" – he looked at his watch – "in a quarter of an hour, and don't let us be seen together before that time. He'll be out of the weighing room soon."

Burke had arrived ten minutes before to ride the Glacier, a fine grey horse by Young Snowdon. Now Burke had a quick eye for a Continental bailiff and a legal officer and to his consternation he had already seen one on the road.

The bell had rung for saddling and jockeys were emerging from the weighing room for the next race. Two of the steeplechase horses were already mounted and being slowly paraded before the stand. At that moment a rush was apparent in the middle of the space allotted for weighing and mounting. A grey horse had emerged from the crowd, which parted right and left, its rider was a powerful looking man in an orange and purple belt and he drove the horse hard at the white railing which separated that spot from the course. The rails were about five feet high, but Glacier jumped them with apparent ease, and turning round to the left was in a moment across the Iffetzheim road and away to the forest.

"He's away, sir," shouted Bradhall. "That fellow of mine has frightened him. There are so many writs out, he doesn't suspect the true cause. We must to horse and back to Baden. I know his haunt now. There's a hundred pounds reward out by this time. They're very slow in their justice, but they're very sure."

Long before Bradhall had finished his speech another horse was seen to leave the crowd; this time a gentleman's groom was the rider: and a burst of applause followed as he rushed Kosciusko at the rails, and landed safe on the other side. "Too fast for timber," said Charlie, who could not help admiring the performance, stunned as he was by the unexpected escape of Burke. Daly turned in his saddle. "A hundred pounds," shouted Bradhall, "and a free pardon." but Daly was already out of hearing. The crowd watched the race from the platform till, imagining it to be a runaway gambler who was only leaving his creditors behind him, they turned their attention to the steeplechase in hand, which could be no longer delayed for such a common occurrence as the escape of a defaulter.

A few race goers swayed by interest or curiosity, ran to mount their horses, and amongst them were Charlie, Mr. Bradhall, and his assistant. They were soon on the line spread at a hopeless distance over the country; and Charlie most prudently followed the detective's advice –"The road, and to Baden. Keep him in view if possible!" The foot of the hills was about eight miles distant, and for these Burke made, of course at his best pace. He had every advantage but one – weight. Glacier was in tip-top condition; Kosciusko was not fit to race. Glacier had about a hundred yards start; but Burke was riding thirteen stone (this was a Continental steeplechase be it remembered,) Daly about eleven. Burke had also to judge the pace; for he could allow himself neither to be run up to nor to ride the Glacier to a standstill. Onward they went, Burke preserving the line, and not an apparent fence to stop them between the road and the forest. Daly continued to gain, but it was clear that he was pressing his horse, and as the ground was soft, it must soon begin to tell. Burke, too, was evidently fearful of letting him come near; and so they rode through standing patches of corn, maize, and potatoes, at one time the distance lessening between them, at another increasing. It was clearly Daly's game to press on, especially as he could not hope to hold out against the condition of the other; and thus they sped onward, watched with an intensity of interest by three or four of their followers not known to the others, who soon began to fall away. Tom, who had followed his brother, caught up.

"What's the matter, Charlie? Who is the fellow?" Charlie scarcely heard, as he continued at a moderate gallop along the side of the road. "Is that horse thoroughbred that your groom is riding?"

"Yes; by an English horse out of an Arab mare. He was bred in

Hungary."

"That's lucky. By Jove he's gaining." said Tom, who was enjoying the race more as a matter of speculation than anything else – "No. I'll back the steeplechaser for a hundred. But who is he, Charlie?"

Dissimulation is a mask which suffocates, but Mr. Bradhall occasionally let in the air through some breathing-holes, and he did so on this occasion.

"There's a warrant out against him for forgery, to the tune of several thousand pounds, and there are suspicions of his being concerned in the murder of the late Mr. Thornhill many years ago, which you'll not recollect, maybe. It made a great stir at the time." They had been going for about seventeen minutes, and Tom sat down silently on his horse, and urged him to increased speed. At about this point, a road ran at right angles, or nearly so, to the one they were traversing, so that at the distance of a quarter of a mile it had to be crossed by Burke and his pursuer. We have said that the country here was quite undivided by fences; but parallel to this road ran a dyke of enormous depth, half full of water, and banked up on both sides, perpendicularly, with rough-hewn stones. The width from side to side was as much as eighteen feet, and when the depth of the ground be considered and the bad take off, it was a most formidable jump for any horse.

"Here's an end of it!" said Charlie, "Turn to the right, if Burke gets over it, it's a certain fall for Kosciusko – most likely for both of them. They're nearly done now."

On they came and the band of pursuers were just within distance to see Burke urge his horse still faster as he came to the obstacle, confident in his horsemanship and in the staying qualities of the Glacier who, to tell the truth, had plenty left in him yet. Kosciusko was but thirty or forty yards behind him, and Daly's own life, in a measure, depended on the capture of Burke. The danger of a fall was not even weighed in the balance. Burke's horse rose at the leap, but as he did so, his hind legs seemed to fail him, and he fell with his chest against the bank, throwing his rider into the road, and rolling back to the bottom of the water, where he was hopelessly struggling amongst weeds and mud. Had Daly taken time to see this, the capture of Burke was a certainty; but he did not until it was too late, and, unable to hold his horse, he too, came to the place. The horse, strange to say, cleared the dyke, but over-jumped himself, and fell with a crash on the other side on to poor Daly, who lay bruised and mangled with out sense or motion. Not so Kosciusko, who rose at the instant, not much the worse for the fall; and when Charlie Thornhill reached the spot, he found the servant insensible, and Burke continuing his flight on Charlie's horse.

To save a life is a higher duty than to take one and the delay that naturally occurred in attention to Daly caused more loss of time. When the chase was resumed by Charlie and his brother and Mr. Bradhall, it was clear that it was a hopeless case; and after riding two miles further in pursuit, they returned to Baden, happy in the assurance of the police that his escape was impossible. Charlie never cursed the goodness of his horses till that day; but as Kosciusko disappeared beneath Burke's weight, leaving the hacks hopelessly struggling after him, he sincerely wished he had been the sorriest brute in Germany. Daly was taken on to Baden, still insensible, apparently dying, though not yet dead. Burke entered the Forest with an idea that he had outwitted a bailiff's man, and only wondering how such a fellow came by so good a horse, which rivalled the best of his own Irish career

It was some days before any gleam of intelligence lighted up the features of the wounded Daly. Internal injury, and the severe shock to the system which resulted from a pressure on the spine received in his fall, forbade any hope of permanent recovery. Strange decrees of providence! Here in an effort to make reparation for the great crime of his life, Daly met with his punishment and his accomplice was the unwitting instrument of its infliction. If anyone had suggested to him that hanging by public execution, or penal servitude for life, was the proper recompense, it would have shocked his sense of independent action. When first an opportunity presented itself of helping one of the name of Thornhill, his argument was quite a natural one, and was strong enough to enlist his friend Gipsy George, the illegitimate son of Kildonald, in his favour. "Faith, it's lucky we wasn't found out, or we'd be at some Bothany Bay or Portland Island, or some o' them far off places now, and may be Mister Thornhill 'ud never have had his bullterrier, Rosie, back again. What good would we have been to him if we was just hanged or transported?" and thus he philosophically acquiesced in the decrees of providence.

Meanwhile, Kosciusko had returned to his stable, and, what is more to the purpose, Burke had been taken. In a lonely house, not far from one of the wildest spots in that part of the Black Forest, Burke was found on the very night of his escape. The place was more the natural formation of a rock in a dark precipice overhanging the valley of the river Mourg, and not many miles from Eberstein. It had long been the resort of evil-doers, and was held by the remnant of a gang of coiners when Burke had first sought shelter amongst them. His foreign manners and language were displeasing to them; the violence of his temper, assumption of superiority, and open daring, so different from their own low cunning and desire of concealment, that, like the hunted deer, they left him to his fate. On his return to the place he found no one; and it is believed that the reward offered for his capture tempted one of the gang to betray him.

Burke was physically a bold man. When the Gerichts-diener or Process Server appeared at the door of his temporary quarters, he speculated upon how far resistance might serve him. Foreign prisons are proverbially unpleasant.

"How much for?" said he, folding his arms coolly, in a rough coat which he had assumed over his jockey dress; "What's the money?"

"It's not money, Herr Englander." Here Burke drew a pistol: the German functionary drew back, and Burke advanced. At the same moment, our old acquaintance, as we first saw him, Mr. Bradhall, and his aide-de-camp, presented themselves.

"No, sir: it's a case of forgery and the murder of Geoffrey Thornhill, Esq., late of Thornhills, in the county of Northamptonshire." Burke's hand dropped, and his whole appearance at once underwent a change. Mr. Bradhall seized the opportunity to secure him.

"Forgery? Murder?" said, or rather stammered, he. "You'll be troubled, I'm thinking, to find evidence of such a charge."

"Phelim O'Brian," said Bradhall to that worthy, who appeared in the doorway; "is that our prisoner?"

"No other," said Phelim O'Brian. "Faith, Misther Burke, it's thrue; and the papers, wid the names an all, Kildonald and Thornhill, and the title deeds, is all in the hands o' the lawyers, bad luck to them."

"And you have done this Phelim O'Brian: you, that I brought up ever since you was a child; who ate, and drank, and was clothed by me; who'd have wanted bread but for the man you've thravelled hundreds of miles to destroy. Why have ye done this thing, Phelim?"

"And tell me, Mr. Burke, where is Mary Connor? Could no other serve your dainty taste, but the girl I loved and that loved me, and that would have made a home for me when I was old and worn and broken; that would have shared my lot; ay, that would have changed it? – who would have made the bitter sweet and hard usage soft; and taught me to bless you and all the world, instead of to curse you?"

"You fool!" said Burke, with the rage of a chained tiger; "you fool; Mary Connor! It was Kildonald, not I; she bore him a son and a daughter. Those papers which were stolen by you or your accomplices, those are the receipts of the purchase money from Geoffrey Thornhill."

It was true enough; the purchase money had been received by Burke, and he had afterwards become possessed of the receipts he had himself given. From that period he had treated the estate as his own. And having been employed by both sides to expedite matters, he had used both for his own purposes. Burke had a hold over Kildonald because of his ill-starred marriage to Mary Connor and Kildonald had been fain to accept certain sums of money, as the price of his property, which by forgery at his father's death had been made to appear more. The appropriated rents of the Kildonald estate had never found their way further than the coffers of Burke.

It was necessary at last to take Daly's depositions on oath. It became apparent to all that he could not survive the internal injuries he had received. The necessary authorities were therefore brought together, and the substance of what may be called his confession was as follows.

On the day of the Bidborough Races, in 1848, made memorable by the death of Geoffrey Thornhill, Daly, had been induced by Burke to assist in robbing Kildonald on his way home. Having ascertained where Kildonald would dine and where he would sleep, which was not difficult, following his quarrel with Thornhill, the scheme had been concocted. George, known in the country as Gipsy George, or Handsome Gipsy George, was the son of Kildonald by Mary Connor. The indignities and cruelty with which he and his mother had been treated as he grew up had made him a willing assistant in the design, and there can be no doubt he intended to kill his reputed father, had he fallen in with him. Patiently waiting, therefore, under the dark firs, on the heath where I have stated the murder took place, they had at length heard the sound of a horse's feet. They had hastily thrown across the road a strong rope. The descent between the dark box and firs, where we last parted with Geoffrey Thornhill, was exceedingly steep: he had been riding with the reins on his horse's neck, and in a moment he was down. Daly and George had rushed forward, and a blow from the latter had stretched him upon the ground. It had been no sooner struck, however, than the men had discovered their mistake, and would at once have made their escape. Two things had prevented this consummation – the sudden revival of Thornhill, who had only been stunned, and the appearance of Burke himself upon the field of action. Thornhill had seized Daly, while George had stood aloof, uncertain how to act; and the struggles of Daly had been quite in vain to extricate himself from so powerful a man. Fearful of losing his prey, masked and dressed so as to defy detection, as he thought, and still imagining that it was Kildonald whom he had seen struggling, Burke had rushed to the rescue. Seeing a fresh assailant, Thornhill had loosed his hold of the passive, and closed with the active opponent. The struggle had been severe – both powerful men and in the prime of life – but the violent blow, and the blood which trickled from the wounded temple had began to tell, and Burke's vigorous efforts were gradually gaining the mastery. At that moment the moon shone out, and the mask was torn rudely from his face.

"Burke!" said Thornhill. "Good God! Is it possible? Now I know you." Those words had been his last; the eyes of Burke had seen the gleam of George's pistol barrel as it had lain on the ground, and, seizing it, he had shot the unfortunate man through the head. "Och! Will I ever forget it, though it took less time to do than to tell it!" sobbed Daly.

"And what's become of Gipsy George, as you call him?"

"Wasn't he killed by Mr. Thornhill's horse the night when he went to hand the prisoners over to the police, yer honour? Them's his papers in the little box I carries about wid me."

Such was the sum and substance of the deposition of Michael Daly. The papers found in the box were, besides, perfectly confirmatory of those which were already in the hands of Sir Frederick Marston and his lawyer, and established, beyond all doubt, the right of the Thornhills to the Kildonald estate, with no end of arrears of rent, which it was quite impossible to get. Within a week Daly was no more.

CHAPTER 38

HOW THE BROTHERS FARED APART

Reader. Will you do me the favour to explain one or two inconsistencies?

Author. I dislike explanations; but we have travelled so far on such good terms that I'll do my best.

Reader. Why in the world didn't Daly tell all this before? It would have been easy to have done so.

Author. Undoubtedly it would; but it is not my business to penetrate motives, especially those of an Irishman: merely to state facts. I think Daly acted in the most natural manner possible. It takes a man a long time to acknowledge his passive participation in a murder: besides, when the first brush is over, and the pursuit less keen, there is more time for reflection.

Reader. Then why did he confess at all?

Author. Because, while time and circumstances took him further from fear of punishment, they brought him nearer to fear of God. Teach a man that he is not utterly worthless, and you make him better. Show him that he has sympathies with his fellow creatures, and you bring him in closer alliance with his Maker. Society had been kinder to him of late, and he felt an obligation to society. Besides all men have some natural feelings, which require only the proper chord to *be touched to respond. Charlie Thornhill's kindness of manner and honesty of purpose had done this. Had he been other than he was, Daly might long have felt the obligation without much inclination to act up to its demands. There was another reason, not so good a one, but still powerful – his dislike of Burke, who was selfish, and had pressed his point without mitigation, and Daly now saw that his own ignorance had been imposed upon.*

Reader. *And now of course you mean to give us a trial, with us the suborned witnesses, and enter into legal subtleties, and all that sort of thing; because that's the most interesting part: the women like it best.*

Author. *Naturally; because they understand it least. I therefore tell you at once that Burke was taken to prison, and on the morning that he was to have been tried he was found hanged in his cell, having accomplished that end with considerable ingenuity by means of the sheets of his bed. He would scarcely have been convicted of the murder, though he would have ended his life in penal servitude for his forgeries, which were easy to prove. The betting book which was returned to Sir Frederick Marston by coach, had come from Burke, and was given by him to Daly's brother, who died on Marston's estate after some very incoherent disclosures. The lovers of a sensation regarded the suicide of Burke, as a severe national disappointment. The friends of the Thornhills and the family themselves regarded it, after all Charlie's efforts to discover the murderer of his father, as a merciful dispensation of Provide*nce.

Before Charlie went to London, the Dacres had resumed their journey to Italy. No change for the better appeared in Alice Dacre, and it was desirable that she should have different air from her own. Need I say that Mr. Dacre could not withhold his consent to Edith's engagement with Charlie, though the consent was saddled with some conditions as regards time. What cared they for time? So Edith left the Black Forest with her sister, and Charlie went to visit his brother Tom in Baden.

"I hear you were lucky again last night, Tom," said Charlie, as he took up a cigar, and lighted it. He seemed in unusually good spirits which was not common with him. He was the most equable man alive, was Charlie Thornhill.

"I was, Charlie. Those fools outside (don't you see 'em?) de Rougemont and Carlingford, and half a dozen more, would give anything for my luck, and I'm so miserable, that – that – d--- it Charlie; I beg your pardon, old fellow, but I can't help it." Tom was fairly choking.

"Give up play, Tom," said Charlie, bluntly; "it don't agree with you."

"I wish I could. I could give up the money, but I can't give up the play." Tom took a turn up the room, and poured out a glass of sherry.

"Leave this place, Tom; it's depressing and enervating to a degree."

"Such a life as mine, worthless, useless, with all I feel in me that might have been better, would be so anywhere."

"Don't speak so, Tom; but give it up. Leave this place, at all events. Go to England. Anything but this Continental life. I'm going to England next week. Get half a dozen horses, and go down to Thornhills."

"Ah! Charlie, you don't know what it is. I can't live at Thornhills. I can't keep half a dozen horses – at least, I can't ride them. There is but one thing that keeps me from thinking of – of – her, and that's play".

Charlie's eyes opened to their fullest extent: in his modesty he could have feared for himself, but what woman could have been cruel to Tom? The thing seemed impossible. Yet who was the "she" that had evidently turned her back upon the finest fellow in the world? He allowed himself to run over these facts in a few moments, and then he walked straight up to Tom. He was the taller of the two brothers, not the handsomer; but it would have been difficult to find two more perfect specimens of the high-bred Englishman in their peculiar style. Putting his arm affectionately over Tom's shoulder, and looking cheerfully at him, he said, "If it's only a woman, cheer up Tom. Look at me; Edith Dacre has accepted me. I'm engaged to be married to her. I came to tell you this before I leave for London."

Tom Thornhill took his brother's hand. "Thank God for that bit of good news! How selfish I must have been never to have seen it."

"Tom," said Charlie, suddenly brightening, "go and marry Alice Dacre; she's the best and handsomest girl I ever saw, except, except – you know."

Tom's face grew paler; he bit his nether lip; and then with an effort he said,

"She is the woman, Charlie the woman who has twice refused me. I thought it was her mother, or her father, but this time there was no mistake, But it's over; and at the end of the week I shall go God knows where; it don't much matter. I hear the Dacres winter in Florence; so that I shall go to Spain or the south of France." The conversation continued and when they parted the next day, it was years before they met again.

* * * * * *

Within one month of the events detailed in our last chapter, Charlie Thornhill was summoned from Frankfort to take his place in the house of Messrs. Mint, Chalkstone, Palmer and Co., of East Goldbury, City of London. He came, was kindly received by Roger Palmer and his partners, and installed in a small corner railed and curtained off for the privacy of foreign correspondents especially. He found Roger Palmer unaltered; and he did his utmost by dining in Harley Street to cheer the solitude of his benefactor. It was not long before he succeeded so far that the old man was never happy without him.

"I don't ask you, Thornhill to give up your chambers to come and live with me: it might be irksome for you; it would be to any young man of your connections and habits; but if ever you have an hour to spend, or if ever you want a change, remember your father's old friend in Harley Street."

"You've taken care that I shall not forget you, sir; and if you are alone, and it gives you pleasure, I shall be very happy to come today."

It was very curious to see the friendship or attachment between these two men. The one small, shrivelled, nervous, with closely compressed lips and delicate features, afraid of cold or wind, timid, distrustful, parsimonious, and wealthy. The other tall, active, handsome, with an air of fashion and independence which sat nobly on him; homely, honest, indifferent to money except for what it purchased, despising luxury for himself, but always enjoying it as belonging to his order when it came his way; fearing nothing, hoping everything, and living on his labour from hand to mouth. As they walked into Oxford Street, or along Bond Street, together, they were an extraordinary couple; and still more so as they went to East Goldbury in a cab; huddled side by side, his share of which Charlie most scrupulously paid. The fact is, they were of use to one another, and they felt it; and men usually love what they imagine they can protect.

Charlie's life was now monotonous enough. The Dacres were in Florence. The accounts of Alice's failing health came constantly to Charlie in regular letters from Edith. Sir Frederick and Lady Marston were in Town, and as the spring advanced, many of his old acquaintances reappeared. None appeared more pleased with Charlie Thornhill's improved prospects than Lady Montagu Mastodon. "Not such a fool, after all," said her ladyship.

The summer advanced. Alice Dacre could now be moved: they were going out of Florence: but the letters spoke of no improvement. In the autumn Charlie went down to his mother. Tom's difficulties were serious; he himself had gone to the eastern Mediterranean; an occasional letter to his mother spoke only of his excursions here and there and never touched the subject which Charlie knew to be nearest his brother's heart; and he himself was religiously silent. He too heard from his brother, but it was entirely business, and of a painful nature. Must Thornhills be sold? That was the question? "Apparently," said Mr. Mason, the family solicitor, "it must; but it could be held on to for another year, and an eligible tenant perhaps found." Poor Mrs Thornhill and Mary Stanhope! What a change. Of course they must have moved if Tom had brought a wife to his estate but how differently. "Oh! What a blessing he might have been to us, Mary, had he but married well!"

"You don't seem to think of his wife, Emily. She might have found herself in our difficult position."

* * * * * *

One lovely evening in the waning autumn, just twelve months after our last meeting with him Tom Thornhill was lounging on the walls at Malta Since that time he had been wandering from capital to capital, wherever excitement, above all, the excitement of play, was to be met. He was watching the dark blue sea as he smoked his cigar and his thoughts wandered back to the wasted years and enervating process.

But in Tom's case it was better that he should look back. He had forgotten the true end of existence, Duty, in looking forward only to the false end, Pleasure. He saw a picture, as he turned his face from the sinking sun of his prosperity to the coming darkness of penury. He saw his home afar off, and its manifold obligations. He saw his mother, in advancing age, yearning for her elder and best loved son. He saw his brother, successfully struggling with adversity, and making for himself the place that he had taken by right. He saw a loved and loving girl, wearied and broken hearted, who had refused to link her fate and that of her family with a spendthrift and a gambler. He knew she loved him. He knew the other offers she had cast aside, with one hope to cling to. And he now knew how he loved her. He felt the unsatisfied craving of a heart by nature noble, generous, true, but which had been turned from its course by selfish infirmities and unwholesome vanities. Was it too late? Three times? And what were his hopes? Only in utter self-reprobation: in consistent change. But there needs proof of it. Time. Months, or years perhaps. She shall have it; the latter, if need be, and a life of devotion afterwards.

At that moment, on the other side of an angle of the wall against which he was leaning he heard voices. They were some officers, smoking and enjoying the still night, like himself.

"Beautiful: I never saw such a beautiful girl. Dacre was very fond of her." Tom's ears opened at the name.

"When did she die?" Naturally he felt a little interest in the lady who had captivated a Dacre.

"On the eighteenth, I think. I saw it in 'Galignani' on the mess table this afternoon. Do you recollect her, Dixon?"

"Of course I do. Her father was very civil to us. Poor girl! What lovely hair she had!" Tom listened still. His heart missed a beat at the mention of the peculiarity.

"What did it say in the paper; anything about her?"

"No, not a word. Merely, on the eighteenth, Alice something Dacre; I forget what the second name was. I'm very sorry for Teddy: his favourite sister."

Tom heard no more, or the voices ceased. His head fell between his hands on the parapet of the wall and every sensation left him but one dull and heavy pain. For upwards of an hour he remained in this state. He returned to his hotel.

"Waiter, find me the 'Galignani.'" True enough, it was there. "On the 18th of May, Alice Carington Dacre - ." He read no more: the paper dropped from his hand, and he sought his room, blinded with tears.

* * * * * *

In the meantime Charlie continued to prosper. Everything that was in his hand turned out well. Roger Palmer liked Charlie for himself, so did his partners, but they liked prosperity also. His regular business-like habits were very useful as an example to the house. He was at the bank first, and he left it last. Neither was he without his pleasure in the midst of business. He kept his one modest hack, though his income had now become a good one for a single man. He had plenty of society at the West End of Town. Lady Marston would have given him a home, but his mother was in Town for a time, and she had a prior claim. How the two women sorrowed over Tom. How they loved him!

"Why doesn't he write oftener?" said his mother. "And when he does write, why doesn't he say more about himself?" Charlie had his surmises, but he kept them to himself.

They sat comfortably at breakfast in Grosvenor Place one Sunday morning.

"When are the Dacres coming home, Charlie?" asked his mother at breakfast.

"At the beginning of next season," said he.

"And then we shall lose you, I suppose?" rejoined Mrs Thornhill, with a little, a very little petulance.

"Never, my dear mother, if you mean by my marriage. Perhaps it won't be so soon; and whenever it is, you'll gain Edith, and lose nothing."

Mrs Thornhill did not seem convinced. "Where are you going this evening?"

"To Harley Street. Roger Palmer has been ill; not exactly ill, but unwell: and I promised to go to dinner, so I shall dine with him, my dear mother, if you and Aunt Mary have no objection." Aunt Mary certainly had none; so he went to the stables, which were behind the house, and mounting his hack, rode quietly to the City.

There was a comfortable room kept for Charlie to dress in at Roger Palmer's and about half-past six on this said Sunday, Charles Thornhill dressed to his own satisfaction. The dinner to which they sat down was as simple as it possibly could be; well cooked and well put upon the table, but of the most ordinary kind. One thing was remarkable in a man of Mr. Palmer's habits of economy – the excellence of the wines. Indeed, he entertained rarely and sparingly; for Roger Palmer was cynical as well as parsimonious.

"You like that port wine, my dear Thornhill?" said the old man, drawing up his chair to the side of the table, and sitting with his back to the light.

"Very much indeed," replied Charlie. "I never have drunk any so good."

"No! Port wine cannot be bought, nor made: it can only be kept. That wine is worth, let me see – yes – two guineas a bottle: if it were in the market."

"Have you much of it?" said Charlie.

"Yes: plenty. But why do you ask?"

"I beg your pardon, really – but – Well sir, you never drink it yourself; why not put it on the market?"

"Perhaps my heir might like it, Master Charles." The old man's eyes twinkled, and his ordinary mode of address was exchanged from something more familiar. He helped himself to some old Madeira, and pushed the bottle of port over to Charlie. The people were coming out from evening service as he did so.

"D you know what happened yesterday afternoon in Pall Mall?" enquired Roger Palmer

"Nothing remarkable, that I'm aware of."

"It is thought very remarkable: at least it will be sufficiently startling to some people tomorrow morning. Your uncle's partner, George Hammerton, died suddenly yesterday evening."

"Suddenly!" repeated Charlie after him, as a host of recollections came at once to his mind. "Was it suddenly? What age was he?"

"Quite suddenly – not very old; about sixty-seven or eight. Do you know how far you are interested in this event?"

"To a certain extent, I do know; but you and Sir Frederick Marston are the persons to whom I am directed by my Uncle Henry's last instructions to apply to for an explanation."

"Marston is not precisely a man of business; and if you like, I believe I can place the matter very clearly before you." The old man looked thoughtful and anxious, but there was rather a triumphant tone in his manner which jarred with his words.

"Have you cherished any expectations from your uncle since his death? Answer me, if you will, as a friend."

"I have half guessed the possibility of the time coming when there might be something; but I have regarded it as a remote contingency."

"You did well, my dear boy, you did well. I have been this afternoon with poor Hammerton's brother, he declines all responsibility, and the bank will not open on Monday morning. I cannot advise my partners to undertake it; though I think the speculation might be a good one as regards connection. There is a West End house that is likely to take it over so that every shilling in the pound will be paid; but, beyond that, there is no money even to bury him." Charlie's face fell, as what man's would not? He had told Roger Palmer the truth, he had counted on nothing; yet he had sometimes thought that a few thousands only out of that business might have smoothed the way for his marriage, or have given a few more of its comforts to his Edith. Roger Palmer's face, however, wore no such sympathetic expression as might have been expected.

"And there was no will?"

"No will, but a sort of trust deed in my hands, to be used in your favour, as far as Henry Thornhill's interest in that bank could be so, at Mr. Hammerton's death. Had your uncle or Mr. Hammerton lived a few years longer, you might have been a rich man; but God has willed it otherwise."

"Then sir, we must manage as well as we can without. And now, will you give me the explanation you promised."

"I will. Some few years after your uncle bought, with his younger brother's portion, a share in Hammerton's bank, a terrible crisis arrived which ruined half the bankers in England. Indian affairs were the origin of the panic, and the extent to which speculation had been carried out in that country. Few remained firm and by one finance house alone your uncle lost 200,000*l*. I need hardly say that it takes a long time to get that money back. Assistance from private sources was all they could hope for, as the trade was too much crippled to do much for one another. Since that day your uncle and Hammerton have never been solvent; but their business was so good that a few more years would have made them so. A private meeting was called, of which I formed one, to consult on the advisability of closing the bank, to the certain ruin of hundreds, or of going on with every prospect of paying twenty shillings in the pound in due course and saving their own reputation. The latter was determined upon, and tomorrow morning every one will be paid in full, but Hammerton's Bank will have ceased to exist for ever." The old man drew a long and deep sigh, as if an old and familiar friend had disappointed him by dying, and then he finished his Madeira in silence.

"Shall I ring for the lamp?" asked Charlie, the twilight having deepened perceptibly during the explanation.

"Not yet, Charles Thornhill. I've a word more to say. Do you know that Thornhills is on the market still?"

"I do: an order was forwarded by my brother last year from Malta to have it disposed of, at a price, just as we had persuaded him not to sell it, but to let us find a tenant for it, if possible. We have not yet had a customer: I hardly think we have honestly tried very hard."

"Do you know the price and the condition of sale?"

"No; but they can easily be had from our man of business, Mr. Mason."

"I do," said Roger Palmer – "75,000*l*, the timber at a valuation. How long has it been in your family? Help yourself, my dear Thornhill." pushing the port across to Charlie.

"Since 1672." Charlie sighed a most genuine sigh of regret.

"Would it do for me?"

"It's a larger place than you would care to live in, but very beautiful."

"Perhaps my heir might like that as well as the port wine." The old man seemed mightily tickled by the joke, considering it was not so pleasant a subject to Charlie.

"I should be very happy to think that she did. She's one of the kindest and best wives and mothers I ever met."

In one moment Roger Palmer was on his feet: it was rather too dark to see his face, which was whiter than ever with surprise: in his sudden rise he upset his own wine, and half spilt the glass to which Charlie had so lately helped himself.

"She? – she?" said the old man, almost shouting till the room rang again. "Who told you it was a she? Where did you learn such a story? I see: from your Uncle Henry. And how do you know anything about her?"

"It was my Uncle Henry, I think, or perhaps Lady Marston. But I saw them at Frankfort, struggling against poverty and sickness; and I'm only glad you have the means of rescuing a good woman and her daughter from their stings."

I think the bottle of port must have done something for Charlie.

"No, Charles Thornhill, never! Kildonald stole her from me, and shall not have my money. She liked him, loved him, better than the hands that had worked for her, and the brother that had warmed her; she made her own bed, let her lie on it."

The old man spoke very cruelly, and Charlie interrupted him: "But Mr. Palmer, you forget –"

"I forget nothing: it is because I can't forget. Not a word more, Charles, my boy. You, sir, you are my heir. You shall have Thornhills, and thousands and thousands besides." The old man resumed his seat, and as he drank off a fresh glass of Madeira he became quieter. "There, ring the bell, Thornhill, for the lamp. We're in darkness groping our way; let's have some light upon it." Charlie did so, and the light came.

The declaration of the miser had so astonished Charlie that he sat for some minutes unable to say a word, even of thanks, much less of repudiation. Images of all sorts flocked into his mind, and bewildered him. He thought there was something he ought to do, but it wanted a struggle to do it. At length Roger Palmer spoke again: "The thing is already done. I've made you my heir. I owe all I have to your father. He saved the whole house from ruin and myself from beggary and disgrace. Now, will you have Thornhills, or shall I try some more tempting investment for you?"

"My dear sir," said Charlie, rising with the tears in his eyes, and walking towards Roger Palmer, "I need hardly tell you what you have already done for me. If there is anything in the world I can do for you to give you pleasure but this, tell me. But I can't take Thornhills; there's something tells me I can't. And then, think of poor Tom."

"I have thought of Tom, more than he ever thought for himself; but don't say no: not tonight. You owe me something. Repay it by an act of obedience. Be my son. I never had one; but I could have wished him to be like you."

"You overpower me, sir; indeed you do. There are many considerations. Give me time. The temptation you put before me is too great."

"Then take time, boy; this day week. In the meantime make Mason promise me the refusal of the estate. Goodnight. God bless you."

Charlie went out into the clear, warm night. He lit a cigar: and as he rode to Grosvenor Place he had plenty to think of.

* * * * * *

It was the end of the season. The House was tired out; even the eloquence of Gladstone failed to attract attention. The last *déjeuner* had been given at Richmond, the last dinner at Blackwall. Lumley had closed his house, and Rachel had gone back to Paris. Even the clerks in Goldbury were going up and down to Broadstairs and Margate; and the grouse on a hundred hills were counting the hours of their probable existence. Sir Frederick and Lady Marston were taking their last dinner previous to turning their backs upon drought and solitude, made manifest by the half dozen carriages that still remained in town. Sir Frederick was in better spirits than usual, as he led his wife down stairs apologising for his want of punctuality.

"The fact is, my dear, I have been detained on rather pressing business by old Roger Palmer, of whom you've heard."

"And whom I have seen, Fred. And what had he to say?"

"That Thornhills was sold at last."

"To whom, if it's not an impertinent question, Fred?"

"He's bought it himself."

"It's somewhat large for his wants. Does he mean to live there?"

"It's not for himself; he has already made a present of it to another."

"To our friend Charlie? I thought you told me he steadily refused to accept it." Lady Marston seemed less astonished than she ought to have been.

"Excepting upon conditions: with which Roger Palmer has complied."

"And they are?"

"An allowance to the Kildonalds, which shall place them in comfortable circumstances; and a legacy of 20,000*l* at his death. It was all he could manage to do for them; the old man would do no more."

"And Tom Thornhill?"

"Wrote a week ago a letter, such as few men but himself could write, urging, praying, his acceptance of the generous provision, and declaring it the only means by which he could be relieved from the constant and unavailing regrets for the disappointments he had brought on them all."

"And Roger Palmer himself, is he going to die?" said the Lady, smiling.

"Not of starvation, certainly; for there's a handsome annuity payable out of the estate to him, more than adequate for all his wants."

"And do you approve of all this, Frederick?" Sir Frederick looked up from his plate, and saw so bright a twinkle in his lady's eyes, and so absolute an absence of all astonishment, that he began to feel a little disappointed.

"Why! Kate – "

"My dear."

"You knew of this before?"

"I've heard a little about it, certainly. Charlie was here the day before yesterday; he came to see you; and he couldn't help saying something about it to me. He was in terrible distress: and – I hope you are not jealous, but you know you are never at home, so – I – just – ventured to – advise."

"My love," said the baronet, walking solemnly round the table, and stooping to kiss the tears from his wife's eyes, which began fairly to run over, "I knew how honest and generous and good you were, but I never knew what a counsellor I had so near home, or I might have saved myself many a weary hour. When I want to know how to do right, Kate, I shall come to you."

When Sir Frederick and Lady Marston read Tom's last letter over, one expression much perplexed them. "I never knew," he wrote, "until she was gone, how much I could do for her memory which I failed to do for her. My life is now passed in retirement. And from the day that the fatal announcement met my eye I have lived on the consolation that if she saw me now she would have no cause to blush for her unworthy preference."

* * * * * *

The following spring the Dacres returned to England. Their first visitor was Charlie. He met them in Paris, and returned to London with them. They had but little to learn of his improved fortunes, as Charlie was too glad to communicate his happiness to trust to surprises. When Edith Dacre walked down the steps of St. George's, Hanover Square, a happy bride, she had known for some few months that Thornhills was to be her home.

"Well!" said Lady Montagu Mastodon, looking at the bridegroom as he stuttered and stammered his acknowledgements, "a man may not know the difference between a bight and a bite, and yet get through the world remarkable well. He's not the Dunce of that Family."

CHAPTER 39

CONCLUSION

We have very nearly finished. Indeed to have landed our hero and his bride safely in the family domain, and to have shuffled his brother off to Alexandria or Cairo seems to be about as much as the most exacting could require. It was from the former of those places that Tom's last letters were dated; and for the next three years he was only heard of at long intervals. He spoke of returning to England for a time, and looking forward to catching a glimpse of his brother's happiness, which was now complete. That gentleman, indeed, seemed to be made for enjoyment; and when Mrs Charles Thornhill presented him with a son and heir his exultation was far beyond all proportion to the event. He had his troubles, however. He was very desirous of exchanging the cares of a banking house and the onerous duties of a foreign correspondent for the responsibilities of a country gentleman. There needed to be a resident landlord at Thornhills, and the estate could well support him and his little additions to it. Besides, London was not to his taste. There was one claim, however, greater than those of Thornhills and his own inclinations – that of Roger Palmer; and for the old man to have seen his *protégé* turning back from the golden furrows in which he was ploughing, would have broken his heart. So he rented a small house in Belgravia and contented himself with running backwards and forwards as often as time would permit.

"Some day," thought he, "we shall all find ourselves at Thornhills again. Let my mother have it till then; and we must be her guests." His wife was more beautiful than ever: marriage had wonderfully improved her, as it does most people. It strengthens the weak, confirms the unstable, softens asperities, and teaches us to bear and forbear. It is a universal panacea, the offspring of affection and hope, and the parent of perpetual sunshine and self-denial.

At length Tom Thornhill was heard of, and in a way that few could have conceived possible. About the beginning of the third summer after Charlie's marriage a book appeared in London on the drawing room tables of most people who have any regard for their reputations as to literature. It was not light literature, and yet it was as fit for a drawing room table as elsewhere. It was not a religious book. It neither dealt in polemical divinity nor abstruse speculation; yet there was a tone of seriousness running through it which told of deeper thoughts than those which usually force themselves to the surface on the streams of fashionable society. It was not cheerless, not egotistical, but it was easy to detect a wound unhealed through the flimsy veil of adventure which the writer had thrown over it. At all events, "*Uranothen*" obtained a deserved and decided success, and men of learning and research, as well as women of taste and education, united in unqualified admiration of the author. And this was Tom Thornhill. And everybody read it. Those who did not know him were delighted; those who did scarcely believed their senses. The Marstons read it, and the Mastodons; the Robinson Browns, and the Dacres. It was read in fine bindings, in one volume, in three, in railway stations, and in Elizabethan parsonages, and always with something of approbation and sympathy. The East is a favourite subject with most men; and there was then much untrodden ground which required a delicate and trembling foot to traverse it. And there was one who read it, and who dropped tears of genuine love and sympathy and pity.

One beautiful winter's morning after Christmas, Charlie and his wife were at Thornhills. The hounds were meeting at the bottom of one of his own covers, about three miles distant, he desired his groom to take his horses on, and Mrs Charles Thornhill would take him to cover in the carriage. In a few minutes Edith arrived, ready to give the Squire his breakfast, and ignorant of the new arrangement made for her. To a stranger she had the happy, joyous smile of early womanhood, though she led her second child, a little girl of nearly two years old, by the hand. To an old acquaintance she had gained in loveliness by the loss of that over-buoyant joyousness for which she was so remarkable some years before.

"You'll have to put your bonnet on, Edith, after breakfast: I've ordered the carriage for you." Charles was buckling on his spur as he spoke.

"There goes my favourite ottoman. Do look, Charlie, your spur has caught the cover."

"Oh! I beg your pardon, dear. It will easily sew up with a bit of brown silk."

"It's not so easy to sew up, as you call it, with brown silk. Look, sir, at the mischief you have done."

Charlie picked up the baby for the time being, who was staring with open eyes, and wondering whether mamma and papa were really quarrelling, as she and her brother Geoffrey did occasionally.

"How sorry I am: now for the breakfast. Where's my mother, Edith, and the rest of the royal family? Don't forget that you have to dress."

"Why didn't you tell me that upstairs? I shall have to alter my hair."

"Would you rather I did not come with you in the carriage? I can always order my hack?" "What! Are you going to cover in the carriage?" The whole manner was changed: alacrity and good humour and a blush that might have sat on a maiden cheek lighted up his wife's face as he said –

"Of course I am, if you and – "

"Oh, how enjoyable! There's your tea. We shan't be a few minutes." The door opened again and again, and in a few minutes the whole family party busily engaged at breakfast.

The fact is that "dear Edith" had been a little disappointed. There had been a discussion in the dressing room as to the propriety of her riding on horseback to the meet. Charlie had put a prudential and very decided negative upon it; and, although the most indulgent of husbands, when he made up his mind that he was right, he usually stuck to it.

The cover near which the hounds met was a hanging wood, with the river running rapidly below it. An open country, of a most formidable character to cross, stretched away in deep grass meadows on the opposite side. In fact it was *the* vale *par excellence* of that part of England; and we all know what that means. Heavy galloping, rasping ox-fences, and water on its way to the never ending currents of the ocean.

The hounds were no sooner in cover than they spoke to their fox: in a minute they were running him along the side of the hill, whilst the horsemen were hallooed back to give him room to break. A fox is either very timid or very bold; on this occasion he was an incomprehensible anomaly, for, catching sight of the carriage, Reynard veered to the left, went straight down the hill, and in one moment was swimming the river at its deepest part.

The first along the road to pass the carriage was Charlie Thornhill;

and he was not long in turning short through the gate at the top of the cover, and galloping through it towards the point where he heard the whip's cheerful "Gone away!" As he emerged from the wood on the sloping meadows below, he saw the body of the pack stemming the current, and the leading hounds already dragging themselves up to the hollow banks, and shaking their sterns hastily before they settled to the scent. For a moment he contemplated swimming, but a recollection of the banks opposite deterred him: he had once been very nearly drowned in an attempt to do so. He turned, therefore, as quick as thought towards the ford. A quarter of a mile away, he could just see the gate that led out of the meadow towards it and by which he knew the exact spot at which to hit it.

"Not a soul with them," said he to himself. "What a pity! And such a scent in cover. By Jove! There is someone with them! And somebody who knows the country. How the deuce did he get there?" For at that moment a horseman emerged from the waters, and made straight for the only practicable place in the stiffest fence in the country. Charlie watched him as he held on his own way, while behind him thundered the field,

"Well done!" said the Master. "Who is that, Thornhill? I hope he don't override the hounds, sir, whatever he does." The Master and Charlie kept on: the unknown huntsman was a little to their left, slightly in advance, and the whip, having seen as many of his hounds out of cover as he thought orthodox, was in the thick of it.

"There they go; look at the beauties; 'Gad! What a head they carry. We shall never catch them. And there's that man in the black coat again; damn it, how he's overriding them."

I don't think he was; but it was enough to make even a Master of Hounds swear. For a quarter of an hour they had been flying: a stern chase is proverbially a long one: the horses, a little short of condition after a frost, were beginning to feel it; and a few casualties had already taken place while the black-coated man continued to hold his own as very few men can. He was a tall, graceful man, with great power over his horse evidently, by the way in which he rode him. He swerved neither to the right nor the left, but sailed along (the pack quite under his command, whichever way they might turn).

"It's Jim Mason," said one.

"It's that confounded parson from Stickbury," said another.

"No it's not; look at that fellow, he's a bigger man: besides, I think he has a beard."

However, they were not more than two fields behind: one strong post and rails separated them: a nick would soon satisfy their curiosity. Their hopes rose.

"He has a beard;" – the front rank men of the ruck could almost see it. At that moment the leading hounds headed short up to the right, and almost before the field could acknowledge the turn, certainly before some of them could steady their horses, the hounds, the stranger, and all were over the brow of the hill, and had once more disappeared from sight.

In the meantime the carriage had been hunting the fox, as ladies will hunt him, against all hope. The coachman, too, was an enthusiast, and not a bad pilot. So they went down one lane and up another, over a piece of turf, and then through a farmyard – in fact, in the most mysterious holes and corners, now stopping to listen, then making a spurt, until they reached, in a roundabout manner, an ornamental bridge.

"If we don't see 'm here, ma'am, we shan't hear nothing of 'em again." So Jehu pulled up and sat still. He had been sitting, perhaps, five or six minutes, when he rose on his coach box. At that moment he was joined by his master's second horseman, who, seeing the impossibility of catching them by following over the ford, had come round by this bridge.

"Ride on, Jim, and look if you can see anything of 'em." Jim had been gone a minute, when he reappeared, and began beckoning to the coachman to come on.

"They're close here, running like blazes, and only one gent with 'em. It ain't the master, he's got a black coat."

At that moment the hounds came down the grass field at the same pace, while the fence at the top opened, and the hounds crashed through an ox-fence with the single horseman in close attendance. Down he came, with all his might, towards the gateway near to which the carriage was drawn up. He never raised his head nor checked his horse till he got close upon it; then he looked up, pulled his horse into a walk, and put out his crop to unhasp the gate leading towards the bridge and buildings by which they had come in.

Edith was not alone in the carriage. But she was standing up in her excitement and watching the hounds as they took the fence, crashing through the broken underwood with that dash which distinguishes a foxhound from all other animals. She suddenly heard her name sharply called by the beautiful girl who sat beside her, and looking down, she saw that every spark of colour had left her cheek.

"Edith, Edith; Look; pray look, dearest!"

"Yes, yes: I see. Charming! Beautiful! Isn't it? But where's the field?"

"Did you see him? Tell me, did you. Surely you didn't know of this?"

"See him. See what? That man with the beard, who seems to have had the best of it today? Charlie'll be out of temper."

"That was Tom Thornhill, Edith, if ever I saw him in my life."

"My darling child, he's in Alexandria. You're dreaming."

"No dear, I'm not dreaming. That *is* Tom Thornhill."

"Alice!! Home, William, as fast as you can go."

You see, Alice was not dead – never had been dead. Her aunt, godmother, and namesake was dead; which was but natural seeing she was about seventy years of age, being very much older that her brother, Mr. Dacre of Gilsland. In fact, polite old women – and she was a polite old lady – feeling that they lose their good looks about that age, make a point of going about then. If Tom Thornhill's eyes had not been blinded by tears when he checked the officer's conversation in the paper so long ago in Malta, or had he looked again the next day, he would have seen that this lady died in Bruton Street instead of Florence or Gilsland.

At home the sisters waited patiently enough; but neither mentioned his name. Two; three; four hours. At half-past four a step, an unmistakeable step, was heard upon the stairs; the door opened, and a much damaged hat, very watery looking boots, and a well splashed scarlet coat entered. He stood a moment; his wife jumped up and ran towards him; but he shut the door, and placed his back against it.

"He's there, Charlie; I know he is," said the lively little woman, struggling in the arms of the giant.

"He! Who? What do you mean? Be quiet. Down, tigress; down."

"Who? Why, Tom. *My* brother Tom; he's my brother now. Let him come in. Tom, Tom!"

"He can't come in; he's covered with mud. Don't you see Alice is here?"

"Is he worse than you? You've been at the bottom of the Sludge. He shall come in."

Charlie stood to one side and the door opened. There, once more, in the full blaze of that winter afternoon, stood Tom Thornhill and Alice Dacre face to face. Charlie and his wife melted out of the room while Alice gazed at Tom. She saw not his muddy attire; instead she looked upwards to a visage altered by his youthful failure to understand or to curb a madness. The once animated, handsome, confident demeanour was drawn by desolation; but also by a firmness of purpose hewn from his climb out of the vortex at the eleventh hour. For his part he looked down at the face he thought he would never see again. The girlish softness had become leaner, the bones of her face betrayed her suffering while the grave dark eyes, lit by gladness in that moment, carried only a distant hint of melancholy.

Dinner that night was joyful and yet thoughtful and the next morning Tom lost no time in borrowing a horse from his brother and setting off to Gilsland where a solemn Mr Dacre consented to his plea for Alice's hand, hedged about with demands and promises that we can understand and which Tom was at last able to give.

Tom before very long was seen in town buying carriage horses and furniture. He is as good a fellow as ever, and a better man. He has made a name for himself, a higher and more honourable one than that which he destroyed. He has suffered, and others have suffered with him. Adversity has done for him what prosperity never did for any. Amidst all his regrets he has but one remaining – that he should ever have caused a pang to his Alice. She declares herself amply rewarded for it all. Tom has been known to speak with some vanity of that thirty minutes, to say nothing of its results. And, though University men have often heard of such things, I believe Tom Thornhill is the only man who ever rode a run entirely to the exclusion of the rest of the field.

Amidst all the wishes for the happiness of our beloved Royal Prince and his Bride, Alexandra, which were showered upon the Royal Pair on the 10th March 1863, there were none more sincere and few more large hearted than the health that was drunk at Thornhills. "And Tom, old fellow," said the Dunce of the Family, at the conclusion of a very uncommon burst of eloquence, "may he only be as happy as we are!"

.

Printed in Great Britain
by Amazon.co.uk, Ltd.,
Marston Gate.